Heat by Ellie Marvel

What's a mild-mannered alien to do when he goes into heat far from home, and the only compatible female is a rough and tumble Terran mining specialist. She's a friend, but not one to just hop into bed. Answer: he courts her. The old fashioned Terran way, at least insofar as his research about the backwater planet can determine. Because if Tarkin can't seduce the tomboyish Sarai before his cycle ends, he won't get a second chance at love.

Breathless by Rachel Carrington

Lark Hogan is a martial arts expert trained to handle almost anything. Seeking vengeance for the death of her sister, she sets out to stop the murderer. Lark seeks help from Zac, a mercenary, independent wizard who lives only for himself. Confronting a common enemy, Lark and Zac battle their own demons as well as their own powerful attraction, and when sex gives way to love, this couple will fight to the death to protect what they've found.

Midnight Rendezvous by Calista Fox

From New York to Cabo to Paris to Tokyo, Cat Hewitt and David Essex share decadent midnight rendezvous. But when the real world presses in on their erotic fantasies, and Cat's life is in danger, will their whirlwind romance stand a chance?

Birthday Wish by Elisa Adams

Turning 30 shouldn't be any big deal, but for Anna Kelly it marks a deadline she's about to miss. Her list of goals she wanted to accomplish before hitting that magic number is almost complete—except for one thing. She's always wanted to spend one night with sexy Dean Harrison. When Dean asks her what she wants for her birthday, she grabs at the opportunity to ask him for an experience she'll never forget.

Ellie Marvel
Rachel Carrington
Calista Fox
Elisa Adams

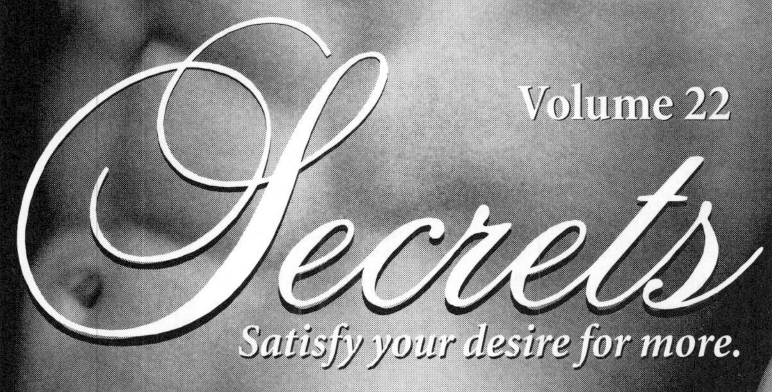
Volume 22
Secrets
Satisfy your desire for more.

SECRETS Volume 22
This is an original publication of Red Sage Publishing and each individual story herein has never before appeared in print. These stories are a collection of fiction and any similarity to actual persons or events is purely coincidental.

Red Sage Publishing, Inc.
P.O. Box 4844
Seminole, FL 33775
727-391-3847
www.redsagepub.com

SECRETS Volume 22
A Red Sage Publishing book

ISBN: 1-60310-002-4 / ISBN 13: 978-1-60310-002-1

Printed in the U.S.A.

Book typesetting by:

Quill & Mouse Studios, Inc.
www.quillandmouse.com

Contents

Heat

by Ellie Marvel

To My Reader:

I love me some nice guy! I also love to turn romance staples on their heads, shake them up like pennies in a pig, and see what falls out. In *Heat*, the romance staple I've twisted is "mating lust" and what has fallen out is… Tarkin. I hope you enjoy reading about Tarkin and Sarai as much as I enjoyed writing them!

Chapter 1

Tarkin and I had dinner at Larry's again. Unbelievers and newcomers might consider it a hole in the wall since it was in the lower district, but it was actually one of the best places to eat in Diggette Colony, if you had the credits to afford it, which we both did, within reason. I wasn't expecting the meal to be any different from the hundreds of times I'd eaten here with my stoic Gitternian friend over the years.

We'd order our food, chat with each other and our friend Heen, a waitress here, and go our separate ways. Pretty much every time. Okay, it was more like, me babbling at Tarkin, and Tarkin interjecting a few wry comments when pressed.

I treasured those comments. I worked hard to get them.

However, tonight when we reached our table, Tarkin handed me a delicate pink blossom, I assumed from the public organics bubble, and pulled out my chair like some courtier of old Terra.

"You feeling okay, bud?" I asked. How could you tell what a Gitter felt, anyway? Their appearance was similar to Terrans, but they always had this expression on their faces as if cracking a smile, or a frown, would cause some galactic incident. Not that many Gitters left their home system to explore the galaxy, but Tarkin was an exception.

"I am in perfect health," he said in that funny, clipped accent of his. Tark scooted my chair as I lowered my butt to it, smooth as you please. Then he seated himself on the other side of the two-humanoid table, straightening the plastene food mat so it lined up perfectly with the edges.

I managed to keep further comments about his health, or his perfection, to myself. Maybe the flower was something new he'd managed to grow in his garden plot, and this was his subtle way of bragging. It could happen. It wasn't like he was an android.

Tarkin glanced up from his food mat and raised his eyebrows slightly. "How are you today, Sarai? Was your workday more satisfying than yesterday?"

"Tempored six tubes of kitium ore. Perfect, I think, but you never know lately." I twiddled with the flower. What was I supposed to do with it? Put it in my hair? Nobody else in Larry's had a flower. There sure as hell weren't any flowers in vases, like fancy restaurants on Terra. Just plain, sturdy tables of various sizes, moldable chairs, booths along the wall, and a bank of screens showing vids, newscasts and trivia contests. In the back were the kongii and other gaming tables. In lieu of a bar, Larry had installed a row of high-tech servo-chutes maintained by robos and living waitstaff. Food and beverages came out, dirty dishes went in, simple as you please, and much more hygienic. Not to mention safer.

Of course, nobody else at Larry's dined with a Gitter, either. For, what, the ninth time in a row? People were going to talk. There was little else to do in this colony when you weren't working—talk, drink, gamble, and fuck pretty much covered the bases.

Or garden. Tark liked to garden. He had his own plot in the organics bubble.

"I am sure you did a more than adequate job." He inclined his head to me as the squat roboserver wheeled out our drinks. Same drinks as the past eight nights. "Your psi is well-honed. Hermana Mining is one of the top kitium producers in this quadrant because of you."

Tark thumbed the server's paypad, and I reached across the table and grabbed him. "Hold on. Tonight I'm paying."

He stiffened. His gaze dropped to my hand, carefully scrubbed after my stint in the ore lab, curled around his wrist. My skin was pale against his kaf-colored arm.

When he raised his dark eyes to mine, I could have sworn something hot, maybe a little angry, flashed in their depths. "It is my pleasure," he insisted.

I dropped his arm like a blistering tube of ore. "Maybe I want that, uh, pleasure."

Besides, as a temporer I had tons more credits. Tark was, well, a peddler. He located things people wanted and fixed things people broke. He had a way with old tech, and there was way too much of it on outbound colonies like this one.

Tarkin's answering frown was the tiniest twitch between his eyebrows. The overhead glims played across his features in warm blue shades. "It would please you to buy our meal?"

"We're friends, Tark. You don't have to buy my food." I placed the flower carefully on the milky grey table, then imprinted my finger on the roboserver paypad.

"It is not custom on Terra for the male to provide? I respect your customs, Sarai."

"Maybe a hundred years ago. What vid have you been watching?"

Tark steepled his fingers. "The Library." He meant the universal database that was the supposed be-all, end-all source of information for every being in the galaxy, which it was not. Though the Librarians poked their noses anywhere and everywhere, the information wasn't always made public.

I snorted. "Like the Librarians spent more than a tenday on Terra when they decreed our backwater planet worth an entry. And that was, I don't know, a decade after first contact? My granmater wasn't even born."

"How interesting," Tarkin said, and knowing Tark, he meant it. "Do you have any ancestral stories of first contact?"

"A few," I answered. Then I grinned. "I'll swap them for more information about Gitternis." The Library, I'd discovered soon after meeting Tarkin, was remarkably devoid of facts about a species that had made first contact long before Terra. Either the Librarians knew a bunch of things they weren't telling or Gitternis was really that uninteresting. I always tried to weasel more details out of him, but he was pretty tight-lipped on the subject.

Tarkin blinked. "Yes, you would require more information than the Library offers. I agree. We shall trade information."

"Really? It's a deal." I could barely conceal my shock. Okay, I didn't conceal it, but Tarkin just nodded.

By Hoover, he was being weird tonight! I tapped out my meal choice on the table's central touchpad and avoided his gaze.

Gitters, who preferred to be called Gitternians except I always forgot, were odd. Solemn and uptight. Standoffish. Tark was more personable than the other Gitters I'd met in my thirty odd years, and I'd grown to like him. A lot. I liked his subtle humor and patience and, hell, I liked his dusky, exotic looks and tight buns. I wondered how his body looked naked, and I wondered how his full, mobile lips would feel against mine. Library or no Library, everybody knows Gitters don't mingle, but what he didn't know about my entertaining little fantasies wouldn't hurt him.

In my fantasies, it was all about pleasing him. Others might find him too short and reserved for sexy daydreams, but he was only small compared to humanoids other than me. Terrans and Gitters were medium-sized on a galactic scale, and thanks to my granmater's Irish heritage, I was smaller than most Terrans. We were a short, fiery, and frequently psychic people. Which is how I ended up thousands of light years from Terra temporing valuable, delicate kitium ore with the freakish powers of my brain.

A humanoid delivered our food—our friend Heen, a Devian with four arms and a dislike for the coveralls most humanoids donned in public. No need for them when her beige pelt kept her warm enough.

For his part, Tarkin dressed in embroidered tunics and trous, which he'd explained patiently were a better advertisement for his luxury item acquisition service—he never called himself a peddler—than baggy coveralls. I just appreciated the view.

"You two again?" Heen handed plates off the serving tray onto the table. No recon food here at Larry's. It wasn't cheap, but it was worth it, especially to a Terran like me who grew up eating almost all fresh. "People are gonna wonder what's going on."

"People around here would talk if you lasered their mouths shut." I grinned. "You didn't get any hair in my soup this time, did you?"

Heen smirked. "It's not in the soup. For you, Tarkin." She placed a dish of bubble tomatoes, brown bread and some kind of white meat in front of him. There were springs of green herb arranged artfully on the side.

I stared. Sure didn't look like my veggie soup and fried egg sandwich.

"Thank you." Tarkin inclined his head at Heen. "I appreciate your attention to detail."

"You let her in your garden again, didn't you?" I accused him.

Heen made a gesture with her right hands I didn't recognize, but it looked rude. "Jealous?"

"He won't let *me* in his garden. Tarkin, why can't I go in your garden?" I bit into my sandwich, the yolk runny the way I liked it, and wiped a droplet off my chin onto the shoulder of my brown coverall. Hey, it was clean. It was my dress coverall, never worn in the mines. Much.

Tarkin and Heen exchanged a glance, and Heen said, "Giblet, you know your ores, but you got the black thumb. He's keeping his organics safe."

She had a point. My psi skills were strong but limited and all about the ores. I couldn't interface, I couldn't push worth mentioning, I could hardly even access the Library without a hard terminal. Lucky for me, what I could do was profitable enough—tempor a rare metal so it could be used for wetwiring before it went inert. Kitium was a sensitive mix of metal and organic when removed from the earth, and if it wasn't in stasis, it had to be worked by someone like me within hours or it was so much sludge. Technology hadn't been able to surpass many things the mind could do, a sore point with species who didn't have psi in their biology. Wetwiring—implanting kitium into a humanoid brain to increase psi—could only take you so far.

"You have never shown interest in gardening before." Tarkin unfolded a cloth napkin, another of Larry's extra touches, and placed it on his lap. "Perhaps you would like a napkin?"

I paused in the midst of swiping more egg off my face and glanced at the creamy napkin rolled around the utensils. "I guess my table etiquette leaves something to be desired, huh?"

Heen laughed out loud. "She can be taught, Tarkin."

Blushing, I unrolled my napkin and dabbed at my lips with exaggerated finickiness. "Goodness me, how could I forget my years of finishing school?" In truth, after secondary, I'd gone straight into psi voc training, and after that, started refining kitium ore, which I'd been doing for nine years.

"Terran years must be shorter than galactic years," Heen said. "Clean your plates or Larry will be angry. Wanna catch a vid soon, Sarai?"

"If it's a new one." Heen loved to rewatch old favorites while I preferred new-to-me vids.

"I'll buzz you," Heen called over her shoulder as she left.

"Sarai, I apologize if I have been remiss. Tomorrow I will escort you to my garden." Tarkin sliced his meat into small pieces before eating it.

"I'll bring the rake," I said, despite the fact Tarkin was right. I had little interest in gardens unless it was harvest. Organics weren't my thing. But I'd let Tarkin show me the inside of a cleaner pod if it meant spending time with him, so I nodded to emphasize my willingness and cover my sarcasm.

Heen was too busy to join us, as she sometimes did. We continued our meals in companionable silence as Larry's ramped up for the night's revelry. The food was expensive, but after twenty hours, the booze was not. And the gaming tables had a loose reputation that may or may not have been earned.

Tarkin tilted his head to one side as two Irts at the next table raised their voices in debate. Normally, the large, rough humanoids didn't frequent Larry's, but every time I'd come here recently, there were Irts nearby. I blamed the fact Larry's had just been voted one of the "best-kept secrets" of the colony in the quarterly blips, which was dumb when you thought about it, because if you keep telling a secret, eventually it wasn't a secret any more, and where does that leave Larry's? Overcrowded, that's where.

The Irts, as Irts tend to do, started snarling as they argued. Tarkin tensed when the anger in their tones increased. I smiled at him reassuringly.

"Tell ya, it ain't the thing to do," the Irt in the purple coveralls insisted, pounding his fist on the table. Heen was covered by short, silky fur, very strokeable, but Irts put Devians to shame in the hair department—and many humanoids to shame in the size department. His paw was a good three times the size of mine.

"Bazzit, you slag burner." The other Irt, a larger individual and female by the looks of her chest, crooked a meaty finger at her companion. A hint of bone white claw glistened at the tip. "You tell me we buzz up another useless politico? You try to get my money."

Tarkin twitched in response and gripped his table knife.

I frowned. What was up with him?

The male Irt half-reared out of his seat. "You on glister. Nothing to do with me. Not right, this, not good. I quit."

Tarkin turned in his seat towards the Irts, a bundle of repressed energy.

The moldable material of the responsive chair swiveled partially from the table. "The lady and I would appreciate if you lower your voices. You are disturbing our meal."

I gaped at my suddenly psychotic friend. "Tarkin, what are you doing?" I hissed across the table. "Ice it."

"What you say, Gitter?" The male flipped his nose at Tarkin. Irts evolved from the dominant predatorial species on their home planet, and though they'd discovered spaceflight eons ago, their claws were still like razors, and longer than my fingers. I did not want to antagonize an Irt, here or anywhere.

"Do not call me that. I am Gitternian. I asked that you moderate your tones." Tarkin lowered his chin, annoyance twisting his normally impassive features, and the Irt growled.

The female hunkered on her elbows. Her muscles bulged, obvious even through her fur. "We talk if we wanna," she said to Tark, but she included me in her bitter glare, her tiny black eyes piercing me with animosity. "Public place."

"You challenge?" the male asked. He laughed, his fangs gleaming. "Gitters don't fight. Terrans a joke. Baldies."

Tarkin's hand gripped the edge of the table, and I swear it quivered. I tensed my legs to jump up and run like the tiny hairless humanoid I was.

The female shrugged and turned back to the male. "Leave the squirts alone, Bazzit, I not done with you. You can't quit. You signed. We all did. That's the problem, rockhead. Only one solution. You wanna be problem or solution? You wanna be problem, *I* be solution on your ass."

A tall, armored robot wheeled up to the quarreling Irts and Tarkin. "Would you like your meal to go?" asked the robobouncer. It directed its speech primarily at the Irts but spared Tarkin a metallic glance.

The female glanced at the male, then at us, and held up her paws with the claws sheathed. "Nah, 'bot, we settle."

"We settle," grumbled the purple-suited Irt. "Female hotheads. All war, no care."

"Best that you do." The robot glided away.

"What the slag is your problem?" I asked Tarkin when the Irts weren't paying attention any longer. "Since when do you jump in the middle of other people's brawls?"

"I am sorry." He slumped against the back of his chair, which cupped his shoulders helpfully, and stared at the knife in his hand as if unsure how it had gotten there. "I fear things have progressed further than I'd thought."

I glared at him. "What things?"

Tarkin set the knife on the table and waved an elegant hand. "I will explain later, Sarai. Let us finish our meal in peace."

"Whatever you say, Slasher." I eyed him as his face smoothed into its normal mask and thought about Diggette Colony's little eccentricities. And how Tarkin didn't fit in here. This was a rough place full of rough species and few amenities. If he hadn't been able to finagle old tech, he'd never have been able to support himself here with, ah, luxury acquisition.

I mean, that part of his job was sophisticated and all, and it imbued Tarkin with an air of gentility, but damn! We were in the outbound here. The barely settled part of the galaxy. Who in Diggette Colony outside management and Tarkin wanted to wear embroidered trous? Or drink from etched tir-glass flutes and log entertainment vids that didn't revolve around sex and violence?

Which brought me back to the question, why had the Irts gotten my mild-mannered friend so bent out of shape? Anywhere besides Larry's, intervening in an Irt confrontation would have been a ticket to the infirmary, but even the biggest, dumbest Irts minded a version of civilized manners at Larry's, with his staff of robos. Good thing. I couldn't imagine getting trapped in a bar fight with Tarkin. Gitters were slow to act, and pacifist, and I'd have to rescue him and me both. I'm weak on the galactic scale of humanoids and can barely protect myself.

As was Tarkin. Though I'd never seen a Gitter insert himself into the argument that was none of his business. Or get angry. I couldn't even get Tarkin to argue with me, and Land knows I'd tried to get under the man's skin.

But my friend wasn't himself tonight. I studied the eating knife beside him and noticed he'd arranged it precisely opposite my flower, echoing the bloom's position.

Tarkin caught me staring and smiled. "Do you not like your meal, Sarai? I can select something for you I promise you will enjoy more."

"I'm good," I lied. The food was fine and I'd never for a minute worried about the Irts, at least not until Tarkin started acting like an agro warrior. A rambunctious Gitter was something I never realized existed.

I knocked back the last of my drink and wiped my hands on my pants. "Are you about done?" I wanted to get out of here and question Tarkin, vigorously, about what the hell was going on. Why we'd eaten dinner together nine nights in a row. Why he'd brought me a flower. Why he'd antagonized two Irts—at Larry's, of all places, where the robobouncers would have geeked him into tomorrow without hesitation, as if the Irts themselves weren't enough danger for anybody.

Why my dependable, unflappable friend was suddenly behaving like someone of an entirely different species.

Chapter 2

Out on the sidewalk, Tarkin took my arm and tried to escort me past a trio of drunken shiprats who passed Larry's halosign for the less tasteful bar next door. Vehicles, battered personal models and cabs, whizzed by along the narrow street, a warm, metal-scented wind in their wake. A sturdy railing separated the pedestrians from the drivers.

Even through my coverall sleeve I felt the heat of his touch. My nerves clanged like a gas alarm, and it wasn't because we were in a low rent district after dinner. Unsettled, I wriggled away, and he halted in the middle of the grubby walkway, forcing the shiprats to split around us. They twitched their long tails out of our way.

I could count on my collective digits the number of times Tark and I had had any physical contact. He exuded this large personal space, so I'd never thought much about it. I thought about it now.

He lowered his eyes and bowed. "I have offended you."

"You're being strange tonight." I took a chance and punched him lightly in the chest. There was no give. "But no. Not offended."

The growing crowds on the sidewalk, bent on seeking pleasure, or just drunken oblivion, flowed around us. Holosigns blinked and danced, sometimes projecting images onto the sidewalk. Overhead, the Diggette sky was dark and full of blips as hoppers and other ships navigated the busy port.

Tarkin watched me with an expression I couldn't identify until I began to fidget.

"And more weirdness," I said. "Tark, have pity."

He reached out and brushed a curl off my cheek. This time I didn't flinch. "Would you like to come to my apartment?"

"Uh." Creepy… but this was Tarkin. I'd been to his place many times and emerged unscathed. Jealous of his possessions and sense of decor, but unscathed. "Why?"

"I would speak to you in private. About why I'm behaving… unlike myself."

Tarkin was my pal. Next to Heen, my best friend on this space-forsaken rock. He was acting peculiar, but there was no reason to be worried about going to his apartment. "Sure."

At the next crosswalk, we caught a cab to Tarkin's sector near the organics bubble where all the fresh was grown. You couldn't grow much worth eating on Diggette thanks to the mineral composition of the soil, not to mention all the heavy mining Hermana and other companies were doing. Most of the inhabitants of this city who had families lived in Tark's sector, as well as beings like Tarkin who valued their peace and quiet.

My apartment—practically a closet, it was so small—was closer to the industrial district so I could roll out of bed for work at the last possible minute. Noisier, dirtier, and what did I care, since I only used my closet to sleep, bathe, store my crap, and vid my landbound family on Terra. I saved my credits for a ship and sent the rest to my Mom. When I had leisure time, I spent it at Heen's, Tarkin's or the vidmall.

And sometimes in the lab. Hermana, one of the three mining outfits on Diggette and the only one that produced refined kitium, had been having setbacks lately, particularly in kitium stability, and I'd been putting in practice time with my technique, honing my temporing skills. I was no novice. There was no reason ore I primed should destabilize so frequently, unless there was something unusual about the kitium composition on Diggette I couldn't sense. If my reputation didn't go to crap because of this, I could find another position, but most mining planets where I'd have to set up shop were even rougher than this one. Luckily, kitium temporers were rare enough that a slightly tainted one was better than no temporer at all.

Still didn't mean I wanted a bad rep. I had my pride. I was also in danger of becoming more than slightly tainted, and without reliable psi there wasn't much a puny, inexperienced humanoid like myself could do that I wouldn't outright detest.

Tarkin paid the cabbie and engaged the retinal scan to access his building. I had to be scanned, too, as a registered guest. Couldn't be too safe in a colony like this one, not even in this sector where patrols hovered at nearly every crosswalk. They drove the only flitters allowed inside city limits. Everyone else was relegated to the slower magnevehicles that the cops could freeze with a single flick of the demag button. Tark had a rather nice vehicle with a supplemental rotor installed so it could go outcountry as well. Not that he let me drive it, after what happened the first time.

The flat was on the eighth above-ground floor of the building. The lift released us into a long, silent corridor of understated taupe tiling and intermittent doors. The occasional holoinsert in the walls displayed a changing variety of plants, stars, and artwork, testament to the fact this was one of the higher credit buildings in the city.

Tark retscanned his door sensor, unlocked it, and motioned me inside when it opened with a hiss. “May I take your coat?” he asked when the door closed.

“I’m not wearing a coat.” I plucked at the fabric of my coveralls. “I don’t think you want me to take these off.”

“However you are most comfortable, Sarai.”

I snorted. “Yeah, I’ll just hang out in my skivvies.”

Tarkin smiled, a mere tilt of his lips, and eased past me out of the small foyer. “My home is your home,” he said, and disappeared into his kitchenette.

Something clattered, and I caught a waft of a heavenly odor. What was that? I recognized it, but… Distracted I sniffed the air and wandered into his apartment. Aside from the small kitchenette and sunken den, his flat boasted a large toilet, a storage closet where he kept some of his trade items, and a decent sized bedroom.

“Did you change something?” I called to him, peering around for the source of the odor. It was a game we played—see if the unsophisticated Terran could spot the home improvements. At least, I played it, because I knew it pleased him for me to take note of such things.

His place was as spotless as ever. Expensive candles, Terran, no doubt, as most species disdained open-flame items, clustered on the small table in his den area, which was lined with curved leather chairs and a lush sofa that must have set him back a year’s peddling. A painted screen in muted blues and greens concealed his vidset, as if Tark couldn’t bear to acknowledge advanced technology when he retreated to his cave. Not that the cave metaphor was accurate for his species, but considering what the Library didn’t reveal about them, who knew?

My favorite Tarkin-object was an ancient wooden chest wrapped by three gold bands. I’d never seen it open and loved to speculate what it contained. I told Heen it hid all the humanoid porn and vidgames Tark didn’t want us to know he owned, but she just looked at me like I was being weirder than usual. Tonight the chest’s carved lid boasted an arrangement of pastel stones on a tile plate perched in the center.

When Tarkin returned to my side, I still hadn’t spotted anything new besides the stones. I sure didn’t see any incense or aromachines to explain that odor. The candles were unlit. Discreetly, I inhaled. It seemed stronger toward the kitchen.

He noticed the direction of my attention. “Would you care for a beverage? I have terwine, laager, soda, kaf. Water.”

“No, thank you.” Oh, there was the home improvement! “I see you got some new fresh.” Last time I’d visited, he’d had a couple plants, but several large decoratives of various origins lent the room an *al fresco* atmosphere. Was it a plant that smelled so good? I didn't recognize them, and I definitely recognized the subtle, sweet odor tantalizing me into a near-fit. My mouth began to water, and I doubted the plants in Tarkin's living room were edible.

Tarkin acknowledged my powers of observation. "Several new ones—tropicals, I believe you would call them. An importer from Ysaltris had need of a new shaver."

How could he be so casual? The odor was driving me crazy. I stepped closer to him and glared. "I give up, Tarkin. What is that smell?"

His brow wrinkled, and a little tendril of black hair fell over his forehead in that delightful curl I always wanted to tug. "Do you mean the chocolate?"

"What?!"

"I have a chocolate dessert in the kitchen. It is called brownies on Terra."

Oh my stars! True chocolate was impossibly hard to come by in this part of the galaxy. It had become such a sought after delicacy even Terrans—on Terra—had trouble getting their hands on any. Apparently the endorphins it released in Terran brains were relatively universal, and some species even… well, no need to go there.

But real brownies! Here! Unable to contain my joy, I grabbed Tarkin in an impromptu hug.

I jumped up and down, squealing like girl, and the top of my head cracked into his cheek. "Whoops, slag it, I'm sorry."

I tried to step back, but Tarkin didn't release me. I became conscious of his arms around me, returning the embrace, his hands low on my back. His fingers supported my spine and brushed the top of my butt. His eyelids half-lowered to cover his dark irises.

"It pleases you? This is very encouraging, Sarai." An expression I barely recognized on Tarkin, a glimmer of satisfaction, flashed across his features.

"Heck yeah, it pleases me. It's amazing you could get your hands on chocolate." This close to him, I could barely smell the dessert. Tarkin's own scent replaced it. I loved his fragrance, and I'd never gotten such a delicious snootful. His scent was woodsy, with undertones of spice, nothing like a Terran. Fuller, maybe, as if it tickled more sensors than the ones in my nose.

The ones in my brain? But that was foolish. I didn't have that type of psi.

This close, I was reminded Tarkin was slightly taller than I, lean, but strong, with solid shoulders and trim waist. His species grew no facial hair other than eyelashes and eyebrows. Our bodies didn't mash together, but there was something about the splay of his fingers on my lower back that unnerved me. Something almost possessive.

"Uh, Tarkin?"

His eyes opened completely, the pupils dilated almost as wide as the irises.

"Yes?" His breath feathered across my lips. Did I imagine it was chocolate tinged breath, or was that just the brownie in the air?

And either way... why was Tark worried about pleasing me? He was always gracious, but not to the extent of procuring chocolate. It wasn't my birthday, and I'd hardly been promoted with the kitium temporing issues I'd been having.

I dragged myself away and used the vestiges of my willpower not to kiss him senseless. First I went bunko over brownies, and now this. My God, he'd never speak to me again! "You said you wanted to talk to me about something."

"One moment." He disappeared into his kitchenette again and emerged with something dark brown and crumbly in his hand. "For you."

It was a brownie. An honest to goodness brownie that looked a whole lot like the ones my granmater made for special occasions. Most thoughts of kissing fled my brain to be replaced by thoughts of chocolate. Chewy, moist, mouthwatering chocolate.

His breath had definitely smelled of chocolate.

I held out my hand, and he shook his head. "Open your mouth."

"You're kidding." But I complied, and he popped a bite of the dessert between my lips. His thumb brushed my cheek in what would have been a caress if it hadn't been Tarkin doing it.

I savored the brownie. The rich taste spread across my tongue, through my body, like the warmth of a yellow sun.

Tarkin watched me as the brownie dissolved on my tongue, then fed me the rest. "I believe it is customary on Terra for a male to give a female valued gifts when he wishes to court her."

Court her? What was going on? I swallowed and cleared my throat. "Did you get that from the Library, too?"

He smiled. His teeth flashed white against his mocha skin. "Gift-giving is not unique to your species."

He stepped closer to me, and I hopped away. "What are you doing?"

His voice lowered into some husky baritone I didn't recognize. His shoulders seemed broader, his legs longer, clad in the soft, expensive materials he favored. His eyes glittered. Even his black hair, neatly in its tuck, glittered. "We are friends, are we not? You said much the same earlier tonight."

"I like to think so," I hedged. Frantically I searched my memories of conversations with Heen, articles in the Library, offhand comments by anyone, to explain Tarkin's out of character behavior.

Gitters didn't, ah, mingle with other species. This, I knew, one of the more solid hearsays about their race. They didn't hug, they didn't touch, and they didn't ooze sex appeal. They didn't court Terran females who favored grubby brown coveralls and considered the vidmall high culture.

"My gift has pleased you?"

"Y… yes."

"I have paid you marked attention this past tenday. We have shared our time. You would like to know why."

I nodded. Our nightly dinners were starting to make sense.

That was a lie. They still made no sense. My head whirled.

He took my hand. His thumb stroked my palm, my sweaty palm, in a slow, circular gesture that felt a lot like the taste of chocolate. "Do you wish to please me?"

He had no idea. Oh, slag, please say he had no idea. Was this some weird Gitternian mockery of my crush on him?

"Does it involve sharing my brownies?" My voice came out in a squeak I didn't recognize. Something rubbery happened in the vicinity of my knees.

Tarkin leaned toward me and whispered, "It would please me, Sarai, if you would mate with me."

Chapter 3

Sarai seemed nervous and confused, but I was encouraged by her response. I had prepared for this moment to the best of my abilities, studying both Terran culture and her preferences in a circumspect manner. Even for those who follow the path of the Wanderer, such as myself, the joining does not wait upon any convenience. I counted myself lucky I'd located a compatible female when my time came upon me. There was no other female on the planet or the sector, so far as I had been able to determine, who would suit me as would Sarai.

That I was fond of her and found her person attractive was an unexpected bonus.

The moment had arrived for me to put my request to her. I had courted her in the Terran fashion and given gifts that pleased her. She was my friend. Terrans had been verified by our scientists as compatible if they had sufficient psi, so I had no qualms on that score. I had reported to the Gitternian Council several tenday ago, and they had been pleased by my choice of a Terran. My petition would be without pressure or any mention of consequence, the only honorable way to issue such an invitation.

In fact, I had waited almost too long to ask Sarai to mate, as the joining had already begun to alter my behavior. Why my progression was so accelerated this cycle, I did not know.

I leaned toward her, to catch her unique scent. Other humanoids are sadly lacking in the subtleties of olfactory discernment. "It would please me, Sarai, if you would mate with me."

As I said it, I hardened. An image of Sarai's pale, soft body unclothed and spread upon my bed invaded my inner eye, and I barely kept it from her mind. I would take her quickly, for I would not be able to help myself, then in the following days I would explore every centimeter of her, feel her hands upon me, join mentally and physically in the manner my species required.

The prospect of Sarai as my lover excited and pleased me more than my choices from previous joinings, and more than I cared to dwell on at this time.

I was out of time.

I edged my hips away from her so she would not note my urgency. To allow your choice of mate to detect your need before she had accepted would be uncouth.

"What?" she asked, then repeated herself. I had caught her off guard. "What?"

"Would you mate with me?" I asked her, slowly and plainly, resisting the urge to lick her pink lips, savor the chocolate she had eaten combined with her own sweet-salty taste. I wanted so much to touch her flame red hair, unbind it and curl it around my fingers.

I expected an onslaught of her colorful Terran slang, perhaps expressions of her peculiar humor or even anticipation.

I expected, and was prepared for, avid questions about my physiology and the cultural practices in my home system. I could reveal what was allowed and satisfy her curiosity, even though the situation I found myself in—trapped too far from Gitternis to slake the crucial urges with another of my species—was a challenge.

But what I did not expect from Sarai was complete incomprehension.

"Mate? You mean, like, do it?"

I considered her turn of phrase. "If by 'it' you mean sexual intercourse, yes."

"You're kidding."

"I am not."

Her face turned scarlet, and her scent sharpened with anger. "You're mocking me, aren't you? Everybody knows Gitters, I mean Gitternians, are eunuchs or something."

"We are not castrates, my dear." On Gitternis, the females outnumber the males three to one, so we are not accustomed to difficulties when our time is upon us. More, a surfeit of choice and females vying for our attentions, even when we are numb to them.

However, part of the path of the Wanderer is to adapt to other cultures. Terran courtship was a practice I found particularly exhilarating, if stressful. Pursuing the female I wished to bed had roused latent predatory instincts, which might also explain the accelerated progress of the joining.

Sarai rubbed her forehead. "I thought Gitternians didn't mix. I'm Terran. We're not… the same."

I did not think Sarai had mated outside her species. I had discretely quizzed Heen on that matter, for it would not do to interrogate one's selection. That would reveal doubt in her desirability and your confidence in her. And Sarai's desirability was near boundless, with her white skin and colorful hair, with her striking blue eyes that concealed nothing. Now, they spoke to me of her bewilderment. The soft brown flecks on her skin that danced upon her nose, like sugar. She was small and rounded, made to fit in the circle of my arms. So different from typical Gitternian appearance and yet so enthralling.

What would a Terran do if his advances confused his partner? Would he attempt to confirm his prowess?

"A member of another species is not the optimum choice for many humanoids, but I will endeavor to see to it your experience is not unpleasant." Though it was presumptuous, though it would reveal my craving, I caught her hips and pulled her against me, nearly shuddering as I encountered her warmth. I allowed my hand to cup her plush derriere.

"We are not so different it would frighten you," I lied. At least, the physical joining should not frighten her.

Sarai's eyes widened as my erection prodded her. They were such pure cobalt, like the blooms of a helia. She excited me, this Terran woman. She interested me before my cycle peaked, and now what I felt bordered on obsession. It unbalanced me, but I had no option at this point.

"I would please you, Sarai. Countless ways." My voice was raw in my throat. "Let me."

Sarai gulped. Her lips parted. I brushed my mouth against her flushed cheek, and she moaned softly. Her scent shifted from anger to arousal. So close…

Another mental image nearly inflamed me beyond reason. Her rounded ass bare, her spine arched, as I pushed her face forward across the couch. Her sweet, pink cunt parted, moist, inviting. The wet, quick slide of my cock plunging into her.

She flinched. "I… my head."

Damn! Had I tapped her psi? It was too soon. This loss of control had occurred too frequently the past tenday as the joining built towards its inexorable conclusion.

She struggled. I released her with effort. Her form tempted me, and my basic urges growled at the edges of my being. It was almost beyond the point where I would be able to restrain myself in her presence. I could sense her interest. Why did she resist? In a short time, I would be on her like a primitive, taking her whether she permitted it or not, or I would suffer the consequences of failure.

The eternal consequences.

But she could not know that. To lay that part of my dilemma at her feet would be without honor. A Gitternis female would understand, and choose accordingly, but Sarai—I would not burden her so.

"I don't understand." She bit her lip. I longed to do the same.

There were disadvantages to approaching a non-Gitternis female during one's time. This was the primary one.

I took a deep breath. The hard-won chocolate teased my senses. Sarai teased my senses. Her female musk. The electricity of her presence. "I am sorry. I thought my intentions clear. I wish to have sexual intercourse with you. Now."

"Why?"

"I want you."

"Why?"

It was becoming difficult to stay in one spot. I wanted to pace. I wanted to prowl. I wanted to rip her clothing off and mark her skin with my teeth. On Gitternis, the joining would never evolve to this level before being tended. There were reasons for our biological complexities.

"Sarai, I must warn you. Comply or go."

She blinked rapidly. "So, what, we can't be friends now? This is crazy."

I would not beg. My muscled bunched. My groin began to ache. Stars popped in my vision.

"Comply or go," I repeated.

She backed toward the door, and my soul plummeted. She had no idea—she could not know. I'd failed. There was nothing I could do. Nothing except force myself on her, which I could do without injuring her. I'd been trained.

The animal inside me roared. I closed my eyes.

"I, uh, I have to… to go," she stuttered.

"Don't," I whispered, but she was gone.

"Don't freak out, don't freak out, don't freak out," a frantic voice chanted inside my head as I huddled in the cab after leaving Tarkin's as fast as my short little Terran legs could carry me. I went straight to Larry's since Heen would be there and I had to talk to somebody about the fact a Gitter had just propositioned me. Not just any Gitter, but a friend I had known for years.

It had occurred to me I could take him up on it. For about a second. Five or ten seconds. He'd given me brownies! I could have kissed him. Hugged him. Licked him all over. But I wasn't about to let a horny humanoid near me until I knew what sex with one of them entailed.

Some species considered sexual contact tantamount to a marriage certificate. Some were capable of reproducing across species boundaries. Talk about potent sperm. Some engaged in, shall we say, alternate sexual practices I had little interest in sampling.

Some species went psycho at the end of an affair. That included a lot of Terrans.

Tarkin hadn't exactly been forthcoming, now that I thought about it in the smelly privacy of the robocab. I had no knowledge about Gitternian sex beyond my previously held belief they didn't have any. Many people joked the galactic stork brought their young to them.

The lights of the city whizzed past the windows and soon the cab dropped me at the crosswalk nearest Larry's. Avoiding the others on the sidewalk, especially any who looked like they might proposition me, which at this time of night was half of them, I made a run for the sanctuary of Heen's section in the restaurant.

The dinner crowd had thinned, replaced by the gambling, drinking and pre-fucking crowd, since Larry didn't allow public sex any more than he allowed public brawls.

Heen, the delicate hair on her face in little swirls that indicated she'd been rubbing her forehead a lot, popped up at my table before I punched in a drink order. Her apron featured several unidentified spills, a patch of hair on her leg was matted, and I wondered if this was one of the nights she wished she'd put on coveralls like those of us not blessed with pelts.

"What are you doing back here?" She held her datapad in one hand, a stingstick for rowdies in another, and her remaining arms were akimbo.

My fingers flew on the table's touchpad as I ordered something swift and alcoholic. "I need to talk. Can you take a break?"

She holstered her stingstick. "I'm due one. What gives? You look white around the lips, baldie."

"You aren't going to believe me. Come back when you can stay. And bring a Library portable."

Heen returned in five with two servings of my drink but no Library unit. "I figured you'd want double." For herself, she had kaf. She untied her apron and sank into the yielding chair opposite me with a groan. "This job is so menial. I'd go back to sex partnering if this rock didn't have so many Irts on it."

I took a long, deep drink of my rika, a facsimile of Terran sake made from a native rice plant, one of the few things safe for humanoid consumption—but only after it had been fermented. It burned all the way down, and when I exhaled, I noticed a lemony tang.

"You brought me the good stuff again," I accused Heen. "I ordered the cheap crap."

"You can afford it."

"Where's the Library unit? We need to do some research." Though what good it would do me considering the available information on Gitternis, I had no idea.

"There wasn't one free." Heen scratched beside her flat nose, more of a broad, pink feline sniffer than anything Terran looking. Her large, delicate ears were canted up on her skull, her eyes round and lavender. She was taller than me by a head—my head, anyway. I'd grown up familiar with many alien species, and the variety out there never failed to amaze me. Humanoids—bipedal primates, essentially—made up the bulk of our galaxy's inhabitants, but there were also multipeds, morphs, aquatics, arthropods. You name it, somewhere it had achieved star-faring capability.

Terrans were basic two-armed humanoids, as were Gitters. Gitternians. Damn.

Which didn't necessarily mean we were sexually compatible, alas—or what I'd consider compatible, which was a less flexible definition than some.

"I won't be tasting anything by the time I'm halfway into this." I hefted the plastene mug. "Seems like a waste." I took another swill. It really was good. Tarkin and Heen were always trying to educate my Terran palate, which was funny because I was the one who grew up on a planet that still had green spaces.

Though who knew about Gitternis? Oh, Tarkin. What was I going to do?

Heen sipped her kaf and eyed me over the rim. "I don't have forever. Quit stalling and tell me what's bleached your face like a moon."

I held a third sip in my mouth until it threatened to burn my tongue. The pain gave me courage. "Tarkin asked me out."

"To the bubble? I knew that."

"No, I mean… he asked me to do it with him."

Heen chuckled. "Is he taking you on a sex trip to some Terran vacation island?"

Tarkin's declarations of undying love were a joke of long-standing between Heen and myself. She knew how I felt about him and had always warned me not to store my goods in that cargo hold, though she wouldn't say anything beyond that.

"I'm not kidding." As my agitation grew, I talked faster. "He had brownies at his apartment and asked if I was pleased with his gift and when I said I was, he said he'd been courting me this past tenday and asked me to have sex with him. Heen, he had a… he kind of hugged me? And I'm pretty sure he had a hard-on. No jokes."

"All right, all right. I suppose it couldn't have been a laser in his pocket, considering what a pacifist he is." Heen rubbed her forehead. "It could be time. But… a Terran?"

"Time for what, the stars to fall?" I snapped. Just as I'd always suspected, she seemed to know more than she'd told me. "Why does everyone say Gitters don't interbreed if Tarkin wants to sleep with me? Why can't I find anything about Gitters in the Library?"

"Some species manage to preserve some mysteries from the Librarians," Heen said. "Did you give him a chance to explain or run screaming?"

"He told me to put out or get out."

"He almost picked a fight with those two Irts tonight, didn't he?" Heen sighed and leaned into the chair, pressing two of her palms against the back and cracking her spine. "Poor Tark. That is not good. If he asked you, he had to have a reason for thinking it would work." She narrowed her eyes and inspected me.

"Don't stop there," I demanded. "Level with me."

Heen glanced at the servo area, where drinks and plates of food continued to be shuttled through the chutes for the roboservers and waitstaff. "I should get back to work." But a little smile flickered across her lips as she said it.

"Heen, please."

Heen pressed her finger to her lips, the universal gesture for secrecy. "I only know what I heard when I was a sex partner. I've never spoken with any Gitternians to verify it. They're very private with outsiders, including the Librarians."

"No kidding." I thought of Tarkin—polite, reserved and always careful to sidestep questions about his home system that went beyond public knowledge. He'd told me once his species was divided into proficiency-based classes. He belonged to the Wanderer faction, which meant he was one of the adventurous ones who left the home system to learn about other cultures first-hand, rather than through the notoriously unreliable Library system.

"I heard if a Gitternian male came to you for sex, not to turn him down, unless you had a handy escape route."

"Do they get pissed?" I gulped my beverage to wet my suddenly dry mouth. I couldn't imagine Tarkin hunting me down and shooting me with the laser not in his pocket, but before tonight I'd never imagined Tarkin had sexual appetites.

"I think they get sick if they can't have sex when they need to."

"Sounds like a line," I said. "Baby, I've got the horny flu and I'll die if you don't do me."

Heen's nose wrinkled in a Devian scowl. "It must have some grounding in fact or my mentor wouldn't have warned me. Tarkin might be desperate at this point, Sarai."

"Starfrack," I cursed. "I thought he'd clued in to my silly crush on him and was making fun of me. Or crazy. Is he crazy?"

She shrugged, a fluid gesture she'd picked up from interaction with Terrans. "Perhaps that's why you're supposed to have an escape route."

I half rose from the table. "Why didn't he explain? How sick will he get?" Panic rose in my throat like a piece of bad recon meat.

"I'm sure it's not that serious. Even the Gitternians couldn't have concealed death by horniness from the rest of the galaxy."

"What should I do?"

"That depends on what you want." She swirled her drink and gestured towards me. "He's apparently fixated on you, so he might come looking for you. There are several species who go through a cycle like this, and the sufferers can become very aggressive."

"Looking for me?" I sank into the chair, then popped back up. "He'll come here."

Heen tilted her head to the side. "Larry wouldn't appreciate a scene like that smudging his reputation."

"A scene like what?"

She averted her gaze and ran a finger around the rim of her cup. "Maybe you should go somewhere else. What about The Black Hole? He'd never look for you there."

The Black Hole, a bar a couple streets over, was the anti-Larry's. The snacks were lousy, the beverages limited, and the crowd rough. Not a great place for a small, solo humanoid to venture alone, without combat psi or mech armor.

I nipped a fingernail, then said, "I could get a motel room."

"Won't work. He can track you anywhere you use your ident chip. You sure you don't want to change your mind about this?"

It might have been my overwrought imagination, but a glint of amusement—at odds with the concern in her voice and words—crossed Heen's face as I grew more agitated. But Devians, and Heen in particular, found the strangest things humorous, so I wasn't sure what that implied.

I gnawed on my poor, abused fingernail and considered her question. Heen had mated right and left in her days as a sex partner, but I obviously didn't have her experience. In my own sex life, I'd stuck with Terrans. There was that one near miss with a friend of Heen's a couple years back, but nothing had come of it. Not that I was xenophobic, but, well, sex complicated matters for me, no matter who I did it with. Where my body went, so did my heart. Stupid, unsophisticated Terran.

Sex with Tarkin, considering my friendship with him, my feelings for him, and my lack of knowledge about his kind beyond Heen's man-in-heat hearsay, was a bad idea. And I still had the nagging suspicion Heen was leaving details out.

"Is there something you're not telling me?" I asked. "I get this feeling you're hiding things."

"In this apron?" she asked. "Terrans are so suspicious."

Unconvinced, I tried digging for dirt a more roundabout way. "Do you really think it's a good idea? Tark and I being different species and all?"

"If my mentors said I could fuck a Gitter, you can fuck one, too, Sarai."

Yeah, but I wasn't a trained professional. I waved my hands in the air. "I can't without understanding his intentions. Or any ramifications. It's too weird. He's our friend, Heen."

"You like him," Heen said. "You always have. Take a chance."

"I don't have enough facts." I also didn't have enough courage. "Let me hide at your place."

Heen got up and adjusted her apron. She pulled a plastene card from a pocket and tossed it on my table. "That's the third place he'll look, right after here and your place."

I raised a finger. "The mine. Or the lab."

"He knows you too well, Terran. You'll have to go somewhere unexpected." She squeezed between a table of Ventx and a roboserver, then called over her shoulder. "I'll come get you at The Black Hole when it's safe. That's a generic vidchip. It's not traceable."

"You'd better." I glared at her retreating back. To myself, I added, "You'll probably have to rescue me from a bunch of drunken spacers."

At The Black Hole, I ducked through its doorway, wincing at the fierce music throbbing from the giant holoscreens over the fight cage. I found a corner stool at the vid bar close to the back door. I waved the tall humanoid server away—no expensive roboservers here—because I didn't want to use my ident chip. If I got thirsty before Heen came to fetch me, I'd hit up one of the Hermana employees I'd spotted in the crowd. Raka, from transpo, maybe. Or wC'in, who I ate lunch with sometimes, when he didn't have a live meal.

Lucky for me, I hadn't seen or been seen by any of the, shall we say, disgruntled individuals who resented the higher salaries and safer environs of lab techs like myself. Or resented Terrans. Or species with psi. Or red-headed females in brown coveralls.

You name it, in a place like this it could piss somebody off if you weren't careful.

I used Heen's vidchip and dialed up the tamest in the Hole's selection of vids. Nothing too sexy that might put me in mind of Tarkin and my long-held fantasies about him. Fantasies I was passing up the chance to fulfill.

Sometimes I hated myself and my unsophisticated Terran ways.

Chapter 4

I could not have Sarai, but I could not stay cooped in my apartment, like the angry beast caged inside me who would in a few hours be tamed forever. She had fled, doubtless to some location known only to her. In any case, I would not seek her.

Not until she was safe. Not until the process was complete. I had known of Gitternians who chose not to accept their fate, and indeed in the past I had fought it myself.

I had done things, things I'd been trained for, yet with Sarai I could not bring myself to do them. Not with Sarai.

This was the last night I would be… myself. I would not spend it bemoaning Sarai's decision, or mine. I would behave with honor and courage. I would not shame my kin and kind with the cowardly fits of the unevolved.

Sarai's choice would be my choice.

I ate two of Sarai's brownies in a row, relishing the dark, buttery taste, before catching a cab to Larry's. My skin prickled as the call for joining mounted inside me, unanswered, and I forced myself to be still. I had no fear I would encounter Sarai. She had been so alarmed by my behavior she would likely not surface for days. She favored avoidance when troubled, avoidance or flippancy, I had observed in the past.

When she did return, I would not be the exact man she remembered. Would she have chosen differently, had I broken decree and confessed to her?

When Heen appeared beside my table, it was all I could do not to beg her to tell me if Sarai had contacted her. I could tell from the expression on her elegant features Sarai had.

Before she could speak, I made my intentions clear. "She has made her preference clear. I will not pursue her."

Heen snorted and clunked a large mug of something alcoholic in front of me, something I had not ordered and did not want. I drank it anyway. "So you'll just let yourself suffer? Tark, I heard things as a sex partner. I have an idea what it means for you to—"

"Do not speak of it." It was possible Heen knew some version of the truth. I felt the primal urges inside me swell. My vision reddened and cleared like a warning light blinking on and off, on and off. I could smell Sarai's distinct fragrance on Heen's fur. She'd been here.

It nearly undid me. The beast inside me growled. It wanted Sarai. It did not want to die without a struggle.

Without a fight. This gave me an idea.

"I need the location of a brawling venue," I told Heen. "It will not suffice, but it will make the situation… easier to bear."

Heen watched me for a long moment before she answered. "You're my friend, Tarkin. I don't want you to get hurt."

I picked up the mug I had drained. With the adrenalin coursing through me, I crushed it in my fist. The destruction felt good to me. Violence. Lust. Anger. All the primitive emotions male Gitternians had not allowed to control our behavior in eons, except for these brief, unavoidable cycles.

I'd never thought to be caught alone at my time. It had come upon me too quickly, unexpectedly, and I had courted Sarai in haste. Who besides the Holy Ones planned for the dwindling as one's path? No one, though all Wanderers prepared for the possibility.

Or they were supposed to. And that did not make it welcome.

I finished crumpling the mug, and Heen's eyes widened as I dropped the useless vessel to the table. "That is not the Tarkin I know."

"I am not," I concurred.

"You frightened her."

"I regret that I was unable to approach her in the manner she deserves." I bowed my head and studied the twisted metal. My arms itched. My face felt tight and hot and I longed to dig my fingers into the hard table. Into a woman's flesh as I pounded senselessly into her body.

"Why couldn't you explain it to her? She would have listened. She cares for you, Tarkin."

"Emotional blackmail is not a moral path." Would Sarai ever think well of me again?

After tonight, I would not care so much. I would miss caring. I would miss pain and joy and taste and touch. I would miss Sarai.

I had been taught to accept this, should it be necessary.

I gripped my thighs under the table, barely feeling the bruising strength of my fingers. "You will find me changed when next we meet, but I will still be your friend. And Sarai's. Please tell her, Heen, that I asked not in desperation."

"I didn't think so."

"And now I must fight, or perhaps you would be so kind as to sedate me with your weapon. You may have to use it several times." The muscles in my arms and legs bunched and swelled. My veins filled with repressed energy.

She must have noticed my state, as her brow ridges flickered. "If you're this twisted, how did you expect to have sex with Sarai and not scare the galactic shit out of her?"

I could give Heen a partial explanation, but to do more would violate centuries of law and tradition. I attempted to keep my tones level and unthreatening. "Fighting is a release, while lovemaking is fulfillment. A connection. We… require that from time to time. I cannot explain more. Do not ask."

She leaned toward me, lowered her voice. "I used to be a sex partner, my friend. I have connections in the business. Are you sure only Sarai will do?"

"Yes," I snarled, growing more provoked by the second. Heen was too close, too much a reminder of what I had just lost. "Only Sarai."

"Well, then." She seemed to reach some decision. "The best fight cage is at a bar called The Black Hole. Know where that is?"

"I do." With lingering civility, I bowed my head to Heen. Nearly every atom inside me wanted to leap on her and force Sarai's location from her lips.

But I would not. Sarai had rejected me, and to track her was not honorable. I must avoid her. I would not be able to control myself in her presence. I would go to this Black Hole, and I would fight, I would crush, I would bleed, until the first stage passed and the dwindling began its inevitable course through my body and soul.

I'd reached the middle of the documentary I'd chosen about a thirty-system kongii tournament when the back of my neck began to prickle.

Psi or no psi, somebody in the Hole was watching me.

Prostie? Terran hater? Person desperate for a vid terminal? I was almost afraid to turn around and find out.

As it happened, I didn't have to move a muscle.

A huge brown palm, claws glistening, landed on my shoulder, and an Irt twice my size yanked me out of my chair. "Techie," she growled, barely audible above the thumping music and shouts and screams from the fight cage area. "You come to the wrong place. No bots save you here."

Contrary to popular belief, all Irts do not look alike. I recognized this one from Larry's, one of the pair Tarkin had antagonized.

Slag! She was drunker than a shiprat off a six-month haul, and apparently she recognized me from Larry's and Hermana both. How else would she have known I was a Techie?

"Do you want a vid terminal?" I asked hopefully. Irts retained grudges like Terran females retained water.

"Want you to bow and kiss my hairy ass," she said. "You be nothing without diggers."

"I'd be nothing without diggers," I agreed, because it was true. Diggers went into the earth, both with and without machines, and excavated the kitium and other ores. Kitium in particular was a sensitive substance. Exposure to too much high tech at any stage of the process and it fizzled.

I mean, I could dig the shit myself and tempor it in the mine, which believe me I'd been considering lately with my ratio of successful kitium tubes, but that was even harder than what I did in the lab, not to mention backbreaking, depressing, and dangerous. I wouldn't have the energy to psi-nudge the ore after I mined it.

"You not hafta bow to face my ass. Smaller than a child." The Irt palmed the top of my head and pressed. I barely stayed on my feet. Her fingers wrapped almost completely around my noggin. A claw tickled my ear.

Oh boy, I thought. Don't squeeze, Big Bertha.

"Can I…" I realized I'd almost offered to buy her a drink, but I wasn't sure if that was an insult. It might imply she couldn't buy her own. Irts, Irts, Irts. What were you supposed to do if confronted by an Irt besides scream and run? My brain blanked. My knees locked, which was better than buckling. I didn't fancy being held aloft by my head.

She wanted me to kiss her butt. I had more survival instinct than pride, okay? I could do that if it meant keeping my body parts intact.

She leaned down, way down, until her small, black eyes peered straight into mine. She was like a nightmare version of Heen—flat nose, a broad mouth with protruding incisors, wiry hair and whiskers. Dark brown with blond tips, in a species caste-marked by their pelts. I wasn't sure what hers meant besides, "Hates Techies, likes to drink."

I could smell the cheap alcohol on her breath. Her coverall was quite a bit more stylish than mine. She rubbed my head roughly, and my hair sprang out of its braid, pieces flopping around my face.

"So much trouble for psi," she muttered. "Goes against everything. Fracking Hermana. Slagburners. Criminals."

"Erk." I squeaked in agreement with whatever she was ranting about. I tried to scooch away, but her hand tightened on my skull. Red that had nothing to do with my escaped hair started to pulse in my vision. "Please, can you ease up on the head?"

She did, slightly. "Can't mash the precious psi, no."

The weakness of relief trembled in my knees but I stayed upright. "I'm more worried about the skull in general."

"You're an egg, not the bird, Techie. Breaking you won't solve anything. But it would help." She transferred her giant paw to my chest and shoved.

Next thing I knew I was flying across the Black Hole and bouncing off patrons. Luckily they slowed my progress. Unluckily, so did gravity, still a law on most planets. I landed on my ass with a jolt of pain and skidded across unidentified greasy substances on the floor. My hair tangled in my face. Lights flashed around me, and somebody kicked me in the back.

Next thing I knew after that, the Irt flew across the Black Hole in my wake, knocking patrons aside like bowling pins.

She howled with rage. I scrabbled out of her way between the many legs either rushing toward or away from the bar fight. My hands slipped and slid on the grimy floor. I found an opening and leapt up, ignoring the bruises on my rear.

Somebody grabbed my arm before I could take off.

"Nooo!" I yelled. "Help!"

A rough voice near my ear growled orders. "Sarai. Be silent. Do not move."

Tarkin! My mouth dropped open and my hair invaded it. I spat. Spat again.

He shoved me behind him when the Irt stormed across the bar. She had a hand laser and I bet she knew how to use it. We were dead, we were dead, poor us, I started to drag him away, but…

He moved so fast I could barely see his hands and feet. He vaulted into the air, kicked her in the head a couple of times, and grabbed the laser out of her paw. He landed and tensed to spring again.

She stumbled and guarded her pate. A spurt of dark blood appeared at her nose.

He poked the laser at her large chest. "Run or die."

For a minute, even the other patrons froze. Not that they were intimidated by an unholstered laser, but because a Gitter held it, rage burning in his black eyes like an imploding star. It was as if a domestic ticit had suddenly morphed into an agro warrior. I would have bet my entire savings even those with minimal psi could sense the jeopardy everyone in the proximity was in. Far as I knew, Gitters didn't have psi, certainly not combat psi, but I could taste the power building inside Tarkin's lean, deadly frame like salt in the air right before you spot a Terran ocean.

The Irt, no fool despite her species' reputation, bobbed her head and placed her fingertips on her brows, acquiescing way more easily than I expected. I blinked about ten times, convinced I hadn't just seen what I'd seen. Tark, leaping into the air twice his height. An Irt, backing away from a fight with a dapper Gitternian peddler.

"Unfortunate. I would have picked die." Tarkin pocketed the laser and turned to me.

His face was tight, alien. I didn't know this man. How had he found me?

"Are you injured?"

Even the voice wasn't his, rough and low. He again took my arm, drawing me close, and ran his hands over my body. It was… sort of impersonal, but then his nostrils flared and his hands lingered at my waist. My hips. Between my legs.

I tried to jump away, but his grip was even more secure than the Irt's had been.

I wasn't sure if it was any safer.

He seemed satisfied when I quit struggling. "This is not how I would have wished this, but I cannot…" His face twisted. The crowd, already ignoring us, pushed us against each other.

"What are you doing here?" I asked. Our thighs brushed. Our hips bumped. There was no mistaking his erection.

"Heen sent me here. Come." He propelled me toward the rear of the bar.

Damn bossy-ass matchmaking Devian! Heen would pay for this. After I paid. Oh, man.

"I don't think so." I tried to sound as fierce as he looked.

He ignored me. He kicked open the door of an all-species wash up, happily empty, and locked it behind us. There was a multipurpose, body-conforming waste receptacle, a sink, and a slot to purchase the various items one might need in a wash up beyond disinfectant.

"I don't need to pee."

He dragged me to the sink. "Wash," he ordered.

I did. I wanted to, anyway. It wasn't like he'd scared the spit out of me and I'd do pretty much whatever he said at this point.

"I do not have much time." He placed a hand on my neck as I scrubbed the ick off my hands and disinfected. "Sarai, what did Heen tell you? I know you saw her."

I blushed. He was going to make me say it? The overhead glims flickered half-off, back on, like an old neon sign. "She said you might be in heat or something. And you'll get sick if you can't do it."

"Yes."

After all his freakishness, that was all I got? "She said you were dangerous."

"Yes," he said again. And then, "I am sorry. I must do this."

The first kiss wasn't gentle, a lover's first greeting. It was hot and wet and impatient. He parted my lips and tasted the inside of my mouth. I let him. Did I have a choice? Did I want one? Stars, he terrified me, he coursed with power, he felt so…

My back bumped against the sink. His body pushed mine. He gripped my hips and slanted his head to the side to access my mouth.

My heart raced with fear and something else. His warm breath feathered across my cheek. His arms wrapped me. His presence overwhelmed me. Panicked, I shoved his chest, but he growled.

"No," he said.

"Tarkin, please." My voice wobbled.

With an abrupt gesture, he released me, but only to rip open the top of my coverall, revealing my support tank. I tried to scream, but he muffled my protest with his mouth.

He kissed me, and kissed me again, kissed my neck and earlobes and collarbone, as if he couldn't get enough of my skin. He rubbed his cheeks against me like a scentmarking cat. Tension began to pool at the base of my spine. Muttering softly in what I took to be his native language—it sounded like music—he smoothed his palms down my arms. His fingers had calluses at the bases.

"Not enough," he said with a curse. He trapped me against the sink with his legs and shrugged out of his tunic. He, too, wore a soft tank, brilliant blue like sapphires. His arms were corded with muscle, and the tank delineated well-developed shoulders and pecs. I'd never seen him this unclothed.

His skin was like pale chocolate. His hair, normally queued, was black as space, unkempt against his neck. I closed my eyes, but they popped back open.

Groaning, he rubbed the insides of his arms against mine, across my half-bared back, increasing our direct contact. He caught my hair and rubbed it against his lips.

Suddenly I wished he'd take off his tank. Oh, stars, to have his skin rubbing against mine, all along my body, it would be like…

And he did. He yanked it over his head and tossed it to the floor. Tentatively, I rested my palms against his chest, not sure if I wanted to shove him or caress him. He needed this, but did I, considering my feelings for him?

He drew in a breath and watched me, his eyes black with compulsion. His chest was sculpted like a statue, his nipples small and dark. He was, indeed, not so different from a Terran, as far as I could see.

His gaze trapping mine, he reached underneath my tank and cupped my breasts.

My nipples pebbled like moonstones. His hands trembled with the depths of his heat. He pinched the sensitive buds, and something inside me switched from fear to arousal.

Click. Just like that I forgot all about what a bad idea this was, how intimidating he was, and remembered my fantasies. I remembered how I'd always felt about him and what I'd always dreamed of.

When he kissed me again, I slid my tongue across his and into his mouth. Electricity sliced through my body.

I tasted fire and spice. I closed my eyes and I could still see lights. Flashes. Images of us that made me wet and achy. One thing about a man close to my height—things fit. When he rotated his cock against my pussy, I groaned.

"Sarai," he breathed. "You will not deny me again."

I wasn't sure if he'd issued a commandment or a question. But he was right. I'd run and he'd caught me.

I think… I think if he'd kissed me, back in his apartment tonight, we'd be on tango number three, not the sleazy wash up at The Black Hole, wrapped around one another like teen-agers.

Cool air puffed over my chest. Tarkin had pushed my tank up and buried his face between my breasts. Then again, maybe there was something to be said for a sleazy quickie when I'd been celibate for so long, lusting after… Tarkin.

The sink behind me was sturdy. And, I'm sure, fully christened. I leaned back and gasped when he devoured my nipple. His teeth were sharp, his mouth sweltering and slick. I dug my fingers into his hair. It was satiny, heavy. He licked and suckled first one breast, then the other, and finally I grabbed him by his ears and dragged his face up to mine.

The way I kissed him now, the drugged intensity of it, would leave no doubt in his mind I'd say yes to whatever he wanted. Even here. Even now.

What he wanted was soon obvious.

I helped him wriggle my coveralls the rest of the way down my legs and kicked off my boots. He lifted me onto the sink. It hurt the bruises on my ass, but I didn't care. He didn't say anything, just watched me with those eerie black eyes and wrapped one hand in my underpants. His fingertips brushed my pussy. Was he going to touch me? I knew I was wet. Did Gitternian women get wet? They'd have to in order to…

He tugged sharply. The fabric of my panties cut into me, hurting, and finally tore. With my sock-clad feet, I joined him as he shoved his trous and underwear to the floor. Black hair curled around his cock, which looked normal enough to me.

Not that I had time to admire it. Or play with it, the way I wanted to, to make sure his body was on the up and up. I mean, you heard things about alien penises.

With no further ado, he spread my legs, positioned himself, and thrust his swollen organ into my not-quite-ready vagina.

I let out a yelp. My pussy burned and stretched. I tried to relax inside to accommodate his abrupt heft. It was too rushed to thrill me, but maybe Gitternians didn't go for foreplay.

I could deal with that. For Tarkin. It wasn't all about self-gratification when you had feelings for someone, right?

He closed his eyes, and his jaw clenched. The glims flickered. I heard voices outside the wash up door and really, really hoped nobody tried to come in.

"Sarai," he gritted out. "This will pain you."

"I'm not a first-timer," I said. Though he was sort of acting like one.

"I promise this will be the only time it hurts, sweetling."

Aw, he called me sweetling! I smiled.

He thrust into me further, withdrew, and returned. The slide of his cock, of flesh. Fullness and heat. Again and again. My juices began to assert themselves. His pelvis nudged my clit and I felt the first stirrings of a build towards climax.

Tarkin began to pound into me faster, grinding against my pussy and inspiring shards of delight. He bent his head and bit my breast. Really dug his teeth in, growling softly in a way that should have been funny but was very sexy. The bite hurt. I wanted him to do it again. Was that what he meant, about paining me? But then he sucked, and the combination of his mouth on my nipple, his stiff cock in my pussy, and I knew Gitternians weren't so amateur after all. I escalated, gasped, and he dropped a hand to tug my clit.

My hips bucked. I whimpered. He pushed inside me deeper, and harder, and I thought, is his dick growing? when suddenly something jerked my brain open like a tear in the fabric of space. Visions, lights, pain, flashes, Tarkin's black eyes, a vortex, I cried out, feeling my throat rip, my heart rip. His body slashed into mine. My psi filled and overflowed with him, cracked, shattered. It was an attack. It was a flood. I saw colors, I saw nothing, I felt intense pleasure/pain, I felt nothing.

I felt nothing.

Chapter 5

The sun rose, sending beams of dry warmth through the half-open blinds, and still Sarai slept. Her long eyelashes formed two perfect semicircles on her pale, freckled skin, and her chest, tucked carefully under my finest bed sheets, rose and fell with her even breaths.

She sighed in her sleep and shifted, the covers revealing the tops of her creamy breasts. Her sleep seemed peaceful, but… Again I stopped myself from waking her to ascertain her mental and physical condition.

She needed the healing sleep after the first joining, and I knew this well. If I were honest, I wanted to wake her for different reasons.

One mating with Sarai was not enough to satiate my inner beast, though this did not surprise me. I had thought of her long and often prior to this, and a cycle could last through several joinings. A first cycle could last a tenday. Would she be compliant when she woke or would she resist me?

My loins fired at the thought of Sarai's resistance. And her compliance. Yes, I wanted to wake her.

I wanted to drag the covers from her body and rouse her with my hands and mouth.

I wanted to taste her essence and feel her hot, slick walls close around my cock, this time without the desperation of the previous night. This time with her urging me on and moaning in pleasure. Last night had been necessary, but left much to be desired.

I wanted to touch spirits with her, again, and help her see how close two people could be, when joined in body and soul.

I wanted her, I wanted to…

My hand hovered over her soft shoulder. I drew it back. My lovely Sarai was the Library definition of unpredictable. Stimulating. How would she react to my explanation of what mating with a Gitternian meant for a Terran? With laughter? Fascination? Curses? Would she feel I had taken advantage of her? Would she cry?

I could promise her the opening of our minds would never be painful again, only pleasurable. I had not expected her to become unconscious during the act, so the experience could not have been agreeable for her. That, I regretted with all my being, but had I not taken her… It no longer mattered, because I had, and now I must deal with any and all consequences.

As would she. If I'd warned her in more detail what lovemaking with me would mean for her, would she have acquiesced?

Even I could not be sure how much it would affect her. Gitternian females had the same psi powers as males, so mating in-species spawned no changes, but Terrans and others we mated with—another story. In those cases, we functioned as catalysts. We had known our mental joining affected non-Gitternians in unpredictable ways for eons, but had managed to keep it hidden from the rest of the galaxy.

It would not do were the galactic government to learn what sex with a Gitternian could do to psi, not with psi the commodity it was. Our people did not have the biological capability to function on command in the way of most other species. Our joining time was not to be tampered with.

Not with the dangers inherent in mishandling it. Not with the type of psi it sometimes awoke in our partners.

Unfortunately, these were issues I could only skirt with Sarai when she woke. I must first determine any changes in her psi before alarming her in such a fashion. Not only was it against Gitternian regulation, with severe punishments inflicted upon those who disclosed prematurely, but it would panic her, and she would be unsettled enough. My interest, despite my efforts at courtship, had been unexpected—had "freaked her out", as she was so fond of saying. Our joining had altered her psi, potentially, and would alter our friendship.

I did not want to lose her. Chances were our mating had gifted her with the ability to bond with me during intercourse and nothing else. Such was usually the case, so we were required by our laws to conceal other possibilities until actual transformation was confirmed. Revealing confidential details about Gitternis was forbidden, even for Wanderers forced to take a nonstandard partner during their cycle.

Though with Sarai, I cannot say I had been forced. Another thing I must confess, to myself if no one else. I had not looked for an alternate partner after I met Sarai.

She was my choice.

She was still asleep.

I coughed.

A small sound woke me. I was sprawled on my back in a bed. A soft bed. Fancy sheets on my bare skin. No city noises. Definitely no infirmary noises. Smelled nice.

Smelled Tarkin.

I was in Tarkin's bed, and I was totally buckers. Which meant I hadn't dreamed last night's encounter in the bathroom of the Black Hole.

Something rustled beside me, and I realized not only was I in Tarkin's bed, but Tarkin was in Tarkin's bed. I lay as still as I could, and he made no move to touch or wake me. I resisted the urge to roll over and protect my boobs. The sheet slid further down my body, and I concentrated on sleepytime breathing and no eyelid flutters.

Was he asleep? Was he going to say anything? Man, he smelled good. All clean and rich.

Were there any brownies left?

Wait a minute. Why didn't I remember getting into Tarkin's bed? As many times as I'd fantasized about Tarkin's bed, you think I'd remember that. Additional images from last night trickled to the front of my brain, especially the part where something so weird and painful happened to my psi at a crucial moment I'd passed out. Which didn't explain why I was naked, unless Tark had…

I sat up and screeched, "Did you do me when I was passed out or something? That's some crazy near-necrophilia, buddy, and I won't stand for it."

Tarkin, covered from his midriff down in a pale blue sheet, quirked a dark eyebrow at me. "You are already not standing, Sarai."

"Uh." Whatever I was going to say trailed off when I got a full gander at Tarkin in bed.

His chest was elegantly sculpted, lean and defined, and unless I missed my guess his abs were sculpted as well. His dark brown nipples provided a perfect contrast to his paler brown skin. A strong neck curved into broad shoulders, and his arms, his biceps, holy cowpox! How did a peddler come to have a body like a galactic athlete? The whole package was covered in flawless, lickable cocoa skin that brought to mind all the flavors of the milk chocolate rainbow. Were Gitternians naturally perfect or did he work at it?

His hair was mussed and shiny. Some of the longer strands actually had curl to them, freed from their preternaturally tidy state. No stubble: he was Gitternian. Just a clean jaw and dark, magnetic eyes.

"Good morning," Tarkin said. But he wasn't looking at my face. The sheet had fallen to my waist, and he eyed my breasts with the same hungry look that was probably on my own face. Like he thought I was lickable.

I didn't remember much licking from last night. Just some hopping onto the sink and some hard thrusting. No time to absorb the details.

I really wanted to see the rest of him. So did my privates.

"I asked you a question," I said, ignoring my saucy nethers. His hips were angled to the side so the sheet didn't reveal anything interesting about his own groin area.

Tarkin blinked. His serious look. "I did not take advantage of you when you were unconscious. Only when you were awake."

"I got a migraine or something right before I… finished," I said. "What happened?"

"I brought you home."

"Why didn't you take me to my apartment?"

Tarkin smiled, a long, slow, lazy smile I'd never before seen on his face. "I could care for you more efficiently here."

What did that smile mean? Had I done something embarrassing besides pass out? "Was I sick?"

"How do you feel?" he countered.

"Wigged," I admitted. I tugged the sheet around my shoulders. "A little sore. And hungry."

He cocked his head to the side and a frown creased his brow. He'd taken me to bed, and he was adorable. Ruddy stars!

"Wigged? You feel that your hair is false?"

Nearly everyone in the galaxy knew commerce tongue, but several species added idioms that approximated their native language. Tarkin and I had this issue when I reverted to Terranisms. But commerce tongue was so bland, I couldn't help it.

"Freaked out," I explained. I knew he understood that phrase. He may have accused me of being overly fond of it once or twice.

His eyebrows rose and he guessed, "You are referring to the opening of your psi last night. If your head aches, there are remedies."

It was good he wasn't going to try to pretend it hadn't happened, but what the hell? "My head is fine, but why in the world did my psi go haywire?" A new notion crossed my mind, a very unpleasant one. "Do you think I have brain fever? Maybe that's why my kitium temporing hasn't been taking. Oh, slag!" My superiors had been displeased with me lately, considering how much of the company's income hinged on my well-paid ability to handle the fragile ore.

I wasn't worth squat if my psi fritzed.

"The two things are unrelated. I am sure of that." Tarkin pursed his lips a moment, and the sheet dropped lower on his torso. I kept my tongue in my mouth. "I must be able to trust you, Sarai, in order to explain. It involves confidential information about Gitternians." He met my eyes and my heart thumped. "Can I trust you?"

"Don't you already trust me? Heen said you picked me for this—" I waved my hand over our bodies "—which must mean something." Even my bravado couldn't hide my blush.

He nodded. "I hope you understand. My options were not plentiful."

"Thanks a quadrillion," I snapped, a little stung. "I'm a last resort."

"I would not describe you as a last resort, Sarai." Tarkin reached out and touched my… hand. How terribly mild. Had he returned to normal, albeit naked, Tarkin after slaking his lusts? Maybe last night was the end of it.

Not fair! I hadn't even gotten off. I wanted to whine to him that I deserved more than last night, that I'd wanted him in a carnal way for ages—but the explanation of my mid-coitus migraine took precedence. He seemed positive it had nothing to do with the kitium, and Tarkin was rarely mistaken.

"You can trust me." I strove for a jolly, non-lusty tone and tried to relax.

"When Gitternians mate, it involves a joining of psi. A mental mating, if you will."

"Our brains did it, too?" I asked. Interesting, if disturbing. "Like mind -reading? Everyone knows mind-reading isn't possible. Psi doesn't work that way. No wonder you don't want anybody to know. The government would—"

"No," he said hastily, interrupting me, "not mind-reading." He removed his finger from my hand. Strange how bereft I felt when deprived of that tiny contact. "However, the rumor we cannot be intimate with other species is because we cannot if they do not have sufficient psi. It is more of an opening than a reading." He paused to consider his words, something he often did. "We also must be in our cycle for such an act to occur."

Normally, Tarkin was the epitome of coherent, but right now, he seemed unsure. He wasn't being very… clear. Did he mean he couldn't have sex unless he was in heat? That he couldn't have sex outside his species unless he was so randy he couldn't help himself? If so, what did that mean for our future? Was this a one-cycle stand?

I couldn't ask that outright. Even though he claimed I wasn't his last resort, that didn't mean he wanted a romance with me. I'd prefer not to pressure him, and I sure as hell didn't want him admitting he wasn't interested beyond the demands of his biology.

I'd try to get the information slyly. Because I was the sly master. Yep. "Your cycle is when you go into heat and have to get some?"

"That is not an inaccurate description. There are many species who have fertility cycles. It is not that different."

I couldn't imagine being that subject to biology, though lots of species couldn't imagine bleeding like a stuck pig once a month, a lovely Terran female characteristic advanced science had yet to completely outwit without major surgery. "Would you get sick if we hadn't done it?"

And were we going to do it again? Because I'd be up for it, if he was.

Maybe.

Depending.

Tarkin's face smoothed into an emotionless mask. Not that he had mobile, expressive features, but you could see glimmers if you were observant. It was a myth Gitters had no emotions. Obviously it was also a myth they had no sex.

"I would have lost the ability to mate and certain other aspects of my emotive nature," he said evenly.

I gaped at him. "You're shitting me!"

"I am not."

"Would your winky have fallen off? I saved your winky!"

Tarkin's mask cracked, and he smiled. "Ah, Sarai. It is a delight how you reduce things to the most basic levels. But no. It would have been a hormonal shift, and a shift in my psi."

"So you'd keep your winky, but what?"

"There are certain responses I could not have without the missing hormones."

"You'd be a limpy for life." I threw myself back on the pillows and stared at the ceiling, creamy squares of insulated tile striated with gold. Fancy and sophisticated. Like Tarkin.

But not like me. I had to face the facts. We didn't mesh romantically, but now that I understood what had been at stake, I'd try not to be a bitch about it. Hell, I'd have tried to seduce an Irt—or Tarkin, pre-cycle—if it meant I'd be saved from everlasting abstinence.

"A limpy," Tarkin repeated. It sounded dumb coming out of his mouth, but I didn't laugh. The sheets rustled as he adjusted to face my new position. "I believe I understand your meaning. And yes, I would have been."

"You so owe me," I joked. "Now I know you can get your paws on brownies, this could work out great."

"I am thankful you do not seem to be angry. I trust you will have no regrets."

I didn't look at him. He didn't want to know about my regrets, and I didn't want to dwell on them myself.

"Or is it Heen you owe for setting us up? I took off and nearly cursed you to the limpy life. She prefers prysallin to chocolate, by the way." I swallowed a lump in my throat and babbled to ease my discomfort. "I can't believe you beat up an Irt at the Black Hole. I've got bruises on my butt, but I bet she's got bruises on her ego. Knocked around by a Gitternian."

I had bruises on my ego, too, or was that not my ego? Shut up, heart! Just... leave me alone.

"I am sorry I was not more prompt and the female hurt you."

"Do you have any idea how many bar brawls I've been in? Tons," I lied. I had distinct talent for avoiding them. "Anyway, you should have explained this limpy thing last night. I would have taken one for the team. No biggie."

"Sarai!" Tarkin exclaimed, his voice thick. "I..."

He choked on his words, and I didn't prompt him to continue. For a long moment neither of us said anything. I couldn't tell what he was thinking, but as for myself, I could barely wrap my head around what the stubborn cuss had risked last night. I bought what he claimed about Gitternians and sex. Not only did it answer a lot of questions, but something in my heart, or maybe deeper, believed him. Something instinctual, like I'd be able to tell if he lied. Besides, he was Tarkin.

All of which didn't answer the question of why his people would hide that little tidbit about themselves, minus the funky psi sex. Wouldn't public knowledge about their cycles make it easier to find a hump buddy in times of crisis? Or did they fear other species would take advantage of the weakness? Sure, I'd love for him to have chosen me because he had feelings for me, but I wouldn't have forced him into a lifetime of celibacy when I could prevent it.

Fracking stars. When it came down to it, it was just my body and psi he'd needed. I could ignore my heart. The confusion and disappointment would melt away like starshine in the daytime.

Tarkin finally spoke, prissy and stiff as hell. "It would not have been honorable for me to pressure you with that knowledge."

"You're an idiot." I waved my hand at him, and it came into contact with his smooth, warm chest. I flinched away. "Oops, sorry."

With something that sounded almost like a snarl, Tarkin rolled on top of me. The sheet separated us, but his erection pressed my thigh. His hands gripped my upper arms.

"This is not a joke." His eyes flashed, and a pulse beat in his temple. Wow. I'd made him angry for the first time in our acquaintance. "Do you think I did not consider every option? Do you think I wanted to risk... what we have, knowing your feelings about lovemaking?"

My face burned. "What do you mean?"

"You and Heen, you speak in front of me as if I am not there. Heen enjoys casual encounters. You do not. Should I have ignored this preference?"

"That's just girl talk." My breathing came faster. He had a boner!

Maybe… maybe his cycle required more than one orgasm. Oooh, but then there'd be that headache thing.

"I courted you, Sarai. I respect you."

I stared at his left ear. Even that looked sexy to me. "I know you do."

"I am fully aware this will alter our relationship." His stare was so intense I swear he was reading my mind, or trying to. However, mind-reading had never been proven to exist, which was for the best, all things considered. The galactic government already tread the ethics line when it came to folks with strong psi. My psi was so limited there was only one thing I could do with it, so I hadn't been indentured.

"You sound like you regret it a lot more than I do," I said, slipping from understanding friend into bitchy territory. Which I'd just vowed not to do. So much for maturity.

His thumbs smoothed the tender skin on the inside of my arms, a caress at odds with the annoyance in his face. "You do have regrets."

"Heck, no." Tarkin's mixed messages were making my brain and libido equally crazy. Damn, if he'd just shut up and let me know whether he needed another screw, we could argue this exact same topic afterwards. "Sex in the bathroom at a seedy bar. I get to check a lifelong goal off my list."

"I asked you to stop making jokes." His eyes narrowed, and his fingers tightened, biting into my flesh. "You must understand. It may alter… many things."

"It doesn't have to change anything. I'm okay with it." Why was he going on about changes? Was he saying our friendship was over? Like a big baby, I teared up. His weird behavior the past few tendays, his proposition, the rough sex, and now? I wanted to scream and cry and hit him. And kiss him and make him love me the same way I loved him.

His hand moved from my arm to clasp my chin and immobilize my head. "Are you?"

"Totally." *Don't cry. Don't cry.*

He lowered his head until his lips were only centimeters from mine. His cock prodded my thigh, obvious and urgent. "Do not lie to me."

"I'm not lying." My heart beat a painful drum solo in my chest. Did he have a hard-on because he needed to do it again or because he was mad? Or—scary—both? Or—scarier—did I care as long as he used it on me? "Why would I lie?"

"I know you well. You resort to levity when you are ill at ease." He bent further until he could speak in my ear. His breath sent shivers through me. The side of his smooth face brushed mine. His chest, his hips, his legs, pinned me to the bed. "What can I do to ease you?"

Kiss me. Hold me. Tell me you chose me especially. "Quit bullying me."

Tarkin jerked away as if stung. I took advantage of it to squirm out of the bed, gripping the edge of the sheet to hide my nudity.

He frowned. Because I'd tried to run off with it, the sheet barely covered him. One long, toned side of his body was revealed, neck to toe. Everywhere I could see, his muscles were taut—as tense as I was. "We cannot pretend nothing happened."

"It happened, and now the winky is saved. Yay." I dragged my gaze to his face and realized staring anywhere else, even his cock, would be safer than the fury in his eyes. It was such an alien expression, it made me remember he was an alien—to me, anyway.

Did I even know him?

He propped himself on his elbow, as if preparing to come after me. "Sarai, you are making me angry."

I hovered at the side of the bed. The sheet was tucked in at the bottom too snugly to wrap it around myself like a dress. Distance between me and Tarkin's body, his smell, his skin, should help me think more clearly.

And clearly I didn't want to have this discussion if he was about to end our friendship. "If you're ticked at me, I should leave."

With one hand, he pulled the sheet. I couldn't tell if he was trying to yank the sheet off me or onto him. "No."

"I need to go."

"You cannot, Sarai."

I gave him my most annoying 'Duh!' look. "Yes, I can. You're not my boss."

He rolled closer, under the sheet, which gave me leeway. I hopped back until the sheet was like a trampoline between us. "Come here," he said.

"Why?" Beneath the sheet, cool air wafted across my skin.

"We have unfinished business."

I heaved a deliberately disgusted sigh. "You need to screw again?"

Tarkin's lips tightened. "I am still in cycle."

That wasn't an answer. Did he or didn't he? Or did he just want to get this painful conversation over with? "If last night was enough to save you from the limpy, I have stuff to do."

"No, you don't. This is not a day you are scheduled to work."

I'd failed in my effort to be unbitchy. Churlishness and disappointment possessed me, and as much as I wanted to see Tarkin naked, as much as I wanted to make love to him without passing out, I couldn't and wouldn't keep bluffing. I was a terrible liar, and in another minute I'd be bawling like a Terran cow and begging him to be my boyfriend because I'd loved him forever and ever.

Best I vacated the premises before I humiliated myself. "Work isn't the only thing in my life. Just buzz me if last night didn't take, and I'll pop by for a quickie. Or will it be quick? I mean, how long was I out?"

Tarkin growled—growled!—and snatched the sheet so hard I nearly tumbled onto the bed. I let go just in time, and there I was, starkers, in his bedroom. He stared at my body, licked his lips. With movements as slow and calculated as a drowsy cat, he climbed out of the bed. The sheet fell to the ground, and there was no mistaking his wonderfully humanoid arousal. Or his intentions.

Bravado? Or cowardice?

Tough choice—not!

I shrieked and ran.

Chapter 6

When Sarai fled, pure instinct consumed me. I was on her before she got halfway through my common room, my hands buried in her silky hair, my arm wrapped around her ribs. Her body, plush and soft, against mine. Like velvet and satin. She wriggled and dug her fingernails into my hand, but her resistance only made it worse.

We had unfinished business.

Her scent enticed me, as did her nudity, her panic. I buried my face in her neck, sucking heat to the surface.

"Where exactly do you think you're going, Sarai?" I murmured.

"Leaving!"

"But you are so delightfully naked."

"Heen runs around naked all the time." She squirmed, yanked at my arm, but the joining was full inside me, and my strength was quadrupled. I shifted against her back, our skin sliding. Because our height was similar, I could slip my cock between her buttocks.

She squeaked and tried to bend away. I released her hair and trapped her hips against mine. "Why do you fight, Sarai? This time will be different. I promise you."

"You're freaking me out."

"Imagine that." I had tried to be the Tarkin she knew, the Tarkin she was comfortable with, but my cycle possessed me too fiercely. My desire for her was too overwhelming.

It consumed me. And I wanted to consume her.

I nipped her ear. She shivered, and the partial bond we'd established last night let me know it wasn't merely fear. She gasped when I picked her up and walked to the sofa, where I set her on her feet.

"You're very strong," she said, her voice breathless.

"Yes." There was no need to explain my physical strength was enhanced. It might intimidate her. More.

She tried to twist and face me, but I held her in place. "Are you going to let me go?" she asked.

"No." I pushed her hair aside and nuzzled her neck. I loved her sweet-salty Terran flavor. I could not wait to taste the inside of her mouth, the rest of her body.

"Do you have to be so bossy?" She grabbed the upholstered couch and shoved.

The movement ground her buttocks against my cock in a way I suspect she hadn't intended. I felt myself leap against her soft skin and adjusted so I could again slide into her cleft. The tip of my erection probed her crevice and bumped her pussy, hot but not as wet as I would make it.

She froze. "Let's get one thing straight. The back door's off limits, buster." Her defiance, when she could do nothing to prevent me from taking her as I chose, was exactly what I would have expected from her. Exactly what delighted me about her.

She was angry with me now, but she would not be angry long. Our lovemaking would not always begin in anger, once she understood.

I cupped her breast in my hand. She was soft and warm. In the corner of my eye, I saw her lips part. Her nipple hardened. I brushed my thumb across it, feeling it tighten even more, and licked her ear. Almost involuntarily, I curved my hips against her, then pulled back. She tensed, and I shoved forward, my cock plowing the channel between her legs.

She leaned her head against my shoulder in partial acquiescence, exposing her neck, but her nails still clawed my arm. My Sarai. Mine. A quick twist, and I slid deeper into her folds.

She inhaled sharply. I rubbed my cheek against hers and burrowed again. Her juices began to slicken my cock, sensitize the head. I forced a knee between her legs and nudged her thighs apart. Her slit was creamy and hot, topping me as I rubbed her.

I reached around and sought her pussy with my fingers. I checked her clit—softness, wetness, the pearl inside. I pushed my hips forward until I could reach my cock, which I rubbed against her until she dripped with moisture and her breathing came fast. The feel of my wet fingers below, her heat above, hardened me like titanium. I craved the clasp of her body around me, her psi in harmony with mine. I craved the joining, with Sarai.

"Bend over," I ordered. I didn't recognize my own voice.

She hesitated. I bit her neck like a mating feline and pushed the head of my cock into her sheath, despite the awkward angle.

"Mooley crap!" She jumped. My cock slid out of her. "You haven't even kissed me."

"I have not." Red swam across my vision. I recalled my vow to taste her and dropped to my knees, turning her body until I was level with her sweet center. I had never mated with anyone outside my species, either. The sight of her white skin aroused my inner senses, and the taste… I parted her outer lips and licked her pussy, savoring her tangy essence. I drove my tongue into her slit, around her nub, then delicately kissed her clit.

Sarai bit back some exclamation. I captured her bud between my lips and flickered my tongue, gauging her excitement. Through our partial bond, I felt her psi begin to pulse, ready itself. Mine, too, sprang to greet her. I buzzed her with my tongue, darting it over and over the knot of sensitive nerves until I felt her legs quiver. Her hands gripped, digging into the couch. I inserted two fingers into her sheath.

Heat. Pressure. Tension. Her inner walls compressed my fingers. I pumped my hand with the same rhythm I licked her, escalating her to a point where she would open for me. She had to be raw for this to fulfill us. She had to be out of her head, and in mine. It would not be like last night.

Tonight the joining would be elemental, and permanent, and the changes fated to happen to her would coalesce. I would report my actions as a catalyst to the Gitternian Council, and the wait would begin.

I planned to keep her content and unafraid with more lovemaking. And chocolate, if necessary. The next while would be like her Terran Heaven, for both of us.

A cry caught in Sarai's throat. Her body shuddered. Her psi sparked against mine, seeking what she didn't yet understand. I rose, grabbed her head, and kissed her, a kiss she returned without qualms.

She wrapped a leg around me, drawing me close. Our tongues danced, and our skin clung. She reached down and encircled my hard cock with her hand. Rubbed it against herself. Her palm on the head, her exploring fingers on the underside, sent chills up my spine. Her grip inflamed me. My sac tightened and ached. She probed herself, sighed into my mouth, and smeared moisture over the head of my cock. Squeezed it. She was so hot I felt I might burn. She tilted her hips and inserted my tip into her sheath.

She squeezed tight, her inner muscles a vise of delight. She took me out, reinserted me. Never letting me plunge. Controlling me. Pleasuring herself with my cock like it was her toy.

I gritted my teeth and tolerated it—for a time. It would ease her fears if she thought I would allow her the lead. Pressure built inside me as she fondled me. I forced myself not to move, to concentrate on kissing her and enjoying her flesh. Every time she allowed me inside her body, she inched onto my cock, took me deeper. She longed to ride me, I could sense it. I longed to ride her, to fuck her until we connected.

It was nearly time. I massaged her behind, my fingers tipping into her rear crevice. Parting it. Her psi began to blossom, and her pulse beat in her throat. The scent of rain and musk surrounded us. Her kisses became wild, and she gripped my hair. She whimpered, deep in her throat, and the jerk of her hips sucked me deep.

Warmth engulfed me. Slick, glossy flesh squeezed my cock, all along its length. Sarai buried her face in my neck and did not move. I did not move. We concentrated on the feel of my cock in her body, her pussy filled with my hardness. Our psis fluttered at the edge of union. I could not believe, after my urgency earlier, how I was able to remain this patient for her. How I was not taking her until she screamed.

"Is this how you have to do it? Sitting up?" Her lips moved against my neck. She kissed me, licking my pulse.

"No." I placed a thumb against her temple, my fingers in her hair. It curled in soft ringlets.

She turned and suckled my thumb, took it into her mouth. My cock jumped at the feel of her slick tongue. "I might like a different position. My, um, bum is kind of bruised."

Slowly, I disconnected our bodies, and she grumbled. I pulled her off the sofa, turned her, and bent her, unresisting, over the back. She was a dream, a fantasy. Her hair spilled down like a waterfall of red fire. She had faint bruises on her buttocks—I did not know if I was responsible, or the Irt. Carefully, I took the round, pale globes in my hands and parted her. Her anus was pink and tight. Her pussy glistened with moisture. Her slit gaped slightly, beckoning.

I reached around and plucked her clit. When she wriggled her ass at me, I slid into her tightness until my sac met her flesh and was rewarded by a breathy groan. She trembled, tightened, and I withdrew, little by little. I rubbed her bud, wet with moisture. She rose to her tiptoes and pushed her buttocks against me.

How could I resist? I thrust quick and hard, our bodies slapping. She jolted forward and gasped. I flicked just the tip of her clit, rapidly, and pistoned in and out of her.

Before our psis had a chance to merge, before I sensed her spill, she convulsed around my cock, luscious but badly timed. Her ripples tried to pull an echo from me, but I was not yet ready. She let out a huff and shivered.

I removed myself from her sweet cunt and helped her straighten. "That was fast." She seemed a little disappointed. Her eyes dropped to my cock and she raised her brows. "Too fast for you. Do you want me to…" She looked me with uncertainty in her blue eyes and licked her lips.

"No." Not this time. I picked her up, and she twined her arms around my neck, trusting. She weighed nothing to me in my current state. My erection bounced against her ass as I carried her to the bedroom.

"Do Gitternians not get off physically? Did you have a brain 'gasm?

Because I couldn't tell, I'm sorry."

I laughed. "Oh, we have orgasms." I dropped her on the bed. She bounced and uttered a startled exclamation. I crawled up her body, starting at her feet. Her eyes widened. "We share them, actually. Allow me to demonstrate."

Her cheeks flushed. She parted her legs, and I nestled between them, in the traditional position of male and female. Her beneath me. Accepting me into her body. Into her soul. I slid home.

She draped her arms over my shoulders and propped up her knees. It shifted her pelvis so I was able to sink deeper into her wet heat. I established a steady rhythm, watching her carefully, holding myself back. In and out. Slow and alluring. This had to be perfect. Had to be right.

Sarai was soon caught by the motion and began rocking her hips gently, a boat at sea. Each time I delved into her, I twisted, to stimulate her clit. She closed her eyelids with a flutter. With twined fingers, I held her hands down, on either side of her head. This would end only one way.

And still, I moved. In and out. In and out. Her dampness, I could feel it increase. Her temperature rose. Friction and moisture. The rub of flesh against flesh. Her exhalations became more forceful as I trapped her in the wave.

With her excitement, mine ascended as well. It was the Gitternian way: part of our arousal was knowledge of our partner's pleasure. After tonight, when with me, she might be the same, and she might not. I did not know how her Terran structure would react to the joining.

My breath came faster. I called out her name, and she responded. Kissed me. My hips pistoned against her, our flesh pounding. She drew her knees further up, her thighs wide. Twisting her head to the side, she focused on our joined hands. She tugged at them, but I did not release her. I did not think she wanted me to. She closed her eyes and whimpered. Panted.

I pressed deeper, deeper into her body, searching for the conclusion I craved, and felt an answering flutter against my psi.

There. There she was. I swiveled against her clit, withdrew nearly all the way. Her lips parted on a cry, and I plunged into her body, slashing open her psi, the mating urge taking over.

Inside her all was tumult. Colors, brighter than expected. Different. Overwhelming. I could hear her in my mind, chanting, babbling. Actual words I should not have been able to discern. What did it mean? Her emotions poured into me, her sensations, as I knew mine poured into her. We shared. I thrust. We came closer. She squeezed me, unquestioning, and gloried in the union. Her orgasm, my orgasm, crested, exploded. Our psis mingled. We joined. Entirely.

I could not breathe. I could not see. She filled me with pleasure. The joy she experienced, the electric thrill I'd given her, I had never felt anything like it. Inside my head, inside my skin, I heard her voice, feathery, intense, whispering, "I love you I love you oh God. I love you" in such a rush of emotion it sealed off my psi. Cast me out.

This time the feelings, the reactions, overwhelmed me, not Sarai, and my consciousness lapsed, my arms wrapped around her as if she could hold me to this plane.

When I woke, she was gone.

Chapter 7

I probably shouldn't have taken off after Tarkin passed out, but I had to be alone. I made sure he was breathing and comfortable, whispered his name, very softly. He didn't wake but he seemed peaceful. I'd passed out in the Black Hole and woken with no ill effects. No reason to alert a medic.

I could see it now. "Uh, doc, I just screwed this Gitter, and he passed out."

Doc: "Are you a Gitter?"

Me: "No, I'm Terran."

Doc: "You sicko! Did you rape him? Gitters don't have sex outside their species. No wonder he passed out. I'm sending the cops."

Me: "I swear, this was his idea! And he made me pass out first. Just not… this time."

I dressed and went somewhere that would distract me from what had just happened—the lab. Time for kitium practice. As Tarkin had pointed out, I wasn't scheduled to work today, but at the lab, everything else would disappear. In essence I could clear my head by using it for something else entirely.

That was the plan, anyway. My psi was muzzy and tingly, as were certain areas of my body. To my knowledge, psi-sex was unique to Gitternians, though my knowledge could not be described as galactic. Surely I'd have heard of a brain 'gasm, or Heen would have told me, because she loved to try to shock me with tales from her sex partnering days. As it was, I felt fat with pleasure, especially my head.

Me, the fathead.

It was mid-afternoon. After I caught a taxi home to bathe and change, I grabbed a meat wrap from a street vendor to eat in the lab. Hermana only employed one person, me, to tempor kitium, so on my days off, any ore deliveries went straight to stasis. Kitium had to be worked soon after being removed from the earth, and it wasn't like deposits of it ran deep and rich. It was erratic and scattered through the ground, sometimes in the middle of other ores, sometimes off by itself. Made it a real challenge to find and extract. Kitium diggers had to have a sixth sense, metaphorically speaking, about locating it because they couldn't use high tech. If they'd had a sixth sense literally speaking, they'd be in the lab with me, temporing it, or working in some government medlab, installing it.

Diggers. That put me in mind of the big Irt who'd tried to squoosh my head last night after muttering such upsetting things about my lips and her ass. I wondered if she had the day off. She probably had a headache to match mine, thanks to intoxicants and Tarkin's foot connecting with her skull.

Mine was entirely Tarkin related. My psi was jumpy and off. I probably shouldn't tempor today, but I couldn't think of anything else that would divert me enough.

Okay, okay, Tark was right, I had no life beyond work. But I was in my element here. I didn't know how the other branches of the company functioned. I just holed up in my lab and got my nice paycheck. My family needed it, and I liked it. It was a good life.

Though the rest of the company's ugly grey warehouse was as active as ever, the kitium labs in the bowels of the building were silent and dark. The only folks who ventured down here were Hermana employees like the kitium porters and myself, and security was minimal, once you were allowed into the building itself. It was so difficult to handle kitium without ruining it, there was no black market I'd heard of. Plus it wasn't like Hermana had a bunch of industry secrets to hide. The ores they mined, including kitium, were standard, as were the various metallurgical processes used to refine them.

I chipped in and flipped on lights, checking the stasis unit to make sure I had enough viable kitium to work with from last night's delivery. The box preserved it for a day or two, no longer. I'd also need vac tubes, sealant, goggles, tongs, picks, brushes, slides, lab whites, gloves. I'd have to disinfect everything first, myself plus all the pieces.

The room where I worked kitium was blinding white, sterile and low-tech, aside from the stasis unit and wetband. Next door was the main lab, which contained the gadgetry I used for testing. I hadn't had full testing facilities when I'd been hired and hadn't needed it until recently. In the past couple months, about a third of the kitium I tempored soured in the tube. The ores were coming in hot and fresh, so the problem was… me. Something I was doing. I'd tested everything I knew how to test, including some of the tubes that had soured, and investigated every phase of the delivery path for any unintentional exposure to stasis malfunction. Nothing—no reason for the kitium to sour outside my lab.

And if I couldn't figure it out, Hermana was looking to replace me. Which would chew rocks.

My six tubes from yesterday were still in stasis in the outer lab, awaiting pick-up. I resisted the urge to check them. The less they were handled, the better, and I'd run them through the gauntlet yesterday.

After I shucked my coveralls and donned my tech whites, I warmed up the wetband in the kitium lab and the elescope, the spectroscope, and a few other devices in the main lab used to test raw ore and verify whether tempored kitium was stable. Picking it apart with high tech nullified that sample, but a smidge from each batch was enough for analysis. It had to be perfectly balanced and hygienic—attuned for bioengineering and medtech. It was used to wetwire humanoids and a few others whose psi was limited or nonexistent so they could access psi devices—Library terminals, starships, computers, mechs, and the like. Psi was uncommon, but that didn't stop the science branch of the galactic government from coming up with new and varied uses for it. New ways for everyone to depend on it. If a person wanted to advance in most careers, he, she or it had to scratch up the funds to get implanted with wetwiring.

Kitium mining was an intense business, and temporers like myself rare. Which didn't mean Hermana would cut me any slack when their bottom line was at stake. This planet wasn't rich in kitium, but Hermana wouldn't want to give up its monopoly. The government would approve another outfit to mine here if Hermana's supply choked.

Or a third of its deliveries soured in the tube.

There was just enough ore in stasis to make my trip to the lab worthwhile. After I sterilized everything, I donned plastene gloves and carefully took a chunk of the kitium ore out of the box. The mass was greenish brown and cratered, with lots of black Diggette dirt and flecks of other embedded stones. I pinged it with my psi to see how much kitium we were talking here—ah, enough for a good melt. My job was to remove the integrated organics and other impurities, tempor the cleansed ore, and deposit it into a vac tube for transport.

First I broke off a nubbin of ore. Pre-temporing, the substance was brittle, like Terran coral. Scientists theorized it formed in a similar fashion, with tiny life forms bonding together and then giving up the ghost to become kitium. The organics and other impurities—the gangue—made up the bulk of the ore.

I inserted the small, dingy chunk into the wetband, washed it, then toted it to the outer lab and slid it in the elescope. Yep, the composition was as normal as kitium ever was. Ran a spectral—nothing I hadn't seen before. Nothing I could detect that would cause souring later.

The elescope and spectral, though I'd been quick, nullified the kitium. I nudged it with my muzzy psi to verify. Inert as granite. That bit, anyway.

Back to the clean room. Sterilized myself… again… and went to work on the original chunk.

Tricky business, temporing kitium, and tedious. There were no real scientific terms for what I did, for what most people with psi did, but I had my own vocabulary. First I fluoresced the ore with my psi to see which parts were kitium and which parts were impurities. Then I had to flake away, wash away, cut away, everything else. That, I had to perform with low-tech cutters and picks, like sculpting.

Tink, tink, tink. Boring, boring, boring. Scrape and brush and flick and scratch. I hated this part. I alternated between psi and tools, determining what needed to be flaked off and what needed to remain.

Each time I used my psi, it clarified, losing the muzziness that felt like wadding in my head. By the time I'd removed the gangue and chaff, my psi was functioning at peak capacity, or higher. Fluorescing the ore was effortless, and the kitium flared like starshine when I psi-tapped it.

Interesting. Perhaps the brain 'gasm had energized my head.

When the kitium was as clean as me and my little wire brushes could make it, I wetbanded it to pare it down to the raw material, a double fisted wad of gnarled protrusions branching from a central node. Young kitium had few protrusions. The biggest piece I'd ever worked had had a central the size of Terran cantaloupe and a hundred tickers of varying lengths. The Irt who'd mined that one had definitely been recommended for a bonus.

This one was small. Manageable. So far I'd only used my psi to highlight the ore, but now I'd tempor it—change its constitution from solid to melt and purify it of lingering organics. Psi was required. The traditional methods of many advanced civilizations had not proven successful.

Why? I dunno. Hey, I was a psi tech, not a geek. I knew what I could do and how to do it, but not the science behind it. I could have gotten a metallurgical degree on top of my psi voc, but I hadn't had the money at the time and hadn't had the time since I had the money.

Now, I wondered if knowledge of the science of how all this crap worked might help me figure out where my process was flawed. Maybe I should ask Hermana to import me a geek with a little psi—not competition but a second head to puzzle this out.

And maybe that would be admitting to such weakness Hermana would dump me immediately.

I didn't want to look for a different job. I liked this one. I liked this planet. I liked the people on this planet, one in particular. One who could make me orgasm in my body and brain simultaneously. One who was probably still naked and still had brownies in his kitchenette, brownies he'd gotten for me. Me!

Well, flit a digger. I couldn't stand here waffling over my future, and I sure couldn't start fantasizing about Tarkin. I had to tempor the kitium, test it, and decant it before it went lifeless.

I placed the kitium on the melting tray and focused on it, concentrating my psi on its internal structure. Slowly, it came into focus, until, in my mind's eye, I could see crystalline lights, intricate, rigid shapes that needed to be nudged into a liquid form, but only after the darker blots of impurities were forced out. I pushed and tweaked until the kitium was unadulterated, and then began the more intense process of changing the kitium's structure.

Temporing was usually like forcing the kitium, and my psi, through an invisible lattice, then another, and another, until the component pieces were tiny enough to reconfigure into liquid. My psi became more scattered with each layer, specks of awareness whizzing around my head like flies. Too many passes and I could lose center and drop the kitium in mid-transition, rendering it worthless.

Today, however, the substance liquefied after only one pass, and while my psi was still open, while I was appraising the tempored kitium in bewilderment, a high-pitched whine sliced through my head. Through my psi.

My control went ballistic. The kitium flared in brilliant, visible detail. I slapped my hands over my ears and crumpled beside the counter. Like huddling on the floor would hide me from the horrific noise making my skin feel like glass about to shatter.

By the stars, what was it? An alarm? Malfunctioning tech? My eyes watered and the knife-like trill escalated, then thinned out of the range of hearing.

I breathed deeply, wiggling my ears and checking my fingers for blood. Nothing. My psi throbbed, sensitive and tender, worse than after the brain sex. I wasn't deafened: I could make out a murmur of sound, a soft hum of machinery, and a faint babble that sounded almost like… words.

Somebody besides me chatting in my hermetically sealed, soundproof kitium lab?

I crawled up off the floor and checked the holocom. Inactive. I punched the call button. "Hey, wC'in," I said, when the receptionist's lizardly face popped into view. "Was there a factory alarm just now?"

"No, Sarai." Off-screen, I heard fingers tap on a hardset comp terminal. wC'in had no psi or wetwiring.

"Did you page me?"

"No." wC'in turned from the camera to inspect its terminal and, in a quiet voice continued, *Why would I?*

"Maybe if, um, somebody was here to see me?" Like Tarkin, tracking me down? The thought excited me as much as it intimidated me. He'd told me to stick around, and if he'd gone to the trouble to find me, he wouldn't be happy. Which didn't mean he wouldn't make me very happy, shortly thereafter. Hopefully I could convince him we should go to his place and avoid the company wash up.

"There is no one here for you," wC'in replied, dismissively, then again in that quiet voice, *Who would come to see Sarai? She has no friends.*

"I have several friends." What was up wC'in's blowhole? Was it because I wouldn't take a meal with it the other day? It had been eating one of its occasional live meals. Turned my stomach. I guess I was culturally insensitive, but so be it.

wC'in swiveled back toward the camera, two deep lines etched in its narrow grey forehead, indicating confusion. "Ahm, I am sure you do. Will that be all?" Then, in a whisper that didn't even cause its lipless mouth to twitch, it said, *Working too hard. They're going to fire her anyway.*

"Thanks for the vote of confidence." I switched off the holocom and returned to the kitium on the melting tray. It had partially hardened into a squiggle of brown goop. Must have been the psi flare-up I'd experienced during the weird shrieky noise. I poked it with a needle, but my psi agreed—it was as inert as the countertop.

Better test it anyway. I scraped some onto a slide and entered the testing lab. To my surprise, I had company. Two Irts dressed in tech whites, their backs to me, hovered near the portable stasis box where I stored the completed tubes of kitium for shipment.

"Can I help you?" I asked.

The Irts whipped around, and I shrieked nearly as loud as the sound that had fractured my wits. It was the female from the Black Hole and her companion from Larry's.

Survival instinct kicked in. I hurled my teeny plastene slide of kitium in their general direction and dashed for the door. One of the Irts caught my lab coat just as I reached the safety of the hallway. The other slammed the door, and I found myself pinned to the wall.

There were no windows in my lab, so nobody could see inside. No security cameras, either, not all the way down here. I opened my mouth to yell again, and the female's wide palm mashed it with more force than necessary. My lips ground into my teeth. I tasted blood.

As I stared at her broad, hairy chest, she said, "Not yell, techie. We deliver." And, quieter, *She better believe. Blast our luck!*

"Mmmf," I replied.

I could see the male, off to my side, out of the corner of my eye. He was smaller and paler than the female but still so tall I couldn't make out his face with my head immobilized by the female.

"What you doing here?" he asked. *She not supposed to be here. Day off. Ruin everything!*

I wasn't dead yet. A good sign.

"Mmf mm mm." I forced myself to relax, as if I weren't scared stiff, and wiggled my head. The female removed her hand. Slightly.

"I work here," I said, my lips brushing her palm. I continued to stare at her chest—eye contact with Irts can be taken as a sign of aggression. "Putting in some overtime. What did I ruin?"

"What you mean?" *Iggit baldie. No plan for this.* The female's claws tipped out. "We deliver."

The male indicated a box of supplies—tubes, slides, I couldn't tell. It was a typical Hermana white crate. "There your crap," he said.

"I thought you said you were a digger?" I asked the female, foolishly reminding her of our conversation the night before.

"Overtime, too." Her claws eased further out of her fingertips, and I couldn't tear my gaze from them. *No kill. She stupid, she never guess.*

"I'm not stupid." At the risk of seeming antagonistic, I tilted my head and looked up, up, up at her face. Why did she and the male keep making comments under their breath? Irts weren't the muttery type. Or quiet.

The female's nose wrinkled, and her pupils slitted as we locked gazes. "Didn't say you were." *She onto us, maybe? She know we not deliver. Slaggit!*

Okay, that was weird. Her lips had not moved for the <u>sotto voce</u> part of her comment.

I had heard those words… in my head. My psi burped, and I realized it was operational. Still in use. I had to consciously seal my psi when I finished with it, and I hadn't done that in the aftermath of the piercing noise.

I tried to click it off and encountered resistance. It wouldn't close. Something large and puffy blocked the mental doorway.

"I, um, thanks for the crap." I tried to slide away from the female along the wall and bumped into a counter full of supplies. I had plenty of supplies. "I needed more stuff. I work so much, you know? I use it up fast. Thanks, really. Appreciate it."

I continued to hear their dangerous mutters. They didn't want me here and weren't sure what to do now that I'd interrupted… something, and it had nothing to do with delivering supplies. What was going on? Why could I hear them in my head? Could they hear me?

They must not, or they'd have been, well, freaking out right now as much as I was. Unless all Irts could read minds and had been hiding it from the government all this time.

Oh, man. I could read MINDS!

This was all Tarkin's fault. Tarkin and the brain sex. Making love with him had altered me internally. Had he known this would happen? Surely he'd have warned me. Surely. He'd denied the psi bond had anything to do with mind-reading.

But he'd denied it really, really fast.

The female muttered something—in my head—about silencing me, and I gulped.

"I won't tell anybody," I said, before I could stop myself. Apparently sex with Tarkin had also made me more stupid than usual.

The female, already twice my size, expanded. "Tell what? We deliver. Supply porters. Approved." She sounded like a broken halo. We deliver. We deliver.

But then, in my head, she said, *Be easier to get her out alive or dead? She can't tell. Can't let her. We'll never get out of the contract if she tells.*

"Let's go, Vi," said the male. "We got more work." *Vi's bristling. Techie gonna bleed. Didn't sign up to kill baldies. Damn Vi! Can't stop her, she bigger.*

Oh frack, this Vi person was going to kill me to keep me quiet! About what? How fair was it to die to preserve somebody's secret and not even know what the secret was?

Vi growled low in her throat, right before the holocom crackled.

"Sarai, there is someone here to see you," wC'in informed me, and I didn't have to read anyone's mind to register the varying degrees of shock.

Chapter 8

It was essential I find Sarai as quickly as possible and quarantine her for her own safety. She could not range freely until we could determine the extent of the psi changes our mating had precipitated and instruct her as to their use—and their concealment.

I had every reason to believe they went much deeper than anticipated. Though one's mate might lose consciousness during an initial joining, it was not normal for the Gitternian to do so, unless he or she was a catalyst for greater change than expected.

After a tense holocall with the Gitternian Council to verify the culmination of my cycle and Sarai's identity, I hacked into the city ident system to see if my runaway lover had flashed her chip in the past several hours. I was in luck. She'd hailed a taxi, visited her apartment, hailed another taxi, and reported to her place of employment.

Ah, with a brief stop at a street vendor for food. Her appetites, at least, had not altered.

The Council was sending a team, but in the meantime I was in charge of keeping her safe. I couldn't do that if we were in two separate places. It would be no hardship to endure extended proximity to Sarai.

Especially since I could abandon all subterfuge. I had the Council's approval for full disclosure, not that I would have remained silent had they delayed, considering the circumstances. I could think clearly after our second mating, the fever dissolving to a manageable level. I gathered the items I might need to retrieve Sarai should she be recalcitrant and left.

In a very short time I arrived at Hermana Mining and requested Sarai at the reception desk. The dB'thx at the controls could not hide its expression of surprise, its leathery, reptilian face dewrinkling in amazement. But with professional efficiency, it hailed Sarai through the holocom system.

"Sarai, there is someone here to see you."

No answer. The receptionist tried again. "Sarai, I know you're there. We just spoke."

The holocom displayed an empty lab. Something black crossed the camera and it switched to audio only.

"Um." Sarai's voice sounded strained and muffled. "I'm busy."

Was she already suffering? Confused? She would be freaked, indeed, if she began to hear the thoughts of others. Damn and blast, I should have id-locked my door to prevent her departure! Her body, her scent, her presence had distracted me. I had not taken proper precautions to ensure her safety.

I gripped the edge of the desk. "Tell her it is imperative I see her. It is an emergency."

"He says it's an emergency," the receptionist repeated. "Can you come up here?"

Muffled noises and a tiny squeak. "No, no," Sarai said. "I… am… very… busy. Tell… him… I'm sorry we, uh, missed each other last night. Eek!"

Another muffled noise. A crash of metal against metal.

The receptionist shuttered its inner eyelids with annoyance. "Shall I send him down with security?"

Something guttural that wasn't Sarai vibrated through the intercom in my lower aural range, still enhanced by my cycle. The dB'thx did not appear to hear it.

There was someone in the lab with Sarai. And she wasn't happy about it.

I relaxed my palms on the desk so my tension would not threaten the receptionist. If denied, could I gain access to Sarai without authorization? How much of my cyclical heightening remained? "I must see her. If I cannot go, you must send a guard to fetch her. Now."

There was no response for a long moment, and I tensed, prepared to force the dB'thx to sound an alarm or let me pass. Then Sarai's voice, tense and high, said, "Don't send anyone. I'll be up later."

"I will go without a guard," I said. "Ident me."

"That's against regulations." The dB'thx ran my ident chip and its inner eyelids clicked open. "You have clearance?"

"I repair low tech," I said, a job nearly as uncommon as Sarai's. "I am a licensed contractor for many businesses."

"Yes, here it is. I see." The dB'thx registered me and handed me a visitor badge. "Stay outside, by the door, and buzz her." It pointed. "Down that hall, take the lift to the ground floor, turn right, pass five doors, you can't miss it. Kitium Lab."

"Did she not sound strained to you?" I asked the receptionist. "Why would she switch to audio only?"

"Sarai often turns off the holo to reduce the tech in her lab," the dB'thx said. "Some kitium thing. If she needs something, call me, but I doubt she does."

"We did not miss one another last night. I believe she wishes assistance."

"Maybe she thinks you're one of her other boyfriends. She said not to send anybody at all, so I'm not involving security without a compelling reason." The receptionist turned away from me and back to its hardset, dismissing my concerns.

I found the lift and the kitium lab where Sarai worked without delay. I was hard pressed to maintain a calm pace. Adrenalin coursed through my veins, and I tried not to burn the latent energy unless, or until, it was needed.

I could hear nothing from inside the lab, not even with my augmented senses. I pressed the audiocom switch at the door. "Sarai, I am here. Let me in."

"Tark, what are you doing here?" she yelled, at a distance from the audiocom receptor.

"We have an appointment."

"I can't come to the door. I'm in the middle of something… hairy. Ouch!"

I did not know how far her psi transformation had progressed, or how far it would progress, but I did know that a Gitternian's mate who gained the capability to mindread could only do so if he or she had visual contact.

Unless her mate wished to speak to her.

I focused on an image of Sarai as I imagined she was right now—her hair in a net, her tech whites on. I thought at her, *If you are experiencing difficulties and want me to enter the room, tell me you want fresh for dinner.*

I activated the audiocom. "We are going to be late," I said. "When will you be finished with your work?"

"I'm busy now, but I want fresh for dinner tonight!" Sarai exclaimed, confirming my suspicions—about her situation and her psi. "Lots of it. I'm so hungry I could eat an Irt. Ouch, frackin'—"

The audiocom sliced off. I considered alerting the receptionist, but it had not been particularly helpful, and I did not want to endanger Sarai should her troubles be related to the psi changes. She had enough fears about her employment status at current. Directing the attention of her superiors to any irrational actions on her part would not be in her favor. Especially not if they had any inkling what was causing their temporer to behave erratically.

But it was obvious she wanted me to intrude. One of the items I had with me, in the event Sarai had been unwilling to return to my apartment and locked herself in a room, was a blank ident chip. Highly illegal, highly useful, and indistinguishable from the implants most humanoids had. There were items a Gitternian peddler knew how to locate, information a peddler could gain, though I did not often trade such goods.

I placed the blank against the touchpad, and the lock clicked. Cautiously, I bumped the door open but did not step through. Yet.

A wise choice. As soon as the door swung inward, it hurled back at me with a blow that would have knocked me into the hall had I been attempting to enter the room. I caught the door before it slammed and shoved with most of my strength.

Something soft yet solid prevented the door from hitting the wall. There was a groan, and someone cursed—not Sarai. I scented; she was not near the door.

She was, in fact, caught against the chest of the female Irt who had harassed her at the Black Hole. The Irt's claws were bared and gleaming, and her palm covered Sarai's mouth.

"Shut the door, Gitter, or blood spills," the Irt growled. Sarai's eyes were wide, her face pallid. "Red's pretty on white."

"Let her go or I will alert the guards," I said loudly, hoping any monitoring equipment in the hallway, any workers nearby, would detect my voice. This entire floor, aside from the kitium lab, appeared to be vacant.

The Irt poked a claw into Sarai's neck. Blood began to trickle onto her lab coat. Sarai twitched, and her eyes filled with tears.

"Come in and seal the door."

I did as instructed. There was another Irt slumped behind the door, one I also recognized from Larry's. In fact, the two Irts, and several others, had frequented Larry's the past month, though their species usually preferred less expensive dining arrangements.

Nothing had come together yet, but there was definitely intersecting information.

"You have no cause to harm Sarai," I said. "If this concerns last night, your quarrel is with me." Neither of them appeared to have a distance weapon, which meant combat would be hand-to-hand.

"Iggit baldie. She in the way. You too." The Irt shook her prisoner slightly, and Sarai's head wobbled. Blood continued to seep onto her coat, a crimson flower against the white. Inside, I felt the fury, the urge to defend my mate, mount like a nuclear reaction.

I balanced on the balls of my feet, watching the female and listening for the male. "What is it you wish?"

"For this one—" She shook Sarai again—"not to come work today."

I wished that myself. "Why are you in this laboratory?"

The Irt tilted her head forward, daring me to disagree. "Delivering supplies."

Sarai made a rude gesture with her middle finger the Irt could not see, but I could. I took that to mean the bigger female had lied.

"If you have made your delivery, you should leave." My primary concern was getting Sarai out unhurt. "Or we will go and you can complete your delivery. We are expected," I lied.

Did it matter the duplicitous Irt would be angry and unsupervised in Hermana's kitium laboratory? In Sarai's laboratory? I did not wish to fight. My aggression level was not at last night's peak. Nevertheless, I would do what was required.

Or perhaps it did matter. Sarai had encountered unexpected difficulties with her kitium stability of late—roughly the same space of time in which I had noticed the increase in Irts at Larry's. Was there a connection?

Sarai might know. She might already have plucked the thoughts out of the Irt's brain. But there was no way I could ask either of them. However, I could send Sarai another message.

I extended my hands out to my sides and attempted to appear like the species Gitternians had the reputation of being—peaceful. Nonviolent. Which we were, unless pressed. Or in our cycles. The trick was to avoid pressing situations and cycles that escalated to the point mine had.

"Ser," I said, choosing the neutral form of address between individuals of equal stature, "I do not know why you must harm my friend because she interrupted your delivery. Were you startled? I am sure she has completed her tasks and would be happy to depart."

To Sarai, I thought, *If they were here to harm you, fist one hand. If they wish to harm you and the kitium, fist both.*

Sarai made two fists, her knuckles as white as her face.

"Neither of you's leaving," the Irt said.

Behind me, the other Irt stirred with a groan. "What hit me, Vi?"

"Door, you smudge. Grab the Gitter, but watch out. Stronger than he looks."

If I incapacitated the male too slowly, the female would have time to hurt Sarai. When the male grabbed my arms from behind, bending them up, I pretended to struggle and gritted my teeth against the aggression that jittered through me. Even though I could only see the top of Sarai's face, I could make out the disappointment that leached even more color from her skin.

It is not the right moment, I thought at her for reassurance. *Be ready.*

Though I could not tell her what to ready herself for. I was not finished with these Irts. Overpowering them could wait until I discovered why they were here and what they wanted with the kitium. Did they intend to steal it? It would do them little good. Even the Council's best agents had never confirmed, or established, a black market for the sensitive ore.

I cleared my throat. "What do you intend to do with us? We are not your enemies." The male shook me, as if in answer.

"Crossfire," the female said. Vi, the male had called her. "Too bad."

The male twisted my arms in unconscious distress. "Can't slag 'em. That would really blow the shaft. We logged in."

"There is no need for bloodshed, no matter what your purpose is here," I said. Hermana's security measures were strict, at least at their perimeter. The Irts could only have entered the building legitimately. They would indeed have to be registered as employees to be this deep in the building. Regrettably, Hermana's internal security was inefficient, or nonexistent, else there would already be guards at the laboratory door. They obviously relied on preventing undesirables from entering. Doubtless it saved them credits.

The Irt glared at me. "We're porters. 'Course we logged. That's all."

Their actions belied their words. Mere porters? If they expected us to believe them, they would not threaten us. "Why does it matter that we intercepted your supply delivery?" I asked.

"This one thinks we not legit. She run and rat, we lose our jobs." The Irt shook Sarai, who clenched and unclenched her hands in rapid succession. "We doin' nothing. But think you, Hermana believe an Irt over their psi freak? No chance for us."

"Perhaps you could let her speak. Reassure you." I suspected Sarai had a great deal to say, were the Irt to remove her hand. Would she be a projector once she was trained, capable of transmitting mind speech, or just a receiver? It would interest the Council to know how we functioned as a team.

However, satisfying the Council's curiosity was not worth endangering Sarai. I would need to end this with a minimum of conflict. Perhaps a discussion might suffice. I would attempt it, though violence might be more… satisfying. I did not like to see Sarai in danger.

The Irt eased her hand from Sarai's face to her neck. The thick grey fingers wrapped around the Terran's fragile throat as Sarai gasped for breath. The Irt's claws had retracted, but she could still kill Sarai with a twist of her muscular arm.

I forced myself not to leap at her. Luckily my cycle was no longer so flush I could not control myself. Were this to have happened at my peak last night, both Irts might already lay dead upon the floor. The Council would not have appreciated concealing such a fiasco from the colonial administration and the galactic government.

Sarai shook her head. "I don't know anything except I walked into my lab and you jumped me."

"You said you wouldn't tell. Tell what?"

"That you were delivering my stuff, um, late?" Her voice rose higher with each word.

Ah, Sarai. She was not skilled in the art of subterfuge. The Council would be disappointed, but I appreciated that aspect of her character. I did not want to change my current employment, which the Council may have required had we been better suited for their purposes.

"We on schedule," the male said.

"You will be late if you do not depart on your rounds." I flexed my shoulders. The Irt behind me was beginning to strain my muscles. My escalating fury did not help me remain calm. "What do you hope to achieve with this assault? Her silence?"

Vi ignored me and squeezed Sarai's neck. "Tell truth. What you think you see us do?"

"Gaack!" Sarai coughed, her face reddening.

"You are going to injure her," I said calmly. I prepared to break the grip of the male if the female continued to compress Sarai's breathing.

The female's eyes slitted as she watched me, but she eased up on Sarai.

Sarai coughed again. "Nothing!" she said, her voice rough. "You scared me because you were… well, you were pissed last night and I thought maybe you'd come after me."

Better, my love, I thought at her. *Very convincing.* I wondered what Sarai knew about the Irts and the kitium.

"It's convincing because it's true," Sarai said, and then snapped her mouth shut.

I realized she had answered me. No, she was no mistress of subtlety. If the situation were not so dangerous, I would have smiled.

The Irt restraining her growled. "Not convinced." She stared at me. "Why here, Gitter?"

I raised my eyebrows. "Sarai and I have an appointment. I came to fetch her. She loses track of time when she works."

"You, Techie, what appointment?"

I am teaching you to cook fresh, I instructed her. *We were going to the organics bubble.*

"We're going to the garden. To get stuff and cook it," she said. "You guys hungry?"

"You eat at Larry's," the Irt said. "You don't cook."

"How do you know that?" Sarai asked.

The Irt shrugged. "Ways."

I was right: the Irts had Sarai under surveillance. They knew when she ate, what she ate. When she worked, when she was away from work.

They had intentionally come into her lab when she was thought to be away from work. Sarai had confirmed it had something to do with the kitium.

I could think of only one answer. Sabotage. It would explain their presence at this particular time, the surveillance. It would explain Sarai's kitium troubles.

But what were they doing? Sarai had described to me how she tested each step of the kitium's processing, assessed everything that happened to it between stasis and delivery, and come up with nothing. With limited individuals who had access—and blank ident chips extremely difficult to come by—why would she have suspected Hermana's employees?

But something had soured a good portion of her tempored ore regardless—something these Irts were doing. Did they intend to spoil Hermana's kitium production or were their actions an attack on Sarai herself?

"You seem to know a great deal about my friend," I observed. "Why is that?"

The male behind me wrenched my arms tighter. "Shut it."

Discomfort knifed through my shoulders and chest. I was losing patience and my hold on civility. "If you harm us, do you think no one will realize who did it? The wC'in at the desk knows we are here, and I have no doubt it knows the porter schedule as well. The colonial administration will not be pleased."

"She'll venge me now she knows who I am," Vi said. "Gotta stop her. Terrans are squabblers. Go to the bosses just for spite."

"And Irts are so peaceful," Sarai said with a huff. "Who tried to mash whose head at the Black Hole last night? I was minding my own business and you waltzed up and squeezed me."

"I was slaggin' drunk. Now you get vengeance. Say we screw around at work."

"Maybe last night you were drunk, but what's your excuse today?" Sarai argued.

The brown hair on Vi's forehead clumped up as she frowned, her fangs gleaming. "You venge from last night. I not even hurt you then. Think non-psis can find jobs so easy?"

"Think a Terran kitium temporer whose tubes sour can find work so easy? Mauling me won't help you keep your stupid job."

Sarai should not antagonize the Irts. *Do not anger them further*, I pleaded with her. *We must calm them.*

Sarai rolled her eyes at me. Her anger at me, at the Irts, was intense. She was not going to cooperate and let me deal with this situation. I might have to go on the offensive after all, before they injured her further. As her catalyst, I felt responsible for her mental state, and I could not bear for her to be hurt. Even without a psi connection, her pain was mine.

"You got psi." Vi cuffed Sarai's temple lightly, but Sarai's mouth pinched with discomfort. I stiffened in my captor's grasp. "You got it easy."

Through tight lips, Sarai said, "Just the one kind of psi." She met my gaze and tilted her chin into the air, daring me to contradict her. "I can't even get hired for manual labor. Terrans are too small and weak."

"Are that." The male lifted me off my feet. "Gitters, too. This one like a little doll."

A snarl built inside me as the male hefted me in the air. My feet dangled. A hiss of sound, the signal that the rush was upon me, began to interfere with my hearing.

The Irt had just made the exact wrong move.

"Mind him!" Vi snapped at her companion. "He flares."

Her warning came too late. Instinct overwhelmed me and my feet snapped back, cracking the Irt's kneecaps like dry wood. He howled and dropped me. The female's claws shot out of her fingers. One of them pierced Sarai's shoulder.

Sarai yelped. *Duck,* I thought at her.

She managed to slither down several centimeters in the Irt's grasp. It was enough. I crouched, then vaulted forward and up. The remaining cyclical influence gave me more range, more strength, than other humanoids. My kick caught the Irt in the face.

She flung Sarai across the lab. Blood splattered from the Irt's face and Sarai's shoulder. The sight of Sarai's wound enraged me further. The Irt clapped one hand to her gushing nose and slashed with the other. I leaned back. The deadly claws raked within a hair of my chest.

An unexpected clout slammed into the side of my head. Her opposite paw, the one I thought was holding her nose. I stumbled sideways. My ear rang and throbbed. I could feel hot agony in two places where her claws nicked me. I do not know if she meant to crush my skull or disorient me but I was tougher than I appeared.

However, the fact she had managed to land a blow at all meant my abilities had waned more than I thought. My rage would not suffice.

A beaker crashed into the female's back, courtesy of Sarai. Vi turned with a snarl, assaulted from two sides. I kicked at her knees, hoping to incapacitate her the same way as the male. More agile and alert than her companion, she leapt back. Two more pieces of lab equipment flew toward us. One struck the Irt in the head and one whizzed past me.

"Get the Terran!" Vi yelled at the male, but he was not made of such stern stuff as she. In the corner of my vision I saw him drag himself up, his face twisted with pain. Not a threat.

Sarai threw random bits of her lab at him anyway. A rock hit him in the chest.

The female, canted sideways to make her body less of a target, circled me warily. She feinted; I remained out of her reach. We traded blows, testing. Mine landed. Hers did not.

"Knock her head off!" Sarai yelled. Then, "Hey, cut that out, that's valuable!"

I risked a glance. The male had begun to hurl things back at Sarai, and she jumped behind the stasis machine where the kitium tubes were stored. Something breakable smashed against the machine and pieces scattered.

The female rushed me while my attention was divided. Grappling with her would be unwise, so I pivoted, latching onto her arm as she passed. I used her velocity to my advantage. With a vicious twist, I swung her body around. At least one of the bones in her forearm snapped, the loud crunch sending a shudder through me.

The Irt gasped and backed away, but the damage was done. She was no match for me, and she knew it. She bent, one hand against her brow. The other flopped uselessly at the end of her broken arm. Irts were primitive and testy, but they were not stupid.

Or, this female was not stupid. The male behind me was of different ilk. Something else flew through the air. Without turning my back on the female, I gestured towards him.

"Stop destroying the lab," I ordered, "or you will not like the consequences." I forced myself not to attack until it was warranted. It was not easy. My blood ran hot.

"Stob off," the female agreed, fury and dismay coloring her tones. "Warned you, he flares. Who'd thunk? A Gitter."

The male paused with a small machine in his hand, by the angle meant for me and not Sarai. He flinched when my attention settled on him. From the way he leaned on the counter, I suspect I'd broken one of his knees.

I would break more of him if he did not heed me.

Sarai found a rag to staunch the flow of blood from her shoulder. She made no attempt to move towards the door. Anger glittered in her blue eyes like twin novas. "We shouldn't kill them," she said to me, "but if you'd be so kind as to hold the bitch down, I want to stab her shoulder with a knife."

"Vengeful Terran," the Irt muttered. She glanced at the door, but I shifted in front of it. Neither Irt would leave this room until I had my answers. Until Sarai had her answers, at least about the kitium issues. The other answers she wanted would have to wait.

Sarai spat something in her native language I didn't understand and then in commerce tongue said, "You tried to pop my head like a zit last night because I have psi. Who are you calling vengeful?"

"Sarai," I said, "are you all right?"

She grumbled another rude Terran phrase, one I had heard before, especially when she hurt herself. "No thanks to them. Or you! You should have warned me that—"

In my head, I cut her off. *Not now. Do not reveal things these Irts do not need to know.*_

"Pfaugh," Sarai answered aloud. "What about what I might have needed to know, huh? Secretive bastard."

I had no defense. She was correct, though I hoped when *I* explained, her anger would diminish. The operatives from the Council might help appease her—or increase her anger beyond imagining.

The female Irt glanced from Sarai to me. "Let us go, we not report the assault," she suggested. "Broken arms, knees? Bad business." Sanctioned brawls in fight cages or rough sectors were one thing. Physical altercations in other areas of Diggette Colony were another. The colony administration did everything it could to avert the coarse reputation other outbound colonies tended to develop. It was better for commerce, and Diggette was a very focused colony in that respect.

Sarai, gripping her shoulder, stomped to the center of the room. From her vigor, I assumed her injuries were minor, if bloody. The Irts were in worse shape, especially the male. "You're crazy. You think you can get us in trouble? You assaulted me first, *digger.* You deserve everything you get. I'm calling the guards. I'm telling them everything."

I help up a hand. "Not yet. Perhaps now these… porters will tell us their true purpose in your kitium lab."

"That's easy," Sarai said with a snort. "They came here to—"

This time I dissuaded her outburst with a hand on her shoulder. Not the injured one. "She will tell us herself. Will you not, Vi?"

"Thought you didn't know nothing," the Irt accused Sarai.

Sarai, tense beneath my touch, jutted her chin forward. "I'm a good guesser. And you're not exactly subtle."

"You not supposed to be here," the male complained. He bent and ripped his coveralls off at the knee to inspect his injury.

"We not tell anything," the female added. "Can't make us." She watched me as she declared that.

"I know everything anyway." Sarai pointed at the Irt. "I know about your sneaky plan to ruin my job, and I know for some whacked out reason you think you're in the right, but what I don't get is how you did it. I checked everything!"

Vi gestured right back at Sarai. "Nothing to do with you."

"Sure looks like it, since you threatened to kill me. Twice."

"Bah!" Vi's fangs appeared as she sneered. "We want you dead, you be dead."

"It could be our altercation roused the guards," I cut in. "If you wish any sympathy from us, perhaps you should explain yourselves quickly." If there was a discreet way out of this situation, with the least likelihood of revealing what Sarai had become, or what items I had on my person, it would be for the best. Hermana's guards might ask questions Sarai was not yet equipped to skirt, and they would definitely conduct body searches.

Hermana might also alert the colony administration, and the Council would not welcome that at all.

The male, his knee bound in a strip of material from his coveralls, hopped to stand beside Vi. "Guards not down here. Think we iggits?"

"You not know slag for months," Vi pointed out. "Today bad luck."

"Well, I know now," Sarai said. "Dummies."

I almost wished I could silence her lips the same way the Irt had. My love was no model of perfection, yet I cared for her no less. I shifted my arm from her shoulder to her back, where I stroked her spine, the lower half, in a soothing motion. Touching her soothed me as well.

"Months. Sarai and I have noticed other things in that span of time." I kept my voice level and risked a jump in logic. "Tell us why you sabotaged the kitium tubes. Do you mean for Sarai to lose her job?"

"Yeah, and how the flip were you doing it?" Sarai began to lean into me as I caressed her. Some of the aggression drained from her voice.

"How you figure that?" the male asked, stunned. He balanced on one leg. "We got second jobs. Porters. Planning a long time. Nobody guess."

"Shut your hole." Vi cuffed the male across the head. He skipped awkwardly to the side as he rubbed it. It had to be sore from the blow of the door earlier. Vi eyed me, us, with new respect. "Not about her. Quickest way to spat Hermana. No use for that psi slag anyway."

Sarai stiffened and I wondered what she might have overheard in the Irt's brain.

"You wish to weaken your employer?" I asked. Disrupting kitium production would diminish Hermana's profits. In fact, according to Sarai, Hermana would lose their government contract if they could not leverage the available ore. "Why?"

"They belly up, good for us," the Irt said.

"You'd lose your job."

"Lose slaggin' contract, too. Fatwads. Crooks."

"I see." I gathered the Irts were locked into an employment contract they felt was unfair. Large companies with government backing often took advantage of species without psi in such a way. If Hermana lost mineral rights, they would have no use for kitium diggers. Or temporers. "Would you care to elaborate?"

"What diff it make?" the female scoffed. "You ruin anyway. Turn us in. Over for us."

"Maybe we won't." Sarai frowned and stared at Vi. "But you'll have to stop. There has to be another way. The politicos. Grievance officers. Something."

I had more questions, but I did not ask them. Sarai could enlighten me of anything I had not guessed later. I held my peace, calming both of us but remaining alert enough to defend.

"Tried everything," Vi complained. "Damn baldies, think talk talk talk can close black holes."

Sarai shook her head. "For it to work now, we'd have to be ignorant, dead or cooperative. You messed up the ignorant part, and I'd rather not revisit the dead part. Besides, Tark would stomp your ass." Sarai patted my shoulder. "Wonder why I don't feel cooperative?"

Sarai's breast brushed my arm. Even in the midst of danger, I became conscious of her nearness in a sexual fashion. I continued to stroke my hand up and down her back, including the top of her rear. It was not as satisfying through her lab wear as it would be once I undressed her again.

Only this time, there would be no secrets between us.

"Let us first hear their suggestion," I said, caressing her. "Perhaps it would be best if this incident were not broadcast." *They might investigate you and me as well, love. You do not want that right now. There are other things you need to understand about me… about us… first.*

Sarai snorted in response to my unspoken rebuke and shifted away from my touch. The Irts eyed us suspiciously.

"Why you help us?" Vi said.

Sarai spoke before I could. "I sure as stars won't help you if your idiot plan makes me look bad. All this time, it's not my fault the kitium has been wonking. What a relief." She lifted the rag off her shoulder. "Or it would be, if I didn't hurt so much."

"Sorry," Vi said, obviously not sorry from her hairy smirk.

"So how did you do it?" Sarai applied pressure to her wound again.

Vi considered Sarai's request and finally pointed at me. "Thank him."

I could not conceal my surprise. "Me?"

Sarai stared at me, every part of her body exuding shock. "You're involved in this?"

"I am not."

The male Irt gestured toward the box of supplies. "Old tech hairdryer. Enough puff to spoil but not enough tech for alarms."

Ah! I had repaired an old tech ionic hairdryer six months ago, which had been purchased by an Irt. With the amount of body hair they had, it made sense to me.

Their plan had indeed been long running. Irts were not usually so patient.

"I guess you didn't help them on purpose," Sarai said to me. The set of her shoulders loosened. "A hairdryer is just... fiendishly clever. I never considered a low-grade heat source in the stasis environment itself since I thought nobody else could open it. I tested the unit and it was clean. How did you break into it? My kitium porters lug the box itself to the foreman, and nobody but me and the foreman have a key. It's DNA-chipped."

"Noneya," Vi replied. She glanced at me again, and I wondered if she, or her companions, had been one of my clients for the painfully expensive and illegal blank ident chips. Either way, it did not matter. The kitium sabotage was done, and now we had to contain the repercussions—just like with my and Sarai's lovemaking.

"What guarantee can you give us you will not pursue this course of action further?" I asked. "Our silence will hinge upon it."

"Silence!" Sarai exclaimed. She paced to the stasis machine and back, gesturing emphatically. "They nearly ruined my rep as a temporer, my head is on the firing block, and they beat me up twice. Who knows what other stuff they'll try to get out of their contract?"

"What do you gain if you report this? The animosity of the entire Irt faction on Diggette?" Irts might be antisocial and warlike, but they were also extremely clannish. Smaller colonies like Diggette typically hosted a single tight-knit tribe that did not encourage rivals.

Sarai flapped her arms. "So?"

"Better if we have leverage." *Otherwise I do not see how we could ensure our safety.*

Sarai shook her finger at the Irts. "You shouldn't have signed such a dumb contract in the first place. I mean, no med benefits at full salary? If you can call that a salary. And the termination clause is criminal."

"What you know about it?" Vi bared her fangs. "You cahoot with management, read our docs? Maybe you in on it, indenture kit-diggers to fasten your own job."

"Those are standard clauses in boilerplate mineworker group contracts," I interrupted smoothly. "Unfair group contracts, at any rate. It's a safe assumption."

"My contract isn't like that." Sarai blushed at her slip. "I used a politico to negotiate it."

"Told you," the male said to a bristling Vi. "Who you use? Somebody on Diggette?"

Vi coughed, her face wrinkled with derision. "Like a psi-friendly politico take an Irt contract. How many times I tell you? And now, all ruined." She turned her back on him, something Irts did when they regarded someone as entirely unthreatening—a mark of disdain.

"What you gonna do?" she asked me while the male smoothed his rumpled fur behind her, obviously embarrassed. "Decide, Gitter. We have rounds."

"You're going to finish your rounds after this? With broken—" Sarai waved her hand in their general direction "—arms and knees and stuff?"

Vi huffed. "A little pain. Bad contract, but this our job, baldie. Think we can call in sick? Come and go as we please?"

"Go about your business," I said after a moment. It was more important to escape this incident with no further danger to us—either from the Irts or an overly curious colonial administration. "As long as we remain unmolested and the kitium sabotage stops, we will say nothing unless Sarai's skills are questioned in the future. Then, you understand, we will be forced to reveal what you have done. It is not right Sarai should suffer for this."

Vi exchanged a glance with the male. "Sure," she said unconvincingly.

I raised my eyebrows. "Do not think I cannot find you, should I wish."

"What are you talking about?" Sarai asked. "I'm tired of all these secrets." She stared hard at the Irt, who must not have thought the information she wanted, for Sarai continued to look confused.

After a hasty exchange they thought I could not hear, Vi grunted and tapped her brow with her good hand. So did the male. "Agreed."

Soon, I said to Sarai. *We need to put an end to this first.* I slipped an arm around her, expecting resistance. When she recoiled, I held her still. To her credit she did not struggle beyond the initial flinch, reluctant, I think, to display any friction between us—any weakness—in front of the Irts.

"Mind your woman, Gitter," Vi said with a smirk. "Never get used to it. Males in charge. Inferior species."

"He's Gitternian, not a Gitter, and he's not in charge and I'm not his woman," Sarai argued, but her pink cheeks belied her claim. "It's not like that."

I dropped my hand, cupping her hip. *Is it not?* I queried, and her face reddened more.

"We can go?" the male asked. He inched toward the door with a pronounced limp.

"Go." I drew Sarai to the side, giving the Irts a wide berth as they departed without a backward glance.

Chapter 9

It did not take Sarai long to begin. "Why the stup didn't you warn me sex with you was going to do… this thing to my brain? Tarkin, I can read minds. That's, like, not possible. Or healthy. Is it temporary? Permanent? Can you do it?" She tugged a wayward red curl. "Slag it! I can't imagine the stuff you've heard in my head."

I often had wished to hear what was in her head, it is true, but most of it came out of her mouth eventually. "No," I reassured her, attempting to lead her towards the door. We needed to return to my apartment before the Council arrived. They would not be pleased I had allowed Sarai to stray before debriefing. "Mind-reading is a skill no Gitternian has, and few of our partners develop the ability."

She wrapped her free arm around her torso. "Is anything else weird going to happen? Am I going to wake up tomorrow and be able to travel through wormholes without a ship? Kill people with a mean look? I can't believe you did this to me! You said the brain sex thing had nothing to do with mind-reading. Was that a lie? Did you realize this would happen?"

I longed to ask her if she would have accepted me as a partner if I had violated Council policy and confessed everything but answered only the questions she had asked. "The possibility was extremely remote. It is an incidental expansion of your psi abilities."

"Incidental my bum," she grumbled, and then glared at me. "Why can't I read your mind like the Irts? Say something in my head."

Because I am Gitternian, I said. *You can only hear my thoughts if I send them. I promise you, nearly all we join with who are not of our species develop only the ability to meld with us.*

"Oh." She picked up a broken plastene beaker and put it in the trash. "And those Irts—they messed up my kitium with a damned hairdryer. All this time. I almost lost my job! wC'in upstairs, it thinks I'm going to lose my job. Everybody at Hermana does. I'm a laughingstock. What if I still lose my job? What if they find out what my psi can do? Will the government come after me? Tarkin, I—"

I placed a finger on her lips, and the flow of increasingly frantic words came to an abrupt halt. She regarded me with wide blue eyes. "Sarai. Let us go home. There are some people you need to meet."

"Who?" Sarai wrinkled her nose. "All the other girls you did this to?"

Was she… anxious? Angry? Jealous? "I have never encountered this with one of my partners. Like I said, it is extremely unusual." I wanted to tell her my strong feelings for her, too, were unique in my experience, but it did not seem like the proper time. "You will meet the Gitternian Council—the ones who will explain everything to your satisfaction."

"A Gitternian Council. Is that like your government?"

"Not exactly. Please, Sarai. Let us go, and there will be no more secrets."

She huffed. "That's a relief. But I'm really mad at you." As she shed her lab whites, her motions twisted her wounded shoulder. "Ouch! I need a medic. We should stop at a clinic."

"There will be a medic at the apartment." I helped her wrap her shoulder, my hands lingering on the pale, delicate skin of her neck. "There is no need to explain to anyone connected with the colonial administration how you came to be marked with an Irt's claws."

"All right, fine," she conceded. I adjusted her white undershirt over the makeshift bandage, careful not to hurt her. "But you and these Council dudes had better explain everything, and I mean everything, as soon as we get there."

The bloodstains concealed by her coveralls, we neatened her lab, confiscated the hair dryer hidden among the supplies the Irts had delivered, recoded the lock on the stasis box, and left. I signed out at the receptionist's desk. The dB'thx gave us a curious look but did not ask questions.

Now all I had to do was introduce my Sarai to the Gitternian Council operatives. The Council was not as reclusive as most Gitternians, due to their responsibilities, but they had not had much exposure to individuals like Sarai. I doubted we would be recruited, but aside from that, predicting what they would think of Sarai was beyond my ken. Instead I imagined what I would do to, and with, Sarai, once we had completed our obligatory debriefing and scheduled whatever training they felt necessary for a newly awakened talent.

I trusted she would enjoy the lovemaking as much as, or more than, our previous encounters. My cycle had ebbed, and the shift in urgency would change things.

Would Sarai still be responsive or had she only mated with me in friendship? I would know soon enough, and I prayed I received the answer I sought.

We traveled home in Tarkin's magnevehicle, but we didn't talk. Tarkin, because that's Tarkin. Me, because—okay, I was sulking.

I couldn't believe he'd let those hairy bastards free after they nearly ruined my life and ripped us to shreds. The sex-mad, whoop-ass Tarkin who was not Tarkin had suddenly turned back into the Tarkin who was Tarkin—the mild-mannered, considerate Gitternian with the dry sense of humor and affection for luxuries. Who was this new man, and what else about him had shifted back to the Tarkin who was Tarkin?

Did the end of his heat cycle mean no more bed play? I still had no answer to that question, and it wasn't one I'd ask these Council people. And why was I obsessing about whether or not Tarkin would want to, or be able to, remain intimate with me after everything that had happened today?

I loved him, yes, but I had larger concerns. What would become of me now that I could read minds? Little bits of stray thoughts jumped into my head if I looked at someone while my psi was active. More than bits if I concentrated. Not that I had much of a chance to test it.

"Please deactivate your psi," was the only thing Tarkin said to me, when I was eyeballing the garage attendant and listening in as she planned her grocery list. "There will be time enough later."

He had retreated to the physical and emotional distance I associated with him. Despite the vibes I'd gotten from him in the lab, he didn't seem lover-like now.

"I think there's something wrong with my psi. I haven't been able to close it this whole time," I complained, but when I made the attempt, it snapped shut like a trap. "I take that back. I got better." Without ceremony, I returned to normal, no hint I was a biological aberration on all known planets.

Or so I'd once thought. Gitternians don't mingle. Psi-sex doesn't exist. Mind-reading isn't possible. I'd thought many things a day ago that were now proven wrong. I never considered myself the savviest, knowingest being in the galaxy, but these revelations made me wonder what other falsehoods I'd swear were true. Did pigs—Terran pigs—fly when no one was looking?

I was tired of things happening to me out of the blue and upsetting my universe-view. Which reminded me, I was about to meet these Council people, and I had no idea what to expect.

When we reached the garage beneath Tarkin's building, despite the lure of a medic I refused to go upstairs. My pain had subsided, mostly, and I needed to prime myself. Tarkin didn't try to drag, push, or persuade me. He lingered beside the low silver vehicle with his face and body language as impassive as the Tarkin I'd known for years.

The Tarkin from last night would have heaved me over his shoulder and toted my ass through the building. The Tarkin from last night would have pissed me the hell off, too. And turned me on.

"I'm not ready for this." I paced in front of his vehicle, avoiding the creases in the prefab paving. It was something I did when I was stressed. "Tell me about this Council. What are they going to do to me? Are they connected to the galactic government?"

Tarkin leaned against the magnevehicle and watched me. It was something he did when I was stressed.

"As you are aware," he said, "Gitternians do not reveal everything about our species to the rest of the galaxy. The Council is in charge of sustaining our privacy. Among other things."

I circled a nearby support pillar and walked back to Tarkin's vehicle. "What things?"

Tarkin shot me a look. "The fact that intercourse with a Gitternian can cause changes in psi, for starters."

That was more acerbic than Tarkin was wont to be. I paused to stare at him, my wounded arm close to my side. The muted lights of the half empty garage on his face revealed little beyond detached tolerance.

"Did you kiss and tell before or after last night?" I asked.

Tarkin blinked, and a puzzled crease appeared between his brows. "There was no need to mention the kissing. I merely informed them I had acted as a catalyst this cycle and specified the identity of my partner."

"Catalyst?"

He inclined his head. "The Gitternian partner is referred to as a catalyst if the joining triggers more than the typical adjustment in psi."

"So there's always the chance—" I tapped my head "—you can catalyze somebody. If you don't want anyone to know about it, why do you go outside your species?"

"Sometimes it is necessary." He straightened and advanced on me, and I accidentally stepped on a crack. "And sometimes it is desired."

"Oh. Um." What did he mean? Did he mean he desired me or that the Council desired its people to get some strange and see what came of it? What *were* they going to do to me? "Isn't it dangerous to create new mindreaders who might not be as cooperative as me?"

"Cooperative," he mused, and the subtle lift of his lips indicated great amusement, Tarkin style. "Not the word I would have chosen."

I hummed with pleasure. I loved to crack his deadpan. "You know what I mean."

He stopped several paces from me, not close enough to touch but close enough to dart forward and hug him madly before he could get away. If I were so inclined.

"Yes, I do know what you mean," he said, happily unprivy to my thoughts, thoughts that kept straying from the serious matter of my future. "Either way, the Council feels the gamble is worth the results. They monitor certain aspects of the galactic government in order to shield us from Librarians and other information seekers. Mindreaders are useful."

A covert organization, then. That didn't want to share its mindreaders. However, the notion of Gitternians directing a crew of mindreaders was a lot less menacing than the galactic government doing it. The notion of Tarkin directing, say, me, with the aid of some silk scarves and a naughty instruction manual, was not menacing at all.

"Do they encourage you to find non-Gitternian partners?" I asked.

"It is not required," he said evasively. He indicated the lift with a hand, not touching me but steering me nonetheless. "We should go. I do not like to delay medical attention to your wound. And they will not be pleased we left my quarters before you could be appraised."

"Why?" The lift, its walls lined with a beige rubbery substance, whizzed silently up to the level of his apartment.

He studied the yellow glow of the indicator light as we passed each floor. "You could reveal your new abilities to someone who would not be as understanding as the Council."

"I wouldn't do that. I'm not crazy." I wasn't convinced the Council would be what I'd term understanding, but I did get that nobody else would be anywhere close to my definition of the word. Mindreaders would not be anybody's best bud, outside the government.

"Unintentionally."

As I'd never been one for secrecy, he had a point. The only secret I'd ever kept had been my huge crush on Tarkin, and considering he figured I'd be game for some action this cycle, it could be argued I hadn't kept that secret, either. The question was, did Tarkin realize I wanted more than action? He'd said our lovemaking would change things, but Mars only knows if he meant my psi, our relationship, or something else entirely.

Dammit, what was the use of mind-reading skills if I couldn't read the person I most wanted to figure out!

The lift slid open, and too soon we reached his door. He indicated I should precede him into the apartment, so the three people on Tarkin's comfy leather furniture focused their glares on me, their dark eyes reproving. With their medium brown skin, black hair, and unsmiling features, they could have been Tarkin's relatives, except that they exuded cold disinterest and Tarkin, well, Tarkin was not cold.

The Gitternian Council, I presumed.

"Are you hiding behind me?" I hissed at Tarkin. I could understand why he wouldn't want to face these ice cubes, but I wasn't going down alone. "Quit fiddling with the lock."

The two males rose from the sofa and inclined their heads ever so slightly, but the petite woman in the curved chair remained seated. Her glossy black hair was caught in a severe queue at her neck, and her figure was what one might describe as rectangular, if one were being kind.

Regardless, they all three exuded an aura of gravity and consequence that unnerved me, as if I were on trial.

"Is this the Terran Sarai Rose McNally?" the woman asked.

"Operative Kinlen." Tarkin performed a stiff bow. "This is Sarai McNally, yes."

"Why did you escort the Terran from your domicile before confirmation?" Now the Gitternian woman stood. Her head barely reached the shoulders of her companions, and they were my height, which made Tarkin the tallest person in the room—here on Diggette, it had to be a unique experience for him.

Tarkin closed his eyes briefly, and an expression flashed across his features that made me want to stand beside him. Support him. I shuffled closer until our elbows bumped.

"I did not escort Sarai from my domicile. I secured her from another location."

The woman's eyes narrowed. She nodded her head at one of the men, who took a small datapad from a hip pouch and made a notation on it. "You allowed the subject to depart?"

"Sarai visited her place of employment today. She puts in a great deal of overtime."

"I'm not a prisoner," I pointed out. "Am I?"

She did not respond to me. "You risk much, Wanderer, when the subject is newly awakened and entirely untrained. Have we any untidiness to conceal?" The one man continued to take notes while the other stood like one of Tarkin's statues. If he wasn't the secretary and he wasn't the bitch-in-charge, did that make him the medic or the muscle?

The muscle option would have been ludicrous, considering the humanoid's relative size, if I hadn't seen what Tarkin could do.

"No untidiness." Tarkin clasped his hands behind his back, which removed his arm from the vicinity of mine. Fine.

"The subject triggered no alarms?"

"Come on," I said. "The subject is right here." Irritated now, I opened my psi and attempted to read their minds. Nothing. Tarkin knew what I was doing, because his lips tightened.

Do not attempt to do that again, he mind-talked me. *They will have a reader on the premises to test you.*

A reader—someone like me? Someone who'd slept with a Gitternian and could now read minds? Boy, did I have some questions for her! Just in case she was listening in on my brain, I greeted her. Or him. *Hi, I'm Sarai. Why don't you come introduce yourself and we'll eat brownies while these dull fish argue about alarms?*

There was no answer.

"All is silent," Tarkin said out loud. I snickered. Everyone ignored me.

"Is the subject ready for confirmation?" the woman asked.

This was ridiculous. "You need confirmation? How about the subject confirms you Gitternians pulled a fast one on her and logs a complaint with a grievance officer?" Something I'd never do, but they didn't have to know that. Unless their reader scanned my thoughts and told them I was bluffing.

The woman hmmed. "I am surprised by your selection, Wanderer. The subject is belligerent and hostile. Have you placed the entire Council in jeopardy? Perhaps your schooling was faulty."

"It was not faulty," Tarkin said. "I chose well." I detected a rare trace of exasperation in his tones, but it didn't phase the Queen Bee.

I had no idea why Tarkin had picked me, but no matter what happened, I didn't regret the fact we'd made love. Okay, if they locked me up the rest of my life I'd regret it, but Tarkin was the most thoughtful, intelligent being I knew, not to mention the sexiest, and he must have known what he was doing. He could have caught a zip ship to Gitternis and had risk-free rumpy. He could have located another humanoid with psi if he was merely wanted to fill the annual mindreader quota—someone the Council would value. But he'd opted to remain on Diggette Colony when his time came.

For the first time, I considered the fact Tarkin had chosen to spend his cycle with me. He may have cut up stiff about optimum selections and cycle escalation, but zip ships were fast, and he'd courted me for ten days. We'd had dinner together that many days, anyway. As minimalist and, okay, feeble at courting as he was, he could have been at it longer, and I'd never noticed.

It gave me hope. It gave me confidence. I stomped toward the woman and pointed at her with my good arm. The man I'd pegged as the muscle stiffened.

"If you trained Tarkin in anything, I'm sure he made top scores. Now quit talking about me like I'm not here, or I'll leave—then you can talk about me however you want. I need to go see a medic, and there doesn't seem to be one here."

Finally, I snagged Her Highness's attention. "A medic?" she said. "Why did you allow the subject to be injured, Wanderer?" One of her eyebrows arched in an irksome fashion. It was irksome when she did it, anyway, though not when Tarkin did it. When Tarkin did it, it was kind of hot.

But she bugged me, and I'd never been good at keeping my gob shut when somebody bugged me. "This little gash in my shoulder." I unzipped the top of my coverall and revealed the bloodstains on my torn undershirt. When the heavy fabric of the coveralls peeled away, it yanked off the crappy bandage and semi-scab that had formed. "Shit, that hurts."

"An incident in Sarai's lab," Tarkin said before I could mention crazy Irts and kitium plots. "I thought it best if she were not examined by a non-Gitternian medic at this time."

"The subject may see our medic after the confirmation," the woman said.

"Oh, that's polite. It matches your greeting. Do most Gitternians have absolutely no social skills or is it just the Council?"

The woman spoke to me directly, as if acknowledging a particularly annoying child. "What would you suggest, Terran?"

I held up a finger. "First, don't pretend I'm not here." Then another finger. "Second, how about, 'Hi, I'm a really short secret agent and you must be Sarai. Nice to meet you.'" In an impressive display of maturity, I didn't hold up the finger I wanted to hold up.

The woman pursed her lips. "Nice to meet you? That remains to be seen."

"I don't think you're in a position to be snotty. Where do you get off sleeping with folks and not warning them it could mess with their heads? Not letting your people even give hints about the possibility?" I put my hand on my hip and laid it on as thick as the humidity in a Terran swamp. "What gives you the right to co-opt my life without my consent?"

"Normally the only transformation involves—" she began, but I cut her off.

"I'm not normal."

Beside me, Tarkin shifted his weight and guilt darkened his already dark eyes. "I am deeply sorry, Sarai. I did not realize you felt your life had been ruined."

"I wouldn't say ruined. More like churned," I whispered.

Shame riddled me as well. I'd exaggerated to put the Council operatives on the spot, not Tarkin. I knew how I felt about him, but I hadn't sorted through my emotions about the psi changes. In the past hour I had resented it, tried to ignore it, and eavesdropped on someone's shopping list. My acceptance of my new brain would depend on how much danger it put me in.

Out loud I said, "I get that you weren't allowed to tell me, Tarkin. Though how they would have figured out if you squealed…" I turned back to the Council operatives and captured the woman's steady gaze. "What now?"

"Assess you, train you, and consider your future as a reader."

"And protect me?"

"You are now our responsibility. Tarkin's, to be precise."

That meant there would continue to be a connection between me and Tarkin. I'd figured we'd remain friends, but how did Tarkin feel about Council-mandated togetherness? I glanced at him, but his attention was focused on the operatives.

"What does this responsibility entail?" I asked.

"I trust you see the wisdom of concealing your abilities?" she asked.

I nodded.

"Tarkin is responsible for ensuring you do so and aiding you when necessary."

I didn't like the sound of that—"ensuring". I doubted they were as concerned about exposing me as they were what I'd learned about Gitternians. What would Tarkin be expected to do if I tried to rat them out?

Maybe I didn't want to know. Besides, I'd never! I could imagine what the galactic government would do if they realized Gitternians could make mindreaders out of ordinary citizens. The poor sods would become sex slaves, and not everyone would enjoy that as much as some species.

Nope, betraying Tarkin's entire people was not something I'd do.

But what I might do… is have some fun with it. Make life easier.

"As long as I keep it secret, does it matter how I use my abilities?" If I were unethical, or bored, grocery lists wouldn't be my only listening material. Mind-reading would be easy to exploit. I hadn't considered how far I'd take it, but it would rattle their cages if I asked.

The woman glanced at the secretary before answering. His datapad beeped madly as he pecked away. "If you abuse others with your gift, controlling you is another of Tarkin's responsibilities. One hopes it would not escalate to the Council level."

I elbowed Tarkin. "They think you're in charge of me. What do you think?"

The corner of his mouth curled up. For Tarkin, that was akin to a belly laugh. "I think the operatives would like to proceed to the test phase and schedule your training so they may return to their posts."

"What posts?" Why was he smiling? Was he… enjoying this confrontation?

The woman answered me. "Do you think we spend all our time confirming readers in the outbound, child? We have other responsibilities."

"Like what?"

The woman's left eyelid twitched. Then the left side of her face. Slag, was she going to stroke out on us? "There is no reason for you to know that."

"It's my future. What do readers do after you run them down? Work for you? Tarkin said you guys have a reader nearby. I hope he's getting a head full."

"A reader accompanied us, yes, but she is not hiding. It is courteous for a reader to remain out of eyesight until her skills are needed."

"Why?"

The twitch in her eyelid increased. "A reader cannot probe someone who is not in her line of vision."

So I couldn't read somebody I couldn't see. Useful information. "You keep saying she. Are all readers female?"

"No." She took a deep breath. "Citizen McNally, all these questions will be answered during training."

I gave her a break. "I'll take the training, but I don't want to work for you."

"I agree. I do not believe you are compatible for Council service," the woman said dryly. "It is a shame. Tarkin has been a promising candidate for years. I suppose he could attempt another partner, though two such… responsibilities would be demanding."

The thought of Tarkin with another woman chapped my buns. I wanted to believe he hadn't chosen me in hopes of creating a mindreader, but what if they pressured him to try again?

He seemed to sense my concern because he answered immediately. "I did not select a Terran in order to further my candidacy. I have no interest in Council service, as I have indicated in the past."

So I wasn't part of some mindreader quota. His selection was personal, not political. Unless it was reverse political because he assumed, even if converted, I would be undesirable to the Council. Hmm. Well, I'd always known he was smart.

"We had such hopes when you informed us you had selected a Terran. When you spawned a reader, even the Chair took an interest." The woman sighed, evidencing the first touch of emotion that wasn't bitchy or cold. "The subject… Sarai… is obviously unsuitable."

"Thanks." I took it as a compliment. I wouldn't want to be whatever they considered suitable. If that had been any part of Tarkin's motivation, he'd guessed right.

"More importantly," Tarkin added, "it would not suit her."

"You would not consider, next cycle…?" Her voice trailed off when Tarkin frowned.

He moved close to me almost possessively. "I would not. Can we proceed to the confirmation? Sarai should not have to wait for medical treatment."

The woman nodded her head toward the Gitternian guy who didn't have anything else to do besides stand there, and after another moment a tall humanoid female walked out of Tarkin's bedroom. She, too, was Terran—a strapping blonde in a dress that danced around her ankles. As she stepped, the sound of tiny bells swirled up from her feet.

"Sarai." She held out her hands to me, and I took them. Her fingers were strong and warm and not even a little sweaty. "I'm Candy Dawson from Florida, American Continent."

"I'm Sarai McNally." Our eyes met, and suddenly I could feel her inside my head, rummaging around like my granmater sorting through the attic in search of that damned bird cage she knew was up there somewhere.

"Hey, now." I jerked my hands away and swiveled my head. "Who invited you in?"

"I thought you consented to be tested?"

"So you jump my brain without buying me dinner first?" I joked. In truth, I hadn't considered what it would be like to meet another mindreader. Like I'd had time to consider it. "Not even any foreplay?"

Candy's brown eyes widened, and then she laughed. "Oh, it's a joke! I've been with the Gitternians so long, I forgot." Almost guiltily, she glanced at the operatives, none of whom had cracked a smile.

Tarkin, however, was having trouble pressing his lips in a straight line.

"Citizen McNally, please do not resist the assessment," said the female Gitternian. "Then Operative Dawson can tend your wound."

"You're the medic, too? Were they too cheap to spring for two people?"

"My abilities are at the green level. I'm higher in empathy than straight mind-reading, which means I'm suited to the healing arts."

She seemed so normal. Why would she want to hang out with Gitternians who weren't Tarkin all the time? "When did they convert you?"

"Martin and I met ten years ago. It's been interesting." She indicated the Statue, which nearly made me hoot—I mean, the height differential alone. I wondered if they still had a hot love thing going or if they were merely coworkers now.

I didn't ask. I just said, "I can imagine."

She smiled. "I'm sure you can. From what little I could see, your psi skills are physical or earth-related. Right?"

"Metallurgy. Mostly kitium."

"Also interesting." She crossed her arms and tapped her fingers against her opposite bicep. "Those types of skills don't usually develop into mind-reading. But it's not an exact science. We really don't know how or why it happens."

"You're not reassuring me."

She uncrossed and held out her hands again. "It doesn't hurt and doesn't take long if you don't resist. It'll also go even faster if you open your psi and hold it—hm, ready but not active."

I supposed we should get this over with so she could get the Irt germs out of my wound. "Let's at least sit down."

She led me to the couch, and we got comfortable while the three operatives and Tarkin watched with varying degrees of interest. It was kind of creepy, having an audience while this chica explored my head, but I took her hands and relaxed the barriers that held my psi dormant.

It was neither pleasant nor unpleasant and was over with, as promised, quickly. Candy turned to the operatives. "Purple," she said. "Good clarity potential, no empathy, minor projection. More of a receiver than anything."

The female operative's lips tightened. "We could have used a purple in quadrant three. What intensity?"

"High," Candy said. "Language-unspecific. Not much distance."

I was purple. And intense. And unempathetic. On Terra, purple represented royalty and bruises. "What's that all mean?"

"It means you can hear thoughts, as long as the in-vision target imagines words, but you can't read emotions any more than you can naturally. You can't compel anyone to hear you."

"No more than I can naturally," I added. "By yelling."

She cracked up, and the Gitternians glowered. After we quit giggling, she explained, "The downside to lack of projection is you and Tarkin will only be able to maintain a two-way conversation when you're intimate."

Wait, she assumed we'd be intimate again? Did that mean Tarkin's sex life wasn't constrained by his biology? Could he or couldn't he do it outside his cycle? He hadn't really clarified that issue earlier today. He couldn't do it before his cycle, so it made sense he'd go back to Monk Man afterwards. Unless he could pre-cycle and just didn't want to do it with me until his crotch was afire with lust.

I eyed Tarkin, standing between me and the guy with the datapad and watching me with a hooded expression. No help there. I opened my mouth to ask Candy, but she peeled my coveralls away from my shoulder.

"Ouch!" The blood that had trickled from the gash since I'd shown the wound to the operatives had glued the fabric to the laceration again.

Candy flinched as well. "I'm sorry. From the sensory impression I got, it's a flesh wound, but painful."

"You felt that?"

"That's why I'm a medic. Martin, may I have my kit?"

Tarkin, unexpectedly, placed a light hand on my shoulder. I drew in a tiny breath. "It is not serious," he said. "Good."

Candy's dude retrieved a silver case from beside the vidscreen and knelt beside her. It held a myriad of hyposprays, vials, and other quickie med tools. While Tarkin clasped my shoulder, she cleaned and bandaged my wound with antisep-foam. I was so distracted by his touch, I hardly felt the sting.

"When the sealant dissolves, the wound will be gone," she told me. "I'll leave an extra vial in case it peels off. The foam wasn't designed to withstand how frequently Terrans bathe."

"Cleanliness is the next best thing to friendliness," I quipped. "And if you're going to be next to a friend, it's best to be clean."

Candy laughed again. "I haven't visited Terra in way too long."

"What's stopping you?" I asked, then tensed when Tarkin moved his hand from my shoulder to the nape of my neck. His fingers curled into my hairline, caressing the base of my skull. It was a gesture both affectionate and sensual and reminded me I would soon be alone with him and able to discuss… oh so many things.

"Working for the Council is time-consuming." Candy shrugged and packed away her med supplies.

In a slightly breathless voice, I said, "Glad it won't be me."

The lady Gitternian looked glad too, inasmuch as Gitternians looked like anything besides bored out of their minds.

After Candy finished, we scheduled my first official training session. I tried not to balk the date selection much, considering the steam coming out of the Queen Bee's ears, but after the Irts' hair dryer trick, it wasn't like Hermana would be anxious to give me vacations. It would take a few tendays of shiny, flawless kitium tubes to get back in Hermana's good graces.

When I asked where we'd meet and how long it would take to get there, everyone except Tarkin went all shifty-eyed. They wouldn't give me a location. A secret rebel base, I supposed, from which the Gitternians hoped to take over the galaxy. Or something.

Tarkin, on the other hand, exuded an increasing degree of impatience for the operatives to scram. He mentioned their imminent departure twice—twice!—even though the Head Lady seemed determined to pound the basic guidelines for mindreader conduct into my head before she was willing to leave.

"I will ascertain Sarai is conversant with the protocol," Tarkin assured the operatives. "It is under control."

Not that I wanted them to stick around, though I'd have loved some one on one time with Candy, but Tarkin was not being normal. "Why are you being so rude?" I whispered to him. "Is there something you're not telling me?"

"It has been a stressful day for you," he said. He touched my arm shoulder lightly, drawing his finger from my shoulder to my elbow. "Do you not wish to be alone?"

Alone how? I blinked a few times, and Tarkin raised his eyebrow. In that kind of hot way, not in the irksome way.

Candy glanced between Tarkin and me and something seemed to dawn on her, because she grabbed her med kit and hastened to the door.

"We should go," she said. "Medic's orders. Sarai won't go rogue. She's a purple, not a black."

The female operative pursed her lips. "I am merely doing my duty."

"Now let Tarkin do his."

Tarkin seemed to agree. Without the Boss Lady's agreement, he held open the door. If they ignored it, they'd look uncouth, and I guess even Council members have some social skills. With a last frown at me, the female operative exited, the others on her heels.

Candy went last. "Watch out, woman. I think he's still cycling," she murmured. She winked at me right before Tarkin closed the door.

Chapter 10

Was Tarkin still cycling? He wasn't behaving like last night, or even this morning. I glanced at him warily as we hovered in his foyer.

"I am not," he said to me.

Damn.

"How did you guess what I was about to ask? You reading my mind?" I said with a nervous laugh. After such a tense couple of hours with the operatives, not to mention the Irts, I was surprised I didn't crumble into a thousand disconnected bits as soon as Tarkin shut the door.

But then, the tension had started this morning, with the two of us naked in Tarkin's bed. Had that really been this morning? Had the sex really been that good?

Tarkin ruminated on my question—the one I'd asked out loud—before answering. "I do not need to read your mind."

Good thing. Best that he had no idea what I was thinking.

I wandered into the living area. "Long day," I commented. "Stressful, like you said. Boy, I'm tired."

Funny thing about Terran women. We often say things we don't mean when there's something we really want to know. Worse, we pretend disinterest or agreement when in fact our wishes lie elsewhere. It's a sneaky way to solicit opinions without committing your own or admitting you're interested in the topic.

When you think about it, it's also a stupid way to gather information. Asking Tarkin if he wanted to have sex would be more efficient. Painful but honest. Yet discussing his cock on the down cycle would be easier than admitting how desperately I wanted to discuss our future as a couple. As something more than friends. What would I say, something casual? Nonchalant? *Hey, are we dating now or what? Because I'm a hip momma either way, groovy to the max and all those ancient slang terms.*

No doubt his face would settle into that "You are the oddest being I know" expression I'd been known to inspire in him, and it would crush me. If I could get him to make the first move, I'd at least know he wanted to talk.

So I didn't goob out and ask about "us". I covered it up and said, "I should head home. Gotta work hard tomorrow and restore my reputation." If he had things to say to me, he'd…

"No," Tarkin said right behind me.

I whirled, startled. "You don't think I can restore it?"

"No, you should not go home." Although close enough to swap smells, he made no move to touch me. Instead, he regarded me with that intense stare, the one I'd always pretended was a look of secret passion.

I stared back. He didn't speak. I didn't speak. I squinted and opened my psi. He stared some more.

Nope, still couldn't read his mind.

Did he want to talk or not? Impatient, I ended the silence. "I'm tired," I repeated.

He tilted his head toward the bedroom. "That can be remedied here."

Shivers raced up my spine at the memory of what had happened in his bed this morning. "Are you tired?"

A humanoid male with a Terran-style libido, which was the majority of humanoid males, would never admit to being tired because that would be like saying, "Sure, let's not have sex." What would Tarkin say?

He said, "I do not require as much sleep as a Terran."

I shoved a piece of hair behind my ear, careful not to bump him with my arm. Be damned if I'd touch him first! "That doesn't answer my question."

"I am not unusually exhausted."

His steady gaze unnerved me. I swear, he had reptile eyes. He could go without blinking for hours.

I mimicked his proper tones. " 'I am not unusually exhausted.' Does that mean you're exhausted the usual way?"

"I could not be. Today has not been usual."

"So you're tired."

"I did not say that."

I closed my eyes and squeezed the bridge of my nose. I wasn't too tired to have the talk, but I was definitely too worn out to decipher Tarkin-speak for hidden meanings. I stifled, not very well, a small scream of frustration.

Two gentle hands cupped the sides of my head, fingers lacing into the hair to massage my temples. "If you are tired, we should go to bed."

My eyes popped open. A tiny smile curved Tarkin's lips, sparked in his eyes. He continued. "I would prefer you be well rested the next time we make love."

My breath caught, and I nearly coughed. My version of being coy had actually worked! Tarkin started the conversation. Tarkin made the first sally.

Tarkin brought up sex and continuity.

"You said your cycle was over?" My voice rose on the end of the sentence, turning it into a question.

"It is."

"You don't have to be in heat to… you know?"

"During our cycles we forge the initial connection with a partner." He placed one hand on my hip and drew me against him. "Afterwards, biology no longer dictates us."

I came to rest softly against him. "Then what does?"

"Our hearts, Sarai."

There was no urgency in the light touch of his body against mine, none of the insistence of last night and this morning. I could easily escape his grasp, easily refuse his offer. This was no favor for a friend in need, no necessary act to preserve his manhood.

This was Tarkin reaching for me, one hundred percent of his own volition.

And it was more astonishing, more perfect, than anything that had previously happened between us.

My throat swelled a little and my eyes felt hot. Tarkin wanted me. Wanted me to stay with him. Tarkin wanted to go to bed with me and sleep, before making love.

But why wait?

I cleared my throat, feeling foolish. "I'm not tired."

Tarkin's brow creased. "You just said—"

In a move I'd longed to make for years, I leaned forward and kissed him.

I meant it to be brief, but Tarkin's fingers tightened on my head and he held me there, and he kissed me back. His lips, teeth and tongue made short work of my tentativeness. In moments we were wrapped around one another, tasting, holding. I rubbed his shoulders, tracked my fingers down the indentation of his spine. He tilted my head to the side to gain better access. But our embrace was not frantic or driven. It was—genuine.

I was making out with Tarkin, and he wasn't in heat!

A whoosh of relief weakened my knees, and I drew away from him to suck in a restorative breath.

"What is it?" His pupils had dilated, and his dusky skin was flushed.

"I can't believe this is happening." I ran a shaky hand through my curls, shoving them away from my face. I really needed a hair band.

"Do you not wish it?"

"Oh, I wish it!" I outlined his chin, his high cheekbone and strong nose, with a single finger, coming to rest on his bottom lip. To touch him this way, after years of being close enough to touch but not brave enough to try, was intoxicating.

"This has already happened twice." He moved to kiss me again, and I stuck my finger between his lips, delaying him. He licked it, then nuzzled my palm.

"But this is, like, real. You're not doing it to save your winky."

Tarkin laughed. "That was a side benefit. I was prepared to face the dwindling if you did not wish to be with me."

"You're talking about the impotence thing, right?"

"It was real, Sarai. It is real. Can you not know, now, how I feel?"

I rolled my eyes. "Why would I know, when you haven't told me?"

Tarkin took my hands from his face and splayed them against his chest, where his heart beat steadily. "I have known for a long while whom I would approach at my next cycle. And I have known for almost as long that no one else would suffice."

My insides bloomed with joy like the fat yellow marigolds in my granmater's window boxes. "You couldn't have dropped a hint?"

"Would you have accepted that I could not function physically if I had approached you before my cycle?"

"Absolutely," I said, but then I wondered. Would I have? Or would I have convinced myself it was some funky alien excuse to avoid a real relationship? Or that I didn't turn him on? I smoothed his shirt over his chest, staring at the wrinkles that formed and unformed in the fabric of his tunic.

"I would have been unable to explain my status," he reminded me. He caught one hand and kissed it. "It is against Gitternian law to reveal any details, even to those we care about."

My fingers, idly stroking his pecs, stilled. "And you care about me?"

I regretted it the moment it blurbed out of my mouth. What a dork I was, fishing for reassurance and hints of commitment. I should welcome what I'd been granted, not cry out for more.

"I do," he said, echoing the Terran marriage vow. Something lurking in his almost-smile hinted he was fully aware of the significance of the phrase. "I love you, Sarai."

"You do?"

"I do," he repeated.

"Then I love you too. I mean, I love you, but not because you love me. Because I love you. Fracking stars!" I interrupted my idiot-speak with a sniffle. I wasn't crying, I swear, it was allergies.

"I do," he said for the third time, placing a kiss on my forehead followed by one on each cheek. Lastly on my lips, as if sealing a promise.

"I am definitely not that tired," I said.

"I did not think so."

And he was right. I wasn't too tired for two orgasms for me, one for him; half a pan of brownies—shared; a shower—also shared; and a little something Heen described to me once involving the shower head, soap foam, the shower curtain, a white undershirt, a personal communication device set to vibrate, some soda from the kitchen, the empty soda bottle, and all Tarkin's towels.

Okay, Heen didn't exactly describe it the way it happened, but we Terrans are good at improvisation, and Tarkin didn't own any sex toys.

Yet.

When I was finished, or, rather, when we were finished, increasing our orgasm count one apiece, Tarkin looked up at me from the ruin of the bathroom floor.

"That quite freaks me out," he said, his handsome features alight and lightly sheened with perspiration. "But I like it."

So I did it again.

About the Author:

Ellie Marvel is a Southern gal with an accent to match and writes romantic fiction that doesn't leave out the naughty bits. She collects books, cats, vintage clothing, antique kitchenware, dust bunnies, dings in the car bumper and souls. Okay, no souls. Find out more about Ms. Marvel at www.elliemarvel.com.

Breathless

by Rachel Carrington

To My Reader:

I've always been fascinated by wizards, but for the longest time, they'd always been decent and upstanding. No roguery allowed… until Zac. When I got the idea for this storyline, I knew the heroine would have to be someone who could match a rogue wizard in both skills and wit. Lark is exactly who and what Zac needs. I hope you feel the same after reading *Breathless*.

Prologue

"You cannot stop this monster! He isn't human!" Shanae gripped her sister's shoulders and shook them fiercely. "This is beyond your control."

Lark looked into her younger sister's dark eyes, so like her own, and shook her head. "Regardless, I have to try."

"If you go out there, you could be killed." She stood in Lark's way, her eyes wild.

"You must stay here. I need to know you'll be safe." Lark turned her gaze toward the gaps in the wooden slats. A flash of black whipped by, and she knew he waited, hiding like an animal.

Diaz—a monster who thrived on tormenting his victims. No doubt he took great pleasure in watching the people scurry about searching for safety. Her father had warned her about the sorcerer's cruelty, his relentless desire for domination.

The approaching storm, growling thunder, and sparks of lightning heightened the intensity of the moment. "My place is with you," Shanae protested.

"You have not yet been trained. You will stay as I have instructed." Squaring her shoulders, Lark tugged her black leather shirt down over her stomach while her sister made a noise in the back of her throat like she always did when disgusted.

The rattling metal door nearly came off in her hand as she tugged it open. The shed creaked against the onslaught of the wind, the dilapidated structure offering little protection from the elements unleashed a scant hour before.

Lark stepped out into the driving rain and wind. The stinging rain slapped at her face, but she kept her eyes trained straight ahead. She couldn't falter now, no matter how difficult the path lay ahead of her. Finding him wouldn't be easy, but the other option was failure. Unacceptable. Diaz had taken too many lives not to be held accountable.

Her lips curled as she walked two feet away from the shelter. From the corner of her eye, she saw a flash of light. Tin creaked and popped, shearing into deadly missiles. Agonizing screams rent the air. Pleas for help. She caught the scent of blood. Another win for the monster.

Masses of people poured through the metal door, desperate to escape the raging storm. Mechanical gunfire rang out. Diaz's victory cheer. One by one, Lark's friends and neighbors fell to their knees.

The wind whipped away her screams, tossing them into the air where they lingered like tiny droplets of moisture.

Staggering out of the shelter, Shanae's hands clutched her blood-stained chest. "Lark!" She could barely be heard above the wind.

Slipping and sliding over the wet ground, Lark raced toward her sister. Sinking to her knees, she reached for a handhold, anything to keep Shanae from falling farther away from her. "Hang on. You have to stay with me."

Dark eyes now held only pain. "Promise me."

"Promise you what?" The rain beat down, soaking them to the skin.

"That you won't confront him. You cannot defeat him."

Their fingers linked. "I can't." Sobs tore through her chest. "I'm sorry. I can't."

Shanae coughed and winced. "Please. Not alone. You can't defeat him alone."

One promise. A simple thing, really. "No, not alone. I promise I won't confront him alone."

With a small sigh, the youngest of the Hogans closed her eyes for the last time.

Lark tipped her face back to the elements and screamed aloud. "You bastard!"

As the winds faded and slowly died to a slight breeze, taunting laughter echoed across the valley.

Chapter 1

Las Vegas, Nevada
Two months later

Standing at the corner of the bar, Zac watched the poker game unfolding two tables away, and while he'd been implored to join in the fun, cards weren't his game of choice. He eyed the buxom blonde behind the counter of the all-night bar. Now, she, on the other hand, could very well be his choice… at least for the evening.

A gust of wind tore open the outer door, and several of the patrons cursed, protecting their cigars and cards. High heels crossed the solid wooden floors with sharp clicks.

Long, sexy, and curved in all the right places, the dark-haired beauty dressed all in black strolled into the smoke-filled room. Her long hair flowed down her back, licking at her waist, and her lips, painted a tantalizing red, beckoned him from the corner of the room.

He straightened and pushed away from the bar. Whoever the woman was, she'd caught his attention. Held it prisoner.

Her almond-shaped eyes swept the room, and though no lights provided her assistance, he didn't doubt she could see very well. Her gaze pinned him, and a knot formed in the pit of his stomach.

"I'm looking for someone." Her voice, a wicked combination of smoke-filled rooms and hot, sweaty nights, punched him in the solar plexus.

"Aren't we all?" A guffaw accompanied the question from the back of the room.

The brunette didn't turn around or acknowledge the voice. Instead, she approached the corner, her back held stiff, steps never faltering. "I'm looking for the man they call Wolfe. Would you know were I could find him?"

Zac eyed her, raking an insulting gaze up and down her sexy little figure. Damn. "And if I do?"

The beautiful face hardened. "Then you will tell me where he is."

The room erupted in a chorus of riotous laughter before he silenced the noise with a wave of his hand. "What makes you so sure I'll tell you anything, lady?"

Her hand swept up, but his wrist blocked the intended smack. Their eyes clashed, connected, and breaths mingled in the heat of the room while silence dropped. Her eyes widened, and recognition flickered for a brief moment before her muscles relaxed. "You must be the man I'm looking for."

Dropping his hand to one side, he leaned one hip against the mahogany bar. Biding his time. Her forced smile shouted her irritation louder than any words could. "Actually, I'm not. The man you're looking for doesn't exist."

"I'd say that's for me to decide."

He pushed himself away from the wood. "Then you're an idiot. You shouldn't be here, and you damned sure shouldn't be here looking for Wolfe."

"He has something I want." The woman followed him as he tried to make good his getaway. Her high heels punctuated every step.

"Oh, I'm sure he does." He paused and looked over his shoulder. "Just as I'm sure you could offer him something in return."

Her eyes narrowed, assessed him. "Funny. I never took him for a coward."

The words settled in his stomach like a kick, and memories crashed down upon him, raining over the decent, fluffy images he'd stored there to erase the bad ones. He shook his head and took a sudden step backward, so suddenly his hip bumped against a table littered with cards.

"Jesus! Why don't you watch where you're going?" A chair scraped against the wood to accompany the complaint.

Zac ignored the gripe and pushed open the exit door, needing the clean, night air and the rake of the wind over his face. His booted feet hit the concrete, and he dragged breaths into his lungs.

"Why are you hiding your identity?"

He lifted his head and fixed her with a cold stare. "I'm not hiding anything. Wolfe doesn't exist, at least not the Wolfe you're looking for."

Her lips curled into a sneer. "Do you think I haven't seen you? That I don't know who he is?" She walked closer, stopping within an inch away from his face. "I've seen you in my dreams for the past two months. I've thought about nothing else save finding you, and now, I'll be damned if I'm going to walk away before I get what I came for."

Snagging a handful of her hair, he gave the soft waves a tug which caused her to wince. "Did you come for this then?" His lips fastened on hers, savage and brutal. He kissed her long and deep, savoring the taste of her until the warning bells rang inside his head. He thrust her away. Staggering back, he lowered his head to the brick wall behind him. "You shouldn't be here."

"I need you. The world needs you."

If only she knew how little he cared. "The world can go to hell. I don't work for it or anyone else. I work for me." Slapping the wall with his palm, he stalked away, never looking back, hoping she'd take the hint and leave.

Lark watched the broad shoulders disappear around the corner of the building before giving into the desire to smack the same wall. The brick chafed her palm, but she didn't feel the pain. *Arrogant bastard.* Her father hadn't warned her, but then, Wolfe had been blessed with immortality. He'd had plenty of time to perfect the art of nastiness. Well, regardless of his disposition, she hadn't come this far to fail now. Did Wolfe even knew about the problems Earth faced?

She sailed forward, streaming around the side of the bar as fast as a whippet. Instantly, she collided with a wall of muscle. Solid arms enfolded her, and she found herself staring up into eyes the color of onyx. Her breath snagged in her throat. She didn't have time to acknowledge the man's inordinate sexiness, and yet, the beauty of his face compelled her to.

Lifting one hand, she cupped his cheek. He didn't flinch. "You are, by far, the most beautiful man I have ever seen." *What the hell?* The thought sprung out of nowhere!

His gaze flickered slightly. The compliment served to earn her release. "Why are you following me?" Arms folded across a chest honed to perfection—a gesture meant to intimidate, no doubt.

Lark didn't back down, nor did she allow his stance to strike fear within her. "I didn't seek you out only to hear no."

His lips twitched. A chink in his armor, perhaps? "Too bad. I hate to send you home empty-handed." One eyebrow warred with the tousled hair drooping over his forehead. "So, would you like to hear my suggestion?"

Her gaze burned into his face. Her fingers curled into the palms of her hands, the urge to slap him powerful. Better yet, she wanted to send him spinning into outer space. Only his abilities far exceeded hers… at least, she assumed so. Her father had trained her well. Perhaps she underestimated herself. "What I would like to hear is why you refuse to help me."

"I owe you no explanation." The words shot out like machine gun fire.

"I've made you angry."

He turned his back to her. "Demanding women always do."

"Oh, so that's it. You're much more accustomed to weak women who fling themselves at your hard muscles and beg to be kissed." Her foot ached to kick him squarely in his perfectly chiseled ass.

He angled a look over his shoulder, and his lip definitely twitched then, just a slight uplifting, but enough to send Lark's temper soaring. Before he could respond, she came at him, eyes narrowed, lips held in a thin line.

She wanted to catch him off guard, but as if he read her mind, he whipped around, effectively deflecting her charge. Arms raised, they battled in the back alley, bone connecting with bone.

She spun high into the air, building up her speed. The kick she aimed at his solar plexus never met its mark. He slapped her foot down. She rebounded with a left hook, but he caught hold of her wrist, flinging her arm away. She realized quickly he only fended off her blows, nothing more. He didn't need to exert any energy beyond that.

A red haze coated her gaze, blurring her vision. Images of her sister's dead body, the destruction Diaz had left behind, and her own ineffectual attempts to stop him fueled the burn in her heart.

Having mastered the techniques of *hyung* at an early age, Lark's jump kicks were always lethal and delivered with such deadly accuracy her opponents rarely saw them coming. She leapt into the air once more with a cry of victory, her right leg extended, her body a combination of precision and determination.

As quick as a lightning strike, her new enemy snagged hold of her right foot and snapped her body to the ground like a fallen electrical line. Her ass hit the pavement, and though the contact made her want to scream in agony, she wouldn't give him the pleasure of seeing her wince. Arching her back off the ground, she came to her feet, hands poised in warning.

"You're fighting a losing battle," he said in a calm, almost unaffected tone.

Damn him. He wasn't even winded. "You anticipate my moves."

One shoulder lifted in a shrug as if bored by both the conversation and the company. "I would hardly be the man you believe I am if I couldn't defend myself, now could I?"

She had to try one last time. Lunging forward, she aimed a fist at his stomach, but he twisted neatly, catching one arm behind her back. His own arm bracketed her body, and the scent of his aftershave filtered into her nostrils. So powerfully intoxicating.

"You don't learn very well, do you?"

"I learn what I need to." She heard his inhalation, felt the hardness of his cock pressed against her spine. "You can release me now."

"I could, but I like you better this way." Still holding her arm with one hand, he gave his free hand permission to glide over the flat plane of her stomach before sliding upwards to cup one full breast. "In fact, I can think of a million other ways I'd like to have you."

"You selfish bastard! Let me go!"

"If I let you go, what will you give me in return?" His busy hand had now drifted lower, brushing over black leather, stopping at the waistband of her pants, fingers tilted downward.

She smacked his hand away, but it only returned, naughtier than ever. Her nipples drew taut, and she tried to control her ravaging hormones. He cupped her pussy, and she bit her lower lip, barely managing to hold the moan back. "How about I give you a swift kick in the nuts if you don't?" The words were softer than she intended.

The low rumble of his laughter sent a dart of heat down her spine. "Do you believe in fate?"

I have to get away from this man. Every ounce of sanity she possessed screamed at her to put as much distance between her body and his. He was dangerous territory. "Getting philosophical now?" The huskiness of her tone spoke of her building desire, and she cursed her decision to speak.

"If I were to touch you now, to cup your pussy, would you be wet for me?"

Her knees threatened to buckle. "Stop this."

His lips dropped to her neck, and unable to resist herself, she tipped her head sideway to give him better access. Insanity had taken hold. Why else would she cooperate so freely? She'd never been this attracted to a man with such urgency. His slightest touch ignited her.

Releasing her arm, he turned her, pulled her closer until her breasts flattened against his chest. "It's only a matter of time."

A lump formed in her throat. "I don't know what you're talking about." Her throbbing pussy told her otherwise.

To refute her words, Wolfe palmed her cunt through leather, grinding the placket of her zipper against her clit. *Sweet Jesus.* A burst of pleasure made her tremble, and for a brief moment, she wanted to hold on, let him continue this overwhelming assault. All too soon, sanity returned, and she broke away, stumbling backward.

"Don't touch me!" *At least not yet.* She damned the unspoken words, the longing she felt for this stranger.

Calmly, he held out his right hand. "Come. We will have a glass of wine and talk."

She stared at his peace offering. "I don't believe I want to talk to you now."

His hand dropped. "Suit yourself, but you claimed to need me. Has that now changed because I felt your desire for me?"

Yeah, she could definitely grow to hate this man. Head held high, she marched past him. "Fine. We'll have a glass of wine, but I choose the place." Her body still hummed from the electric touch of his fingers. She increased her pace, pausing long enough to throw over her shoulder, "and the wine."

"So now that we have the wine," Zac tipped his glass to prove his point, "you should probably introduce yourself. Ordinarily, I know my enemy's name before I engage in hand-to-hand combat with them."

She sat across from him, her long dark hair spilling over her shoulders like a black waterfall. With every movement she made, she enticed him, drugged him. His cock hardened beneath the table, and he drew in several deep breaths to restore proper blood flow to his brain. How long had it been since he'd been so aroused by just the scent of a woman?

When he'd held her in his arms, tasted her skin, and cupped the warmth of her pussy beneath her pants, he'd teetered on the edge of an orgasm. Impossible, but the urge had been so strong, he'd had to release her.

Her hands cupped around the wine stem of her glass, and she leaned forward. Even in the shadows of the dimly lit bar, twin dark orbs reached out to him. Her eyes were a magnet, ensnaring him without regret.

He would fuck her. The thought came unbidden, but he didn't fight it. In fact, he embraced the power of the knowledge.

"I would hardly call that hand-to-hand combat. You barely moved."

Her words caught his attention, and he inclined his head. He waited for her to supply the information he required, needing the time to rein in thoughts.

She stared at him for a long moment, long enough to make his pants grow tighter, and when she finally spoke, the sound wafted over him like a silken breeze. "Lark. My name is Lark Hogan."

Sitting up straighter, he raked a lock of hair away from his eyes. "Hogan? As in Marcus Hogan?" She'd definitely captured his attention this time.

She nodded. "He was my father."

"Was?"

"He… was killed two years ago." Her voice cracked.

Stretching one hand across the table, he touched the back of hers. "I'm sorry. I didn't know."

Her eyes flashed. "How could you have?"

"I can see you really don't know me."

"Then perhaps you would care to enlighten me. You do have me at a disadvantage since you now know my name, and all I know of you are the legends I've heard."

Touché. "I'm Zac Wolfe, but I'm surprised you don't know more than just the childhood fairy tales. Didn't your father teach you better than to track down someone you don't even know?"

Impossible. Marcus Hogan spent his life training warriors, teaching them how to defend themselves and how to take down the enemy without a sound. To learn each and every weakness. Go for the jugular. Most of all, Marcus taught his pupils about life.

Damn. He wished he'd had the chance to say goodbye to the old guy. They hadn't spoken in years, but Zac remembered him well. As sharp at sixty as he had been at thirty, Marcus had treated him like a son.

"I'm sorry. Am I boring you?"

The sultry question brought him back to the sexy brunette sitting across from him. For a long moment, he watched the play of emotions across her face. The grainy sounds of an old rock band filtered through the speakers overhead, and the scent of cigarette smoke stung the air while she struggled to control her temper. Her ability to reach into the deep part of herself and respond in such a polite manner earned his admiration.

"You could never bore me." The swift intake of her breath made him smile. "I believe you were going to respond to my question about your father. I assume he trained you as well as he did me."

"Better actually. Ordinarily, I'd follow his guidance word for word, but this time, I was in a hurry."

Definitely Marcus' daughter. The bite to her voice sounded so reminiscent of the man who rarely lost his patience. The one time he did see Marcus' explosion of temper, he knew why the man always controlled it.

He drummed his fingers on the table top. "What could be so important you wouldn't listen to your father's advice?"

"Will you stop bringing him into this, please? You act as if you know him."

He gave a short bark of laughter which made her eyes narrow. "I can see we really didn't do our homework, did we? Lark, Lark, Lark. Never," he leaned closer, violating her personal space, "and I mean never, confront an enemy you don't know."

"Are you my enemy then?" She issued the challenge with a spark in the ebony pools of her eyes.

His wine glass skidded across the table, and he rested his palms flat against the scarred wood. "What else would I be?"

"I didn't come here to fight you, Zac."

The way she said his name ignited a fire in the pit of his stomach. His cock responded with another powerful surge, a violent demand for release. Shifting on the wooden bench, he cleared his throat. "No, you came on a fool's mission—Diaz's mission."

If his words surprised her, she didn't show any emotion. Her restraint continued to amaze him. "I've heard you have potent gifts."

He certainly didn't need her to remind him, but if she thought he was in the do-gooder business, then his assumptions about her lack of knowledge were accurate. "Yes, but they're mine. They belong to me, and I use them only when I choose—not because of someone's need for a hero."

She chuckled low, surprising him even more. The intimate sound of her laughter was as compelling as a naughty whisper. "You talk as if you know my father. If so, I'm sure you knew his views on helping your fellow man."

Zac's teeth clamped together so hard his jaws ached. "I did, and he would never expect me to help with a cause I don't believe in."

For a long moment, she only stared at him. Then, she shoved his glass back toward him. "Finish your wine. It's expensive."

His eyes narrowed. "I'll pay the tab."

"Diaz won't stop until he's taken over the world... or we stop him."

Shit. He didn't want to sit here with a gorgeous brunette discussing the nasty bastard who intended to make all of their lives miserable. He'd crossed paths with the monster over fifty years ago, and he'd give up anything to be able to rewind that day.

"Diaz makes sure everyone knows about him, and he's always had grandiose dreams. He hasn't succeeded yet. So what makes you so hell-bent on stopping him?"

A loud, harsh sigh rent the air. "He killed my sister."

Not surprising. Zac managed to look appropriately sympathetic. "My condolences."

"You could give the bastard a run for his money when it comes to coldness," she returned.

"You don't get many places in this world by having a heart of gold. Sorry."

"So, I'm wasting my time then?"

He ignored the still, small voice whispering in his ear—the tiny conscience he'd shut out years before when he'd learned the world wasn't his friend and even his closest friends couldn't be trusted anyway. "You already know the answer."

Lark slid out of the booth and walked around the table. She moved with the lethal grace of a jaguar, her curvaceous body packing a powerful punch in black leather. She placed one hand on his shoulder, and he tipped his head back to see her face.

What she did next surprised him, and he was rarely surprised.

She cupped his face, and Zac had just enough time to catch his breath before she gently traced his mouth with the tip of her tongue. He forgot how to breathe, and when the vixen pressed her lips to his, he didn't really require the knowledge. Every nerve in his body went on high alert. He rose up to deepen the kiss, but she pulled away.

Her long black hair sifted over her shoulders, and she gave him a sultry wink. "If you change your mind," a gold-embossed card landed on the table, "you know where to find me."

As she walked away, Zach's raging erection told him he'd go looking for her.

Chapter 2

The air stifled him. He didn't want to be anywhere near the humans, but alas, he considered this journey a necessary part of his plan. Narrowed eyes swept the streets of the quaint town, and his lip curled. He could obliterate them all with barely a flick of his wand, but that didn't suit his purpose.

The people were so busy, scurrying to and fro, paying no heed to the darkness among them. He liked seeing their ignorance, the obliviousness to anything save their own lives.

Diaz's long, black cloak swept behind him, but to the residents of Las Vegas, he fit right in. Face lifting to the air, he caught the scent of fear. Ah, yes. Lark Hogan. She feared him now. Doubted her own skill. Just as he'd wanted.

Flexing his fingers, the sorcerer strolled down the busy streets, hearing the laughter and the chatters of conversation. Soon, he would control them all.

Most importantly, he would inherit the powers long denied him. Ah, yes, his next meeting with Mr. Wolfe would go exactly as planned.

Then he would walk away with the biggest prize of them all.

Lark knelt by the tombstone, her palm pressing against the cold marble. "No matter how long it takes, Shanae, I will avenge your death. I swear." Withdrawing the athame from her boot strap, she sliced the lethal blade over her wrist and allowed the blood to drip down onto the fresh mound of earth.

"Revenge won't bring her back."

Leaping to her feet, she spun, crouching into a defensive posture. How had the man snuck up on her? She'd always prided herself on the ability to detect the approach of the enemy. Eyes narrowed, she swiped the blade across the grass before tucking it back into place. "What are you doing here?"

"I thought we needed to discuss your situation more."

She straightened, trying not to notice the way his snug, black pants hugged his crotch. The bulge hypnotized her—this demon she'd released. "I believe you're the one who told me I was wasting my time."

God, he exuded perfection… or damned close. Huge. Strong. Wearing leather. She'd always had a weakness for men in leather. As she studied him, his eyes flamed, and she bit back a curse.

She'd known he would come after her. The heat had been too high, and when she'd turned it up a notch with the kiss, she'd guaranteed his arrival. "You know, you really are a cold-hearted bastard."

"I believe you've mentioned that already."

"You're not here out of any desire to help."

His shoulders lifted in a careless shrug, and leather rasped against muscles. "I won't deny what you read in my eyes, Lark, or what you felt when you kissed me. I am nothing if not brutally honest. You need help, and I have certain needs as well."

"You expect me to strike a bargain with my body?"

He came forward with slow, methodical steps. "I expect you to do what your father taught you."

She raised her hand to strike him, but he caught hold of her wrist. "He never taught me to sacrifice my soul to battle a demon."

His fingers tightened around her flesh. "No, but he taught you about your gifts, the abilities you've been given to protect innocent people." Lips curling into a sneer, he continued, "As much as you'd like to convince yourself that avenging your sister's death is protecting someone, it isn't. Revenge makes people do stupid things, and going head-to-head with Diaz is a very stupid idea."

Lark wanted to hit him. "Someone has to stop Diaz, and it's apparent no one else has the balls to even confront him."

One dark eyebrow lifted—too casually for her liking. "So, you're thinking you can stop him all by yourself?"

He toyed with her, much like a cat with a fallen bird. "That wasn't my original plan, but then you were clear you weren't interested in being a hero."

Those dark eyes bored into her soul. "Perhaps I've reconsidered, had a moment of enlightenment." He brushed his knuckles over her cheek. "There may be room for compromise."

Damnit, why couldn't she break away from him? She still struggled against the hold he had on her wrist, but every move proved ineffectual. Each twist only tightened his hand, chafing her wrist.

God, she hated admitting her own weakness, but she'd hate it more if he knew. The calloused fingers curled around her wrist excited her in spite of her desire to escape him. She needed to push him away, but mostly, she wanted to dive into the wealth of silky, black hair and taste his lips again. Energy zipped through her body, revitalizing her. "Compromise, my ass. You're saying you'll help me if I have sex with you."

Zac chuckled, brushing the tip of his finger over the fullness of her lips. "Don't simplify my offer. I will help you defeat Diaz, but in turn, you will become my…" his pause had her supplying the distasteful word.

"Odalisque?"

Seductive laughter brushed over her skin. "I hardly have a harem of women." His thumb traced the line of her jaw. "I prefer to think of it as a sexual companion."

Her temper spiked as it did often around him. "I was under the impression you just wanted sex. As in one night." Her thighs trembled at the thought. What would one night with this man be like? Her imagination wasn't that strong.

His breath bathed her cheek when he dipped his head low to whisper in her ear. "Do you really think one night would be enough?"

Shivering, she tried to push him away again, but her hands encountered hard flesh. Taut muscles. Warm skin. She closed her eyes as the whispers slid over her skin in a breathless taunt. This man should be her enemy. He'd turned her sister's death into a mockery, using the tragedy for his own personal gain. She should hate him, but, as she lifted her eyelids and met his heated gaze, her own lusts betrayed her.

She needed him… for Shanae. And the gods curse her, but she would have him for herself. Standing on tiptoe, she licked the corners of his lips, trailing her tongue along his lower lip before she responded against his mouth. He might have made the offer, but he wouldn't be the one calling all of the shots. "You have a deal."

His arm swept around her, bringing her into hard contact with his erection. "Then we will begin tonight."

A lump lodged in her throat. "How do I know you won't back out once I give you what you want?"

His hand snagged in her hair and tilted her head back. He loomed over her, dark and dangerous. "I give you my word, and I never go back on my word. Ever."

She read the blazing rage in his eyes and doubted he'd ever been questioned before. "If that's not good enough for me?"

He released her, thrusting her far enough away from him so she stumbled over her sister's grave. "It will have to be. I will not sacrifice my reputation for a good fuck." He tipped his head to one side. "That's exactly what tonight will be. Maybe even an excellent one."

Control snapped, and she launched herself forward, on the offensive.

It didn't matter that she couldn't defeat him. She needed to strike him, to hurt him. To touch him again. The tortuous thought nearly shattered her determination, but she'd already initiated the attack.

Zac caught her around the waist, and the wind began to whip and swirl, spinning them out of control. Breathless and disoriented, she could only hold onto his unyielding muscles as he carried them higher, scaling the buildings surrounding them to sink into the cottony white clouds.

The temperature dropped suddenly, and the coldness chilled her body. Icicles formed over her head, dripping around her like diamond glaciers. Only the heat of his body kept her teeth from chattering.

God, she felt his body everywhere. His solid thighs pressed against her softer curves. His hands held tightly to her waist, and his chest caressed her breasts with each move he made. Just a slightest motion, but enough to make her nipples peak with each sensation. His breath sloughed over her ear, sending little nips of delight galloping down her spine.

The threat to Earth melted away then, and as he lowered their bodies until their feet finally touched the ground, she stared up at him. His face seemed implacable. Untouchable. She touched his cheek anyway. "Where are we?"

"Look around," he commanded, his jaw clenched.

Lark stepped out of his loose embrace and followed the sound of rushing water. The sun gleamed brightly, breaking the chill of the air. She didn't recognize the place, but the beauty overwhelmed her. The darkness of the world, the evil, fell away, and here she stood encased in a shrine of breathtaking glory.

The colors were so vibrant. Even the vivid green grass hurt her eyes. She crossed over a slight hill and followed a winding path down to the crystal blue water. She heard Zac's footsteps behind her, but didn't turn around.

"This is my home." He sounded close enough to touch her, and the thought alone made her shiver. She wanted him to touch her. Again and again.

"It's beautiful."

"It is now."

The harshness of his tone captured her attention, and she pivoted. "Not before?"

"Diaz," he bit out.

"He was here?" She hadn't felt the touch of evil. Could her craft be failing her? First, not sensing Zac's approach, and now missing the touch of evil?

"Since you're wondering, you haven't missed Diaz's trail. This place has been swept clean." The abruptness of his voice yanked her head upward, and Lark sought the answers to her questions in the depths of those dangerously dark eyes.

"You read me well." Perhaps she shouldn't have made such a confession. As her father always said, one shouldn't give a stranger ammunition without knowing if he was friend or foe.

His lip curled. "I brought you to nirvana. Is it so surprising I can read you as well?"

"Why did you bring me here?"

Movements controlled and lethal, he paced around her. She didn't doubt he could be a deadly enemy. The rumors she'd heard were undoubtedly true.

"You wanted proof I would keep my word." One hand swept in an arc. "This was a barren wasteland after Diaz finished his assault fifty years ago. My grandmother died on these grounds, and as she breathed her last, she made me promise to restore her homeland."

"You loved her."

"Meaning?"

"You had a reason to keep your word." The minute she spoke, she braced herself for an attack which never came. Instead, he turned from her and walked to the edge of the river. "I'm sorry," she finally relented.

He pinned her with a steely look over his shoulder. "Don't."

"Don't?"

"Don't lie to appease me. You need me, and I want you. That's the truth. We don't have to like each other to make this a mutually beneficial relationship."

"Why can't you help for the good of man, or has life hardened you so much you forget what my father taught you?" She stood beside him.

"I gave up the lessons with Marcus long before you even knew what you were."

"Why?"

"We're not here to discuss ancient history."

She surprised herself by sliding her hand down his arm. "Then answer my question."

"Don't touch what you cannot control." The warning came a second too late. He snatched hold of her waist and dragged her into his arms. She caught a glimpse of the raging desire in his eyes before he tasted her.

Passion swirled and climbed, as wild as the ride which brought them here. He consumed her, drawing her into his world. Magnetic sensations danced up and down her body, and every ounce of resistance in Lark's body evaporated. His fingers were magical as they glided up her skin underneath the tight, black blouse she wore.

Heat ratcheted through her, splintering into tiny shards of electrical sparks. Zac's lips left hers to travel down her neck as she tipped her head back. She found herself leaning against the arms behind her, allowing him free rein to travel lower. The deep vee of her blouse gave him ample play space.

He dipped his head and kissed the tops of her breasts, just a light grazing of his lips against her flesh. Lark let out a breath on a sigh and dug her nails into his arms. His tongue swept a warm, moist path from her cleavage to the pulse point at her throat, and her stomach muscles clenched.

She should stop him. Sanity demanded it, but desire overrode it. She'd lost the ability to think, to reason, and as the moment began to spiral out of control, the winds increased. As quickly as he'd captured her, he let her go, keeping hold of her hand. He lifted his eyes to the sky and stared into the brightness.

"Don't let go." His fingers tightened around hers to emphasize the command.

An eerie shrill penetrated the perfection. A thick, black conglomeration of angry clouds fastened together into a giant time bomb. Hurling toward them like an angry swarm of locusts.

"Diaz." The word came out as an epithet as Zac braced his feet.

She tugged her hand free, and he turned to look at her. "He never lets his victims see him."

"People change."

"Not monsters."

Chapter 3

Zac sensed Lark's fear, but she retained control, and raised her hands to counter the attack. She shouted out a warning before the bullets began to fly, hundreds and hundreds of bullets with deadly aim. With lightning fast precision, she dodged them, ducking and weaving just as her father had taught her.

Her skill impressive, she challenged Diaz's power, daring him to come closer. Her eyes never wavered, and her eyes bore no trace of hesitancy.

He found himself wanting to protect her anyway. "Get behind me," he instructed over the whine of the ammunition. His shoulders bunched, and he inhaled deeply, unleashing his power, claiming the magic once more. "So, you've come back for a rematch, Diaz. You fucking coward. Why don't you come face-to-face with me for once in your miserable life?"

He held up both hands and swept them in a circle. The bullets began to bounce off the protective shield, dropping to the ground and disappearing in the grass.

She remained crouched beside him, her eyes ever alert. With an overabundance of energy, she could hold the bullets at bay for hours, and were she to learn how to harness her own supernatural qualities, she could be quite deadly.

Zac stepped closer, his shoulder brushing against hers. Hands raised, he spoke calmly, guiding the destructive bullets toward the river flowing behind them. "Stay with me," he commanded, then turned to make sure she followed his lead. He knew the exact moment her powers united with his. Like a surge of electricity, the jolt rocked him.

He met her gaze, hesitating long enough for her to smile at him. The connection intensified as their abilities joined, and focusing his attention back on the conglomeration of ammunition took great effort. His fingertips lowered, sinking the violent funnel closer to the water. Inch by inch, it disappeared beneath the rushing liquid, leaving silence in its wake.

She blew out a breath which caused his skin to tingle. "Diaz's games are becoming nastier."

"That wasn't a game. More like a warning."

"He doesn't want you to help me."

Zac grunted. "I don't want me to help you. So, Diaz's disapproval can't come as a surprise."

She crammed her hands into the back pockets of her leather pants. "Why don't you want to help?"

"Saving the world isn't what I do, sweetness." He cupped her cheek before allowing his hand to fall back to his side. "I take it. One piece at a time."

Red crept up into her cheeks. "Am I one of those pieces?"

"I would never be so crude as to call you a piece." He winked.

Lark muttered something below her breath and brushed her hands down the front of her pants. He didn't want to notice how her hands shook or why the proof of her frailty bothered him, but it did.

"Does using your powers take that much out of you?"

She stuffed her hands pack into her pockets. "Why do you ask?"

"You're shaking."

"Couldn't have anything to do with our just facing a hailstorm of bullets, could it?"

He placed his hand at the small of her back. "I'm sure you've faced others." Her acquiescence as he guided her across the grass revealed her exhaustion.

"I guess I haven't mastered the art of cruelty as you have."

"Protecting my own ass isn't cruelty; it's self-preservation. Maybe you should learn a little about protecting yourself first instead of trying to save a world that couldn't give a fuck about you."

"Care to tell me how you came to be so cynical?"

"No." The one cold word could have frozen the outer bounds of hell. Snagging hold of her wrist, he towed her forward.

"Where are we going?"

"To my house."

Lark leaned against his shoulder. "So, I take it you weren't joking when you said this is your home?"

"I don't joke." Anger simmered within him. He couldn't explain the overwhelming desire to protect her, and he didn't want to understand. Maybe one night would be enough to get her out of his system, but just as the thought entered his brain, the wind brought the sweet scent of her perfume. He dragged the drugging aroma into his lungs.

His suggestion had bad idea written all over it.

"You're not listening to me, are you?"

Why did her voice wrap around him like a lover's hand? It captivated him. Made him want to chain her to his side. He wanted to protect her, to save her from the demon she intended to face.

His hand slid down to her hip. "Actually, I'm doing more thinking than listening."

She inhaled swiftly, deeply. "Why doesn't that surprise me?" She held up one hand. "Never mind. I should have known better than to assume a man could think with something other than his dick. So, why don't you take me back to Earth now?" Pulling away from him, she broke free of his embrace. "I have a lot of work to do and very little time."

"The only thing you have to do is stay here tonight. After all, we do have a deal."

Her eye color changed to a darker shade of brown, a sign of her irritation, perhaps? He looked forward to learning all of the nuances, the ways he could make them change. As he moved toward her, the ground shifted, rumbled.

"Diaz isn't happy," he chuckled.

"Don't think you can toy with him, Zac. He's a monster."

He chucked her under the chin. "Were you not listening when I told you he killed my grandmother? I know all about Diaz, but in case you need more information, I'll fill you in." He circled around her. "At last count, he's at least 3,500 years old. No one knows exactly where he lives or if he even has one home. He doesn't let anyone get close to him, and he doesn't have minions as he doesn't need them."

Dragging his hand through his hair, Zac continued. "His powers are extraordinary and come from years of dark magic. He has honed his mastery until he's one of the most powerful demons this universe has ever seen or will ever see again." A long pause. "Oh, and the current score is in his favor."

Lark whirled, and fire lit her eyes. "How can you be so glib?"

Zac gripped her chin between his fingers. "Life is a bitch, baby, especially our lives. So, I prefer if you didn't give me any shit about our being born for higher purposes. Because, quite frankly, I would much prefer to be normal. Just a man."

She slid her hands up the wall of his chest, and her touch caused his cock to surge to life again. "Somehow, I don't think you could ever be accused of being just a man… even without your powers."

His heart pumped faster as blatant, erotic images rolled through his mind. Her long, black hair swinging free around her waist. Pert, high breasts beckoning him with dark aureoles and a patch of silky dark hair between her thighs, covering her mound. Every muscle in his body aching with tension and the desperate need to take her, he settled his hands around her waist. "Tonight, I will have you."

Her breath caught in her throat. "What if I change my mind?"

"You won't. You're a woman of honor."

"How can you be so sure?"

The question held a challenge, and he smiled, studying her face for a long time before he finally responded. "You want me as much as I want you." Her eyes widened, then narrowed as he flicked one nipple with the tip of his finger. Even now, he'd lay good odds moisture coated her panties, and were he to place his palm against her heat, she would unravel.

Rock hard, he took her hand and brought her index finger to his lips. Suckling gently, he kept his eyes on her face. Her expression softened as she surrendered. "Let me feel you, Lark."

Her breasts bumped against his chest as she rocked forward, and the feel of the soft mounds of flesh made his cock jerk. God, how good it would feel to push inside her heat. He could only imagine how tight her body would be, how perfect.

A low, husky moan spilled from her lips, and she locked her arms behind his head, dragging him down. Zac went willingly, sinking into the warmth of her lips caressing his.

A maelstrom of emotions stormed his soul. How had this one woman created them, caused such damage to his own sense of security? Soft and pliant in his arms, she shattered his defenses, crumbled his walls. After just one day. He could only imagine what one night would do to him.

The scented feel of her body made every muscle in his body tense. Her fragrance, a heady combination of jasmine and heather, intoxicated him, and he drew the scent deep into his lungs.

He nibbled her lips, swallowing her moan, or perhaps it was his own. His eyes closed, he explored the sweet cavern of her mouth while his heart pounded against his chest. Blood pressure rising to dangerous levels, he groaned low in his throat and pulled her even tighter. His cock throbbed painfully, demanding release.

She snatched his hand and brought his palm lower, settling it between her firm thighs. His palm pressed against the heat of her pussy, and his vision glazed. Even through the thickness of her pants, he felt the dampness. The knowledge became an aphrodisiac, sending his senses whirling. Sweat trickled down his spine, and his breaths became desperate inhalations.

Tangling his hand in her hair, he dipped his head to feast on her golden skin, his tongue swirling and tantalizing until he felt the torture as much as she did. "God, Lark," he whispered against her pulse point. As he ground his fingers against her mound, she arched against him, pushing into his hand, wanting the release as much as he needed to give it to her.

Fuck. He wanted, no, needed, to feel the plump petals of her pussy against his hands. A desperate craving took hold, shutting out everything but the sound of their own labored breaths.

Wild, wanton, and without reason, they tore at each other's clothes, needing the feel of flesh on flesh. Zac felt alive for the first time in years. Everywhere Lark touched him sparked with fire. He sizzled, and his cock grew painfully harder with each nip of her teeth, each brush of her tongue. Sparks danced in front of his eyes, and he couldn't get enough of her.

His palms glided over her silken skin from her arms to her hips and back up, and he delighted in the sweet, little purring noises she made in the back of her throat. "Say it."

She lifted her head and fixed him with a sultry look. "I want to fuck you."

Every ounce of blood in his body zinged from his head to his cock. He tried to lift her in his arms, but she resisted.

"Here," she instructed, pointing to the grass. "Right now." Lowering the zipper on her pants, she tugged the leather material over her hips while he held his breath. He waited, knowing her naked beauty would prove his undoing.

Lark stood before him, wearing nothing save a scrappy piece of lace, more string than material. Through the wispy panel, the dark outline of her pussy beckoned him. His lungs constricted. She hooked her fingers in the thin straps, lowering the thong, and the compelling urge to touch her pushed him forward.

She defied perfection. Pure honey and silk—a goddess, carved with infinite care. Then, holding her hands away from her body, she whispered, "Is this what you wanted to see?"

"This is what I wanted to feel," he returned, yanking her back into his arms. His hands couldn't stay still. He glided his fingertips over her breasts, pausing to pluck at the taut nipples until Lark gasped. His hand moved lower to caress her bare abdomen, circling around to cup her ass.

He kissed her throat, and she leaned her head back. Gripping her hips, he pressed his erection against her stomach, needing her to feel what she did to him. "I want to hear you come."

One hand dipped low. A small patch of hair grazed his palm as he cupped her mound. Lark jerked and whispered his name. The calloused pad of his index finger slipped in between the petals of her pussy and nudged her clit.

She let out a startled cry and pushed forward, urging him to increase the pressure with the movements of her hips. Moving in time with his finger, she pumped against his palm, sweat beading on her upper brow.

He needed more of her. Now. Sweeping her into his arms, he carried her to a bed of soft grass and lowered her. She smelled of honeysuckle and cinnamon, and the soft, musky scent of her sheath called to him. He answered the summons immediately, drifting down her body until he could hover over her there.

Lark lifted her legs and placed them over his shoulders, granting permission much as a queen gives audience. Zac groaned low in his throat and accepted the invitation, lowering his head, his mouth, until his tongue could make contact with her softness. Beneath him, she quivered and gasped, holding her breath with anticipation.

Then he stroked her. Just one light touch. Enough to taste. To sample the delectable pleasures she offered, knowing once would never be enough. He sank into her. Feasting. Suckling. Tormenting. His tongue danced around her clit, lavishing the sensitive bud with seductive strokes. Her muscles grew taut as her legs clenched around his shoulders.

"Oh, yes," she whispered, hands grasping fistfuls of earth.

He raised his head. "Look at me. Look into my eyes. I want to see you come."

She opened her eyes and met his gaze. His tongue circled and swirled around her clit. Tasting her essence. Feeding the orgasm building within her.

Eyes still locked, he licked her once more—a long, lavish stroke, and she exploded, unraveling with whimpers and cries. Her face flushed, and her lips parted as the climax held her within its grasp.

The moment of pure pleasure came to a sudden halt as Zac's internal alarm alerted him to a possible threat. He whipped to one side and yanked Lark to her feet. "We have to go." He didn't give her a chance to respond before he clothed her with a blink, whisked her into his arms, and began to spin.

Chapter 4

"What the hell was that about?" Lark snapped when she could catch her breath.

"Being out in the open isn't safe."

"It's funny you didn't seem to think of that a few minutes ago when you were—"

"I know what I was doing, sweetness, and I enjoyed every minute of it. Now, it's time to move on to other pleasures." He swept his hand wide. "Welcome to my home."

She turned slowly and caught her breath. The wonder of the structure in front of her eyes held her spellbound. She had traveled the world over, had visited Paris and London, sailed the high seas and dined with kings and queens, but this place—this nirvana as Zac called it—simply amazed her. Her feet glided over the gold-lined pathway as her head swiveled back and forth. She'd never seen such perfection before.

Trees dripped with platinum icicles, and small ponds glittered like polished sapphires, surrounding the house several paces ahead. Crafted of solid bluestone, the two-story manor boasted a circular driveway with a three level fountain a few feet away from the front door. Large weeping willows adorned the front lawns, and low-hanging gas lamps reminiscent of an earlier century illuminated the landscape.

"Is this really nirvana?"

"It's mine." His whisper was close enough to touch.

The heat of his chest warmed her spine. "Why did you bring me here?"

"Diaz wasn't through playing his tricks." He caught hold of her hand and led her up the walkway. "Come inside. There's much more to see… and do."

The inference in his words came through loud and clear. He had every intention of sealing their deal tonight.

And she had every intention of allowing him. After all, a deal was a deal.

"Yes, Mr. Wolfe. Touch her. Hold her. Grow to love her," Diaz whispered, his gaze intent on the images scrolling in front of him like an old movie reel. The voyeuristic nature of his actions brought a smile to his face, and his cock grew hard, pushing against the thin material of his robe.

No! He had no time for dalliances. Darkness shielding his eyes from the glowing light of the moon, he paced back and forth in front of the narrow wooden altar, a place where he would soon be worshipped.

"You cannot imagine how long I've waited for this day." His breaths came in spasms, blood racing through his veins like a rabid dog. The fifty years since his last encounter with Zac Wolfe had been the longest of his life.

His need had been simple. One woman. He'd found her in Wolfe's wife, and but for the interference of the old wizards, Diaz would have had her.

That mission had failed, but not this time. He wouldn't allow another defeat.

"I have waited too long to achieve my goals, Mr. Wolfe, but soon, my patience will be rewarded." Shaking from the force of his emotions, he clenched his hands into fists. "Surely Lark Hogan will be a more fitting vessel for my use than Rena Wolfe."

The building began to tremble, and the clouds turned a smoky gray as the storm intensified. An outlet for his wrath, the turbulence wouldn't satiate him long. "This victory is mine, Wolfe! Do you hear me? It's mine!"

Ripples of maniacal laughter swelled in his chest. "You don't have much time with Lark. I would suggest you not waste it."

Though the couple couldn't hear what he said, Diaz knew Wolfe sensed a change in the atmosphere, and as he watched the wizard follow Lark into the monstrous house, he couldn't take his eyes away.

Now, they would seal their bargain. His teeth flashed into a grin. Once again, he would take what Zac Wolfe wanted most—a chance for happiness.

As Lark walked through the formal dining room, Zac followed her, enjoying the view from behind. While she *ooohed* and *aaahed* over the cathedral ceilings and floor-to-ceiling windows overlooking the back gardens, he allowed much more erotic images to cloud his mind. Visions of Lark lying naked atop his bed, arms and legs open. He could taste her even in his mind.

"This place is incredible."

She caught him off-guard, and he couldn't respond for a long moment. He simply stood staring at her, watching the way her head tilted to one side, her full, lush lips parting questioningly.

"You're thinking about fucking me, aren't you?" She didn't mince words. He liked that. A lot.

"Yeah."

Her tongue moistened those lips which had taken center stage in his sexual fantasy. "So, I guess the rest of the tour is out then."

He walked toward her, his cock throbbing with each step. "There's plenty of time to see the rest of the house."

She held out one hand, her palm connecting with his chest as he came in closer. "This is only for one night, right? Then we focus on taking down Diaz."

His eyes dropped to her hand, and he lifted his own to cover hers. "Sweetness, I'll fuck you many more times before we actually win our battle against Diaz." Catching hold of her wrist, he brought her hand lower and stepped closer. "And you will enjoy every time."

Eyelids drifting low, she personified every erotic fantasy he'd ever had. "What makes you so sure?"

"When I ate you, did you not enjoy the feel of my tongue?" His body temperature escalated, his chest rose as he drew in a deep breath. Did she know what she did to him, or that she was the only woman who'd made him feel this alive in a long, long time?

She seduced him with just the touch of her hand, and his body became hers. His cock responded to even the slightest sound of her voice, and his temperature spiked to dangerous levels.

Face flushing, she opened her eyes and looked into his. He could drown in those chocolate pools, and when her lips parted in a breathless whisper of a sigh, his cock jumped.

"You haven't answered my question, Lark." His hand fisted in her hair. "Can't you speak?" If she didn't speak soon, he wouldn't be responsible for his actions. At present, his cock was in the driver's seat, demanding release.

"Very much." A sultry blend of sex and heated promises, her eyes flicked up to his face. Her gaze both innocent and alluring—a damnable combination.

He trailed his fingers up her ribcage. "Then what are we waiting for?" The honeyed scent of her shampoo wafted over him, and his balls grew tight. God, the anticipation of plunging into her sweet pussy nearly drove him to his knees.

Her fingers gripped the hem of her blouse and began to inch the material up over her abdomen. Zac's eyes dropped, and the sight of her soft, golden skin increased the pressure between his thighs. Any minute now, he would explode.

Several torturous seconds later, she tugged the blouse over her head and tossed it to the floor. He had to touch her. The palms of his hands slid over the warmth of her stomach and around her waist.

"You're so soft," he murmured, pressing his crotch against her thigh.

She didn't respond. Instead, she reached behind her and unhooked the clasp of her bra. Her breasts spilled out of the lace cups, and he captured them immediately. He filled his hands with the heaviness and plumped them, bringing the nipples close to his lips.

Her hands braced the wall behind her, and she arched her back. "Kiss me."

His eyes met hers. "Kiss you here?" He drew a lazy circle around one nipple with his tongue, and she moaned, the sound breathless and enticing. The dusky tip peaked in the air, and he drew it into his mouth, suckling gently.

She clasped his head, threading her fingers through his hair. "Oh, that feels nice."

He switched his attention to the opposite peak and lavished it with gentle, loving strokes. Growling low in his throat, he pressed her back against the wall, taking more of her breast into his mouth.

She tasted better than he'd imagined, and while all of the blood pumped into his cock, he couldn't get enough of her. Her breasts were like the ripest of peaches, plump and juicy, and were lightning to strike, he wouldn't move.

Lark's leg hooked around behind one of his, dragging him closer. She murmured her approval and rocked against him, shoving her breast further into his mouth.

Zac licked a few seconds longer before raising his head. "Let's get you out of the rest of these clothes, shall we?" Without waiting for permission, he waved a hand, and the leather fell away, leaving long, silken limbs and a thatch of dark hair visible beneath lace.

"I want to feel your pussy," he intoned, absorbing her shivers against his chest.

Her hands began to glide over his face, his neck before sliding over his chest. "I want you naked."

He jerked back, nostrils flaring. Her words had the same effect as a punch in the gut. "Your wish is my command." As he finished speaking, his clothes dropped from his body, and her eyes crinkled with her smile. Control tenuous at best, he could only imagine her next move—the one which would send him over the edge.

"Oh, really?" Her voice took on a husky quality. "In that case," she pushed against his chest, "I want you against the wall."

His heartbeat thundered in his ears, but he did as she commanded, turning until his back pressed against the plaster. He held his hands away from his body. "What now, my lady?"

She placed a finger against her lips to indicate her request for silence. *Dear God.* As she began to drop to her knees, Zac bit his lower lip, swallowing the groan. Her breath bathed his stiff cock, and he closed his eyes, hands clenched into fists at his sides. When she touched him, he would fragment into tiny pieces.

Her fingernails crawled over his thighs before she cupped his scrotum. The breath left his lungs on a rush of air. Applying light pressure, she massaged his sac while her cheek brushed the length of his cock, causing the skin to tighten.

Muttering imprecations, he snatched a handful of her hair and gave it a tug. "Suck, dammit!" God, he needed to feel her hot, wet mouth sheathing his dick.

She licked instead, and he nearly jumped out of his skin. "Not yet." The whisper nearly unraveled him. "I'm making the decisions now, remember?"

He couldn't remember anything, not even his own name. Those same wicked fingertips tiptoed beneath his balls and tickled the sensitive area. "Jesus," he cried, bouncing off the wall.

Her lips replaced her fingers, and his ass clenched. She suckled one ball into the cavern of her mouth, and his cock began to twitch while sweat beaded on his forehead.

"I don't know how much more of this I can take, Lark." Already his muscles were tensing, readying for the inevitable propulsion.

She released him and stroked her way up his cock with her wet, clever tongue, making appreciative noises which drove him wild. Finding all of his erogenous zones, she tortured him, stroking and laving his sensitive skin until his palms slapped the wall behind him.

His balls drew up, and he pumped his hips. Close to begging, he tried to inject authority into his voice. "Take me in your mouth."

Her head tipped back, dark eyes twinkling. "Are you really a wizard?"

Lungs constricting, he didn't even didn't even try to breathe. "What?" The only thought in his brain was how to get her lips back around his cock.

An impish smile crossed her lips. "If you come, am I going to be left out in the cold?"

Shoulders relaxing, he clenched his hand around her shoulder. "Don't worry, baby. You'll still get fucked."

With a low laugh, she took him back into her mouth. God, her mouth was so wet, so tight, and hot. Perfect. He moved his hips slowly at first, fucking her mouth as he would her pussy. Then the pace increased, keeping time with his erratic breaths.

"God, yes," he groaned, winding strands of her thick, black hair around his fingers. "That's it, baby. So good."

Lark murmured her own pleasure and withdrew her mouth, laving a wet trail down to the line separating his balls. She spent an inordinate amount of time massaging him while he panted.

"You like that?" she whispered without giving him time to reply. Her clever fingers worked between his ass cheeks while her mouth explored even lower.

"Dear God!" He didn't know how much more he could take. Even now, his balls were so constricted the slightest amount of pressure was a mixture of pleasure and pain.

While her index finger played with his anus, she returned her mouth to the head of his cock. Drawing her lips over her teeth, she took him fully into her mouth again, taking him almost to the back of her throat.

He flattened himself against the wall, his chest heaving with each tortured breath. She worked her mouth up and down his cock while her finger worked into his ass, twisting and turning until his breaths slowed.

She sucked him so perfectly, using her mouth and tongue to nearly drive him to his knees. He never wanted this moment to stop, and yet, his body rushed headlong toward a powerful climax.

As she drove him over the edge, every muscle in his body clenched as the orgasm ripped through him, and his hot seed spurted into her mouth. He groaned while the spasms continued to ratchet through him. Lark rocked back on her heels, but he still felt her hands on his thighs. His shoulders relaxed, his hands fell away, and he bumped his head back against the wall.

"Sweet Mother of God," he muttered. His knees bumped against each other. He'd never felt so drained, so completely satiated. Almost as if she'd sucked the life from his body.

Laughing lightly, Lark slid up his body, her hips bumping against his. "Well, let's see if you can keep your promise, wizard." She cupped his cock, and as it rose in response to her touch, she smiled.

Zac flicked one finger toward the kitchen table, and the placements scattered, floating to the tiled floor. "I always keep my word," he replied, the words thick in his throat. As the strength returned to his limbs, he lifted her, hooking his hands underneath her ass.

"Lucky me," she murmured, wrapping her legs around his waist. His cock touched her pussy, and he nearly dropped her. Soaked, her labia dripped with need. He carried her to the table and laid her back against the unpolished oak. Her thighs fell open, baring her pink, swollen pussy to his gaze.

"You're ready for me, aren't you?" One finger stroked the valley between her legs, and she moaned, jerking at his touch. "Did sucking my cock make you this wet?" At her low murmur of agreement, he lightly pinched her swollen pussy lips before asking, "Does your clit ache?" He touched the sensitive spot, and her legs quivered.

"Yes," she breathed, pushing up against his finger. "Push your fingers into me." The command surprised him, but her forwardness only made him harder.

He shoved three fingers deep inside her, and her vaginal muscles clenched, convulsing around the digits. His lungs filled with oxygen as his imagination took flight. That same tight hold would be around his cock in seconds, and he would burst.

Lark began to wiggle atop the table, her breaths coming in staccato pants. "Now, fuck me." Her hips bumped up and down against the oak.

Withdrawing his fingers, he positioned his cock at her opening. He stood there for several seconds, bracing himself for the ultimate impact of sinking into her tightness. He didn't need anything to tell him this time was different. This woman was different.

And this wouldn't be just a fuck.

Without giving himself time to consider the consequences further, Zac flexed his hips and pushed his cock into her. Instantly, her muscles gripped him, and stars danced behind his eyes. Vibrant colors, bright lights, and rippling waves of electrical sparks all combined together to nearly blind him.

Could such perfection exist in a woman? He didn't need to ask the question. As the walls of her pussy closed around his cock like a silky hand, he knew he'd found his own Utopia.

Lark moaned and writhed beneath him as he pushed and thrust, harder and harder until the sweat ran in rivulets down his spine. He brought her legs up higher, dragging her ass closer to the edge of the table.

Her palms slapped the oak, and excited noises escaped her throat. Fingers digging into the underside of her thighs, he rammed into her one last time. Then her muscles began to spasm, the orgasm tearing through her, almost pushing her upright.

Then the clenching and sweet heat of her pussy pushed him over the edge. His second orgasm of the night ripped a series of growls from his throat, wringing him completely dry until he collapsed on top of her.

She stroked his hair, his shoulders, purring like a contented feline. "It's nice to see you do keep your promises."

Laughter made his chest rumble. "Vixen."

Her hands fisted in his hair, dragging his head upward so she could see his eyes. "You haven't seen nothing yet."

He couldn't decide which of them to hate more, but at present, Diaz knew he had a bigger problem on his hands. Since Wolfe decided to offer his assistance to Lark, the entire wizard population had sat up and taken notice. Diaz sniffed and caught their scent on the wind again. They were near. Maybe not all of them, but certainly more than he wanted to deal with at one time.

Eliminating one wizard was a challenge enough which was why Zac Wolfe still lived, but ridding the world of several wizards all at once would be damned near impossible. Definitely not in his plans.

Swallowing the lump in his throat, he paced inside his temple, alternating between short furious steps and longer strides. Damnit, he had a plan, one that didn't include tangling with magic out of his reach. After surviving 3,500 years, he didn't relish putting his life on the line now.

He massaged his temples while his heart burned with animosity. He loathed Wolfe as much as the wizard did him. So, they'd both managed to stay out of each other's way, respecting the power they both wielded, but now, they were in each other's playgrounds.

Had the crafty son-of-a-bitch now summoned his family to help him, knowing he couldn't defeat Diaz on his own? Fingers curling into fists, Diaz stomped toward the small window at the top of the tower. Well, regardless, he would not go down without a fight. He'd make sure he took more than a few of them with him, too. No matter who won.

The elements responded to Diaz's hatred. Thunder rolled in the sky, shaking the foundations of the temple while thick, black clouds dipped low. Lightning scorched the earth, creating sizzling sounds as the electricity snapped the ground.

The sorcerer stood at the window, staring out into the darkness while the winds whipped the stringy length of his hair around his face. "Hear me well, Wolfe. This time, I will show no mercy. No matter how long it takes, I will end this with your death and with Lark Hogan at my side."

The words echoed across the valley below, spinning through the air and into the storm, winding their way across the distance as a threat. A warning. Most of all, a promise.

Chapter 5

All of three seconds later, Lark sensed uneasiness in the air. She pushed against Zac's shoulders, and he moved with a reluctant groan.

"Someone is here," she whispered in his ear.

"That's impossible. I would know if I had an uninvited visitor in my home."

"Then why do I feel as if there's someone here?" Without giving him time to respond, she dropped to the floor. "Where are my clothes?"

He cursed below his breath and quickly clothed her. "Is this your way of telling me you're nervous?"

She cast a glance over her shoulder, noticing he'd clothed himself in black jeans and a dark blue turtleneck sweater. She watched the way he pushed his hands through his hair to restore some semblance of order, and her mouth watered. The man moved with a sensual grace, like a panther stalking his prey.

"Lark?"

The sharpness of his tone drew her attention to his face. "Don't be ridiculous. I told you I felt someone here."

His glance encompassed the entire kitchen. "Well, as you can see, we're still alone. Just you and me. Together." His tone dipped a notch. "Tonight."

Her skin tingled and not just in the places he'd touched seconds before. Zac Wolfe had the amazing ability to make love with his voice, a tantalizing blend of sex and seduction which made her toes curl. "You've already had your tonight." She tried to move around him, but he snagged hold of her arm.

"Don't play games, Lark. We're both adults."

She peeled his fingers away from her arm. "Why is it I get the feeling there's something about you I should know?" His shoulders tensed instantly. Apparently, she'd struck a nerve.

"I'm a wizard… a wizard who doesn't like to be questioned. That's all you need to know." He studied her for a long moment before turning away.

"Since you're dressed, I'll give you the grand tour."

"I'm not interested in a tour. What I'm interested in is the truth. Why did my father tell me if I ever needed help to find you? What did he know about you, and why in the hell did he trust someone like you?"

Zac whipped around, eyes turbulent. "I saved his life once. Could be the reason."

She blinked at him, assessing his statement, wondering whether or not she could take what he said as factual. Her father hadn't mentioned any near-death experience.

Folding her arms across her chest, she remained silent, giving him the opportunity to explain further, but he only returned her stare as if daring her to push the matter.

Didn't he know by now she never backed down from a challenge? "How did my father know you?"

"Many years ago, he trained me in certain arts."

How cryptic. His response didn't surprise her. She shouldn't expect more than a scant amount of information. Still, she gritted her teeth. "Would you care to elaborate?" Enunciating the words carefully, she bared her teeth in a semblance of a smile.

"Should I?"

The man could drive the sanest woman crazy. Tired of fighting a losing battle, Lark held up one hand. "You know what? Forget it." Wanting a dignified exit, Lark left him, walking down the hallway to God only knew where.

"Where are you going?"

"To the bathroom, if you don't mind."

"Well, since there are no facilities in that direction, I do mind. The bathroom is down this hallway," he pointed for emphasis, "and to your left."

Faux smile still firmly etched on her face, she spun and walked past him, head held erect. "Thank you." The common courtesy pained her. She couldn't believe she'd had sex with him. The thought made her pause. Well, actually, she could believe she had sex with him. No woman in her right mind would have refused.

"You're welcome."

The taunting words followed her down the hallway. "Asshole," she muttered under her breath.

"Wizards have very good hearing," he reminded her.

"I'm well aware of that. Why do you think I said it?" She slammed the bathroom door before he could respond. With her back pressed against the wood, she pressed her palms to her eyes. "Dad, what in the hell have you gotten me into now?"

Dammit! Why couldn't he have just told her he'd sensed a presence, too? Because that would have helped her get even closer. Zac rubbed his face with his hands and pushed himself to his feet. He couldn't allow another one to get close to him. His heart wouldn't survive another trauma.

In the background, the sound of water running came from the bathroom along with the sweet hum of Lark's voice as she showered. Though his mind still focused on his irritation, his body responded to the images of warm water sluicing over honeyed skin. Droplets of moisture clinging to the soft tuft of hair between her thighs. Soap dripping down the slight indentation in her spine and over the perfectly rounded cheeks of her ass.

Sweet Jesus. His cock pushed against the rough material of his jeans. He needed to pull himself together.

Shortly after Lark had made her elegant departure, he'd traced the presence, easily tracking the mist which had evaporated from his house. His guest had been a fellow wizard. Lips curling into a snarl, he stormed toward the lone window in the room, needing something, anything, to capture his attention. The scenery failed to entice him as he'd hoped.

When one wizard appeared, more followed. The last one he wanted to see was his father. Every nerve in his body crackled with anticipation. Expectation ran high. He didn't doubt, though, any second now, the next wizard he would see would be Edmund, and his father's temper wouldn't be far behind.

The water stopped, and a rush of steam escaped from under the door. He spun, his attention riveted to the bathroom, just ten feet away from where he stood overlooking the back gardens.

Why had he directed her to his bathroom? Why not the guest bathroom? He didn't need the torture right now. Just one time with her had proven to be his weakness. How could a woman he barely knew slip underneath his shell?

He took two steps toward the door, heard her humming, and stopped. Would her nipples be peaked from the air? His cock jumped. Fuck! This was getting him nowhere. He needed air, space, time to breathe, and regroup.

"I'll be back in a few minutes," he barked at the door before cursing below his breath. Why had he felt the need to tell her? He didn't answer to anyone.

At least he hadn't until now.

Shit.

The slamming of the bedroom door halted her humming. Ever since they'd exploded in the kitchen, mating like frenzied animals, Zac had been on edge, moody and irritable. Although that could be his usual nature since she barely knew him.

Oh, but she knew a lot about his body. Physically, the man was a perfect landscape of muscle and hard, slick skin, and though she knew he would deny it, what they'd shared in the kitchen hadn't been just about sex. There'd been a connection.

Which scared her more than a little. She had no use for a relationship right now. She'd been taught her life had a purpose, much more than just an ordinary human. She fought evil, and once Diaz had been eliminated, there'd be another villain to fight, someone to take his place.

After wrapping the towel around her body, she finger-combed her hair and shook the damp strands around her shoulders. Coated with steam, the mirror obliterated reflection as she tugged open the bathroom door.

A broad-shouldered man turned, his glittering black eyes raking up and down her body. "Who the hell are you, and where is my son?"

As quickly as a raindrop disappears on hot asphalt, Zac caught the advance warning his father had arrived. Edmund had a strong sensory wave few wizards could miss. In seconds, he returned to his bedroom to find Lark and his father in a stand-off.

"Where I come from, it's rude to demand someone's name in such a manner," she snapped.

Brows lowered, Edmund folded his arms over his chest. "Where I'm from, insolence is considered a punishable offense."

Her own brows arched. "A punishable offense? What are you, a caveman?"

Zac quickly intervened before his father's temper could explode. "Hello, Father."

The older wizard whirled, his long, black hair swirling across his shoulders. "Well, it's nice of you to finally make an appearance."

Lark's gaze shot back and forth between the men. "Father?"

He acknowledged the question with a dip of his head. "This is my father, Edmund."

"Now I see the resemblance. You both have the same disposition," she replied sweetly.

"This woman does not know her place," Edmund shot back.

The tone caused Zac's shoulders to stiffen. "Why are you here?"

"My place?" She took a step forward, but Zac positioned himself in front of her. Tension coated the room, thick and oppressive, and behind him, he could feel her fury, knew she desperately wanted to respond to his father.

"I have to admit. I never thought you'd have the balls to show up here again."

"I have no reason to be ashamed of anything I've done."

"No? Then perhaps you should check your recollection… Father." This time, he made the word sound like an epithet.

Edmund grabbed his arm as he attempted to walk by. "You can't hide from this, son. Diaz has grown more powerful over the centuries. You will not be able to defeat him on your own."

"He's not alone," Lark finally inserted, her tone one of promise.

Black eyes slid over her face as the wizard studied her. "Are you a sorceress?"

"She has been gifted with certain talent," Zac answered for her, peeling his father's fingers away.

"Does that artistry make her a match for Diaz then?" Edmund didn't relent.

"I'm sure she can hold her own." *Only with my help.*

"Is that why her sister died?" The words dropped like a dead weight in the room, and silence descended for a long moment.

"Who are you, and how do you know about my sister?" She pushed her way forward, despite Zac's resistance. She possessed a strong will, almost as powerful as his father's. In spite of the tense situation, he found himself admiring her. She didn't back down from his father, a wizard whose powers trebled her own, without even a tremble. Impressive.

An elder in the guild, the wizard barely flicked her a glance. "There is little we do not know." He turned his back on her. "Is there somewhere we could speak alone?"

A spark of anger had ignited into a burning flame while tempers simmered just below the surface. Before Zac could diffuse the situation, Lark advanced forward, coming to stand merely an inch away from his father's face.

"For someone who knows everything, you don't appear to recognize when your own life could be in jeopardy." Her voice, pitched low, captured the wizard's attention.

He turned in slow motion, assessing her, perhaps testing her. "You do not want to attempt to match your capabilities to mine, young one."

The air crackled with tension. Oppressive heat swarmed around them as rage became palpable.

"You're not the only one who knows how to kill." Spoken in a soft, feminine voice, the words held an underlying steel.

"Don't expend any energy on him, Lark. He won't be staying long."

Edmund's gaze drifted back to Zac's face. "I did not come alone."

"Figures. Seldom does an ordinary wizard travel without reinforcements. I, on the other hand, work alone."

"Not this time." Clipped and short, the response bespoke of the older wizard's rapidly deteriorating patience.

The two wizards came face to face, nose to nose, both issuing and accepting the challenge. *Why the hell are you here?* The question burned in Zac's mind but remained unspoken… at least for now.

"I can't stop you from being here," he finally relented. "But if you think I'm going to have anything to do with any of you, I can't begin to tell you how mistaken you are."

White teeth gleamed. "We shall see. Just remember we are not your enemy."

When had he heard that before? Hadn't it been right after Rena's death? "I guess we'll see about that, too, won't we?"

"We need to discuss this alone."

The bedroom door banged open with a flick of Zac's hand. "Fine."

"So her name's Lark." Amusement colored his father's voice. "Definitely not named after the bird." He disappeared down the hall.

"Stay in here until I come to get you." Lark's jaw clenched, and Zac figured she wouldn't appreciate his demand. This called for back-up. "My father is a nine-hundred year old wizard whose disposition is much worse than mine. You don't want to piss him off."

He hoped his final parting words would keep her safely tucked away while he dealt with the man who'd sired him but had forgotten to raise him.

"Attractive sex toy," Edmund said once Zac joined him in the greenroom.

The jab went unaddressed but not unnoticed. "Why are you here?"

"Finding you took a while. You've learned much since we last saw one another."

"Don't give me that bullshit. You could have found me anytime you wanted, Father. Tracking is what wizards do best. So, don't blame our lack of communication on me."

Edmund inclined his dark head and strolled toward a ficus plant. Barely touching the leaves with the tips of his fingers, he spoke with his back turned. "Your mother has been worried about you."

"Mother has the same way of finding me you do." *There's no way I'm taking the bait.*

"She didn't think you'd speak to her."

How long had the son-of-a-bitch been practicing that line? A long pause followed before Zac responded. "She was right. I don't want to speak to either one of you." A gust of wind lifted his hair as Edmund spun around.

"What happened cannot be changed. Half a century has passed. Can you not let things go now? You haven't seen your family in so long, I'm surprised you even remember what we look like."

Fury unleashed. Anger erupted like a temperamental volcano. "I remember everything about my family… in vivid detail. Especially you, Father. How could I forget the man who killed my wife?"

Lark gasped. Both men spun to the doorway of the greenroom, and Zac's brows lowered into a scowl.

"Don't you ever follow orders?"

"Not usually." The tension in the room mounted, becoming palpable, but she came into the atrium anyway. "Sorry to interrupt this family reunion, but we're about to have visitors." She slid a glance up and down Zac's taut form. "I don't believe these are guests you're going to want to welcome."

He glared at her, but she didn't even flinch. "Are you talking about Diaz?"

"Has the woman got you so distracted you don't even recognize the presence of the enemy?"

She considered putting the grumpy wizard in his place, but they had little time. In a matter of seconds, the army would surround them—Diaz's welcoming committee. She jutted her chin toward the door. "They're coming over the hill just toward the east."

Striding past her, Zac cursed below his breath. He yanked open the curtain covering the window, and stared out into the light. "Perfect." Suddenly, she got a good look at the powerful wizard he'd kept hidden. She came to stand beside him, unable to resist looking up at his face.

Since she'd met him, she'd thought him formidable in his appearance, but now, with his eyes glittering and jaw squared, he took on a new persona—a dark, dangerous one—as if he had no intentions of taking any prisoners.

"You should leave." He spoke so low she almost didn't hear him.

"I should go?" She bumped her shoulder with his. "I'm the reason you're here."

He looked over his shoulder. "I'm talking about him."

Smiling, Edmund approached and clamped one hand on his son's shoulder. "Do not worry. No army can defeat us."

"Do not touch me."

Lark laid a hand on his arm, surprised he didn't brush her off as well. "Perhaps we should see what we're up against first."

Black eyes so like the man at her side pinned Lark's face. "Since when does a woman decide what a wizard does?"

"Look, I don't know—"

"There's nothing you need to know about him," Zac interrupted. "Or want to know, for that matter. Trust me."

The insult hit its intended target. "You have lost a lot of your common decency, I see."

"Common decency only applies to invited guests."

The thickness in the air climbed a notch. Nostrils flared as the wizards stared each other down, threatening and challenging. Muscles bunched.

"Thank you for reminding me I am not welcome here." A shrug indicated his lack of concern. "However, as you well know, your wants matter little to me at present. We have a more important issue at hand."

"You are still in my home." Zac enunciated each word, his teeth clenched.

Edmund flicked one hand and shot across the room, settling a few spaces behind Lark. "This was your grandmother's home."

"Which she left to me," Zac reminded him. "So you can leave any time."

Arms crossed, the older wizard surveyed his son with narrowed, cold eyes. "Perhaps I have underestimated you, son."

"Don't call me that. You lost the right a long time ago."

"Are you sure you didn't take it away?"

"Do the semantics really matter? The end result is the same." Every word sounded as if it came from deep within Zac's soul, and for a brief moment, Lark wanted to take him in her arms and comfort him. Only the look on his face stopped her. He wouldn't appreciate her sympathy.

Something or someone hit the door, and she cleared her throat, yanking her back to the present situation. "The testosterone match is going to have to wait." She spun on her heel.

"Don't open that door," Zac called after her, but she didn't stop to listen.

While the two wizards behind her had their own battle, she'd face the enemy head-on. She had nothing to lose, and Shanae's death still weighed heavily on her mind, especially after the bout of rousing sex she'd had with Zac. Guilt joined her in the shower, and despite the disruption of his father's appearance, it had hung on.

"For God's sake, Lark, listen to me." Zac leaped in front of her, his speed enabling him to hit the door before she could.

"You still know how to use your magic. I'm impressed," Edmund drawled.

She tried to open the front door, but a firm hand pressed against the wood. "Why don't you go talk to your father about your past?" Another yank proved as futile.

"That's none of your business."

The comment stung, reminding her she was as unwelcome here as Edmund. Perhaps even more so. After all, hadn't she brought him back to this place? "I know." *Bastard.* Could he still read her?

"Back away from the door." His voice carried no inflection.

She thrust her head back to see his face. With his nostrils flaring and jaw clenched, every feature outlined his temper. Was she supposed to be frightened now? She followed the commands of no man. "I can take care of this." Let them both rot in hell. If she had to breathe the testosterone for one more second, she'd go mad!

"Like hell."

A thump rattled the walls of the house, and Edmund gave a vibrant curse. "Shall I handle this then while the two of you continue your lover's spat?"

Lark watched a change take over Zac's face, and she knew the exact moment when the man faded completely away, leaving only the wizard to take center stage. Fire shot from his dark eyes, and lethal rage swirled in the depths of those orbs, promising violence.

"I don't recall asking for your help." Bitterness, crisp and clear, slapped the older wizard full in the face.

Edmund's lips twitched as though trying to contain a smile. "Come now, Zachary. We both know you would never ask for help. You're much too arrogant for that." On that note, the elder wizard disappeared, leaving a cloud of dust in his wake.

"Shit!" Zac whisked his hand, leaving her alone with her palm still pressed against the wood.

Zac welcomed the approaching army. He needed the outlet, and now, with his powers surging through his veins again, the thought of taking on Diaz's obstacle exhilarated him. His father stood at the end of the driveway, flexing his magical muscles, and hate burned in Zac's heart.

His thoughts clouded. He tried to push away the memories, dull the renewed pain, but his father's presence prevented him from doing either.

Why the fuck are you here? He wanted to scream, but instead, he clenched his hands into fists and glared at the back of the dark head a few feet away. "Go home." Though he spoke the words in a whisper, he knew his father heard.

The older wizard's response served as one more reminder Zac and his father were connected by DNA. "I'm not leaving without you."

Diaz watched the father and son square off at a distance, and glee rolled through his body. He couldn't have planned a better distraction. With the arrival of the elder wizard, Zac wouldn't be able to concentrate on interfering with his plans.

Even now the young wizard focused more on his father's arrival than the deadly army Diaz had conjured.

Now to prove his point.

Lark tore open the door just as the dark clouds scattered over the sky. Thunder rumbled in the distance. *You always have to bring a storm, don't you, Diaz?* Stepping out into the rapidly cooling air, she called out to Zac, but he didn't turn around, didn't even acknowledge her. "God, this man can be exasperating!" She walked toward him, but he held up his hand to stop her.

"You should go back inside." His voice brusque, he left no doubt as to his present state of mind.

He didn't sound anything like the man who'd ravished her hours ago. "I should do a lot of things which I don't do." She came to stand beside him. "How far out are they?"

"About half a mile."

"As loud as they sounded, I thought they were right outside the door."

His upper lip curled. "Diaz wanted us to think they were about to overtake us."

Ahead Edmund stood with his arms wide open. "What is your father doing?"

"Inviting our visitors to come closer." The words came from between clenched teeth.

She scanned the horizon as the line of soldiers approached on horseback. Dressed in full battle gear and armed with swords, they were straight off the field in an old Viking movie. "What's the purpose of this?"

"What was the purpose in killing your sister?"

Her lungs constricted, making breathing difficult. "Thanks for the reminder."

He flashed a look without remorse. "Sometimes we need the reminders."

She wanted to hate him for those words, or, at the very least, get angry, but he only spoke what he saw as facts. Ordinarily, that was a trait she admired in a man.

The thundering of horses' hooves grew louder, and with battle cries, the men charged. Even from the distance, the gleam in their eyes was visible. Pure evil.

"Stay back," Zac commanded.

"Like hell!"

With shoulders thrust back, Edmund met the line of soldiers halfway. A long, scarlet robe flowed out behind him, causing Lark to frown.

"Where did the robe come from?"

He held up one hand to silence her. "Our homeland. It's a wizard's battle gear."

She'd never seen a wizard in action before. Oh, she'd seen sorcery, but nothing quite like this display. Edmund held up both of his hands, fingertips aimed straight ahead. "You are approaching your deaths." The threat rang loud and clear. "Turn around. Tell your master he should fight his own battles."

The steeds snorted and pawed the ground, the clang of metal stinging the air. No one spoke, and for a long moment, she wondered if the soldiers would obey. They hesitated, uncertain of their next move, but Diaz's orders were stronger than the wizard's commands. They charged forward.

A long line of electricity shot from Edmund's fingers, and the cries of the dying resounded. As long as the wizard stood, more soldiers kept coming, racing over the hills to follow the dictates of their ruler.

"Aren't you going to help him?" Lark tugged at Zac's arm.

"He wanted to take care of the trouble himself."

"How can you be so cruel?"

Dark eyes fixed on her face. "Would you think it cruel if he'd killed your family?"

She bit her lower lip. "I don't understand everything about what happened."

"You're right. You don't." He strode forward, coming to stand beside his father. "You're wasting time, and that's something we don't have a lot of." With a sweep of his hand, he brushed the soldiers aside, sending them careening across the grass. They stumbled into a heap, swords flying overhead. When not one soldier remained standing, Zac set the pile ablaze.

Minutes ticked by as the two wizards stood side-by-side, surveying the damage.

"Actually," Edmund sniffed, "I was just waiting to see how much of your magic you would really use. Well done, my boy." With a smirk on his face, he disappeared.

Lark felt the full force of Zac's fury as he turned and walked away, across the burned grass.

She couldn't help but wonder if asking him for help had been such a good idea after all.

Smug bastard! Zac could think of a few more words he'd like to call his father, but none would really do him justice. Darkness swelled inside his heart.

He'd never wanted to see Edmund again, had effectively erased his father from his life, but now, all the old images came crashing down on him. The very images that had changed him, created the cold mercenary he'd become.

His gaze dropping to the ground, he pressed his palms against his temples. "No! I will not relive this again!" The shouts hung in the air, aimed at no one in particular. "He killed my wife!"

The guild had been listening. Even now their disturbed whispers reached his ears, and he wondered how long it would take for the summons to arrive. They'd call him home soon because they needed his strength. Fuck them. He wouldn't give them the pleasure, not even for the chance to see his mother again.

Pushing to his feet, he staggered forward, tears streaking his cheeks. "You allowed him to kill the one woman I loved, the woman who meant the world to me. How could you do that?"

Rena had been his life, but the wizards were convinced she'd only entered Zac's world to learn more of them, to take the knowledge back to Diaz. Edmund had erased the possibility without even blinking. He hadn't even given Zac the chance to say goodbye.

"I loved her."

He knew the words wouldn't change the wizards' hearts. They believed Edmund had done the right thing, had saved the guild.

Zac would never forgive them.

Chapter 6

"Zac." Lark approached him silently, uncertain of his response to her arrival.

He kept his back to her. "You shouldn't be here."

"You brought me here." His voice broke, and her determination to remain unmoved faltered, causing her heart to skip a beat. What was it about the man that magnetized her in spite of his harsh demeanor? Was it the wounded soul she now sensed beneath the perfect exterior? Or maybe she simply saw more in him than he saw in himself.

"I didn't mean to my home. I meant here." Sadness drenched each and every syllable, and her gut clenched. Why did it surprise her the man had feelings, emotions?

"What's so special about here?" He seemed so remote before, arrogant and unfeeling. Now, the fine sheen of tears on his face startled her.

"You've been crying." Almost in awe, she reached up to touch his cheek, but he jerked away.

"Don't." Had she every heard such agony in one word?

"You don't like anyone to see you like this."

"Go back to the house. I'll return in a moment."

Her hand settled on his arm. "You're really not the bastard you want everyone to believe you are."

He whipped around, yanking her into his arms. "If you allow yourself to think that for one moment, you could get yourself into a lot of trouble. Look into my eyes. Do you see any emotion other than hate?"

Her breath snagged in her throat, but the raw anger she read in his gaze didn't scare her. Instead, the blaze intoxicated her. Heat climbed up the walls of her pussy. So wild and primitive, he enveloped her, and she wanted him.

Hands cupping his face, she didn't back down from his power. "Like it or not, Mr. Wolfe, I do see something more than just the loathing you want me to see. I see pain."

His nostrils flared, his hands relaxing slightly on her arms. "I don't want your sympathy."

One hand boldly cupped his cock. "Does this feel like I'm offering sympathy?" Heat sped through her system, blocking out every thought, every sound.

"Is that what you came for then?" He snatched a handful of her hair and tugged her forward. His lips fused to hers, dragging the oxygen from her lungs and into his.

She fell against the grass, yanking him down with her. His eyes swept over her face, creating a gnawing hunger in her gut.

"You still shouldn't be here." The reprimand burst from his throat seconds before he whisked their clothing away with a sweep of his hand. His fingers sank deep into her pussy, drawing her hips up off the grass.

"Talk later, wizard," she commanded, feasting on his skin with nibbling kisses.

Maybe he needed this—something to take his mind off the memories which had driven him to this point. She could give him something to take away the sadness, at least for now.

He rolled, tucking her body beneath his. The head of his cock tantalized her pussy, and she let out a soft moan. His hand went to the base of his dick to guide it into her channel.

"Do you still want me to leave?"

"No." The word was torn from his throat as he thrust into her heat with one flex of his hips.

Lark's nails dug into his hips, meeting his frantic movements thrust for thrust. "Yes, yes."

Zac took her like a wild animal, mating with a ferocity which caused the clouds to boil in the sky. Grabbing her legs, he yanked them up over his shoulders and drove his cock deep into her soaked cleft. Her pussy clenched around his cock, and the sensation of her muscles holding soft steel made her groan aloud.

Taking hold of his face, she drew his head down closer, her lips capturing his again. Their tongues danced around each other's, savoring each taste. Breaths connected in short pants as he retreated and plunged into her once more, savagely grinding her hips into the grass.

She didn't wince or even acknowledge the animalistic fucking hurt. She gave back as good as she got, biting his shoulder and his neck while her nails raked up and down his spine.

"Oh, yeah. You're so tight." He ground into her, sweat beading on his forehead. "So wet. I could stay inside your pussy for hours." Just as he said the words, his body went stiff, and a burst of juice shot from his cock deep into her pussy. He let go with a cry, his head tossed back, teeth gritted while the veins in his neck strained against the pressure.

Lark continued to move beneath him, seeking her own release, and with just a few short jabs of her hips, she got the reaction she wanted from his cock.

He could stay inside her for hours. Why leave such a perfect place? "Are you ready to come, baby?"

"That's what I'm here for," she panted.

Gripping her hips, he pumped his hips furiously, sliding his cock against her sweet spot over and over until her muscles constricted. She held onto him tightly, wanting this moment to last as long as possible.

The release started with a tingle at the top of her scalp before sliding down her face, over her skin in warm waves. She buried her head against his chest, bucking beneath him while the orgasm gripped her. Until finally she relaxed, her limbs going slack against the grass.

Zac leaned down and kissed her swollen lips once before rolling to his side. "We'd better get back to the house. I don't know when my father will return for the next round."

She sat up straight, her eyes flashing. "What? No further conversation? We're done? Why don't you just slap me on the ass and light a cigarette?"

Propping his head up in his hand, he gave her a long, studying look before his lips curled. "I don't smoke, but the other part I could do, if you insist."

Scrambling to her feet, she waved a finger at his face. "Don't touch me. I've fulfilled my end of the bargain. Now you fulfill yours, and we can both go our separate ways."

Chuckling, he pushed to his feet. "Do you really think this is the last time I'll fuck you?"

Her breath hissing out from between clenched teeth, she snatched her clothes from the ground. "I'm thinking I would have been better off if I had faced Diaz alone."

All humor drained from his face, and he snatched hold of her arm. "He will kill you."

Her gaze dropped to the fingers digging into her muscles. "I think that would be preferable at this moment."

A sigh filtered into the air as if all the fight had gone out of him. "Just go back to the house."

"Fuck you. I should have listened to my instincts and left you to wallow in your self-pity." Without bothering to dress herself, she stalked back up the hill and toward the house, her back ramrod straight.

Zac sank to the ground, dragging his hands through his hair.

"You sure know how to treat a lady." The drawl sparked an instant response.

Clothing himself, Zac leapt to his feet. "You were watching us?"

"Oh, only the ending scene." Edmund folded his arms over his chest. "Good thing for you, I'm not here to talk about your love life. The guild wants a meeting."

"I don't particularly give a shit what the guild wants." He started to walk away, but his father caught hold of his arm.

"You might want to think twice this time."

As his father's eyes flashed, Zac stared at him. "Why? Give me one good reason why I should?"

"You don't want me to have to kill Lark like I did Rena."

Keeping her temper in check had never been one of her strong suits, but now, Lark gladly gave the lack of control free reign. She moved swiftly through the corridors of Zac's house, searching for a back entrance. Fuck the deal she'd made with him. He'd never keep his end of the bargain anyway.

And she had better things to do than watch a wizard wallow.

She took one last look around his home before starting toward the door. "Good luck with your life, Zac. I hope you can find whatever it takes to put you out of your misery."

The wind whistled through the treetops as she stepped outside. Her determination took a rapid nosedive as she realized she had no idea how to leave. "Dammit!" Hands on hips, she stared up at the sky. There was no way in hell she would go back to that man to ask his permission to leave. The very thought galled her. What had she been thinking to get him involved anyway? His reputation alone should have been enough to make her realize she walked into a nest of vipers.

Blowing her breath out from between clenched teeth, she weighed her options, neither of which she liked—go back inside and wait for him to stop sulking or hunt down his surly father to ask for assistance. She'd just as soon ask Diaz.

Being at anyone's mercy definitely wasn't her style. Perhaps now was as good a time as any to test out some of these "abilities" her father assured her she'd been gifted with. Of course, she could end up in Bumfuck, Egypt, but even that legendary city couldn't be any worse than where she found herself now.

Could it?

Every nerve in Zach's body tensed as he faced the circle of wizards. They were all familiar to him—too familiar. He'd never wanted to see them again, but as much as he hated his father, he would not let anything happen to Lark—not if he could prevent it.

"Well, young Zac, how nice to see you again." The drawl came from the back of the room and set his teeth on edge. His brother, Jacob, strolled forward, dark hair brushing his shoulders, wearing the same smug smile he always wore. "It's been a long time."

Animosity burning in the depths of his soul, Zac extended a hand. "That it has, brother." Here sat a man who could have helped to prevent the death of his wife, and yet, he could greet him amicably. Understanding eluded him.

Surprise flickered in Jacob's gaze, but he accepted the handshake. "You've changed."

"I've had plenty of time."

"Is that what you've been doing since you've been gone all this time?"

The snide question only added to Zac's building irritation, but as he opened his mouth to responded, Edmund interrupted. "We have no time for idle chatter. The guild asked me to bring you here, Zac, as it is time for you to rejoin your family."

A chill shot down Zac's spine. "I believe we already had this discussion. I do not intend to rejoin the guild—now or ever." He spun to face the man who had sired him. "I am quite happy with my life right now." Not altogether the truth, but then, he supposed they recognized the lie.

"What about your grandmother? Does her passing not inspire you to avenge her death?"

His hands clenched at his sides. "Leave her out of this. You know this has nothing to do with her."

"No?" Edmund walked around the table. "You'll forgive me if I find your words difficult to believe. She was, after all, your flesh and blood."

"Grandmother knew how much she meant to me." Zac dragged a hand through his hair and thought he caught a glimpse of sympathy in his brother's eyes. He had to be mistaken. Jacob had never been the sympathetic type—not even when he'd learned of their grandmother's ascension to another plane of existence.

"Then it is time we all unite together for justice."

He ignored the announcement and swept a glance around the council chambers. Little had changed in the years since he'd left his family behind. The air still smelled of old leather and rosewood. The aged portraits gracing the onyx walls reminded all the room was as steeped in tradition as the wizards who graced the table.

Squaring his shoulders against the flood of memories, Zac shook his head. "I will unite with none of you." Spinning around, he took one step toward the door when a soft sound, a whisper of silk, captured his attention.

"Zachary, please don‘t go."

Tension coiled at the base of his neck. "Mother." He could fight any army, bring down any evil force, but he didn't have the power to walk away from his mother's pleading voice. Standing still, he awaited her approach, the aroma of lavender reaching his nostrils before her hand lightly touched his arm.

"We need you, son," she whispered.

He looked into her upturned face. With jasmine eyes almost identical to his brother's, Brianna Wolfe could still captivate a man with her beauty. Reaching out, he stroked her cheek. He could never blame her for his father's cruelty. "Mother, you're still as beautiful as ever."

Her smile wobbled, and she reached up to cover his hand with hers. "Will you at least listen to the council before you make your decision?"

He closed his eyes for a moment, knowing his answer even before he spoke. His mother had that kind of power over him—which was precisely the reason he'd stayed away for so long. With a slight inclination of his head, he turned toward the table. "I'll listen."

Edmund bobbed his head. "Excellent." One hand indicated a vacant chair next to Jacob. "Be seated then. We have much to discuss."

Zac could think of only one thing they had to discuss. "You mean Diaz."

A snort came from his brother. "You've been away too long, brother. Diaz isn't our only problem."

"He should be the most important one at present." The bite in Zac's tone didn't go unnoticed.

"Perhaps if you were to make an appearance every so often, you would be aware of the problems which faced us—all of us."

Before Zac could square off against his brother, Edmund banged his fist against the table.

"Enough! Diaz is one of our problems, yes, but I'm afraid before we can deal with him, we must deal with Lark."

His attention captured, Zac pinned his father with his furious gaze. "She has nothing to do with this."

"No? Did Diaz not kill her sister?" Edmund folded his hands together in front of him, head tipped to one side.

"You already know the answer. Why ask me now?"

"Because her quest for vengeance is just what Diaz is looking for."

Shit. Her transporting skills definitely needed some work. Brushing the dust off her knees, Lark straightened to survey her surroundings. Definitely not Earth. Damn. She'd missed her mark.

Darkness enveloped her, issuing a silent unwelcome. The chill seeped through to her bones, and she wrapped her arms around herself. Teeth chattering, she took a step forward, the ground crunching beneath her high-heeled boots.

Everywhere she looked she saw nothing but ice dripping from the trees and snow-packed earth. The landscape stretched ahead, an endless stream of frozen ground. "Where in the hell am I?" she whispered. The words echoed across the distance.

"I think the most important question would be: am I alone?"

The rasp chilled her worse than the wind, and she didn't have to look to know the enemy had found her.

Now, it was kill or be killed.

Zac left his relatives behind, disappearing in a flash, only to find his home empty without a trace of Lark. *Damnit! Why couldn't you just listen to me?* A knot formed in the pit of his stomach, but he closed his eyes, attempting to push the anxiety back, to focus.

"Use your ability." The whisper brought a frown to his face.

"You know nothing of my ability."

Edmund gave a short bark of laughter as he came into view. "Your grandmother was the most powerful wizard in our guild, and when she ascended, she gave her gifts to you." He touched a hand to Zac's shoulder. "Don't you remember?"

He didn't try to break away from the touch. "I can't talk about this now. I have to find Lark."

"If you will use what your grandmother has given you, you will find her."

Fuck. He hated the knowing tone of his father's voice, but he didn't waste his energy on responding. Instead, he reached out into the vast emptiness of space, searching through the clear skies, his mind touching each and every corner of the galaxy.

"Zac." The sharpness of Edmund's tone forced a reply.

"How do you expect me to use my gifts if you will not give me the silence I need?"

"There is something you must know… about Rena."

"No! Now is not the time. Leave me."

"You have to know this!"

With a frustrated wave of his hand, Zac disappeared, his body dissipating into tiny molecules.

As he sailed through the air, his senses alert to the microscopic trail he'd found, anger burned in his heart. The cocky son-of-a-bitch had chosen the time when he most needed every ounce of his magic to bring up Rena! He fought the murderous rage which threatened to consume his soul. He couldn't deal with this now. There would be plenty of time later for confrontation.

For as much as he hated to admit it, he did need to know why his father had killed Rena. Somewhere, deep in his heart, he desperately wanted to believe her murder had been a catastrophic mistake, an accident, something other than a cold-blooded kill.

A gust of wind swept upward, and he quickly solidified, lowering his feet to the ground before the angry tempest could scatter the cells in his body. "This certainly feels familiar," he muttered below his breath.

"Ah, Zac, so nice of you to join us."

He turned slowly, his gaze zeroing in on where Lark stood several inches away from Diaz's cloaked frame. "Are you all right?"

She gave him a disgusted look. "Of course, I'm all right. Do you think I can't survive without you?"

Diaz clicked his tongue against his teeth. "Lover's tiff?"

Zac ignored him. "Why did you leave the house?"

"Your home is not mine, and I had every right to leave."

"Do you always take risks like this?"

The disgust in her eyes segued to anger. "Do you piss off every person you meet, or am I just one of the lucky ones?"

"Enough!" Diaz shouted, his rage causing the ground to tremble beneath Zac's feet. When silence descended, the sorcerer clapped his hands. "Excellent. Now then, where were we? Oh, yes. Love. Lark and I were just discussing love and the incredibly stupid things the emotion can make you do." He lifted one shoulder in a half-hearted shrug. "Tell me, Mr. Wolfe. Have you ever been in love?"

He wouldn't play Diaz's game. Zac's gaze shot past the sorcerer's shoulder to the dark castle looming in the distance. Diaz's lair. He'd no doubt Lark had played right into the lunatic's hands. Or… maybe she hadn't.

For a woman who now faced serious peril, she didn't appear to be shaking in her sexy, black boots. He shot her a shrewd look. Had she planned this? Or was she just now taking this as an opportunity?

"Stop trying to read my mind," she muttered just loud enough for him to hear.

"I could never read a woman's mind. It's far too complicated," he said with a bite to his voice. He whipped forward and snagged hold of her wrist. "If you'll excuse us, Diaz, the lady and I have something to discuss."

"There's nowhere for you to go, Mr. Wolfe. You see, your lady made the unfortunate mistake of coming to my planet. Here, I make the rules, and my very first rule is no one leaves without my permission." Diaz folded his arms across his chest while his eyes glittered. "What do you think are the odds of my giving either of you permission?"

Zac held her close to his side. "You obviously haven't figured out by now I've never been very good at following rules." Hoping like hell he still had the use of his magic, he closed his eyes and focused on his homeland.

Lark gave a squeak of dismay and dug her nails into his arms with a ferocity that made him wince. "Didn't you just hear him? He said we can't leave!"

"I said I don't follow orders, so just shut up and hang on. I know what I'm doing." His words came back to haunt him the moment his feet touched ground. His magic hadn't taken them where he'd wanted to go.

"Shit."

Lark blew out a breath and brushed her hands down the front of her black shirt. "Why do you sound so surprised? Please don't tell me you actually thought you could take us off of this crater." His eyes narrowed, but she forged on, ignoring the growing fire in his gaze. "Just because you're capable of doing a lot of damage on Earth doesn't mean you can handle things in Diaz's world."

Shivering, she took a few steps away from him, her arms wrapped around her waist. "You only succeeded into taking us—" head tipped back, she surveyed their surroundings—"to who the hell knows where. Scratch that. I can guarantee Diaz knows where we are."

"Are you finished?"

One eyebrow lifted, she arched a look over her shoulder. "You're angry? What right do you have to be angry? I don't recall anyone inviting you here."

"You left!"

"I come and go as I please."

"No, you come when I please and go when I say." Zac's fingers curled around her wrist. "We had a deal."

"The deal ended with your pity party. I thought you'd appreciate the time alone to mourn your sorry lot in life." She tried to tug her arm free, but he held on tight. Her gaze dropped to his crotch. "If you want to keep your boys happy and healthy, you'll let go of me."

He shifted his stance but otherwise ignored the threat. "Do you realize how foolish you were to leave?"

"I gave you what you wanted." As much as she wanted to regret that, she couldn't. Since the first time he'd touched her, he'd ignited a spark inside of her, and now, each stroke threatened her self-control.

Drawing her in until her breasts touched his chest, Zac cupped her cheek with his free hand. "I gave us what we both wanted, but you don't make the rules. You belong to me until Diaz has been destroyed."

Fury clawed at her stomach, a restless, writhing entity. "I don't belong to anyone. I sacrificed my body to avenge my sister's death. If you think there's any more to our involvement, you're sadly mistaken."

His hand moved to fist in her hair. "Do you really think so?"

She had mere seconds to gauge his next move before his mouth slashed across hers. Heat exploded in her veins, engulfing every nerve in a fiery maelstrom. She wanted to drag him closer, to sink into his kiss, but this was just his stamp of possession, a way to claim her. Pushing back with all of her strength, she managed to break the kiss. "That proves nothing." She dragged her hair away from her face.

Zac folded his arms across his chest. "I like you, Lark."

Her heart fluttered. Why did those words do that to her? "Am I supposed to feel privileged?"

His jaw tightened. "Do you always respond so negatively when a man says something nice to you?"

"You call that being nice? I certainly don't." Turning her back to him, she walked a few steps away. "This has all been some kind of sick game to you, hasn't it? You planned on going after Diaz all along. I was just icing on the cake for you."

"Actually, you were the cake," he whispered right behind her ear.

Damn his ability to move so quickly. "Why didn't you tell me you intended to come after him?"

"What makes you think that was my intention?"

Though she knew he'd be close, so close she could feel his breath on her skin, she turned around anyway. His eyes glinted like polished steel. "You haven't challenged him or attempted to draw him out. You've just been playing along."

Zac's knuckles grazed her cheek. "You're as smart as you are pretty."

"You think this is a joke?" Palms open, she smacked his chest. "This monster killed my sister, and you're toying with him like a ball of catnip?" She lifted her chin and stared into his brooding eyes. "Well, you can go to hell, Wolfe. I'll take care of Diaz myself."

Before she could move, his hand shackled her wrist. "Don't be ridiculous. You came to me because you knew you couldn't take him on all by yourself."

"You knew, didn't you?" She didn't give him time to answer. "You knew who I was and why I was there the moment I arrived at the bar. Did you know about my sister, too? Did you know he'd killed her?" Her eyes widened. "Did you know he was going to kill her?"

As the air grew heavy with condemnation and guilt, Lark's blood ran cold. "My God. My sister's death could have been prevented."

He yanked up her arm. "No, it couldn't have. Did I know Diaz was on the loose again? Yes. Did I know your sister was the target? No."

"You knew he had a target, though..."

"He always has a target."

"You're telling me you knew this... this... creature was going to kill again, and you did nothing to stop him... nothing to prevent someone's death?"

"I can't save the world."

She pried his fingers away from her wrist, but she suspected he'd relaxed his hold. "You make me sick." Her legs trembled, and she braced herself against the trunk of a rotting tree.

He studied her for a long moment before replying. "You can't blame your sister's death on anyone else, not even yourself, and this can't be about revenge."

"Why the hell not?"

"Diaz will feed off your anger." He approached her slowly, like a panther on the prowl. "You'll never win that way. As long as he can feel your desire for vengeance, he'll anticipate your next move, counter it with his own attack, wear you down, and in the end, he'll kill you."

"So, I should be like you then? Shut myself off from all emotions? Feel nothing?"

Zac's breath hissed out of his throat. "You think I don't feel?" He snagged hold of her hand and placed it over his heart. "Do you feel that? I'm as alive as you are. I bleed like you do, and I hurt as much. Just because I don't show my pain doesn't mean I'm incapable of feeling it."

The steady thump of his heart beneath her palm made her gaze flick to his face. For a brief moment, he looked vulnerable, almost fragile.

Forget it, Lark. You're crazy if you think this man hurts like a normal man would. After all, hadn't she thought he'd been wrought with grief earlier? His cavalier attitude had quickly proven her wrong, and though she'd barely known him two days, she recognized a man who cared only for his own life. Hadn't he told her as much?

He tucked a stray lock of hair behind her ear. "Go ahead. Try to make sense of what I am. Tell yourself what you see is what you get." He leaned in and drew in a deep breath against her neck. "It changes nothing. You still heat up when I touch you." His hand slid down to cup her breast. "Now that I've held you in my arms, tasted you, heard you come, I'm as addicted as you are."

She shook her head, trying to deny the obvious. "I'm not addicted to anything, least of all you. I'm with you for one reason only—to get rid of Diaz. After that, we'll go our separate ways."

A husky chuckle danced its way over her skin. "Do you really think so?" His hand slipped lower, across the flat planes of her stomach, to cup her sex through the thickness of her leather pants. "Then tell me you're not wet right now."

She could barely breathe. "That has nothing to do with whether or not I'll leave once Diaz has been taken care of. You're a mercenary, remember, and mercenaries don't need anyone else."

Too busy lowering the zipper on her pants to pay attention, he murmured a vague response in her ear.

Her head bumped against the tree, and she closed her eye. His fingers crept beneath the thin elastic of her panties before sinking deep into the damp patch between her thighs. She cried out, arching her back.

Making a growling noise in the back of his throat, he flicked his thumb over her clit. His teeth nibbled at her neck while his fingers pumped in and out of her heat.

"Oh, God," she moaned, one hand grasping his wrist.

She shifted to open her legs wider. The pad of his thumb eased the ache building within her soul as he gently rotated her clit. She dropped her head to his shoulder, biting her teeth into the hard flesh.

Zac groaned aloud and pressed his erection into her thigh. "Feel me, Lark. I want to be inside you. I need to fuck you."

The orgasm wrapped itself around her, and she barely had time to breathe before he gave her more. He yanked her pants and panties down her legs, letting them fall to her feet. Then freeing his cock from his pants, he positioned it at the gate to her pussy, locked eyes with her, and then surged into her heat, stretching, filling, completing her.

She felt so… full… so… she couldn't think of a more fitting word. No mere adjective could describe what she felt. Yet, as her hands dug into his shoulders, and his hips bumped against hers, she knew she'd found something she desperately wanted to keep.

Hitching her legs higher, Zac thrust into her, slamming her back against the tree. She felt him everywhere, touching every inch of her sheath, sliding in and out of her warmth. So hard and yet, so soft at the same time.

Clenching her vaginal muscles, she made him groan. She opened her eyes and found his. Sweat had beaded on his forehead, and his breath sloughed against her face in short pants.

"I'm coming," he whispered, his hands digging into her thighs.

She nodded, eager to feel the hot rush of his seed.

He came on a long, low groan—half growl and half plea. His head buried against her neck, he pumped his hips a few more times while she milked him with her muscles. "God, you're incredible," he whispered against her skin.

"Yes, she is. I might just have to try her out myself."

Zac spun around, cursing himself for allowing his defenses to drop. He should have been paying attention, but he couldn't think with Lark so close.

"I don't think I've ever seen a woman quite so... agile." Diaz's voice bounced off the rocks, echoing around them.

He couldn't pinpoint the monster's position. Adjusting their clothing with a wave of his hand, he walked away from the tree, toward the middle of the stony clearing. "I'm surprised you would hide this time, Diaz."

Laughter bounced off the rocks. "Hiding? Oh, no, my dear boy. I was observing. I did hate to keep the two of you waiting, but I had some other invitations to send. I hope you didn't mind the inconvenience. Although, I did see you found something to amuse yourselves. How creative of you."

As Diaz spoke, Zac circled, catching hold of Lark's wrist to keep her behind him. "Thanks. I've always been quick on my feet." He scanned the mountains above them, reaching deep within himself to track the sorcerer's voice patterns.

Lark nudged him between the shoulder blades. "Could we skip the small talk, please? Unless you've forgotten, we have a job to do."

"How could I forget?"

Diaz clicked his teeth, the sound as loud as metal knives against a plate glass window. "Here I thought I was being magnanimous allowing the two of you to say your goodbyes. After all, you didn't get that chance with your wife, did you, Zac?"

Lightning flashed, allowing a glimpse of the sorcerer's figure standing atop a rocky ledge. A long, black cloak swirled around his feet, and the wind lifted his stringy hair, giving him a feral look. Keeping his eyes on his adversary, Zac issued a command. "Don't talk about my wife."

Tapping one finger against his cheek, Diaz looked up at the inky black sky as if trying to recall something he'd forgotten. "What was her name again? Oh, yes, Rena. What an absolutely beautiful woman. Of course, she didn't look anything like you, Lark, my dear, but then, I've always heard once a man loses a wife, he'll seek out a woman who is her total opposite."

"Shut up, Diaz."

When had she stepped out from behind him? Zac glared at her. He wanted to shove her back behind him, but doubted she'd stay. Did she really think the two of them would fight this monster together? No, he'd handle Diaz much better knowing she was safe.

"Stay back."

She ignored the instruction and focused her attention on Diaz. She stood next to Zac, her long silky hair flowing down her back like liquid silk and dressed all in black, like an avenging angel. As he watched her, he felt something tug at his heart—something which shouldn't be there.

"So, you like to kill innocent women and children, but what about those who can stand up to you? Are you brave enough to take them on?"

The smile disappeared from Diaz's face. Zac cautioned, "Be careful, Lark."

"My dear, perhaps it is in your best interest to listen to your lover and stay back. After all, I don't really want to have to kill you." The ground trembled as if kneeling in allegiance to its supreme commander.

Her eyes narrowed, and Zac sensed an impending explosion. He had no way of knowing the full extent of her capabilities, and he doubted even she knew. Though he sensed the magic in her, much as he had in Marcus, he had yet to see her really test it without his assistance.

There was no way in hell he would let her try anything without his help now.

Snagging hold of her arm, he dragged her closer to his side, lowering his voice to a whisper. "He's baiting you."

"Do you think I don't know that?" she said, snapping the backs of her fingers against the hand holding her. "I've studied this monster. I know how he thinks."

One eyebrow lifted, he released her arm. "I seriously doubt that. No one has ever fully understood how he thinks."

"How right he is, my sweet," Diaz drawled, surveying his fingernails with the utmost interest. "So, did you have a large funeral for Rena? I would have so liked to have been there, but I'm afraid my presence wasn't welcome." Another slash of lightning illuminated the sky, and the sorcerer's grinning face.

A snarl built up in the back of Zac's throat, and red flames shot from the tips of his fingers. "Don't test me, Diaz. I'm not as weak as I once was."

"No doubt. I've been watching you for some time. You're quite the industrious fellow. Though I never thought you'd start using your magic for your own personal gain." Taking one step down off the ledge, his eyes glowing like twin rubies, he rocked forward on his heels. "Tell me. Did her death make you what you are today?"

Lark took hold of Zac's arm before he could lunge forward. "He needs us to lose control."

Taking in deep gulps of air, he forced his temper to simmer, to ignore the taunts, and focus on the task at hand, no matter how difficult. The vision of Rena's lifeless body lying against the cold marble still haunted him—almost as much as the steel glint of the blade his father had held in his hands that day. The pain still ran as deep today as it did then.

"It's a shame your father killed Rena. I had such big plans for her."

He froze in place, his eyes traveling from Lark's face to Diaz's. He didn't speak because he couldn't. A lump the size of a golf ball lodged in his throat, and as much as he wanted to drown out the sorcerer's words, he wouldn't.

"Did you know she was to be my protégé?" Diaz blinked rapidly, long nails scratching at the side of his cheek like sticks on sandpaper. "Oh, I can see by your expression you didn't know. Yes, she was perfect, and she would do anything for me. Such a charming lady. I loved her smile, didn't you?"

"You didn't know her." Evil laughter sent a chill through to Zac's bones. He didn't want to look in the sorcerer's eyes for fear of what he might see. "My wife isn't a part of this." He heard Lark's swift intake of breath, but he couldn't bring himself to add deceased in front of Rena's name.

In a pseudo-sympathetic manner, Diaz inclined his head. "She would have been a perfect companion for me on those long, cold, lonely nights. As much as I do love this planet, the cold can ice your blood." Teeth flashed in a sinister grin. "Oh, yes, I had big plans for your wife."

Lark's nails dug into Zac's arm before he could make a move. "Don't. He wants you to react to everything he's saying. He's feeding off your fury now."

"Then he should be full by now," he spat the words. His eyes focused on Diaz's throat, and all he could think about was wrapping his hands around the thick column and squeezing until the monster's body went lifeless.

He drew in a deep, steadying breath. No. He would act on his time, not on

Diaz's. For now, he'd give the sorcerer the reins, allowing him the moment of glory he desired. For in the end, Diaz would be eliminated… forever.

"So, tell me, Mr. Wolfe." Thin, bony fingers formed a tent. "Why do you think I wanted the two of you here with me?"

"You didn't plan this. It was a matter of circumstance." Every muscle in his body grew taut. Need for revenge clawed at his intestines, and while instincts urged him to give into the craving desire, he wouldn't. Lark was right. Diaz wanted the satisfaction of seeing him lose control.

The sorcerer flicked a glance toward Lark. "Perhaps, but I've never really believed in happenstance. In fact, I prefer to think of life as a perfectly structured orchestra with one conductor. Now, who do you think deserves to be that conductor, Mr. Wolfe? The man who couldn't protect his own wife or someone like me, who can control the world with a flick of his finger?"

Zac took a threatening step forward with Lark still clinging to him like a determined vine. "How do you know so much about my wife's death?" He kept his tone conversational, but inside, his gut knotted.

"You mean your father didn't tell you?" The clouds boiled overhead, as if the sorcerer's temperament demanded synchronization with the atmosphere. "He left the pleasure to me. How considerate of him."

Lark shook Zac's arm, bringing his gaze to her face. "Don't listen to him. Whatever he says now won't change what happened in the past. Your wife is dead, and if you make one wrong move, you'll suffer the same fate. He's going to get too complacent, too relaxed, and that's when we make our move."

She gripped hold of his chin. "Look at me. Look into my eyes." As their gazes locked, she continued. "Now focus."

He peeled her fingers away from his skin. Though he understood what she said, he couldn't pretend the sorcerer hadn't gotten under his skin. Diaz knew how well his taunts were working and exactly what he needed to say to snap what little control Zac had left.

Before Zac could move, Lark positioned her body in front of his. "I'm not letting you throw yourself into the lion's den."

He took hold of her shoulders. "Didn't you hear me the first time? I said, stay back. This battle is between me and Diaz."

"Well, as much as I admire the testosterone flowing through your veins, you and I both know we can't defeat this… this… creature without one another. Why do you think I came looking for you? Certainly not for your people skills."

He dropped his gaze to her face, considering what she said. Divide and conquer. Always Diaz's method of choice. But the trap was already set.

"I have to finish this."

She reached up and clasped her hands around his wrists. "*We* have to finish this. We're in this together."

"He could kill you."

Did he actually sound worried about her? She dismissed the notion. Not Zac. He'd made it perfectly clear he only thought about himself. Her hands dropped. "Worry more about your own life, wizard. I can hold my own."

The bravado in her voice didn't reassure him. "Lark, I—"

"As much as I'm enjoying this enlightening conversation, I do have other issues to tend to." Diaz had moved, whipping forward so rapidly Zac could smell the foul stench of the lunatic's breath.

He turned slowly, a pirouette as graceful as a ballerina's, but much more lethal. "You'll get your chance."

"My chance is now."

"Look out!" she cried.

Diaz lunged, his vicious black talons curled into lethal daggers.

Whirling, Zac dropped to one knee, fisted his hand, and held it straight out. A flash of lightning shot from his knuckles, but Diaz moved quickly. Ducking, the sorcerer whirled mid-air, righting himself without so much as a wrinkle in his black robe.

"I wondered if you'd gotten rusty with your magic. I hoped I'd have a worthy opponent."

Zac stood, shoulders squaring. "Well, far be it from me to disappoint you." As his eyes touched the sorcerer's face, he knew today would be the final time he would come face-to-face with Diaz.

There would be only one winner in this battle.

The air rippled with energy. Lark inhaled the scent of wood burnt from the sizzle of Zac's fingertips. The sorcerer and the wizard faced off, and she positioned herself at Zac's side, waiting with tensed muscles for the next move. Too focused.

She didn't anticipate the first strike.

Diaz struck her hard, his hand crashing against her cheek like a forty-pound sledgehammer. The blow sent her reeling, spinning her into the air. Pain shot through her temple. Blinding. Agonizing. She struggled to right herself before the ground rushed up to greet her.

In an instant, strong arms captured her, protecting her, lowering her gently to the ground. She barely had time to thank Zac before he whipped around and directed his fingertips toward the center of the sorcerer's chest. Flashes of lightning zigzagged across the sky, slashing around their feet.

The dry ground ignited, creating circles of flames.

Diaz shot up into the sky and landed back on the ledge, roaring with laughter as destruction danced overhead. "I seem to have upset you."

Hand still holding her cheek, she stared as the slow metamorphosis took place once more. The man faded away, leaving behind only the remnants of a human. Standing in front of her now was a powerful, almost overwhelming wizard… dressed in full battle gear.

The robe suited him, the deep scarlet enhancing his bronzed skin, but his eyes captivated her. As cold as six feet below the Antarctic, they shimmered, reflecting back her own image, and she shivered.

This was why her father had sent her—the wizard standing in front of her. Pushing to her feet, she took hold of his arm. "You knew my father would send me to you, didn't you?"

Zac's eyes didn't flicker. "Marcus had his own ways, just as I have mine." His knuckles brushed down her cheek. "This battle isn't really yours, sweetheart. Diaz was only using you."

She closed her eyes for a moment. She'd known there'd be a reason Diaz had targeted her city, her friends, and family. "He wanted me to bring you here. Somehow, he must have overhead what my father told me… or read his mind… or something. He knew I would bring you to him."

"You were the bait."

"You knew?"

"I always knew Diaz and I would meet again. It was just a matter of time."

"Excuse me," Diaz sing-songed. "Could we wrap this up? I have a wedding to plan, and well, I'm sure by now the guests are on their way."

Zac barely moved and yet, he now stood at the base of the ledge. "Why don't you take me on, or don't you think your magic is strong enough to compete with mine? Are you worried you may be too old to win this time? Is that why you struck out at her first?"

The smile faded from the dark face. "I will take you on, Mr. Wolfe, but first, I'd like you to know once I kill you, she will belong to me." He inclined his head in her direction. "That smack was just to show you who is in control."

"You don't know me as well as you think you do, Diaz." She rushed forward, leaped into the air, and planted her feet in the center of his chest. Twirling, she dropped back to the ground and took a fighting stance, hands extended.

Zac dropped to the ground and rolled, catching Diaz by the ankle and spun him into the air. He released him with a whip of his wrist, and only by a couple of inches did the sorcerer manage to prevent a collision with the rock face.

Zac took deep breaths while sparks tap-danced along his forearms, and twin, blue lasers illuminated the ground at his feet as his power flowed from every pore. He called upon every ounce of his magic, his ability, knowing he would need it to defeat this monster who'd tormented his family for the past century.

Smoothing the wrinkles out of his robe, the sorcerer flashed a grin that belied his foul mood. "I commend you on the excellent move. Your skills are much improved since we last met. Remind me again. Wasn't that when I had the unfortunate duty of killing your grandmother?"

Diaz opened his mouth and roared, the horrific sound sucking every ounce of oxygen from the air. As the deep cry pounded on the eardrums of his victims, he began to rise, his feet kicking the air to propel him forward.

Unable to breathe, Lark fell to her feet, her hands clutching her throat. Zac let out a loud curse and rose to meet Diaz in the air. Whirling forward, he closed his hand around the sorcerer's throat, silencing the howling.

Lark gasped for breath, and Zac remembered to breathe again. He squeezed his hand tighter around the thickness of Diaz's throat. "You bastard. You almost killed her."

Eyes bulging, Diaz bobbed his head as far as Zac's grip would allow. "I'd never kill what's mine, Mr. Wolfe, but you should know by now I will win, no matter the cost."

Catching hold of Zac's wrist, Diaz flipped him backward and spun to take a stance in the air. Like two aerial swordsmen, the two enemies collided in mid-air. Zac hooked one hand around Diaz's bony wrist to shackle him, and as they traded blows, sounds of sizzling flesh and electrical sparks filtered out into the night sky.

Curses became louder and more violent. Diaz reached for a handhold, something to help him gain control of the battle, but Zac anticipated his every move, diving and weaving until the sorcerer was exhausted, even with his own power.

"Damn you, wizard. You're not in this fight alone!" Diaz shouted, lunging forward with one last attempt.

"Wizards never fight alone!" His father's voice startled Zac, and he barely had time to flick a glance downward before the attack came again.

Diaz's fingernails extended into lethal daggers, and he lunged, but an impenetrable wall surrounded Zac, preventing even the sharpest of blades from reaching him. One by one, scarlet-robed wizards ascended into the air, each taking flanking positions around him.

Then the shield lowered, and a burst of energy, enhanced by the wizards now surrounding him, gave him the speed to surge forward, catching Diaz off-guard. His fist shot out with the force of a two-ton truck, blindsiding the sorcerer and sending him reeling.

Diaz spiraled out of control, headfirst toward the stony ground. Virulent epithets littered the air just as he struck bottom. He tried to push himself up, but Zac had already landed on his feet inches away from the fallen sorcerer.

"Your reign ends here." He didn't need to look back over his shoulder to see the guild had joined him, and as he held his fingertips toward the sorcerer, the wizards raised their hands in unison. Flames lanced the air, and Diaz screamed with pain as the fiery streaks consumed him.

Breathing hard, Zac lowered his hands to his sides. He didn't know what to say, how to respond to his family's arrival—his father's arrival. A hand fell on his shoulder with a reassuring grasp.

"It's all right, son." Edmund spoke in gruff tones.

He closed his eyes, guilt a bitter pill. "You killed Rena because she was evil, didn't you?" All this time, he had blamed his father for killing his wife. Only to learn he'd done what he had to do to protect the family… to protect his son.

The hand squeezed. "No, she wasn't evil. She'd just been controlled. There was no way to save her. The guild and I tried for weeks to break the spell, but Diaz was just too powerful at the time."

"If he's so powerful, how could we kill him now?" Pain streaked through his heart as he stared at the ashes at his feet.

"We killed him together. All of us, including you. We've never worked together against him." His voice breaking, Edmund stood in front of his son.

Zac accepted the words with a short inclination of his head. "Perhaps if we had, we could have saved Rena." He paused. "I could have saved her. When Lark came to me…" he broke off, his head snapping around. "Lark? Where is she?"

"She left."

Zac spun to face his brother. "What do you mean she left? She wouldn't just leave, not when Diaz had killed her sister. When did she leave?"

Jacob's eyes widened. "Once you'd killed him. She said to tell you goodbye."

Goodbye? He stood still for a long moment before anger set in. "Like hell." He left his family standing amid the smoke and ashes.

Lark felt him long before he approached her. She stood with her back to Zac, sensing his hesitation. "It's over."

"Yes."

Warm breath bathed the back of her neck, and the heat from his body touched her as he drew close. For a long moment, she couldn't think. His essence surrounded her, enveloping her in a pool of sensuality, making every inch of her body throb. When she found her voice, it shook like she hadn't used it in a while. "Why did Diaz hate you so much?"

"I don't know. I never got the chance to ask him. I would imagine it was because of my family, everything I had that he didn't." His shoulder bumped hers as he stood beside her, and Lark kept her hands at her side to keep from reaching out and touching him.

"I'm sorry about your wife." She didn't know what else to say.

"She died a long time ago."

"But you still love her."

"Yes, I'll always love her."

How was she supposed to respond to that? She remained silent, allowing the cool breeze to wash over her, sweeping away the past few weeks of agony, hatred, and lust. She should leave, but her feet wouldn't obey. She wanted, no, needed him to say something, anything.

"You didn't leave."

Her knees went weak. "I tried to. I even told your brother to tell you goodbye for me."

His hand caught hold of her elbow. "Did you really think I wouldn't come looking for you if you'd really left?"

"Why would you do that? We had a deal and—"

He pressed his fingertips against her lips. "Will you stop talking about the deal?" His breath sloughed out against her face, a warm rush of air. "We didn't just make a bargain, Lark." He lowered his head and his hand. "It was the only way I could think of to help you without looking like I was giving in."

She turned to face him, and the full effect of his gaze fell on her. He was so beautiful it almost hurt to look at him. "Would it have been so wrong to give in?"

He cupped her face, his thumb rubbing her lower lip. "For a wizard, yeah."

"But for a man?"

"Even worse." His lips curled upward. "So, do you really have to go?"

"Are you asking me to stay?"

The air hummed with electricity. "Yes."

"Why?"

"We have something here. I don't know exactly what that something is." He gave a short, abrupt laugh. "Hell, I don't think I could figure it out by myself if I had all the time in the world." He pulled her closer, into a tight warm embrace. "So I guess I'm asking you to stay so we can find out together."

She nuzzled his neck and pressed a kiss against his neck, her tongue tasting the salty tang of his skin. "You feel so good," she whispered.

He dropped his hands and dug his fingers into her hips. "Lark, I need to be inside you. I want to feel you pulsing around my cock."

How could she refuse such a pleading request? She gave his throat one last lick before pressing her breasts against his chest. "Then fuck me, Zac. Make it hard and fast." She barely got the words out before Zac snagged hold of her arms and danced her toward the nearest tree.

Sweeping his hand over her body, he removed her clothing before stepping out of his own. He pushed her back against the rough trunk, and his fingers dove between her legs to find her pussy, wet and swollen. He pushed inside in, driving so far into her channel that she gasped with the invasion. "You're ready for me, baby." He withdrew his fingers, hooked his hands below her ass and lifted her. "Put your legs around my waist and hold on."

Lark obeyed his order blindly, panting and clamping her legs around him with ferocity. He drove into her with such force her lungs protested.

Hips pumping wildly, he thrust in and out while the walls of her pussy contracted. He touched the spot inside of her that made her wild. Her nails scored his shoulders, and her teeth nipped at his skin, everywhere she could taste him, touch him. She felt full. Complete. And she never wanted it to end.

"Hold on," he ordered, driving into her furiously, wildly. The sensations overwhelmed her, dragged her under. Her muscles tightened, gripping his cock.

Zac pushed once more, and the orgasm punched her, releasing her into such intense pleasure she cried out. He continued to pump for a few seconds and then he jerked, coming with such force that he slammed against her, pressing her breasts flat against his chest.

He dragged breath into his lungs, his arms braced above her head. "This."

She lifted her gaze to see his face. Could her heart beat any faster? "This great sex could be what's doing the talking, you know. You might only want me to stay because of that."

This time his laughter sounded sexier, deeper. His arms wrapped around her waist, pulling her away from the tree and into his embrace. “The sex is great. I’ll give you that, but,” his head lowered, and he kissed her gently, just a faint brushing of his lips across hers, “you unravel me. No one else has done that to me.”

“We haven’t known each other long, Zac. This could be just lust.”

He cupped her ass and shifted, allowing her to feel the rising of his cock. “What if it’s more?”

She sighed and pressed her palms against his cheeks. “I’ll make you a deal…”

About the Author:

Rachel is a multi-published author of fantasy and paranormal romances and currently writes for Ellora's Cave and Samhain Publishing. She previously participated in a charity anthology with such best-selling authors as Susan Grant, Mary Janice Davidson, and Patricia Rice. A freelance editor and non-fiction writer, Rachel is also a business consultant specializing in helping start-up companies. Making her home on the East Coast, she also runs a publishing company dedicated to historical romances. For more information, you may visit Dawn's website at www.dawnrachel.com, *or you may read more about her at* www.moongladeeliteauthors.com.

Midnight Rendezvous

by Calista Fox

To My Reader:

I'm an adventurer at heart, so I enjoy creating characters with the same passion for life and excitement of the unknown. And what's more exciting than having a gorgeous man whisk you away to exotic locales for romantic, decadent midnight rendezvous?

For Cat Hewitt, all of her wildest dreams are about to come true…

As always, my deepest gratitude and appreciation to Alex and Cindy, my publisher and editor.

And to Mary J. Leader, a dear friend and mentor who inspired the topic of CVD in this book, and the importance of heightening awareness of this disease, especially with women. And to Dr. Maguire for his insight in this area.

Chapter 1

"He ditched me, didn't he?" Cat Hewitt asked with a sigh of resignation as she plopped into the red-velvet upholstered chair in front of McCarthy Portman's desk.

Rendezvous' attractive dating guru stopped typing on her laptop and lifted her green eyes from the screen. McCarthy smiled ruefully. "You really do have bad timing, Cat."

"Not intentionally," she said in her defense. "I had to go to Jersey. The printer screwed up the invitations for the Healthy Hearts Gala. I'm only, like, what? Five minutes late?" Cat consulted her Cartier watch and cringed. "Ouch. Okay. So I'm *twenty*-five minutes late. Damn it. That's twice in one week."

Cat had already taken care of the majority of the details for her upcoming fundraising event, but these crazy little blips that cropped up were beginning to wreak havoc on her personal life.

She craned her neck and glanced toward the lounge behind her, hoping to find Jeremy Lorenzo somewhere in the crowd. The club, stylish and intimate as it was, was devoid of one seriously good-looking ad exec.

Cat's attention returned to McCarthy, who gave her a sympathetic look. "Jeremy left ten minutes ago with Mia Casey."

"Just my luck," Cat muttered as she snapped her fingers. For six months now, she'd been a member of the Rendezvous dating service, which was housed in this upscale Manhattan wine bar. She had yet to find her perfect match, and the search was becoming a bit disheartening.

Her gaze drifted to the far corners of the club, sweeping over the cozy lounge with its plush red-velvet furniture and soft lighting. Everywhere she looked, couples were hooking up. Some huddled close together on the crescent-shaped sofas. Others slow-danced in the far corner. A sultry jazz tune wafted on the air and mingled with the lowered voices surrounding her and the occasional soft, evocative sound of feminine laughter.

The intimate moments Cat witnessed at Rendezvous made her painfully aware of the one thing her life lacked. Admittedly, it stung a little to see so many other women who were part of the exclusive dating service find their perfect match. Cat desperately wanted to find hers… but her track record of late suggested that dream might remain unrealized.

Tamping down the pang of loneliness that had crept up on her, she forced herself to be optimistic as she pushed aside thoughts of Mia and Jeremy.

More fish in the sea, and all that good stuff…

She was just about to ask McCarthy who was next in her golden database of possible Mr. Rights when Cat's eyes scanned the far end of the lounge and landed on a gorgeous male specimen sitting at the bar. Her gaze homed in on the mysterious man.

In a heartbeat, she forgot about her missed date with Jeremy Lorenzo. In fact, she pretty much forgot all about McCarthy, too.

Instantly mesmerized, she watched from afar as her mystery man lifted the crystal glass sitting in front of him. He took a long sip of what Cat guessed to be scotch. Likely the really expensive kind, if his appearance was any indication.

Dressed in black pants, a crisp white dress shirt with the sleeves rolled up to the elbows and a crimson-colored tie, the man who piqued her interest looked more Wall Street than secret agent, which should have made her discount him right away.

Cat wasn't looking for another Country Club Clone. She'd had enough exposure to stuffy, conservative types who didn't understand or accept her need for sparks. Adventure. Intrigue. Excitement.

In Cat's book, monogamy did not have to equate to monotony.

Yet, something about the hunk at the bar made her think he wasn't at all the staid, boring executive-type she'd been in a dating rut with for the past few years. In fact, there was a distinct edge to this man. Confidence and raw sensuality oozed from him. The determined set of his jaw, his casual movements, his very essence screamed cocksure sexuality.

Only once before in her life had Cat run across a man who exuded this sort of animal magnetism, which was disturbing and uncomfortable in a purely erotic way.

Her gaze remained locked on him, like he was a tractor beam, pulling her in. His body language spoke volumes, captivating her further. He was cognizant of his surroundings, yet somehow disconnected from them. He obviously hadn't found what *or who* he'd been looking for at Rendezvous. That notion sent a little thrill shooting through Cat, for it meant he was still *looking…*

She felt drawn to him for some inexplicable reason. Lured by the contradictory mixture of casual nonchalance and intense sensuality. He was aloof yet alluring. Unapproachable yet… tempting.

And terribly familiar.

"Dreamy isn't he?" McCarthy's gaze had obviously followed Cat's.

"That's an understatement." Cat heard the lust that had crept into her voice. Actually, it infiltrated all of her senses and left her feeling a bit off-kilter. Her insides tightened and the sudden, mysterious throbbing between her legs forced her to cross them in hopes of staving off the dull, achy feeling.

What the hell was that all about?

Despite the fact that she guessed the man at the bar to be a business tycoon of some sort, Cat's interest was quickly zooming off the charts. He had dark brown hair that was trimmed at a respectable length, yet still managed to look a bit unruly and unkempt. Like he was prone to running his fingers through it. Or perhaps he enjoyed driving around town in a convertible.

From what she could see of him, he had a strong profile, a broad-shouldered, muscular body, and a commanding presence. Cat eyed him intently, her curiosity mounting with every second that passed.

She didn't have to look around the bar to know he'd garnered a great deal of attention. Most of the single women who hadn't made a love connection or even a successful hook-up for the night tended to linger there, sipping cocktails and hoping their luck would somehow change. No doubt, every woman within a fifty-foot radius had her sights set on Tall, Dark and Dreamy. Cat was certain he didn't leave a dry thong in his wake. Hell, even she was feeling the effects of his sexy presence.

And the familiarity that settled deep in her bones made this experience even more exciting. Cat was sure they'd met before.

Curiosity gripped her. Suddenly, she was desperate to see his eyes. She suspected whatever color they were, his gaze would be enhanced by his tanned skin and dark hair. If she could just get a good look at him head-on, maybe she'd recognize him.

As though he sensed her gaze, knew on some cosmic level that he'd piqued her interest, he turned in his chair and stared right at her.

Blue. His eyes were a mesmerizing ocean blue. Clear and lustrous. Captivating.

Cat's breath caught. Getting the full effect—his intense gaze, his devastatingly handsome face, his powerful build—made her heart skip a few beats. He was even more gorgeous than she'd anticipated.

"Oh, my," she whispered, feeling a peculiar flare of exhilaration rocket through her body.

"No kidding," McCarthy agreed with a hint of lust in her voice. Obviously, she wasn't immune to his raw sexuality, despite the fact that she hob-knobbed with sexy single men on a daily basis. "His name is—"

"David Essex." Cat tore her gaze from the entrancing vision before her and turned her attention to McCarthy, whose mouth hung open for just a moment.

She recovered quickly. "You know him?"

"Sort of." David was the man she'd thought of earlier—the only man she'd ever met who'd sparked her libido within seconds of meeting him.

Absently tapping the corner of her small, red crocodile clutch against her chin, she called forth a bevy of extremely pleasant memories. Cat would never forget the night she'd met David Essex.

"The Plaza. Three years ago," she mused. "My father introduced us, then promptly disappeared—the only time my father has ever been so discreet, I might add. It took less than five minutes for me to decide I was hopelessly in lust with David."

"I can see why." McCarthy slid a quick glance in David's direction before returning her gaze to Cat. A blonde eyebrow lifted. "So? What happened?"

Cat recalled the evening. Meeting David had certainly been a high point. Not only was he extremely good looking, but he possessed a natural charm that had made her weak in the knees… and unbelievably aroused. But as was her luck, just when things were heating up between the two of them, duty had called.

"I literally left him mid-sentence," she told McCarthy. Her heart sank as she remembered the disastrous events that ensued. "The catering manager was threatening bodily harm to the wait staff for not getting the hors d'oeuvres out quickly enough and I had to intervene."

"Oh." Disappointment registered on McCarthy's face, making Cat feel like she'd somehow let her friend down. "That's it?"

"Well, let me think…" Cat searched her mind, piecing together more of the evening. Unfortunately, no juicy details were forthcoming. "He found me later in one of the corridors mumbling the standard 'what the hell made me think I could do this?' diatribe that all event planners mutter during their first solo event." David had been extremely kind. "He brought me a glass of champagne and assured me the gala was fabulous. He even wrote a donation check for ten thousand dollars."

McCarthy whistled under her breath. "Hell of a guy."

Cat nodded. "He was terribly sweet. I was completely captivated by him. And then…"

"Yeeesss?" McCarthy's green eyes lit up as she anticipated Cat's next words. Leaning forward in her chair, she said in a hopeful tone, "Did you take him home with you?"

"Oh, God, I wish!"

That night, Cat had been able to think of nothing better. The natural flirtation, the intense attraction… her mind had been consumed with thoughts of making love with David.

"Cat!" McCarthy said in a demanding tone. "Don't leave me hanging! What happened?"

The look of anticipation on McCarthy's pretty face clearly told Cat that she expected to hear an erotic tale. She wanted Cat to say that she'd taken David to her apartment—or, at the very least, had engaged in wild sex with him in some dark corner of The Plaza.

Cat wished that was the truth. She wanted very much to give McCarthy the sexy details she awaited. Hell, Cat would love to gloat about a hot and heavy romance with David Essex—that would mean it had actually happened. That they had actually followed the flirtation down its natural, beautiful course.

But…

Cat frowned as she envisioned the fateful evening.

"Shit," she muttered, wishing she could weave a mystical yarn of seductive intrigue and sexual gratification. Unfortunately, reality didn't always cooperate with one's fantasies.

"Now I remember what happened," she said, hearing the dismay that tinged her voice. "I was so nervous about the gala. And, of course, my drooling over David didn't help matters. My hands were shaking so badly that I ended up spilling my glass of champagne on his shoes." She let out a long-suffering sigh. "His really expensive shoes."

Cat had been mortified.

McCarthy made a face. "That's not the least bit romantic."

"It gets worse." Cat cringed at the memories that assaulted her mind. "I bent down to wipe the flood of champagne from his shoes with my napkin and somehow managed to topple the plate of appetizers he was holding. Scallops wrapped in bacon with a pesto-parmesan drizzle on top." Cat felt her body go limp as she slid a bit lower in her chair, somehow hoping to fade into non-existence. She felt her brow furrow. "Is he still looking at me?"

"Uh-huh. He's trying to place you. I can see the hint of recognition in his eyes, but… he's not quite sure he's got it nailed."

"Oh, God." She groaned. If only the floor would open up and swallow her whole. "You have no idea how terrible I felt. I mean, of all the things to smash against a man's chest. First, the green stain was permanent on his white shirt. And if that wasn't bad enough, even Club soda couldn't take out the fish smell and the bacon grease from his tux." Cat sunk a little lower in her chair. "Did I mention he was wearing a tux?" She rolled her eyes. "Armani, don't you know?"

"Jesus." McCarthy's dismay made Cat cringe further. "What did you do?"

"What *could* I do? I started apologizing profusely, and then…" Oh, yes! Salvation! "Another emergency cropped up in the kitchen and I literally ran away. Put as much distance between us as I possibly could."

McCarthy frowned. "That doesn't sound like you."

"I was twenty-three years old and working my first million-dollar event. What can I say? I crumbled under the pressure. I mean, come on, Mac. I completely ruined the man's clothes! What was next? I'd spill the Roasted Duck à l'Orange entrée in his lap? No, no." She knew the horror she'd felt three years ago was reflected in her eyes. "I had to cut my losses. You can bail water sometimes to salvage your pride, but other times you just need to jump ship."

"Well, you're about to get the chance to redeem yourself."

"Huh?" Panic slid up her spine.

"He's headed your way. Still trying to place you, but…" McCarthy could say no more.

Cat turned her head and her gaze connected with David's. His beautiful ocean blue eyes, which sparkled in the candlelight that softly illuminated the club, held a hint of mischief and intrigue. She'd sparked his curiosity.

Oh, how disappointed he was going to be when he discovered her identity!

Shit.

Forcing herself to sit up a bit straighter in her chair, she mustered the nerve that had gotten her through twenty-six years of her crazy existence. Oddly, she didn't have to manufacture a smile for David. It came naturally. Despite the horror of their last meeting, and the embarrassment she felt to this day, she was genuinely pleased to see him. He evoked the most erotically delicious feelings deep within her. Sensations that, until tonight, she hadn't experienced before or after their first meeting.

The humiliation of the past vanished as a sexy grin touched his lips. Fate had delivered David Essex to her once again. She intended to make the most of this unexpected, yet oh-so-perfect opportunity.

A second before he descended upon her, Cat sent up a silent word of thanks to God, the wayward printer in Jersey, and Mia Casey. Without them, she wouldn't be here right now, experiencing the sort of euphoria that settles deep into a woman's soul when she's finally discovered her true destiny.

For Cat, it was David Essex.

Chapter 2

"We've met before." David hated the sound of those words as they slipped, unbidden, from his mouth.

Lame, pal. Really lame.

The beautiful vixen before him grinned knowingly. "Yes, we have." She remembered him and was clearly amused that he couldn't quite place her.

The predicament disturbed him. David was great with names and faces. He usually remembered everyone he met. But there was something about this woman that made his recollection of her cloudy.

Determined to figure out the mystery, he said, "Don't tell me. It'll come to me." He studied her face a moment, finding it familiar. But really, it was her large, whiskey-colored eyes that drew him in, making him think of a time long ago when he'd been completely ensnarled by a gorgeous woman with the exact same eyes…

Aha! "The Plaza. Fundraising event. Two years ago." Thank God, he'd remembered!

Her smile deepened. "Three."

She stood in a graceful, fluid motion. Cresting at least five-foot-ten in her stylish leather boots, she was a perfect complement to his six-foot-three-inch height. She wore an off-white satin blouse and caramel-colored suede pants. She tucked a red handbag under her arm before extending a manicured hand toward him. "Cat Hewitt."

"Yes," he said, instantly recalling the evening they'd met. "You're Martin Hewitt's daughter." His hand enveloped hers. As her warm, soft skin caressed his, he nearly lost his train of thought. Latching onto a small bit of coherency, he added, "I'm David Essex."

"I remember." Her smile was bright and infectious. It made David smile.

Damn, she was gorgeous. An intriguing vibrancy seemed to ooze from her every pore. It was almost as though she knew something amusing the rest of the world did not. He was instantly hooked by her beauty and natural charisma.

Unwilling to relinquish her hand, he simply loosened his grip, yet still held her fingers almost entwined with his. The touch was intimate and enticing, as if they were longtime friends. Lovers, even.

He wished they were.

"The night we met is coming back to me," he told her. "You looked stunning in a lavender gown. Your hair was pulled up on the sides and it was long and curly. But it was…" He regarded her thoughtfully. Something about her was different. It took a few moments for him to figure it out. Drawing on his usually sharp memory, which seemed to be dulled by her alluring presence, he said, "Red."

Cat let out a soft laugh. "That's right." She leaned close to him and whispered in an almost conspiratorial way, "My Julia Roberts phase."

David nodded. "It was damn sexy. Although, I have to admit, this color is perfect," he said of her smooth, shoulder-length, chestnut-colored locks that were streaked with golden highlights. "You're even more beautiful. I didn't think that was possible, but…"

She shook her head while still grinning at him. "I see that wicked charm of yours is still intact."

"It's either a gift," he said as he lifted a shoulder nonchalantly, "or you inspire me."

This seemed to please her, if the shimmering of her amber eyes were any indication. "Quite charming," she said in a soft voice.

David suddenly wondered why the hell he hadn't dated this woman. She was stunning. And her smile was breathtaking. Why had he been so foolish as to let her get away three years ago?

Again, he tapped deep into his memories, conjuring up images of the charity event he'd attended, envisioning her perfectly. They'd had a few laughs, had been deeply attracted to each other. But then something had happened. What was it?

Ah, yes…

David frowned. "You ditched me."

She laughed. It was lighthearted and genuine. The sound seeped deep into his soul. "I didn't ditch you. I had a catering emergency."

"I remember. The pastry chef was chasing the sous chef through the back alley with a butcher knife. For the life of me, I couldn't fathom what a pastry chef would be doing with a butcher knife. But you never returned to fill in the blanks. Nor did you leave me your phone number—or give me any indication that you wanted me to find it out on my own."

Pink patches tinged her otherwise perfect, golden complexion. "Pierre, the pastry chef, was upset with the sous chef because he'd used the berries for Pierre's *crème brulee* to garnish the appetizer platters. And the reason I didn't give my number was because, well, I suspect if you recall the incident prior to that little emergency, you'll know why."

He narrowed his eyes on her. Something else had happened that evening. What? He thought back to the time when Martin had introduced them. They'd talked. She'd disappeared when duty had called—emergency number one. He'd found her again, pacing in a dark, quiet corner. He'd tried to settle her nerves with champagne. And then…

His brow furrowed.

Cat offered, "I suspect you had a very expensive dry cleaning bill."

The sudden recollection had him laughing. "You seemed hell-bent on mucking me up," he said when he'd composed himself. "Male ego made me hope you were just trying to get me out of my clothes, but then you disappeared…"

"I was mortified. And in way over my head with the gala."

"You pulled it off perfectly. Really. It was a flawless event. No one but me—and the kitchen staff—knew about the attempted homicides."

She laughed again. So sweet and natural. It warmed David's insides. "You are extremely charitable. In many ways," she seemed to add as an afterthought.

David grinned at her, extremely pleased that there was already a bit of history between them. He recalled that Cat had sent a check to his office, offering to pay for his tux to be cleaned. He'd sent it back with what he'd thought was a clever note, inviting her to contact him. But then… nothing. He'd never heard from her again. Ego made him hope the note had somehow gotten misdirected and had never reached her.

Despite the fact that she'd never called him, he was very interested in seeing her again. Considering she was here at Rendezvous, he felt safe in assuming she was still single. He couldn't keep himself from seizing this unexpected opportunity. "I'd like to have dinner with you the next time I'm in town."

Her eyes twinkled with what he hoped was excitement. "That would be nice."

"I wish we could do it tonight, but I've got a plane to catch."

"Give me a call the next time you're here. I'm in the book."

He nodded. Reluctantly, he released her hand. "It was good to see you again, Cat."

"Likewise."

He stepped around her and held a hand out to McCarthy, who attempted to appear as though she hadn't eavesdropped on the entire conversation. "It was a pleasure to meet you," he told her. They shook hands. "Thanks for the information."

"Anytime. Let me know if you have any questions about our membership."

"I will." He turned back to Cat. "Seriously? *'I'm in the book'*?"

Her smile was warm and intimate. "I suppose I could make it a little easier for you."

"I was forced to spend the rest of that evening smelling like a fish bin left too long on the wharf. I think you owe me one."

She reached into her small purse and pulled out a business card. Handing it to him, she added, "My cell phone number."

"Much better." He accepted her offering. His gaze lingered on her a few moments more. He really didn't want to leave. Every fiber of his being wanted to spend more time with Cat. It took all the willpower he possessed not to cancel the plans he had for the rest of the week and stay in New York. But he had business to focus on.

"It really was nice to see you again," he told her.

Her smile would forever be engrained on his brain. "It was definitely a pleasant surprise."

"Well, good night." Regretfully, he turned and walked away.

"For a minute there, I didn't think he'd be able to tear himself away."

McCarthy's voice barely penetrated the deliciously wicked thoughts Cat was currently having about David's gorgeous backside. He slung his suit jacket over his broad shoulder as he sauntered away and Cat's gaze naturally followed the path, down the expensive material to where it ended, just above the greatest ass she'd ever seen on a man. Even in loose-fitting dress pants, his well-built physique was discernible.

"Yum," she whispered under her breath. Damn, he was sexy.

"I think that's a mutual sentiment," McCarthy said with a chuckle. "And P.S., you were just coy enough to reel him in."

When David disappeared through the tall doors at the entrance of the club, Cat finally tore her gaze away and looked at her friend. "I'm sorry. What were you saying?"

Amusement flickered in McCarthy's green eyes. "Oh, nothing. Just that I can cross David Essex off my list of potential members. Something tells me he's found what he's looking for. He's totally smitten."

Cat eyed her with mounting curiosity. "Oh, really? You deduced that from our five-minute conversation?"

"It was closer to ten. But, yeah." She shrugged her shoulders nonchalantly. "What can I say? It's a gift."

"I won't dispute your talent," Cat said as her gaze drifted back to the entrance of Rendezvous. She secretly hoped David would return. "But if he's as interested in me as you think he is, why didn't he set a date for our… date?"

"Well, I can't read the guy's mind, but my guess is that he's got a pretty heavy schedule and probably has to consult his calendar first." McCarthy seemed to consider this for a moment, then added, "You know he lives in San Francisco, right?"

"I remember him mentioning it when we first met. So why do you suppose he was checking out Rendezvous? Did he say anything about moving here?"

McCarthy shook her head. "As far as I know, he's not moving. But he travels here a lot for business. I suspect he hasn't found what he wants on the West Coast, so now he's scoping out the East. But like I said, his search is over."

"You can be so cocky when it comes to matches," Cat said with a laugh.

"Are you telling me you're not equally smitten?"

"Oh, no! I'll admit I'm—I'm…" Cat gave serious consideration to the emotions swirling around inside her. *Exhilaration, elation.* Her body thrummed with the kind of sexual awareness people in lust waxed poetic about but which Cat had never fully experienced. Oh, she'd gotten a taste of it during her first meeting with David, but it had been nothing like this. Her insides seemed to be electrically charged, sizzling and snapping with a vibrancy that made her feel super-charged.

In fact, it took a great deal of effort to keep from bouncing around the club in her euphoria. She stayed rooted where she was, though not quite able to get her insides to settle down. She still felt like she was about to jump out of her skin.

Her soon-to-be-sister-in-law, Cassandra Kensington, had once described this feeling to Cat. Cass, who owned Rendezvous, had said that when she'd met Cat's older brother, Dean, she'd felt a peculiar cosmic shift. Like the stars and moon had come into alignment and that perfect moment had been captured between the two of them. Cass had known, in that instant, that she'd found *the one.*

As bizarre as it was to admit it, Cat felt the same way about David. When he'd held her hand—such a warm, gentle touch; yet intensely erotic when his thumb had lightly brushed her knuckles—she'd felt that curious flutter in her lower belly that told her the attraction between them was real and substantial. She felt it still. The stirring in her soul was another indication that David was not just a passing fancy. Fate had brought them together, and every fiber of her being wanted to see him again—to get to know him better.

Cat let out a soft laugh. "Oh, my God," she said in a quiet voice as realization dawned. "I think I'm in love."

"Well, that wouldn't be the strangest thing to happen at Rendezvous," McCarthy said, clearly amused.

"Yeah, well. Considering my track record, it's certainly strange for me."

"So you don't mind that he lives on the opposite end of the country?" She posed the question again, forcing Cat to really consider her answer.

A few moments ticked by. Cat shrugged. "It would definitely keep things fresh and interesting. You know I don't have a lot of free time. I don't necessarily need someone at my beck and call. In fact, I think it might be kind of exciting."

McCarthy hit a button on her laptop computer and proclaimed, "Consider him deleted from my database."

"Ah, it's good to have friends in high places." Cat gave McCarthy a quick hug. "I'll call you when I hear from him. Which had better be tomorrow. If he waits the standard three days to call, I don't think I'll survive it."

McCarthy grinned. "You have nothing to worry about. Trust me. I'm an expert at this, and I can tell you… he's gonna call. In fact, you might want to check your cell tonight. I wouldn't be surprised if he calls from the airport."

"No…" Cat eyed her friend speculatively. Yet a jolt of excitement that targeted her still-throbbing pussy made her breath catch. "You don't really think…? Oh, never mind. I'm not going to get my hopes up." She tucked her clutch under her arm. "I mean, it's just that he's so—*Wow.* Gorgeous doesn't even do him justice." Cat shook her head. "Seriously, Mac. I've never felt this way before."

"Ah, young love." McCarthy whistled under her breath. "So beautiful."

Cat laughed. "We'll see. How about lunch next week?"

"You're on. Call me."

Cat left Rendezvous with a smile plastered on her face. She couldn't seem to contain it. Maybe she really was in love.

Remembering McCarthy's words, she retrieved her cell phone from her purse as she traveled the long, dimly lit corridor. She accessed her voicemail system, hoping David had left a message. True, it had only been a few minutes since he'd left Rendezvous, but she couldn't resist.

As she reached the spiral staircase that led downstairs, Cat heard a peculiar noise that startled her. An eerie, strangled cry echoed at the far end of the hallway. She gripped the black wrought iron railing. Her other hand held the phone. She depressed the disconnect button with her thumb. Leaning back, she craned her neck to peer down the long, dark corridor. Professional suites comprised the opposite end of the floor that housed Rendezvous. Since it was long past business hours, the lights were off in the offices.

Cat couldn't see much farther than a few feet, but she sensed someone was at the end of the hall. Watching her.

A spine-chilling sensation crept through her body and Cat shivered. A moment later, a flash of amber and the shifting of shadows made her jump. A black cat came scurrying toward her, hissing and screeching as though it, too, had just had the bejesus scared out of it.

"Oh!" Cat let out a soft cry as the mangy creature raced past her, sending a sharp hiss in her direction, before disappearing down the opposite end of the corridor.

Cat's heart had leapt into her throat. She laughed softly at her skittishness.

Shaking her head, she spared one last glance down the dark hall. The eerie chill that snaked up her spine told her someone still lingered in the shadows. She still felt as though she was being watched. Snapping her phone shut, she hurried down the staircase. At the landing, the bouncer of The Rage, another bar housed within this upper West Side building, rose from his stool.

"Everything okay, Cat?" Concern registered on his beefy face at her quick descent.

"Yeah, sure, Eddie." She waved a hand in a dismissive manner. "A cat just scared the crap out of me. Ironic, huh?" Her laugh was soft, albeit a bit nervous. She slid a glance up the stairwell. Her stomach clenched. Returning her attention to the burly doorman, she said, "I think there's someone up there."

"Probably one of Cass and Mac's lovebirds looking for a dark corner to f—"

Cat lifted a brow in amusement.

"Make out."

She grinned. "Probably."

"I'll check it out. Want me to get you a cab first?"

"No, thanks. I'll just go around the corner. There are tons of them this time of night." She waved goodbye and pushed open the heavy glass-and-metal door. Stepping out into the summer heat felt like slipping inside an electric kiln. Cat grasped her leather clutch in her hand and immediately began fanning herself. She stopped halfway down the block and bellied up to her favorite vendor.

"What'll it be tonight, Cat?"

She considered her options, then said, "Make it a drumstick, Vic."

"Good choice."

Vic manned a vending cart that boasted spicy Italian sausage served with sautéed peppers and onions on one side and ice cream bars on the other. The tantalizing smell of the sausage permeated the air and enticed Cat, but it was too damned hot to eat anything other than ice cream.

She accepted the drumstick in exchange for her five-dollar bill. "Keep the change," she said. It was a two-dollar tip, but she thought Vic deserved it for braving oven-like temperatures night after night.

As she tore off the wrapper and tossed it into the trash bin next to Vic's cart, Cat reveled in the fact that Manhattan was the perfect city. Whatever one wanted, one could have. No matter where they were in the city, no matter what the hour. She'd lived here her entire life, and couldn't fathom living anywhere else. Though Cat had traveled extensively within the country and abroad, she loved New York more than any other place. Despite the hot, humid summers and the cold, snowy winters, she thought it was *the* place to be.

"You be careful, Cat."

She smiled at Vic. "Always." She saluted him with her drumstick as she walked away.

Though Cat had no delusions about the crime in New York, she felt comfortable walking the streets of this neighborhood at night. For one thing, they were crowded with people. Also, so many of the neighborhoods had been cleaned up lately, and the people seemed to be a bit friendlier. As the familiarity of the city enveloped her, she forgot about her scary moment outside of Rendezvous.

Cat wandered down the street. The excitement she'd felt over her chance meeting with David Essex returned. She happily licked her ice cream, hoping to enjoy most of it before it succumbed to the heat and dripped down the cone. The thick, humid air clung to her skin as she walked, instantly dampening her blouse. Long strands of hair stuck to her now-moist neck. Cat didn't care. She was literally on Cloud Nine. All because of David.

She didn't bother suppressing the smile on her lips. At the moment, life couldn't be more perfect.

As she rounded the corner, however, she was jolted back to reality when she ran smack into a brick wall.

Chapter 3

Or rather, a rock-hard chest that resembled a brick wall.

"Oh!" She gasped, startled yet again this evening. Her eyes widened as she bounced backward and scrambled to maintain her footing. Strong hands shot out and grasped her biceps to steady her. Cat felt jolted to the core. The feeling didn't subside as she glanced up, her gaze connecting with clear blue eyes that glowed in the moonlight and seemed to dance with amusement.

"It's you," she said on a sigh. Her body literally melted under his entrancing gaze.

"So it is."

Cat felt swept away. She smiled up at David, thinking that Fate had intervened once again.

And in that instant, the vanilla ball sitting atop its sugar-coated perch slid over the edge and fell… landing right on top of David's black leather boot.

"Oh, hell." Cat squeezed her eyes shut, as if that would really make the whole thing better. As if she could somehow make the wretched image disappear if she simply ignored it. Cracking one eye open, she peered at his feet. Nope. Still there.

David let out a hearty laugh. "There you go again, trying to get me out of my clothes. You know, all you have to do is ask." The wicked glint in his eyes told her he was serious, despite the playful grin that touched his lips.

God, he was gorgeous. Cat lost all train of thought when he smiled at her. Her heart slammed against her chest and her stomach did an odd series of flips that made her think a three-ring circus had set up camp inside her. Erotic sensations coursed through her from head to toe and that intense throbbing she'd felt between her legs earlier returned. Only it was infinitely stronger this time. Her pussy pulsed like a beacon, demanding attention.

David released her arms. He gave a quick shake of his foot and the ice cream dropped onto the street. Taking the small stack of napkins from her hand, he bent down and swiped at the sticky remnants. He then pried the empty cone from her fingers and tossed it and the napkins into the trash.

Cat should have been mortified. Instead, she was mesmerized.

David's grin widened at her speechlessness. "I forgive you," he said in a soft voice.

"I should come with a warning sign." Was that her voice that sounded so breathy and seductive?

His eyes glowed in the moonlight. "Don't worry about it." His casual demeanor was one thing. The cool temperament mixed with the intense sexuality that exuded from him was enough to make her wet.

"So, why are you still here? You should be on your way to the airport by now."

"And I would be. But either there's an accident somewhere close by or my driver is engaged in a rousing game of craps in some back alley and he's forgotten all about me."

"Let's hope he's just lost."

David grimaced. "He's been driving me around this island for almost ten years. If he's lost, I'm in big trouble."

"Good point." She found it refreshing that he wasn't on his cell phone, barking orders into it as he demanded to know where the hell his driver was. The Country Club Clones she'd dated would do just that. If for no other reason than to try to impress upon her—and everyone else in the near vicinity—how important they were.

David didn't seem too worked up about his wayward driver. Admittedly, his down-to-earth attitude was a huge turn-on.

Add it the list…

A list that was growing by leaps and bounds this evening.

"Would you like me to get you a cab?" he asked.

Cat grinned. "Thanks, but I think I'll walk. It's a bit warm, but that moon is incredible."

He glanced up at the sky and her gaze followed. Narrow strips from the cloudy sky partially shrouded the moon, like three fingers stretching across it, leaving a crescent shape to glow in a vibrant golden color. The light also penetrated the fringes of the clouds so that the outline of a full moon lingered despite the fact that the perfect orb was slightly concealed.

"Interesting," David commented. "Eerie, yet intriguing at the same time."

"It's beautiful," she said.

David's gaze lowered. "So are you."

Cat forgot all about the lustrous moon. She smiled at David. Her stomach did that crazy Under the Big Top routine that had it flipping and twisting and fluttering in a way that made her a bit giddy. So unlike her. But there was a certain lightheartedness that David sparked. Along with intense desire.

It was intriguing and sensual. Deeply arousing.

Cat was about to comment on his evocative charm when a sleek black Town Car pulled up to the curb. The tinted window slid down and the driver said, "Sorry for the delay, Mr. Essex. Ped accident by Central Park. Everyone's okay, though."

"That's good to hear, Tony," David replied, his gaze still on Cat.

As though his driver knew they were engaged in a romantic moment, he raised the window, giving them some privacy.

Cat grinned. "He has really bad timing."

"Yeah, he does."

David's eyes were dark and seductive. They lingered on her lips, which twitched under his sensual gaze. She wanted him to kiss her. More than she'd ever wanted anything in her life.

"Well," she said. She knew she could stand on the street all night and stare at him. He was really too handsome for words. But… "You have a plane to catch."

"Let me drop you off."

She smiled. "I wouldn't want to make you late."

"That's the advantage of having a private jet. The pilots can't leave without me."

Once again, his cool reserve struck a sweet cord. After dating such uptight executives who felt compelled to check their cell phones and PDAs every two minutes—not to mention one who'd consistently reached for his Blackberry just as she was reaching orgasm—David's cavalier attitude was refreshing. And damned sexy.

But Cat didn't want to hold him up.

Okay, she did.

Considering she'd already dumped ice cream on him, she figured she'd made enough of an impression for the evening. "I'm gonna head on home," she said, still grinning. It was impossible to stop.

David nodded. "Okay, then."

She turned to go. His hand reached out and grazed her shoulder, then slid oh-so-slowly down her arm. The soft material of her blouse clung to her damp skin as his fingers swept downward, over her bicep and forearm. His warm skin caressed her wrist a moment before his fingers skimmed over her palm and twined with hers. A gentle pull had her turning fully to him. He took one step forward and closed the gap between them. Cat scarcely had a moment to pull in a breath before his lips touched hers. A whisper of a kiss. So soft and warm and fleeting, she could have dreamed it. But then his mouth touched hers again and her eyelids fluttered closed. This was no dream. This was the most erotic moment she'd ever experienced.

David's lips pressed to hers for only a heartbeat before they simultaneously opened their mouths. His tongue slipped past her teeth and swept over hers. His free hand cupped her cheek as his body melded to hers. The damp clothes and the moist skin from the humidity and the heat that arced between them did a wicked number on her insides. Her entire body went into sensory overload. His tongue delved deeper, teasing hers, tangling with it in a sensual dance that left her molten and damn near singed to the core.

Her fingers skimmed over his side, up his rib cage. She clasped a fistful of now-limp white cotton, literally clutching at him, holding him to her. His hand, in turn, moved from her face and plowed through her damp hair, his fingers burrowing deep in the long strands.

Cat heard a whimper of need lodge in her throat. David deepened the kiss. Their bodies were pressed together, yet she felt the insane desire to get closer to him. Even more so than she currently was. She longed for their clothes to melt away, wanting desperately to press her naked breasts to his warm skin. She wanted their limbs entwined, every inch of their bodies touching each other.

As David's kiss became more impassioned with every second that passed, Cat could think of nothing else but having him inside her. She wilted under his touch, her entire body seemingly liquefying. She could feel the tremble in her legs, a slight vibration that worked its way up to the apex where her sex throbbed in wicked beats.

The sounds and smells of Manhattan at night faded into non-existence. All that registered was the feel of David's lips on hers, the tantalizing sweep of his tongue, the warmth and strength of his fingers as they remained twined with hers, the heat and sensuality that engulfed her.

This was how she'd dreamed of being kissed from as far back as she could remember. This was the kind of passionate, erotic, fully engaging kiss that she'd longed for. David delivered it with such skill, such intimacy, she wondered how she'd live until their next kiss. It was that fabulous. That… perfect.

As he gently pulled away, she knew she should have bemoaned the loss. Her entire being felt the connection being broken as he moved away from her. But it really hadn't been broken. Even as he stepped back, his fingers releasing hers, his hand slipping from her hair, she felt an innate bond. It was mystical, magical. Something beyond her comprehension. It was erotically powerful, yet heartwarming.

"That was one hell of a first kiss." David grinned at her, slow and sexy. The lids of his eyes were at half-mast, as though he was clinging to the memory of their kiss, still entranced by it. His deep, husky voice intensified the sharp stabs of desire between her legs.

"I'll say." She was amazed she had a breath left in her body and a voice to speak.

"Now, I insist on driving you home."

"Are you sure you have time?"

He nodded before reaching for the handle on the door. She stepped past him and slid across the smooth leather seat. David climbed in beside her. His thigh brushed hers. It was a simple touch, yet it seemed so intimate. He sat close to her, despite the spaciousness of the car.

After she gave the driver directions to her apartment, which was only a few blocks away, David turned to her.

"Do you have a passport, Cat?"

"Of course."

A flash of white teeth gleamed in the dim lighting that filled the car. "I have to fly to Cabo San Lucas for business meetings tomorrow, but I have the late evening open. Would you have dinner with me?"

Her heart skipped a beat. "In Cabo?"

"Yes."

Cat could barely contain her excitement. She'd never been whisked away to an exotic locale for dinner. It sounded terribly romantic. "I suppose I could make it," she said. Though her words were casual, her tone definitely wasn't. Even she could hear the thrill that had worked its way into her voice.

"I'll send my jet back here tomorrow to pick you up." The car stopped in front of a tall, narrow building on the corner with a dark green awning out front that had *The Mont de Terre* elegantly scripted across it in gold. "Tony will drive you to the executive terminal to meet the plane."

"Sounds intriguing." Instinct had told her David wasn't a stuffy, conservative type. She'd wanted adventure and excitement, and by all counts, she'd found it.

"I'm looking forward to seeing you again, Cat." His tone was low and sexy. Suggestive.

"Thanks for the ride."

He nodded. Then he leaned toward her and she prepared herself for another one of his warm, sensuous kisses. His lips skimmed over hers for the briefest of moments. Then his mouth pressed to hers. Once again, erotic sensations consumed her body. Heat and desire flooded her veins as his tongue delved deep into her mouth, tasting her, teasing her. When he pulled away, she felt deliriously happy. Filled with anticipation of things to come.

Smiling at him, she said, "I hope you have a nice flight."

"You, too." His eyes sparkled with mischief. "See you tomorrow night."

He reached for the door, but she stopped him. "You don't have to walk me up. I'm sure you're late as it is." She slipped out of the car, her tall heels hitting the concrete curb. She swayed just a tiny bit and stifled a giddy laugh. She'd gone weak in the knees again.

As the car drove off, Cat stood on the sidewalk, watching it go. All she could think was thank God she'd been late to Rendezvous tonight. Otherwise she would've left with Jeremy Lorenzo and missed this incredible, magical meeting with David.

"Everything alright, Miss Hewitt?" The doorman asked.

She turned and glanced over her shoulder at him. "Absolutely, Jack. In fact, it's damn near perfect."

Chapter 4

"Shit."

David stood in the middle of the *mercado* and frowned. He should have asked what Cat would like for dinner. Instead, he'd been wandering the aisles for the past fifteen minutes, wondering what the hell to cook for her.

This is insane.

Those kisses had obviously scrambled his brain. Jesus, he couldn't think straight. He'd even had trouble concentrating on business today. That was something that never happened.

Get a grip, man.

Finally deciding on seafood enchiladas, he started collecting ingredients. Fresh lobster, shrimp and crab. Spanish rice. Vegetables and tortillas. He added a bottle of tequila to the bounty, just in case she wanted some local flavor, though he'd brought champagne from his personal cellar. An exclusive label from his favorite vintner's private reserve, which he sensed Cat would appreciate.

Given her family name, he was pretty certain she had refined tastes. Martin Hewitt was considered to be one of the most respected and well-known criminal defense attorneys in the country. Like David, Cat came from a well-established, wealthy family. His heritage was rooted deep in San Francisco society, hers in New York society.

Back at the condo, he whipped up a small feast. He spooned a creamy cheese sauce over the enchiladas and left them to bake in the oven. He then set the table out on the terrace, complete with white cloth linens, expensive dinnerware and Baccarat crystal. He lit the candles in the large hurricanes until the terrace was alight with a romantic, golden glow, accented by the moon.

It was a clear, starry night. Lights from the harbor and marina, which his condo overlooked, twinkled in the distance. To the south were Lover's Beach and the arch at Land's End, poised on the very tip of Baja.

He couldn't show off the view to Cat tonight, but maybe in the morning they'd have time to hop a glass-bottom boat and head over to El Arco. He wasn't sure how long she could stay; in fact, inviting her to a midnight rendezvous on the spur of the moment was a bit impractical, but David had been desperate to see her again.

He'd been relieved when Cat had accepted his unorthodox date. It said two things about her, both of which were monumentally important to him. One, she liked spontaneity. Two, she was flexible with her time.

And, if he wanted to add in a third point, he'd found it heartwarming that she trusted him enough to meet him in another country. Granted, he came with excellent references, even from her father, but he was still relieved that she felt comfortable being alone with him.

The soft chime that drifted through the open patio doors indicated it was midnight. Cat would arrive any minute. He put the final touches on the romantic setting and turned on the CD player that was loaded with sexy south-of-the-border music.

The ambience was perfect for their first date.

The doorbell sounded, though he'd left the door unsecured, a note taped to it, telling her to come in. His excitement mounted as he stood out on the terrace, sipping champagne, hoping he'd succeeded in creating a memorable setting that would not only impress Cat, but maybe sweep her off her feet. At least a little.

Cat stepped through the patio doors and onto the terrace. Wearing a satiny, curve-hugging dress that created the illusion that liquid gold had been poured over her long, luscious body, she stole David's breath with ease. Though her smile was a bit tentative, as though she was a little overwhelmed, her eyes were alight with mischief and excitement. And David suddenly knew—all the way to the core of his being—that the connection he'd felt last night was real.

She walked with movie star grace. The tall heels of her gold sandals clicked softly on the tiled floor, keeping time with the sultry music that drifted on the night air. She joined him at the intricately designed wrought iron railing that encompassed the terrace. Bougainvilla climbed up the surrounding trellis, the purple and fuchsia buds making a vibrant display against the black railing and the deep green vines. David handed her a glass of champagne.

"*Bienvenido*," he said in a soft voice.

"*Gracias*."

Cat drew in a long sip, her seductive gaze locked with his. She might be young, but she certainly knew how to wield her sensuality. David wondered, not for the first time since Cat Hewitt had invaded his life with the force of a twenty-ton wrecking ball, why this gorgeous, exciting woman was still single. Despite her age, he honestly couldn't understand why another man hadn't snatched up this precious gem years ago.

But then he acknowledged his good fortune, happy she was still available.

When she lowered the glass, her smile turned more confident, all trace of hesitancy vanishing quickly. "This is a lovely reception," she said in her smooth-as-silk voice. "I'm impressed."

Relief washed over him. He hadn't realized how much importance he'd placed on this evening until she'd given her approval. His shoulders, which had been bunched tight without him even realizing it, began to relax.

"I've never been to Cabo," she told him. "My parents preferred vacationing in Europe and Asia when my brother and I were kids, and I really haven't had much of a chance to travel on my own."

"Unfortunately, you can't see the sights tonight, but this is the perfect spot at sunrise. Land's End is over there," he said as he pointed south.

"Do you take time out to sightsee when you travel?"

"Not as much as I should. Sometimes it feels like I spend more time inside conference rooms or on my plane than I do outside."

"Not one to make your deals on the golf course?"

David chuckled. "My game consists of several hours of extreme personal humiliation."

"You don't belong to a country club, then?"

He eyed her curiously. A hopeful glint flashed in her gaze. "No, I don't have time to hang out at the country club."

Cat's grin widened and David couldn't help but smile along with her, despite the fact that he had no idea what they were smiling about.

He studied her a moment as a warm, sultry breeze blew off the gulf, ruffling the long, curly tendrils of chestnut-colored hair that framed her face. She wore her hair up, exposing a long neck he longed to brush his lips over. Her golden skin glowed in the moonlight. Everything about this woman stirred his senses.

David knew he'd made the right choice in bringing her to Cabo.

Dinner tasted as heavenly as it smelled. Not only was Cat impressed by the romantic mood her date had created on the terrace, but the feast he'd prepared was to die for.

As was David.

Cat suppressed a grin as she dabbed at the corner of her mouth with her napkin. She set the linen on the table, beside her empty plate, on which a crumb would die a lonely existence.

"The seafood enchiladas were amazing," she told him. The food was rich and decadent. The champagne was the best she'd ever tasted, and the company…

Warmth flooded her veins at the mere thought of the fabulous man sitting across from her. He was charming and intuitive. He'd asked her intelligent questions during dinner. He'd told jokes. He'd made her laugh. He'd made her smile. And now he was waiting patiently for her to decide whether to indulge in the *flan*, the traditional Mexican dessert he'd made.

Of course she couldn't resist. Even though she'd practically stuffed herself to the gills already. The fact that David had cooked the meal and the dessert made her want to scarf down every last bite.

She lifted her gaze to the man who sat across from her. He eyed her with what looked like curious fascination as she sampled the *flan*. His intense gaze sent a ripple of excitement up her spine.

"*Muy delicioso.*" A sigh escaped her lips.

David's obvious fascination with her intensified. "You speak Spanish?"

"Fluently. As well as French, Italian, Russian and German. My Japanese is a bit weak because I rarely use it anymore, but I can muddle through simple conversations."

"Amazing."

Cat waved a hand in a dismissive manner. "It's really not that impressive. I just had very diligent tutors."

Shadows flickered across David's face as the flames from the candles in the tall, thick hurricanes danced and swayed in the gentle breeze. His ocean blue eyes, large and mesmerizing, seemed to glow in the soft light illuminating the terrace.

"You're an exceptional cook," she told him.

David looked pleased that he'd impressed her. "You're not the only one who had diligent tutors."

He reached for the pot of coffee and poured her a cup. The strong aroma wafted under her nose, teasing her senses. Cat knew even the coffee he served would be rich and decadent.

She eyed David over the rim of her cup. Never before had she met a more stimulating, sexually arousing man. It wasn't just his looks that captivated her. Sure, he had a perfectly sculpted face that would look great on the cover of a magazine. And she could tell he had a well-toned, muscular body beneath the dove gray dress shirt and black dress pants. He'd rolled the sleeves of his shirt up to his elbows and his powerful forearms lent credit to her assessment.

Aside from his dreamy appearance, he had a commanding presence. He seemed to take up a lot of space… as though he infiltrated all of her senses on a visceral level she couldn't quite explain.

Cat could think of nothing better than getting naked with him. She'd waited a seriously long time to find the right bed partner. The few sexual experiences she'd had fell miserably short of hot, but she knew—deep in her soul—that would not be the case with David.

The air around them practically sizzled with sexual tension.

If she had inhibitions—and she really wasn't sure if she did because she'd never been with anyone who'd pushed the sexual envelope—she had no doubt she'd shed them in a heartbeat with this man.

Stifling the wicked grin that teased her lips, Cat finished her dessert and coffee, then stood when David pulled her chair back. They walked to the railing. The black canvas above them was dotted with sparkling stars; the placid water below was illuminated by the moon and the lights from the marina. The air held the hint of fragrant spring blossoms.

David stood next to her at the railing, his elbow propped on the wrought iron. His other hand rested lightly on the small of her back. His touch was so gentle, in fact, Cat wondered for a moment if she were imagining it. But then his fingertips grazed the bare skin and her breath caught. The back of her dress dipped provocatively low, coming to a V just below the spot where his hand currently rested. The dress flowed over her body and the hem skimmed her ankles. Thin gold straps sat on her bare shoulders and the neckline brushed the tops of her breasts.

Cat wore nothing but matching thong panties beneath the dress. No other piece of lingerie could be worn discreetly under the body-hugging material. Fortunately, her breasts were small enough to be suitable for such fashion; *unfortunately*, her lack of clothing had her body in a constant state of arousal, particularly with David standing so close, his fingers grazing her exposed skin.

Her nipples tightened and she was grateful she was facing the ocean, not him. When he leaned a bit closer to her and whispered in her ear, she felt a sharp stab of desire between her legs.

"Do you have to be home early tomorrow?"

Cat's stomach fluttered. She glanced at him over her shoulder. "No. I took care of everything before I left."

David's blue eyes glowed in the candlelight. A sexy grin touched his lips. "I'd like to have breakfast with you."

Cat held his gaze, and her breath, waiting for his next words.

"In bed."

Chapter 5

He was leaving it up to her, putting the ball in her court, so to speak. David didn't want to be presumptuous, and he sure as hell didn't want to make her think he'd invited her to Cabo just to sleep with her. Truth was, if she said she'd prefer to sleep in one of the guest rooms, he'd respect her decision and still want to see her. He wouldn't get much sleep because he'd be thinking about her in such close proximity to him, but he'd honor any request she made.

But damn if he didn't hope like hell that she'd accept his invitation. He wanted her. More so than any woman he'd ever known.

David eyed her from head to toe, thinking he'd never seen such an entrancing vision. She radiated sensuality in a way that made his groin tighten almost to the point of being painful.

She seemed to contemplate his offer for a few moments. The smile that touched her soft lips gave him the answer he sought.

He stepped behind her. Reaching around her, he placed his hands on the railing, on either side of her slim hips. Dipping his head close to hers, he inhaled the fresh, intoxicating scent that was hers alone. His eyes drifted closed and he simply basked in the moment, enjoying the heady sensation building inside him.

He felt her body tense and heard her breath catch as his head bent lower and his lips skimmed over the warm nape of her neck. From base to hairline, his mouth eased over her skin, his tongue just barely teasing her. She shivered, and it spurred his excitement, his need to please her.

He placed a soft kiss behind her ear, and Cat let out a low whimper that was nearly the death of him. His cock strained against the fly of his dress pants, his heart hammered in his chest. Her response to him evoked a wealth of sensations deep inside him, making David's entire body vibrate with desire.

"You are so stunning, Cat," he whispered in her ear. "And you have the most beautiful smile I've ever seen."

She exhaled, letting out what seemed to be a long breath she'd been holding. She leaned back against him and the top of her head nestled right under his chin. They were a perfect fit.

"Mm. That was nice," she said in a soft voice.

David smiled as he wrapped his arms around her waist and held her. "You're one hell of a woman."

"You don't even know me yet."

"I'm an excellent judge of character." He was also a man who went after what he wanted. And right now, he wanted Cat.

She turned her head and tilted it upward. His lips brushed over hers, softly at first. But even the slightest touch ignited a fire deep inside him. His mouth pressed against hers and when she parted her lips, inviting him inside, David took full advantage of the offering. He kissed her long and deep, his tongue tangling with hers, eliciting a moan from her.

When he pulled away, they were both breathless. The passion-induced haze that filled his brain made him a bit light-headed. David couldn't remember the last time he'd been so entranced by a woman, so deeply ensnarled. It was a nice change of pace to push business far from his mind and let his thoughts be consumed only by sexual desire.

His arms loosened around Cat. His hands skimmed her narrow hips. The satiny feel of her dress under his fingertips made him desperate to know what her bare skin would feel like against his. The need to touch her, to hear her sigh with pleasure, to bury himself in her warm depths wreaked havoc on him. He knew he was moving a bit fast, but he couldn't help himself.

Yet he didn't want to scare her off with his hot pursuit. He gauged her reaction to him as his lips swept over her exposed neck again. Then down the long, delicate line of her spine. Her soft moan was all the encouragement he needed. As his mouth returned to her neck, his hands eased over her backside and down to her outer thighs.

"Stop me if I go too far," he whispered in her ear.

Leaning forward, Cat placed her hands on the railing, wrapping her fingers around the warm wrought iron. When David had kissed her neck, it had sent a myriad of sensations coursing through her body. As David's warm lips had trailed over her spine, Cat had seriously thought she was going to lose all control. She shivered at the lingering sensation of his mouth on her sensitive skin, his warm breath teasing her flesh, his tongue sliding so gently, so lightly over her spine that it created the most intense, tingly sensation from head to toe.

His creative kisses intensified the dull ache that had taken up residency between her legs since the moment she'd laid eyes on him at Rendezvous.

David's hands skimmed over her dress. He pressed his hands against her thighs, moving them upward to her waist, bringing the thin, slippery material with him, hitching up her skirt several inches until the hem swirled around her bare knees. The slit that ran up the back of the dress now started just below her bottom. She could feel the breeze that ruffled the material and tickled her exposed skin. Cat closed her eyes and pulled in a full breath.

Stop me if I go too far.

Having sex on the first date wasn't her style, but Cat had no intention of stopping David's hands from blazing their wicked trail. She wouldn't even conjure up excuses for her wanton behavior. She wouldn't blame her reckless abandon on the sultry, summer weather, the flickering candlelight or the sexy salsa beat pulsing from the CD player. She wouldn't blame it on the soft glow of the moon or the glittery twinkle of the stars.

She wouldn't even blame it on the man whose hands were now sliding down the remainder of gold material that covered her legs, then slipping beneath it.

When David's large hands caressed the bare skin of her thighs, she knew there was no one at fault for her lack of willpower.

David Essex was the man Cat wanted to explore all of her sexual fantasies with. He was too damned sexy to resist, too tempting to deny, even if it meant breaking a few of her dating rules. The desire he sparked was simply too enticing, too erotic, and much too wanted for her to pass up.

No, she wouldn't be asking him to stop anytime soon. If ever.

"You have a beautiful body, Cat." The hem of her dress was now draped around her waist. She was bent forward just enough to keep the satin material in place while David's hands explored her body. His long, tapered fingers lightly grazed her bare bottom, sending an erotic shiver up her spine.

Cat eyed him over her shoulder. His gaze was on her backside. He appeared to be deep in thought, making Cat insanely curious to know what wicked contemplations were taking place inside his head.

She wondered for a brief moment if there was anything she would deny him.

Although she wasn't all that experienced with sex, she definitely wasn't naïve about it. She had an active, creative imagination. Cat had some very specific fantasies she'd like to fulfill and positions she'd like to try. She sensed David was the adventurous type, and that excited her all the more.

When David eased down to his haunches behind her, Cat's breath caught.

"Spread your legs for me, Cat."

She widened her stance. His hands slid slowly up each leg, gently caressing her calves, the sensitive flesh at the backs of her knees, then higher still. His thumbs grazed her inner thighs and a shudder of desire made her teeter on her tall heels, but David held her steady. His warm breath on her skin made her tremble. Then his mouth followed the path one of his hands had taken.

Cat's eyelids fluttered closed and she let out a low sigh. David's lips skimmed her bare bottom, his hands inched higher until his thumbs grazed the swollen flesh between her legs.

It seemed to have been a long journey, as though she'd waited ages and ages for him to find his way to the part of her that needed him the most. The intimate, private part of her that begged for his attention.

Both thumbs eased beneath the miniscule swath of satin material covering her and he slowly stroked her wet flesh. Cat's teeth clamped down on her lower lip, stifling a whimper of need that tickled her tongue.

He dragged her thong panties down her parted legs. She lifted first one foot, then the other, and he tossed the lingerie on a nearby chair. David stood, but his hands quickly returned to the apex of her legs, one reaching around the front of her body to caress her sensitive clit while a long finger slipped inside her from behind. Cat let out a soft cry, despite her attempts to remain quiet. She couldn't help it. His hands felt incredible on her body…

And she knew he was just getting started.

"I want to make you come, Cat. It's all I can think about…" His voice was tight, strained. He sounded as though she'd be doing him a favor by letting him pleasure her, yet she was the one reaping the reward.

A second finger pushed deep inside her and Cat gasped. She couldn't remember it ever being like this, couldn't remember ever feeling this turned on or excited. Maybe it was the way he had seduced her, with such subtle finesse. Maybe it was just him, in general, and the innate connection they shared.

As his fingers plunged deep inside her, stroking her, bringing those incredibly delicious, all-consuming sensations within her reach, the pad of his finger pressed against her throbbing clit. Her hands tightened on the railing. Her breath came in shallow, heavy pants. Soft whimpers fell from her lips as every fiber of her being embraced the passion building inside her, working its way toward a powerful crescendo.

When it hit, Cat cried out from the intensity of her orgasm. It gripped her body like a tight fist, squeezing the air out of her. Her inner walls clenched around David's long fingers, keeping him captive inside her as she held fast to the exquisite sensations that consumed her.

On and on it went, until eventually, her body relaxed. David's hands eased away and he wrapped his arms around her, steadying her as she swayed on her heels, her knees nearly buckling.

Holy Christ.

If that was just his opening act, she was in for one hell of a night.

Chapter 6

David held her for several minutes, her bare back pressed to his chest. He needed time to not only let her breath return to her, but to give *his* a chance to resume some semblance of normalcy as well.

When he felt a small measure of control return to him, he loosened his grip on her, but she remained in his embrace. David's head dipped and his mouth grazed her long neck before Cat turned her head toward him. Her chin lifted so he could capture her luscious mouth in another long, slow, sexy kiss. His hands skimmed up the bare expanse of her back, his fingers slipping under the thin straps at her shoulders. His palms slid down her arms, taking the dress with them. The shimmering material dropped to the tiled floor, pooling at her feet.

David broke the kiss, his heart thundering in his chest. His eyes roamed her naked body. She was exquisite. His hands reversed their previous route, sliding up her arms to her shoulders, then down her bare back. His lips teased her neck and she shuddered against him. David's pulse raced and his cock throbbed with the overwhelming need to be buried inside her.

She turned in his loose embrace and smiled up at him. There wasn't a hint of reservation or inhibition in her eyes, but the corner of her mouth quivered slightly as she eyed his mouth.

She wants another kiss. David was more than happy to oblige. Hell, he'd do anything she wanted. Whatever she asked of him, he would willingly consent to.

He dipped his head and drew her into another passionate kiss. She turned fully and wrapped her arms around his neck as she pressed her body against him, making David painfully aware of his need to feel her silky skin against his. He wanted to be naked with her, wanted to explore every inch of her body, wanted to love her slowly, for hours on end.

When she broke the kiss, they were both breathless. Her arms slipped from his neck and her fingers went to work on his tie and then the long line of buttons on his shirt.

"I'm not sure what's causing me to be so reckless, so impatient," she said, her voice tinged with desire. “Maybe it’s the moon again.”

David grinned as she tugged at the hem of his shirt, pulling it from his dress pants.

When his shirt fell open and her hands splayed over his abdomen, she let out a faint moan. “Did you put something in the champagne?”

“No,” he whispered as his eyes closed. Her hands felt like heaven on his body.

“I can’t explain this insatiable need to touch you.” Her palms moved over his chest. She leaned toward him and her warm mouth slid over his pectoral muscles.

David’s hands clasped her shoulders, holding her in place, holding her steady. “Sometimes, you just know when it’s right. I knew it the second I saw you at Rendezvous.”

“Me, too.” Her tongue flicked his small nipple and he let out a low groan.

“Cat,” he whispered. “I want to know all of your fantasies. I want to fulfill every one of them.” His lips slid over her jaw, up to her mouth. He kissed each corner, then stared deep into her sparkling eyes. “I would do anything for you, whatever you want.” He meant it, and he wanted her to know it. “You can ask me to do anything.”

Her mouth quivered. Her small breasts rose and fell with her soft pants. She held his gaze for a moment before it slid down his body. “I want to make you feel as out of control and reckless as I do.”

Her hand skimmed down his abdomen. Lower still, until the backs of her fingers brushed the fly of his pants, making David damn near jump out of his skin.

His jaw clenched as he suppressed a low growl. He closed his eyes, prayed for a bit of restraint, certain he wasn’t going to find any. “Anything you want, Cat,” he repeated.

“I want to make love to you. With my mouth. I want to make *you* come.”

He was halfway there. Her fingers went to work on his belt and then the button and zipper on his fly. Distracted for the briefest of moments when her tongue toyed with his nipple again, she garnered David’s full attention when her hands slipped inside his pants and pushed them over his hips, along with his briefs. Cat eased down to her knees before him.

It was practically the death of him. How the hell he would survive this was beyond him. Not only was Cat gorgeous, but she was bold and daring. The combination did a wicked number on his senses.

Her fingers slid over his tip, then down his shaft. David widened his stance, as much as he possibly could, considering his pants were down around his knees. He braced himself for what was to come, but he had a feeling it wouldn't be enough. Already his body began to tremble with need and anticipation of what she was about to do to him.

While she held him loosely in her hand, Cat's tongue slid up his shaft. David groaned, low and deep. His fingers threaded through her hair, making a mess of her sophisticated hairstyle. He found the pins that secured the thick strands on top of her head and carefully pulled them out, until her hair spilled over his hands and down her back.

As her tongue slid over the tip of his hard cock, swiping at the moisture that pooled there, he pushed his fingers through her hair from temple to crown, lifting the strands off and away from her pretty face. He wanted to watch her as she took him deep in her mouth.

She sucked him hard, and David surged toward a powerful orgasm. As her head bobbed up and down and her warm, wet mouth sheathed his erection, enveloping him in erotic bliss, David held fast to his control. She pulled him all the way in, until his tip bumped the back of her throat. His fingers swirled around the silky strands in his hands. He massaged her scalp with a slow, sensual rhythm inspired by her diligent and wicked ministrations.

"Cat." He murmured her name. "Sweetheart…"

She cupped his balls with one hand, drew him deep inside her mouth and that was all David could take. He let out a loud groan as he climaxed. She continued to suck, taking all of him.

"Oh, God." He groaned again as he shuddered, feeling powerful aftershocks because he was still in her mouth.

Finally, when she eased away, David reached for the railing. He gripped it with one hand to steady himself while he raked the other hand through his hair. Cat stared up at him, a pleased look on her beautiful face. She tried to contain the smile that threatened her lips, but he could see it was an impossible feat. The corners of her mouth trembled and finally she gave up. A slow grin spread across her lips.

David chuckled as he pulled up his briefs and fastened his pants. He reached a hand out to her, helping her to her feet. "That's some technique you possess."

Her smile widened, as though it did great things to her ego to know she'd turned him to putty in her hands. "I was just going by instinct. Responding to your body, letting your reaction guide me."

His arms slid around her waist and he pressed her body against his. Whispering in her ear, he said, "I actually meant that I would do anything *to you* that you wanted."

"You said you would do anything for me. And what I wanted you to do was to let me pleasure you."

"Let me just say, this is one night I will never forget."

"Me, either."

His lips grazed her temple and he drew in a full breath, inhaling her luxurious scent. "It's still early, as far as I'm concerned."

"I slept on the plane, so I'm well rested."

David knew his grin turned wicked as he said, "Shall we take this inside?"

Chapter 7

He collected her dress and panties then scooped her up in his arms and carried her into the condo.

"What about the mess we made on the terrace?"

"I have a cleaning staff that will take care of everything in the morning. Don't worry about it."

Cat snuggled close to him, nuzzling his neck. She inhaled deeply and let out a long sigh. "You smell wonderful."

He set her carefully on her feet when he reached the bedroom. David crossed to the walk-in closet and hung her dress next to his garment bag. He stripped off his tie and shirt, then returned to where she sat, in a hunter-green, oversized chair.

David knelt before her and reached for her leg, gently palming her shapely calf. He slipped her sandal off one foot, then the other.

Cat's smile was slow and languid. As though she was completely relaxed, and maybe reveling, just a tiny bit, in the feminine power she wielded.

David rubbed her feet, his thumbs gently massaging the arch before he slipped the tip of his fingers between her toes.

She let out a soft, sensual sigh. "That feels incredible. Those sandals go perfectly with the dress, but they hurt my feet."

"Did I mention that you completely took my breath away when you walked onto the terrace?"

A deep shade of pink crept up on her cheeks, adding a rosy tinge to her flawless, golden complexion.

David frowned. "I didn't mean to embarrass you."

"It's not what you said—what you say. It's…" She shook her head. A deep furrow marked her brow. "It's *how* you say it." Cat studied him a moment, a mix of curiosity and intense fascination on her pretty face.

His frown deepened. He stopped massaging her foot. "I'll admit that my dating skills are a bit rusty."

The soft, sweet laugh that echoed in the room perplexed David all the more. Until Cat elaborated.

"If you call this rusty, I'm going to be in way over my head when you're back in practice. You are seriously charming."

David finally grinned as relief washed over him. "You had me going there for a minute.

She shook her head. "It's just that you make me feel so special."

"You are special." His gaze locked with hers and he was pleased she didn't look away.

His hand moved up her calf, over her knee to her upper thigh. He was glad she felt comfortable being completely naked in front of him.

"You're beautiful and you're sexy. I want to make you *feel* as sexy as you are, Cat."

He moved between her parted legs. His head dipped to her breast and his tongue swirled around the tight center. Cat's soft sigh told him all he needed to know. She liked his touch, liked the attention he paid her gorgeous body.

But when his mouth moved down her flat stomach to the juncture of her legs, she stiffened. David's lips grazed her inner thigh and he felt her muscles tense. He glanced up at her, curious about her response.

Cat looked contrite. "Sorry. It's just… no one's ever… I mean, that's just so…"

"Intimate?"

She nodded.

"No man has ever made love to you with his mouth?"

She shook her head.

"Oh." For some reason, the knowledge that he'd be the first to love her in this particular way excited David all the more. "I promise you'll enjoy it."

Finally, her body relaxed a little. "I don't doubt that. It's just that I haven't had a lot of experience. Sexually. Most of the men I dated in the past didn't possess your attention span. They were too busy making deals to make me come."

David's hands skimmed over her legs, his thumbs grazing the soft muscles of her inner thighs. He massaged her warm skin, helping her to become familiar with his touch. He wanted her to feel comfortable with him, wholly uninhibited. It was more important to him than anything else.

"I told you to stop me if I went too far," he said. "Just say the words, Cat. So I'll know."

"I don't want you to stop," she whispered. Her eyes shimmered in the soft light that filled the room. Her gaze was intense as she searched his face and his eyes, looking for what, he didn't know. But the soft smile on her lips told him she was sure about what they were doing, if she wasn't quite so sure of herself or her body's reaction to him.

That brought him a small measure of comfort. It also made him infinitely more attentive to her emotional needs, as well as her physical ones.

David's dating skills might be rusty, but no one had ever accused him of not knowing how to treat a woman with respect.

When his head dipped again and Cat knew his intention, she forced herself not to tense up the way she had before. She wanted David's mouth on her, wanted to experience all the erotic pleasure he could bring her.

As his tongue made little circles on her inner thigh, Cat tried not to writhe and wriggle beneath him. He teased her sensitive flesh, causing her pulse to race. Soft sighs and gasps escaped her lips as his mouth moved further upward. When she felt his warm breath on her slick skin, Cat swallowed a moan. She closed her eyes, clamped down on her lower lip. She could only imagine how exquisite it would feel to have David's mouth on the most sensitive, intimate part of her.

She waited with bated breath for the moment to come. When it did, when David's wicked tongue eased over her swollen lips, Cat couldn't contain the small cry that rushed from her mouth.

David gave her little more than a split second to assimilate to his touch, to prepare for his erotic onslaught, before his thumbs opened her and his tongue caressed her sensitive folds then pressed against her throbbing clit.

"Oh, God," she whispered on a hard pant. Nothing about his subtle seduction could have prepared her for the intense pleasure that consumed her. Her hands pressed to the cushion of the chair and she lifted her bottom off the seat, pressing herself against David's mouth, wanting, needing, *demanding* more.

His hands slipped beneath her and cupped her cheeks. His tongue swiped over her wet, swollen flesh in long, languid strokes before he concentrated on the sensitive nub between her legs. He licked her clit. Drew it against his teeth, then soothed it with his tongue.

Cat didn't know how to react. Her legs were spread wide, she was completely open to him and he seemed to be drinking her in. Nothing had ever felt so incredible. So erotic. She didn't want it to end. Ever. But she knew she was close to coming. It was impossible to stave off the powerful climax that was building.

He shifted his hands and pushed a finger inside her while his mouth continued to devour her. Cat's heart thundered in her chest and her breath came in short pulls. She opened her eyes and watched him pleasure her as she surged toward another mind-blowing orgasm.

"Oh, yes." She whimpered. Then she pleaded with him, saying "Please make me come." She wanted it more than she'd ever wanted anything in her life. More strangled cries escaped her lips. "Please, *please…*"

David didn't let up. He slipped two fingers deep into her wet pussy. As every sensation converged and ignited inside her, creating an inferno that raged through every inch of her, Cat cried out his name.

Chapter 8

David knew he should wait. Give her a few minutes to catch her breath. But he couldn't stand the thought of not being inside her. *Right now.*

In a heartbeat, his pants were unfastened and pushed down his hips, along with his briefs. He retrieved a condom from his pocket before he tossed his slacks toward the chair in the corner. After impatiently tearing the foil and rolling the condom down his hard cock, he leaned over Cat. His hands rested on the thick arms of the chair, on either side of her. She gasped for air and clutched at his biceps with a death grip.

Her head was propped against the back of the chair, her eyes were closed. David couldn't hold back another second.

"I want to make love to you."

"Yes," she whispered in a hoarse voice. "Please make love to me. Now."

Her small chest rose and fell with her sharp breaths. The corners of her mouth quivered. David knew he'd never seen a more beautiful sight.

As he eased into her—much more slowly and gently than he wanted to—she wrapped her long legs around his waist. When her grip around his midsection tightened, coaxing him deeper inside her, David knew she was as swept away by their passion as he was, as in need of fulfillment as he was.

But he forced himself to go slow, giving her a moment to adjust to his thick cock in her tight canal. She was wet and warm, enveloping him in an erotic casing. She stole his breath. David closed his eyes, reveling in the sensations she so easily stirred.

When he felt a small measure of composure return to him, he began to move inside her. Slowly, he nearly withdrew from her, then eased back inside her. Cat gasped. Her hands roamed his body, from shoulders to chest to abdomen and back again. Her fingers then twined in his hair and she pulled his head toward hers. He kissed her, long and deep as he plunged into her, increasing the tempo as his tongue tangled with hers.

The long legs around his waist gripped him tight, holding him against her.

She broke the kiss. "You feel so good inside me," she whispered. "So perfect. So full."

David groaned. "Just looking at you makes me hard, Cat."

She seemed pleased by his admission. Her eyes darkened as desire filled them. "Tell me what you want to do to me."

David felt his cock swell even more. It seemed impossible, but damn if she didn't make him even harder. His jaw clenched for a moment. Thinking straight was quickly becoming a difficult feat. But if telling Cat some of the erotic thoughts he had got her hot, he was all for talking dirty to her.

"I want to make you come. I want to take you from behind, Cat. I want you on top of me, underneath me. I want to make love to you in every position imaginable. I want to make you so hot that you beg to have my cock inside you."

"I already have begged."

He grinned down at her. "No. You haven't even begun to beg for it, Cat. But you will."

She bit her lower lip for a moment, then released it. "You know how much I want you."

"As much as I want you." He needed her to know that this was a mutual attraction, that as much as she may beg for him, he would do the same for her. "Now, tell me what *you* want, Cat."

She arched her back and lifted her bottom off the chair, pressing against him. Her hips picked up the rhythm he'd set and, within seconds, helped to increase it. "I want you to come, David."

His growl was low and primal. "You want to feel me come inside you?"

"Oh, God, yes." Her head thrashed from side to side. The breath escaped her parted lips in sharp puffs. "Just thinking about it… makes me… oh, God." She moaned, low and deep. And then he felt her inner walls clutch him tight as she convulsed all around him.

David groaned. "Don't stop," he whispered as he pushed deeper inside her. She held him tight, so damn tight that it made him come. He let out a groan that filled the quiet room. She continued to squeeze him as his body convulsed, as his cock surged and pulsed inside her. A moment later, he felt her come again and he whispered more erotic words into her ear as she rode the wave of desire to completion.

Chapter 9

David placed a tray full of food at the foot of the bed then crossed to the tall windows that comprised the far wall. He drew open the curtains and Cat gasped in awe at the sight of the sun casting stunning rays of vermillion and gold over the choppy water.

"It's beautiful," she said, suddenly feeling very awake, and very alive, despite the early hour and the long night of lovemaking she'd engaged in.

Heat tinged her cheeks at the thought of her night with David. She should be ashamed of herself for being so wicked. And on the first date, no less. But she couldn't bring herself to feel guilty over her decadent behavior. The only thing Cat felt at the moment was incredible.

David settled into bed next to her and explained the monstrosity he'd created, complete with *huevos rancheros, chorizo*, roasted potatoes mixed with sautéed green peppers and onions, and hot salsa.

It smelled fantastic and her stomach grumbled loudly in approval.

Cat laughed. "Sorry."

David grinned. "No apology necessary. We worked up an appetite." He hefted a fork full of eggs and offered it to her.

Cat's toes curled. Could the man be more incredible? She sampled his delicious creation, rolled her eyes heavenward and sighed happily. She might gain ten pounds while dating him, but she'd enjoy packing on every single ounce. He was an amazing cook.

After they devoured breakfast, they snuggled under the thick covers. Cat rested her head on his broad shoulder and enjoyed the feel of his large hand sweeping up and down her bare back. Her palm splayed over one well-defined pectoral and her fingernail grazed his small nipple, causing him to groan.

She smiled, thrilled by her sexual power. David was one hell of a catch. Smart, successful and sexy. Cat couldn't believe her good fortune. And the sparks that flew between them! Unbelievable. She'd finally found everything she'd always wanted.

Except…

She sat up in bed, holding the sheet to her chest. "McCarthy said you were interested in information about Rendezvous. Why would you choose a dating service in New York?"

David looked taken aback. He rubbed his jaw a moment, then stretched his arms toward the headboard. He stacked his hands on the plump pillow and rested his head on them. "Truthfully? I've dated plenty of women in San Francisco and not one of them…" He shook his head, as though searching for the right words. "Compares to you."

Cat eyed him for a moment. "Okay, that was the perfect answer." But there was still a niggling thought tickling her brain. "Except that you didn't *really* answer my question. Are you considering moving to New York?"

He shook his head.

"Are you thinking of opening an office in Manhattan?"

Again, his head moved from side to side on the pillow.

Cat gave this some serious thought. Although she'd told McCarthy at Rendezvous that she wasn't opposed to a long-distance relationship, she suddenly wondered how much of a challenge it might actually be. Especially considering her intense attraction to David, and the strong desire to spend time with him.

"Hey," David said in a soft voice as he reached for her and pulled her back into his arms. Cat had no choice but to settle beside him, her head returning to the hard wall of his chest. "That doesn't mean I don't want to see you when I'm in town. Or when I'm in San Francisco, for that matter. Or when I'm traveling. If you can swing it, of course. Is that a problem?"

Cat wasn't sure. Really, it was much too soon in their relationship to worry about logistics. Still… "So you do plan to spend some time in New York, right?"

He grinned at her, slow and sexy. "Much more so than I'd originally thought."

This placated Cat, set her mind at ease. David let out a long yawn as his hand lazily caressed her bare arm. They lay in silence for a few minutes, and Cat enjoyed the languid feeling that swept over her. She felt comfortable and relaxed in his arms.

Until David expectedly shifted in the bed, forcing her onto her back. Cat giggled as he settled between her parted legs and kissed her collarbone, then the top of her right breast. "How do you feel about Europe?"

She smiled at him. "Love it."

"Good," he whispered. "I spend a lot of time there." His lips brushed the inner swell of her breast. Up and over until his tongue playfully flicked her nipple, causing it to pebble. Cat twined her fingers in his thick mane of hair as she surrendered to his sensual assault.

A soft sigh escaped her lips as he continued to lave and suck her nipple.

"You know, I've always admired people who devote their time to helping others," he said in a low voice, his warm breath teasing her nipple, making it even tighter. "I have a lot of respect for you, Cat."

"I love orchestrating fundraisers. Especially for heart disease research. People just don't understand how serious it is." Cat heard the usual conviction that entered her voice when she spoke of this topic. She continued to run her fingers through his hair, loving the intimacy of the moment. "It doesn't have the emotional pull breast cancer does. Must people don't even realize that cardiovascular disease is the number one killer in America and the majority of people who die from it don't know they have a problem until it's too late."

David's gaze turned intense. "Why is it so important to you to raise awareness and money for research?"

Emotion suddenly welled inside her. "My favorite tutor died of CVD three years ago. She'd had some problems, which she'd promptly taken care of. She felt perfectly fine for a while, then passed away one night in her sleep. It was a complete shock. So unexpected and tragic. She was only forty-two," Cat added on a sad note. "She was a remarkable woman. I miss her every single day."

"I'm so sorry, Cat."

His sincerity and empathy touched her deeply. She had always believed in love at first sight, and Cat was quite certain she'd fallen in love with David at Rendezvous. The feeling had only continued to intensify. He was an incredible man. Warm and sensitive. Not to mention sexy as hell.

A smile touched her lips. Thoughts of David chased away the melancholy that had crept up on her.

"Do we have time for a boat tour before we have to return to the real world?" she asked, ready for a change of subject, a lighter mood.

David grinned. "It's already arranged. We can head over to the marina whenever you're ready."

A wicked thrill inched up her spine. "I'm not quite ready to leave this fabulous bed." One palm eased down his sculpted abdomen to his penis, which grew hard in her hand.

"You're insatiable." He let out a low groan as she stroked him. "I love it."

Chapter 10

Cat retrieved her mail from the appropriate box in the lobby of her apartment building. As she took the elevator to the eleventh floor, she opened the one piece of mail that wasn't a bill or solicitation. Cat unfolded the letter and read it twice, the frown on her face deepening as the words from a man she didn't know sank in.

Dear Miss Hewitt,

I am in desperate need of your help.

My wife suffers from a brady cardiac arrhythmia and her health is steadily deteriorating. Unfortunately, we have limited means to provide her with adequate medical care. Nor can we afford the treatment she desperately needs. I left my job last month in order to care for Lydia full-time. Our insurance has run out and I can no longer afford the care she has received these past few years.

I am appealing to your generous nature and empathy for CVD patients. I hope that you can put us in touch with a specialist who would be willing to help Lydia.

My wife means more to me than my pride, Miss Hewitt. I beg you to help us.

Sincerely,

Carl Henry

Cat's mouth gaped open. She'd never received a letter like this, had never had anyone ask her to help them with such a dire, tragic situation.

She folded the letter and put it in her tote bag, along with her other mail. She stepped out of the elevator and walked down the long corridor to her corner unit.

Carl Henry had included his home address and phone number beneath his signature. He seriously thought Cat could help him.

But what could *she* possibly do?

She was an event planner who coordinated fundraisers. She wasn't a doctor or a nurse. She didn't have close, personal friendships with heart specialists.

Although…

Cat inserted the key in the deadbolt and gave a quick twist of her wrist to release it. She did know a cardiologist well enough to pass along Carl Henry's information to him. Perhaps Dr. Conner could help Lydia Henry. As she pushed open the door, she decided she'd call the doctor as soon as…

Cat drew up short and gasped at the sight before her, shocked to find her spacious apartment filled with vases of roses in every shade imaginable.

She closed the door behind her, dropped her tote and keys on the hallway table and then stood in the foyer, eyeing the vast collection of gorgeous flowers.

David.

She let out a soft laugh and shook her head in amazement at the various arrangements. The vases sat on every available surface, including the hardwood floor.

A knock on the door startled her. She yanked it open and found her landlady, Mrs. Koslov, standing on the threshold, her hands clasped together at her ample chest, a look of sheer delight on her wrinkled face.

"I know I should not have let the florist in without your consent," she said in her thick Russian accent. "But I simply could not resist." The heavy-set woman peered past Cat at the numerous floral displays scattered throughout the place. In Russian, she added, "It is so… *romantic*." Mrs. Koslov let out a lengthy sigh.

Cat couldn't help but smile. "It is romantic. And overwhelming. But mostly, it's romantic."

"Here," the older woman said as she handed over an envelope. "The delivery man insisted I give this to you personally. He said your male friend sent it by Federal Express, and he did not want you to overlook it."

Not a chance in hell, Cat thought. She was dying to know what sweet sentiment David had personally penned.

She couldn't get Mrs. Koslov out of her apartment fast enough. Cat all but shooed her away so she could admire the gorgeous flowers and read the note that accompanied them. She sank into the chair next to the phone and pulled in a full, deep breath. The air in her apartment was fragrant, filled with a rich, intoxicating scent that stirred her senses.

Her fingernail slid under the seal on the back flap of the envelope and she pulled out the crisp white note card that held David's embossed monogram at the top and one neatly scripted paragraph in the middle.

I don't know your favorite flower, but I look forward to finding out what it is. Why don't you tell me Saturday night? Have dinner with me… in Paris.

His signature graced the bottom of the note card.

Smiling at the sight of David's name, Cat reached for the phone and called him to accept his invitation to have dinner in Paris. Then she left a message with Dr. Kevin Conner's service.

Chapter 11

"The complex in Berlin is perfect for professional offices," David said into his cell phone as he paced the spacious living room in his Paris flat. "But it's zoned for residential. I need you to look into regulations and put together whatever documents necessary to expedite rezoning."

"I'll get right on it," said Donovan Kelly, head of David's legal team. "But I'll warn you, my German's not so great."

"Don't worry about that. I know someone who can help us with translations." David drew up short. Throughout the day, there were at least two dozen things that occurred—be it something someone said or did—that triggered a memory of her, making him desperate to see her.

"You still there, David?"

"Yeah, sorry." He tried to collect his thoughts, but Cat still lingered in them. He couldn't suppress the stupid grin that played on his lips. Cat had agreed to meet him here tonight, and he could hardly concentrate on anything else. He was working at half speed, it seemed, because his thoughts continually drifted to her.

And that incredible night they'd spent in Cabo.

Good God. The woman had an amazing body. She inspired the most erotic fantasies, and David intended to explore every one of them.

But right now, he had to wrap up this conversation with Donovan. "Find out what you can and report back to me tomorrow. And fax me the environmental assessment for the Aspen property. That's one hell of a location for a hotel, but we might have some impediments due to prior use of the land."

"I'll get on it. Enjoy your evening."

"You, too." David disconnected the call and placed his phone on the desk in the corner of the living room, where he'd been working all day. He straightened the documents sprawled over the rich cherry wood, then checked the fax machine to make sure it had an ample supply of paper.

Satisfied he had everything under control, he crossed to the gourmet kitchen and put the finishing touches on the salmon and asparagus dish he planned to serve this evening.

He selected his best bottle of champagne, then went to work on the *gâteau au chocolat et aux noisettes*—chocolate hazelnut cake—he intended to serve for dessert. Though he didn't know Cat's favorite rose, she had mentioned a chocolate fetish in previous conversations.

At midnight, the alarm on David's watch sounded. He double-checked the dinner and the dessert and then popped open the champagne. His driver had called from the airport to say Cat had arrived safely and they were on their way to his flat. She'd be arriving any minute now.

When the doorbell chimed not quite ten minutes later, David's groin tightened. He opened the door and his jaw dropped.

"*Bonsoir, monsieur David.*"

Standing on the threshold was not only the most gorgeous woman he'd ever made love to, but said woman was dressed in the most provocative French maid outfit he'd ever seen.

Her short, tight, black skirt hugged her shapely figure and barely covered the intimate part of her body he so longed to taste and pleasure. A delicate, pink lace apron was tied around her narrow waist. She wore a short-sleeved, cropped black blouse, tied just below her breasts and left unbuttoned enough to reveal the pretty pink bra that matched the apron. Fishnet stockings and tall, spiky, black patent leather high heels completed the ensemble.

She'd pulled her long, wavy hair back in an unruly ponytail. Long curls framed her face and dusted her neck. Her beautiful face was subtly enhanced with makeup and her full, lush lips were glossy and wet-looking.

The woman made his heart stop.

David ushered her inside as he collected her overcoat and suitcase from the hallway.

"*Merci*," she chimed sweetly.

He followed her into the apartment, dragging his tongue along with him.

In her right hand, she carried a feather duster, which she promptly put to use.

"Go about your business," she told him in her impeccable French. She swiped her duster over the lamp shade, then bent low to dust the leg of the end table on which the lamp sat.

Desire rocketed through his body. Her skirt was so short that her current position revealed the pink lace thong she wore. She wiggled her perfect ass and he was damn certain they wouldn't make it through dinner before he dragged her down to the floor or onto the sofa and made love to her.

She straightened and cast a seductive look over her shoulder. "Don't let me distract you." She waved a hand at him, as though shooing him away.

David grinned. He was damn glad he'd brushed up on his French when he'd bought this condo last year. But instead of answering her in French, he played the American businessman who was about to have a classic fantasy fulfilled by the sexy French maid.

"I made a large meal. Too much for one person. Would you care to join me?"

She eyed him over her shoulder, her whiskey-colored gaze sweeping over him from head to toe, as though sizing him up. She tilted her head to the side, seemingly contemplating his invitation. Then she said, "I charge by the hour. And I'm very expensive."

"I don't doubt it." David watched her flit about the room, dusting the furniture and straightening the books and knickknacks on the shelving units.

He chuckled as he pulled out the *saumon et aux asperges* and finished his dinner preparation. All the while, his attention drifting to the living room, where he'd catch his "French" vixen in various sexy poses. Bent over the coffee table so he had a perfect view of the enticing cleavage her bra created. Perched daintily on the arm of the leather sofa, brushing imaginary dust from her outfit, her skirt hitched so high he could see the straps from the garter belt she wore and the lacy tops of her thigh-high fishnet stockings.

How he managed to prepare for dinner was beyond him. His cock strained against his dress pants. His heart hammered in his chest. His pulse raged throughout his body, throbbing and vibrating and making him acutely aware of how strongly he reacted to her.

Not ravaging her immediately was the biggest challenge he'd faced in more years than he could recall. Known for his cool head and even temperament, David had given up stressing out over every business deal, every minute detail. But damn if Cat Hewitt didn't have him totally spun up, his usually steadfast concentration shot to hell.

Admittedly, David liked the feeling. He'd forgotten what it felt like to be so alive. So invigorated. Although David's work came easy to him, he'd been so caught up in planning one corporate coup after another that he no longer took the time to even enjoy the fruits of his labor. In fact, this was the first time he'd visited his prime *Champs-Elysee* flat. And he'd owned it for over a year.

Life was slipping by. Much too quickly.

"You are pleased with my cleaning, no?" Cat whispered in his ear, in English.

David grinned. "Almost perfect."

She shot him an offended look. "Almost?"

His grin turned wicked.

Cat reached for the single button on her blouse that was fastened and slipped the small disk through its hole. “You prefer me to clean while *en deshabille, oui*?”

“If that means naked, then *oui*.”

She stripped off the tight shirt and draped it over a chair. “Better?”

“It’s a start.”

One perfectly manicured fingernail grazed the valley between his pectoral muscles.

“*Rouge*,” she said as she flicked the first button she encountered, unfastening it.

“Sorry?” He knew all the blood was surging to his cock, but come on. He couldn’t possibly have missed an entire conversation.

“Red,” she whispered as she continued down the line of buttons until she reached his waist. Yanking the hem from his navy-colored pants, she finished the job. “That’s my favorite rose.”

His shirt hung open and she slid her hands over his abdomen and up to his chest. “*Magnifique*,” she said in the sexiest voice he’d ever heard.

Her wet lips grazed his skin. Her tongue flicked an already hard nipple, causing it to stiffen even more. Excitement coursed through his veins and targeted his cock.

“To hell with dinner.” His hands clasped her waist and he hoisted her up until she sat on the edge of the table.

“*Desirer vivement faire quelque chose*… You’re so eager.”

“Impatient is more like it.” He shoved her skirt up to her waist. “Overcome with desire. Completely enthralled. Desperate to touch you. Take your pick.”

She smiled at him, obviously thrilled by his overwhelming need for her. Cat pushed his shirt over his shoulders and down his arms. She reached for the belt at his waist and unfastened it, along with the button and zipper. Her hand slid behind the waistband of his briefs and her fingers curled around the shaft of his fully erect cock.

David let out a low groan. “God, you are so sexy.” His mouth caught hers in a hot, demanding kiss. His body vibrated with need, his pulse raged in his head, so intoxicating was this incredible woman.

And she was all his.

When Cat had decided to play the sexy French maid, she’d had no idea how passionately David would respond. Admittedly, the role-playing was the most incredible fun she’d had in longer than she could remember.

Cat had realized, when she’d stood in the hallway facing the door to

David's apartment—an opulent flat exceeding her wildest expectations—that her pulse had never raced this fast. In fact, she couldn't remember ever feeling this sexy, this vibrant, this *liberated*.

His mouth covered hers and he gave her one of the mind-blowing kisses she was quickly becoming addicted to. When he pulled away, his lips trailed over her chin, down her throat to her breasts. Cat's fingers tangled in his thick hair.

"This outfit is driving me wild, Cat."

"My name is Damiane, *monsieur*." Her tongue flicked his earlobe. "It means *untamed*."

David groaned. "Just the way I like you."

His tongue slid over her nipple. The combination of heat and moisture, along with the rough material of her lacy bra, tightened the tip of her breast to an almost excruciating degree. The sensation made her restless, dizzy with desire. His mouth moved lower, over her flat belly, down to the apex of her legs. He kissed her through the lace of her panties and a sharp gasp fell from her lips.

David's fingers whisked aside the swath of material covering her and his tongue swept over her slick folds. Cat braced herself by placing her hands behind her on the table. Her head fell back and her eyes closed as David skillfully made love to her with his mouth. He licked and sucked and stroked, heightening her arousal with every talented swipe. His mouth pressed to her and his teeth gently grazed her throbbing clit, sending a wave of excitement washing over her.

He eased a finger in her tight canal as his tongue continued to work its magic on the sensitive nubbin between her legs.

"You know exactly what I like," she whispered. "And you're so good at it." Little whimpers of need and desire tickled her throat, working their way up and out of her mouth until she was chanting his name, teetering on the verge of orgasm.

His tongue pressed against her clit and Cat cried out as she came.

As soon as her breath returned to her, she begged, "*Baise-moi, s'il vous plait*."

Fuck me.

He gave her a wicked grin. "I love it when you talk dirty. Even in French."

Moments later, he was sheathed and inside her, making love to her hard and fast.

"Damiane." He groaned. "You drive me crazy."

And then he came.

Chapter 12

David made love to a geisha in Tokyo. He made love to a Swedish swimsuit model in Stockholm. A gorgeous passenger on the Orient Express. A stranded hiker in Tibet. A cage dancer in Chicago.

When he invited Cat to spend the weekend at his home in San Francisco, he had no idea what to expect, no idea "who" would show up at his door.

When the very beautiful woman with chestnut hair and amber eyes stood on the other side of his door, David's excitement escalated. Dressed in a pair of pale blue leather pants and a matching silk blouse, Cat was stunning.

As herself.

David's cock concurred. He let out a low groan as he slumped against the doorframe.

"Goddamn," he said on a sigh. "You're perfect."

She looked taken aback. "You're not disappointed? My luggage got lost, so you get stuck with me tonight."

She'd flown commercial because he'd needed his private jet to fly his legal team to Germany.

"Baby, I admit the role-playing is sexy." He reached for her and pulled her into his arms. "But nothing's hotter than the real you."

Cat finally grinned. "Such a sweet-talker."

She wrapped her arms around his neck and pressed her slender body against his. Need and desire tore through him. He felt as though he hadn't touched her in years, though they'd only just seen each other last week. Every nerve ending sprang to life, every fiber of his being became acutely aware of her intoxicating scent and her erotic presence.

"So you'll lend me a shirt to sleep in?"

"No." He kissed her forehead. "You're sleeping naked."

She laughed. "I'll need something to answer the door in when Nordstroms' personal shopper delivers panties for me tomorrow morning."

David whisked her inside, still in his arms, and kicked the door shut behind them. "You don't need panties." He pressed her up against the wall and gave her a quick, albeit impassioned, kiss. "In fact, I think a full weekend of nakedness is in order. What do you say?"

She sighed. "A *full* weekend." It was more time than they'd spent together in one trip. "I like the sound of that."

David kissed her, then said, "I'm sorry I wasn't at the airport to meet you. I had to work out some kinks with one of my deals, but I'm so glad you're here. How can I thank you for coming to see me?"

"You could feed me."

He laughed. "Thank God you love to eat."

David took her hand and led her into his enormous gourmet kitchen, which she *ooohed* and *aaahed* over before admitting she didn't understand his need for seven different sauce pans. Nor did she know what half of the fancy gadgets he kept in a stainless steel container next to the stove were for.

"I love to eat food, not cook it," she told him.

So she didn't know her way around a kitchen. David didn't care. She had plenty of admirable attributes. Including her affectionate nature. She stepped behind him and wrapped her arms around his waist. David liked that she was so open with her emotions and desires. He covered her hands with one of his.

"Whatever you've made for dinner, it smells wonderful."

"Lobster Thermador."

Cat let out a sexy mewling sound that aroused him all the more. "I've just died and gone to heaven." She untangled herself and slid onto a barstool to watch him as he finished preparing their dinner.

It occurred to David that she looked perfect in his kitchen, perched comfortably in front of him while he cooked. He felt that intriguing pull deep within him that was quickly becoming commonplace. Every time he was with Cat, a curious longing crept up on him. He wanted her in his life on a more frequent, permanent basis. He wanted to spend more than a few days a week with her. He wanted to make love to her every night and wake up next to her every morning.

The months they'd been together seemed to have passed quickly. Despite the short span of time they'd been dating, David felt like he'd known her his entire life. They were good together, in every way. And he couldn't help but think that she belonged here, with him.

Without thinking twice about it, he asked, "Do you like the city?"

She nodded as she reached for the glass of champagne he'd poured for her. "My mom's a big fan of San Francisco. We come here a couple of times a year to shop and sightsee."

"Crime's not as bad as in New York."

"You'd be surprised at the change that's occurred in New York over the past several years. It's actually become a safer city. Definitely friendlier."

She sipped her champagne. Did she have any idea how hooked he was? Did she sense that he was trying to ascertain whether she'd be amenable to moving? Oh, hell. Why didn't he just come right and ask her? He wanted her to move in with him. It was as simple as that. But it didn't *feel* quite so simple. She loved New York. He could see it in the way her eyes lit up when she talked about her home.

Damn it. He suddenly wasn't so sure he could sway her. So he let the subject drop.

After they'd devoured his three-course meal, they took a cab from David's Pacific Heights home to North Beach, where they found a cozy, intimate club with a live band playing Rolling Stones tunes.

Maybe he could work on her a little more tonight before he revealed his feelings and his desire to move their relationship to the next level.

Cat eyed him over the rim of her beer mug. "How'd you know I love the Stones?"

"You told me when we were in Tokyo."

Her gaze narrowed on him. "You were deep inside me, about to come, and you remember me saying I'm a Stones fan?"

He set his mug down. "I asked you what concert you wanted to see and told you I'd get tickets. Anywhere in the world. Whatever band you wanted to see."

"Yes. You asked me that at dinner, but I didn't have an answer. Then we did the geisha thing and then we made love. And while we were doing that, you said you wanted to make love to me in a dark alley in the Red Light District in Amsterdam, at Carnival in Rio de Janeiro, and in an old castle you'd visited once in England. That's when I suddenly recalled that the Stones were playing in London."

"And under a palm tree in the Grand Cayman."

She laughed. "The Stones are playing under a palm tree in Grand Cayman?"

David chuckled as he shook his head. "No. In addition to the places you mentioned, I also want to make love to you under a palm tree in Grand Cayman. At sunset."

She grinned at him. Slow and sweet. In that instant, David knew he wanted to spend the rest of his life with her. Nothing had ever felt so right.

"I can't believe you remembered that I like the Stones." She took a long sip from her beer then returned the mug to the deeply scarred wooden table. "That's just incredible."

David couldn't explain why he felt so swept away, but he suddenly had to tell Cat how he felt about her. Unfortunately, his cell phone rang before he got the words out. David ignored it as he reached for Cat's hand, but the damned thing just kept on ringing.

"Go ahead and answer it," she said. "It's okay."

Annoyed that their perfect moment had been spoiled, he snatched the phone from his belt clip and said, "This is David Essex."

"It's Donovan. We've got a huge problem."

David relinquished her hand. Cat watched as his head shook back and forth and he muttered curses under his breath. Something wasn't right. He signaled at her that he intended to step outside. Cat knew it was just because he couldn't hear well in the club, but something about him taking his business call away from her suddenly made her feel like an outsider.

She reached for her beer, knowing she was being ridiculous. Nonetheless, a slew of strange emotions began to swirl inside her. She knew the time had come for her to assess the situation.

She was in love with David. She'd felt it from that very first night at Rendezvous.

But they were living in a fantasy world. When she and David were together, it was always in some exotic place, late at night. Tonight, she was on his professional *and* personal turf. It felt more foreign to her than anything else.

She knew nothing about his work.

She hadn't met any of his friends or his family.

It occurred to Cat that seeing each other for three months didn't equate to much more than several nights of hot sex.

Cat sat back in her chair and eyed the people around her. The couples she saw were either dancing or huddled close to each other, lost in conversation.

She wondered what they were talking about. An incredible night they'd spent together in their own apartment, in their own bed, rather than some exotic location? The stressful or exciting day they'd had at work or at home?

Were they sharing their hopes and dreams and fears with each other?

Cat couldn't even begin to guess. Though she'd found physical intimacy with David, emotional intimacy still lingered just out of her reach.

And their geographical distance wasn't going to help them any.

Wondering if it was time to be a bit more cognizant of her situation, and maybe a bit more open-minded, Cat decided to view San Francisco objectively.

Could she live here?

She owed it to herself, and to David, to consider the possibility.

"Hey, sorry about that," he said as he returned to the table and dropped into his seat. "Bit of a crisis. Do you mind if we head home?"

Cat shook her head as she reached for her purse.

When they entered the foyer of his house, David said, "I have some work to do. I'm so sorry, Cat. It's important. Otherwise…"

"I don't mind," she said, honestly. Her thoughts were still jumbled and this bought her a little more time to work through them. "Do whatever you have to do. I'm tired anyway. I'll just head up to bed."

He pointed her in the right direction, gave her a quick kiss, then dashed off to his office in the back of the house.

Cat climbed the stairs to his room, wondering for the first time what it would be like to be David's wife.

Granted, he was attentive and he rarely ever took a call when he was with her, but wasn't it unrealistic to believe that was how it would always be? She couldn't help but wonder what their life together would *really* be like if they were married.

She entered his bedroom and looked around, admiring the elegance and the opulence of the room. The walls were painted a soothing slate blue with white wainscoted accents. A plump, white down comforter covered the king-size bed in the middle of the room. A slate blue sofa and matching chairs were situated neatly in the far corner. Sheer, white curtains covered the floor to ceiling windows. She crossed the room and peered out of one of the glass panes. San Francisco lit up at night was a beautiful place.

But could she live here?

She shook her head slightly, involuntarily. It seemed to happen of its own volition, as though her subconscious mind held the answer and chose now to reveal it.

Cat's heart constricted in an almost painful way. She didn't want to give up her life in New York. Her work was there. Her family. Her friends. She'd grown up there and she'd never considered living anywhere else. And to be so far away from her parents, from Dean and Cass… They planned to have children and Cat wanted to be there to watch them grow. She didn't want to be a long-distance aunt.

It was one thing to traipse around the world for midnight trysts, something entirely different to pack up her life and move across the country.

Damn it. Why'd she have to fall in love with someone who lived so far away? When she'd first seen David at Rendezvous, and she'd felt certain that geography didn't matter. Cat hadn't really considered what a long-distance romance would entail. But now, she had no choice but to face the truth. Being away from David for lengthy periods of time, living completely separate lives on opposite coasts was much more than she could bear.

With a heavy heart, Cat undressed and hung her clothes in the closet next to David's. Tears slid down her cheeks as her fingers grazed his dress shirts.

He was everything she'd ever wanted.

But in her heart, Cat knew she wasn't willing to make the ultimate sacrifice in order to keep him.

Chapter 13

"You're quiet this morning," David said as he shook a small amount of salt onto his omelet.

Cat took a long sip of her Mimosa, then returned the glass to the table. They were having breakfast on David's boat. A decent-sized bay cruiser he'd purchased last year.

"I was thinking I should go back to New York this afternoon," Cat said, drawing his attention.

Her words surprised him. "Is something wrong?"

Cat didn't make eye contact with him. She sat across the table, dressed in a pretty lavender dress Nordstrom's had sent over, along with a shopping bag full of personal items. Her long hair was pulled back in a sleek ponytail. She looked, as always, more stunning than the last time he'd seen her. It amazed David that she was more beautiful, more captivating with every passing moment.

He wanted to make her his. Forever.

But Cat seemed pensive this morning. Something was wrong.

"I left a few loose ends with the gala and I really feel that I need to tie them up. The event is next weekend, and I'm… well, I'm really nervous about being out of town when I'm down to the wire."

She hadn't mentioned any of this before. In fact, he recalled that she'd felt confident all the details for the gala were in place when he'd called to invite her to his home. Something had happened to change her mind.

David recalled the previous evening. Cat had been sound asleep when he'd joined her in bed last night. He'd only worked a couple of hours, needing to do some damage control on a fifteen-million-dollar real estate transaction that had taken a wayward turn.

He'd felt terrible about having to work while she was in town, but he'd had no choice. Even now, he should be in the office, but he couldn't bear the thought of losing any more precious time with her. He'd empowered Donovan to take the lead and hopefully get the derailed deal back on track.

Setting his linen napkin on the table, David said, "I'm really sorry about last night, Cat."

She smiled at him, for the first time this morning. "Please don't apologize. Your work can't suffer because of me, David."

He frowned. Cat was much too standoffish this morning. In fact, she'd hopped out of bed at the crack of dawn and hit the shower while he was still asleep. He had wanted to make love to her, but she'd insisted the delivery from Nordstrom would arrive at any minute and she didn't want to miss it.

Not that he couldn't have handled the transaction on his own. But she either hadn't trusted him with the task or she hadn't wanted to make love with him.

The pain in his heart intensified. She was slipping away.

How?

Why?

What the hell had happened last night to drive this wedge between them?

"Cat," he began. But what the hell was he going to say? She was right. His work *couldn't* suffer because of her, and it wouldn't. He was certain of it. Sure, there would be times when it would encroach on their relationship, but that was life.

Suddenly, he thought he had a much better understanding of what was happening to them right now. "Look," he said, hoping to reason with her. "We've done a great job of keeping our lives and our romance sole and separate. In doing so, we've built our own fantasy world."

She nodded. "Which is completely unrealistic."

"No," he said. "It's not unrealistic. It's perfect. But it's also one-dimensional. Maybe it's time now to start pulling in some elements from the real world."

Her eyes narrowed slightly. "What do you mean?"

"Well, for instance, do you have a date for the gala?"

She laughed, which helped to break the tension that had crept up on them. "Of course not."

David was relieved to hear that. "I'd like to be your date, Cat. I'd like to attend the gala and see what an amazing job you've done. I want to be by your side, supporting something that means so much to you."

Her jaw fell slack for a moment. She stared at him, but he couldn't read her expression. He had no idea what had caused her to pull away from him, but he felt certain he could bring her back to him, if only she'd let him.

"This is really short notice. I mean, you couldn't possibly shuffle your schedule this late."

"It's not a problem. Really."

She gnawed her lower lip, which made David feel unsettled. "Well, I mean, it's just that…" She let out a long sigh. Reaching for her Mimosa, she took a long drink. Then another. After she returned the glass to the table, she cast a steely look his way. "The thing is, I don't think we should see each other anymore."

Chapter 14

There. She'd said it. So what if her hands trembled and her heart raced as though she'd just run a marathon? So what if every fiber of her being wanted to retract each word she'd uttered and tell David she'd just experienced a momentary lapse of sanity?

What the hell was she thinking, breaking up with him?

Stay focused, Cat. You're doing the right thing. You are.

But it sure as hell didn't feel right.

David gave her a dumbfounded look. "Cat..." He shook his head, as though shocked.

"Look," she rushed on before he could change her mind, "this has been an incredible experience. Like nothing I've ever known. But we have to face facts. We live on opposite sides of the country, we both have our own family obligations. Neither one of us is considering moving."

It didn't seem possible, but he looked even more taken aback. "I didn't realize the geography was complicating things between us. I thought we had it worked out perfectly, actually. Cat, if this is about last night, I—"

"It's not," she interjected. "I promise, it's not."

Feeling the tears begin to build, she pushed back her chair and stood. Slipping on her sunglasses so her eyes wouldn't betray her, she said, "I really do need to go."

David stood as well. He came around the table and gripped her upper arms. "Cat, whatever has brought this on, can we please talk about it?"

A huge lump of emotion formed in her throat and she nearly choked on it. "Will you move to New York? Ever?"

"Cat, my office is here. My family is here."

She nodded. "I know. And my work and my family are in New York. Don't you see? This is never going to work between us. And the longer we continue down this path, the worse it'll be in the end." Knowing she couldn't handle the difficult situation and being away from David, she mumbled, "No. I've made up my mind."

She could say no more. The tears were filling her eyes and she knew any second now they'd spill over and he'd see them. Damn it. Why did this have to be so hard?

Because I love him.

She moved away and he released her.

"If you insist on leaving, let me drive you to the airport."

"I can get a cab," she told him in a shaky voice. Time in the car with him meant he'd have an opportunity to talk her out of her decision. She couldn't let him do that. Someday, he'd thank her for cutting him loose before it was too late. Someday, he'd realize that she'd been right to end things now, before it became too painful.

"Cat, you can't just leave like this. I don't understand—"

"I know. I'm so sorry, it's just… I have to go. And you have to let me." She rushed off the boat and down the dock. Hailing a cab passing by the Maritime Museum, she slipped inside and let the tears fall.

Chapter 15

What the hell had happened?

David asked himself the question for the umpteenth time since Cat had turned her back on him and walked away.

To say he was stunned was an understatement. He'd really wanted it to work between them. He was in love with her, for God's sake. But he hadn't had the chance to tell her and now it was too late.

Or was it?

Admittedly, she had a point about their unwillingness to relocate for each other. But still…

As David entered his office, he dropped a file folder on the desk and plopped into his chair, his shoulders slumping forward. He'd never had any intention of moving to New York, and he'd been upfront about that from the get-go. Joining Rendezvous had been a consideration before he'd run into Cat, but that was because he hadn't found what he was looking for on the West Coast. Considering he spent a good deal of time in New York, he'd thought he could make a long-distance relationship work, with the right woman.

Clearly, he'd been wrong. He'd found the right woman, but he sure as hell couldn't make the relationship work from across the country. Cat wanted him in New York. Fulltime. He realized that now.

David absently tapped the end of his Mont Blanc pen against the blotter on his desk. Damn it. Why hadn't he broached this subject with her before she'd gotten all worked up about it? He could have come up with an alternate solution, something viable—*something other than a breakup.*

What exactly would that solution be?

He dropped his pen. Sighing in frustration, he drummed his fingers where the pen had tapped the blotter. Okay, so he'd thought all along that he could sway her, convince her to move to San Francisco when the time was right. Now he knew that wasn't going to happen. Considering the amount of business he conducted in New York, couldn't he buy a place there that he could share with Cat?

He could divide his time between San Francisco, his international locales, and Manhattan. What would be so difficult about that? Cat could continue to travel with him when her schedule permitted, and maybe she'd even consider moving some of her stuff into his house in San Francisco.

Granted, they wouldn't be together *all* of the time, but anything was better than this. David desperately wanted to make their relationship work.

Did Cat?

Well, that was the million-dollar question. One David didn't have an answer to because he'd misjudged Cat's feelings about their relationship. He'd thought she was enjoying the fantasy life they'd created, rather than stressing over the reality of the situation. He'd had no idea that she was moving toward something more serious.

The thought disturbed him because he'd been thinking the same thing. He just hadn't said it aloud. Nor had he figured out in his mind how the logistics would work. Yes, he'd assumed she'd move to San Francisco to be with him. Bad move on his part. But the fact of the matter was, they were, as usual, on the exact same page. They had both arrived at the same place at the same time. They just hadn't known it.

It all became very clear to David and he sure as hell couldn't accept the breakup. Their relationship didn't have to end. Hell, if Cat wanted a commitment from him, he was willing to give it.

Except...

She wasn't answering his calls. He'd tried to reach her every day this week, with no luck. He lifted the phone from its cradle now and hit the speed dial number for her cell phone. When her voicemail picked up, he disconnected the call. He'd already left a half-dozen messages for her. He called her house. Again the machine picked up.

David knew she was probably rushing around this week, putting the finishing touches on the gala preparations. She was probably too busy to take any calls, but damn it—she had to speak to him sooner or later.

In the meantime, he'd just have to think of a clever way to win her back.

Chapter 16

The Healthy Hearts Gala was a huge success. As Cat made her way through the crowded ballroom, she picked up little tidbits here and there that pleased her. The guests were impressed with the elegant décor and the twelve-piece band that played classical music. The champagne flowed freely and the elaborate, passed hors d'oeuvres were decadent and irresistible.

The evening's final headcount came in at just under three thousand. Combined with the auction results and the various donations that would trickle in over the next week or so, the total amount raised would, Cat was certain, exceed her hopes. She felt positive they would raise more than five million dollars. The thought made her deliriously happy, enough to chase away the melancholy she'd wallowed in all week because she and David were no longer together.

He'd wanted to be here tonight. With her. By her side. And she'd said no. It seemed that every five minutes she questioned her sanity.

Making the rounds at the gala, ensuring the entire evening went off without a hitch, she forced herself to ignore the gnawing feeling in her stomach. Guilt swirled around in her belly, leaving her unsettled and uneasy. She'd dropped a bombshell on David. He hadn't seen the breakup coming. She knew he likely blamed himself, and she felt bad about that.

When she spotted her brother and his fiancée, along with McCarthy from Rendezvous, she considered skirting them. But Dean caught a glimpse of Cat and waved her over.

She gave him a hug.

"You did a great job tonight, kid."

"Stop calling me that," she said as she jabbed him softly in the ribs. "I'm twenty-six, for God's sake."

Dean's arm was draped around her shoulders. "You'll always be a kid to me. Get over it."

Cat couldn't help but smile. She adored Dean, and she knew he felt the same way about her. During her entire whirlwind romance with David, her brother hadn't interfered. He'd promised recently that he'd back off and not purposely intimidate the hell out of her dates, or go on and on about how much he disapproved of every guy she met. He'd kept his word. Dean had even bitten his tongue when he'd found out Cat had flown all over the world with a man she had yet to bring home to meet her family.

Although her father knew David well, the thought suddenly struck her as odd.

"Can we talk in private for a moment?" she asked her brother.

Cass and McCarthy looked a little wounded that she wouldn't include them in this conversation, but she hadn't told anyone about her decision to end things with David.

Dean led her to a quiet corner on the veranda. "What's up?" His concern made her cringe.

"Don't look so grim. I just need to ask you a question. Something that just occurred to me."

Dean leaned against the railing and said, "Shoot."

"When I told you I was flying to Mexico to meet David, you didn't try to talk me out of it. Why?"

Her brother looked taken aback. "What do you mean?"

"I mean, Mr. Overprotective, that you didn't once try to stop me from traveling abroad with a man you'd never met."

"Dad knows him. Besides, you told me to butt out of your love life."

"Since when have you ever done anything I've told you to do?"

He shrugged. "I felt pretty comfortable with the arrangement. He has impressive references."

She narrowed her eyes. "So you *did* check up on him."

"Of course, I checked up on him."

She crossed her arms over her chest. "I'm still really surprised that you didn't interfere."

Dean grinned at her. "I couldn't. Cass won't marry me if I renege on the deal to stay out of your business and let you make your own mistakes. Besides," he said as he regarded her with a serious look, "I've never seen you so excited to be with someone. So… convinced you'd finally met the right guy."

Cat frowned. From the beginning, she'd been convinced David was *the one*. There had just been something so magical between them. From that first meeting, three years ago at The Plaza, in fact.

"So where is Mr. Wonderful? I'd like to finally meet him."

"He wanted to come, but… I broke up with him."

"Oh." Dean stood beside her, quiet, waiting for her to elaborate.

"It just didn't work out. No big deal." But even as she said the words, she felt the sting of them. Tears sprang to her eyes and her heart felt like it was being squeezed by a tight fist until she could barely breathe.

"Why do I get the feeling that it really *is* a big deal?"

The fat teardrops crested the rims of her eyes and spilled down her cheeks in a steady stream. "Because I love him."

Dean pulled her into his arms and let her cry. When her sobs subsided, he asked in a soft voice, "Why did you break up with him, Cat?"

"Because he doesn't want to live in New York. And I don't want to live in San Francisco. Everything I love is here. Well, except for David..."

He loosened his arms and held her away from him, forcing her to look at him. "Cat, there are ways to work around stuff like that. If you really want to."

"I don't know what's wrong with me," she admitted. "I love him so much, and I want everything to be perfect. Maybe that's what scares me the most."

Dean chuckled as he pulled her back into his arms. "It's not ever going to be perfect, Cat. Falling in love scares everyone. Trust me. It ain't easy. In fact, being in love can be very painful. It can also be the best thing to happen to you."

"It is," she whispered. "*Was*."

"Does your relationship with David have to be over, Cat?"

She thought about his question for several moments. Finally, she said, "I guess that depends on David."

Dean eased her out of his arms again. "Here's a thought. Why don't you go freshen up in the ladies' room, then give him a call? I'm sure he'd like to hear how much money you helped to raise tonight."

Cat couldn't help but grin. "Cass has really done a number on you."

"Feel free to let her know I'm a reformed man. Maybe then I can convince her to elope with me."

"Elope? Dream on," Cat said as she swatted at his arm in a playful way. "She's waited all this time for her Prince Charming. You can be damn certain she's looking forward to the Cinderella wedding."

"Oh, yeah, that reminds me. She wants you to be our wedding planner."

"Dean, I'm so flattered!" She threw her arms around him and kissed his cheek. "I accept!"

Her brother chuckled. "She'll kill me for telling you, so act surprised when she asks, all right?"

"Of course!" Cat brushed away the tears from her cheeks and drew in a deep breath. "Okay. I'm gonna hit the bathroom and then I'm going to call David and beg him to ignore my moment of immense stupidity."

"Good luck, kid."

Chapter 17

Cat took her cell phone from her purse and hit the speed dial number for David's cell. She fidgeted nervously and counted the rings. One, two, three… *Crap*. What if he saw her number on his caller ID and didn't pick up?

Four, five…

"This is David."

Cat's heart constricted and she felt like crying again. What was wrong with her?

Love, that's what. It was making her do and say and feel the craziest damned things.

"Cat? Is that you?"

Cat opened her mouth to speak. Promptly closed it. Shit. What the hell was she going to say to him? How was she going to get him back? Did he even *want* her back?

"Cat? Are you there?"

Say something!

"Cat?"

"I love you," she said on a rush of air.

Oh God! What the hell…?

Cat's eyes widened. She really had lost her mind!

Her teeth clamped down on her lower lip to keep her from saying more.

Way to put yourself out there, Cat.

She waited, panic and paranoia swirling around in her brain until she could barely think straight.

Why wasn't he saying anything?

"David?" she asked in a tentative voice.

He let out a long sigh. "So that's what happened. You fell in love."

"Yeah."

"And you got scared because of our geographical… difference."

"Yeah."

"And now you're not scared?"

"No. I'm terrified. But I'm also… *Oh*!" A sharp pain suddenly shot through

Cat's brain and she dropped the phone. A moment later, she fell to the marble floor and lost consciousness.

David jerked his phone away from his ear at Cat's loud scream and the clanking noise that followed. He hurriedly pressed the phone back to his ear and said, "Cat?"

No answer.

"Sweetheart? Are you there? Cat!"

He waited several more seconds, his heart sinking to his stomach. "Cat! Talk to me! Say something!"

Jumping to his feet, David collected his briefcase and his car keys. He rushed out of his office and down the hallway, the phone still pressed to his ear as he repeated her name over and over again, hoping for a response. He reached the elevator. Still no word from Cat. The call was still connected, so he knew they hadn't been dropped because of a weak signal.

Something was wrong.

David snapped the phone closed, knowing he'd lose the call in the elevator. When he reached the ground floor, he dialed Cat's number again. He got her voice mail. He tried three more times as he raced to the parking garage. Sliding behind the wheel of his BMW, he dialed McCarthy Portman's number.

She answered on the third ring. "Hello?"

"McCarthy," he said in a rushed voice. "David Essex calling. I was just on the phone with Cat and something happened. She screamed and then I lost her. And she won't pick up."

"I'm sure she's fine," McCarthy said over the loud noise that filled the line. David realized she must be at the gala just as she said, "Cat and her brother are out on the terrace talking. I just saw them a few minutes ago."

"How *many* minutes ago, McCarthy?"

Suddenly, McCarthy's voice was filled with concern. "Oh, um. I'm not sure. Maybe twenty?"

"Shit!" David sped through the Financial District and headed to the private terminal where he kept his plane. "Can you please go find her? I would really appreciate it. She's not picking up on her cell, and I'm just really worried something has happened to her."

The thought of anything bad happening to Cat made him step down harder on the accelerator.

"Of course. I'll call you right back."

He disconnected the call and phoned his chief pilot. "Chuck, I need to fly to New York. Now!"

Chapter 18

Before Cat's eyes fluttered open, she felt the most excruciating pain in her head. Like a jackhammer diligently working on her left temple. It hurt to move. It hurt to breathe. She was afraid to open her eyes, knowing how painful that small action would be, but she needed to know where she was. She needed to know what had happened.

One minute she'd been trying to reconcile with David and the next, she'd woken with the worst headache of her life.

When she gathered the strength to peer through narrowed slits, she didn't see too much that could tell her where she was. A dark room with no discernible objects to help her determine her surroundings. Except that she was lying on a couch.

Coming a little more out of her pain-induced fog, she realized her hands and feet were bound. And a piece of tape covered her mouth. Instantly alarmed, Cat tried to sit up. But the pain in her head was so sharp, she fell back against the hard cushion.

No!

Her mental scream came involuntarily and it intensified the hammering in her head.

She shut her eyes tight and tried to will away the pain. Afraid to move an inch, she lay curled up on the sofa for lord only knew how long. Finally, she heard footsteps coming toward her.

Frightened, Cat forced her eyes open. A small man, likely in his fifties, crouched down so his face was level with hers. The man looked unkempt and disheveled. In the dim light that now seeped into the room from the open curtain, she could make out his features. He had brown eyes and shaggy gray hair. Thick stubble lined his jaw.

"I didn't mean to hurt you," he said in a quiet voice. "Are you okay?"

Cat's eyes grew wide.

Was she *okay*?

Was he *insane*?

She wanted to rip him a new one, but in her current state, that wasn't possible. She couldn't even demand his name or an explanation for what the hell she was doing in his… what? Living room? Let alone ream him to high hell for rendering her unconscious and tying her up.

"Look," he began in a nervous voice. His tongue darted out and licked his lower lip. "I didn't mean to hit you so hard. I got nervous. I just wanted to…" He gave her a confused look, his face scrunching up. He shook his head and then dragged his hand over his bearded jaw. "I don't even know what I was thinking. I knew you'd be at that gala tonight and I just thought I'd go there and talk to you. I've seen you before. I followed you to Rendezvous one night. You seem real nice, but I just…"

He shook his head again. "I panicked when I saw you tonight. I was afraid you wouldn't help me and I couldn't stand that thought so I-I kidnapped you." He let out a low groan and stood. "Oh, God," he wailed, "I've kidnapped you!"

Oh shit. This couldn't really be happening!

Cat managed to reach up and rip the tape from her mouth because he'd only bound her wrists together without securing her arms to anything. The pain from the tape being pulled from her skin wasn't nearly as excruciating as the pounding in her head, but it still made her cry out.

She recovered quickly, realization dawning. The letter she'd received suddenly flashed in her mind. "Mr. Henry?"

He spun back around to face her. "Yes. Miss Hewitt," he said as he dropped back to his knees in front of her. "Please forgive me. I just—I had no other choice. There's nothing else I can do, there's no one else I can turn to."

"I'm not a doctor," Cat squeaked out. So much for reaming him to high hell. For one thing, it hurt too much to think up words scathing enough to make him crawl under the table and hide from her. Worse, she actually felt sorry for Carl Henry.

Which was utterly ridiculous. The man had *kidnapped* her!

Cat couldn't quite collect her wayward thoughts or her conflicting emotions. Her eyes had finally adjusted to the wee bit of light that filled the room and she could see that they were in a tiny studio apartment.

"I can't help you," she said. "I gave your name and number to a physician I know. That was the best I could do. I only plan the fundraisers for heart disease research. I don't know how to treat it!"

"No one called me. I didn't hear a word," Henry said. "So I kept writing to you."

Cat cringed. She'd been so swept away by her whirlwind romance with David, and so busy planning the gala, that she hadn't kept up on her mail. In fact, there was a stack of unopened items sitting on her hallway table. The only thing she'd paid much attention to was her bills. She'd put everything else on hold, planning on catching up after the gala.

"I don't always open my mail immediately, Mr. Henry. Particularly when I'm planning a major fundraiser. I'm sorry that Dr. Conner didn't phone you. Why don't you take Lydia to a hospital if she's so ill?"

"I can't afford for her to be treated at a hospital," he said, the anger creeping into his voice.

Cat tried to remain calm. "There are free clinics. And I'm sure there are government-assisted programs that can help her get the care she—"

"We haven't been able to qualify for any! I made good money at my job. We had insurance. It wasn't until several months ago that she became bed-ridden, too weak to move. And then the insurance term ran out and I couldn't afford to pay for her care or her medications. I can't go get a job because I can't leave her alone."

His distress alarmed and saddened Cat at the same time. She felt a tremendous amount of sorrow and pity for the Henrys' predicament, but what the hell was she supposed to do about it? Unless...

"Maybe I can help you raise the money you need," she said. "Just cut me loose so we can talk about it."

He seemed to consider her offer for a moment, but then vehemently shook his head. "No, I can't. I've kidnapped you and if you go to police, they'll lock me up and then no one will be here to take care of Lydia."

Panic rose within Cat. This situation was going from bad to worse.

David spoke to McCarthy before his jet took off from San Francisco, but she had no news for him. As soon as the plane touched down in New York, he was on the phone again.

His heart sank when she said, "Her brother found her cell phone outside of one of the ladies' rooms at the hotel."

Damn it! She'd been at the Healthy Hearts Gala. He should have been there with her. He should have been by her side, protecting her.

"Dean is a private investigator, but he used to work for the NYPD," McCarthy said. "He's at the station now, with his father. Cass is at his parents' house with his mom. And I'm at Cat's apartment, in case she calls here. Martin is afraid someone might have kidnapped her for ransom money. Or revenge. He's received plenty of threats over the years. He's afraid someone has finally made good on them."

David's stomach took a dive south. If either of those scenarios turned out to be the case, he doubted very seriously they'd find Cat alive.

David could hardly process the dire thought.

"I've just landed. Tell me how to get to Cat's apartment."

He took down the directions then climbed into the Town Car that awaited him on the tarmac. He handed over the instructions to the driver and told the man he'd triple his rate if he got them to the house in short order. The driver stepped on the gas.

David felt utterly helpless. He couldn't call Cat's cell phone in the hopes that she'd pick up. Dean had it. He couldn't call Cat's apartment because McCarthy was there. There was no hope whatsoever of reaching her. He would have to wait for her—or her family—to reach him. With good news or…

David couldn't bring himself to think of the potentially devastating news he could receive. He knew Dean and the police would do whatever they could to find Cat. And Martin Hewitt would willingly put up any amount of cash for his daughter's safe return. Hell, David would match it.

But what if her captor didn't want money? What if, as Martin feared, they wanted revenge?

If so, the chances of finding Cat alive were slim to none.

Shit.

Chapter 19

"She looks peaceful," Cat said. She peered at the woman asleep on the narrow cot across the room from the sofa Cat had been confined to for so long her limbs had nearly gone numb. She'd managed to convince Carl Henry to unbind her ankles. But he'd adamantly refused to release her wrists.

He'd helped her off the sofa so the blood could circulate to her extremities. When she'd finally been able to move on her own, she'd slowly made her way to Lydia's cot. Escaping was at the top of Cat's list, but she couldn't move fast enough to elude Carl. Yet.

So she decided to further assess the situation. As she peered down at Lydia, she felt a pang of guilt for not having done more to help the Henrys. Cat could understand that kidnapping her was an act of desperation.

She was still angry about her current predicament, and even still a bit frightened because there was no telling what a desperate man, facing a tremendous loss, was capable of doing. She had no idea how he'd react if she tried to escape and failed. She had no idea what he'd do to her if she *didn't* escape.

Not that she blamed him. Cat couldn't imagine being in Carl Henry's shoes. If it was David lying in that bed and she had no way to help him, no viable means of getting the treatment he needed, would she feel just as desperate? Would she risk everything to help him, even if it was a long shot?

Yes.

Christ. Now she had empathy for the man who'd kidnapped her.

"She'll sleep most of the night. She's very weak. Lydia has an intermittent brady arrhythmia that's caused her decreased energy and weakness. She has coronary artery disease and is at a high risk for heart failure."

"We're going to have to do something about her condition," Cat said.

"She needs a pacemaker."

Cat lifted her gaze and her eyes locked with his. She didn't know these people, but now that she was involved in their lives, she couldn't just let Lydia Henry die. If saving her life was a matter of medical attention and a pacemaker, there had to be a way to raise money for the treatment. "Let me call Dr. Conner again."

Carl swallowed down what appeared to be a very large lump of emotion. His gaze stayed locked with hers for a few moments before his eyes dropped to his wife's face. He shook his head slowly. "If I let you call someone, they'll find out what I've done."

"I'm not going to deny that you've done something wrong. And I don't necessarily want you to get away with it." He could have killed her, for God's sake, with that blow to her skull. As it was, her head still throbbed in sharp, wicked beats. "But that's not the immediate concern, is it?"

His gaze snapped up to hers. "You'd help Lydia? After what I've done to you?"

"I told you, I'm not a doctor. And I can't force a cardiologist to make time for a new patient, but I can try. We can check her into a facility that will provide her with the medical care she needs, and we'll find a way to raise the money to pay for the treatments and the pacemaker." She gave him a smile, though she knew it was a weak one considering her own physical condition. "If there's one thing I know how to do, it's raise money for a good cause."

Cat had no idea what treatment of cardiac arrhythmia might entail, but she did know how it felt to lose someone to CVD. Though she didn't know Carl Henry from Adam, she did know that anyone who would go to such extreme measures must possess a vast amount of love and devotion. And when it came down it, Cat—as odd as it sounded even to her—found Carl's determination to save his wife's life terribly courageous.

Because Cat lacked her own brand of courage—the kind that would have kept her from running away from what she and David had begun to build—she had to respect Carl Henry.

"Any word?" David asked as McCarthy opened the front door of Cat's apartment.

"Not since the last time you called me. Which was, oh, two minutes ago?"

David shot her a hard look.

McCarthy smiled. "So it's like that, is it?"

He stepped past her and into the foyer. "Yeah, it's like that."

"I figured as much."

Despite her light-hearted banter, McCarthy looked worried sick. She led him into the living room and gestured toward a chair. "Why don't you sit down? I just made some tea."

"I'm gonna need something much stronger than that."

McCarthy crossed to the wet bar. "Scotch?"

"Yeah."

She returned with a glass and the bottle, which she set on the coffee table before him. He downed his drink then refilled the glass, hoping like hell the alcohol would help to slow his racing heart.

"Dean and Martin are still working with the police. No one has called to demand money or declare vengeance. Dean thinks that's a good sign."

"He's sure that's what this is about?"

McCarthy gave a helpless shrug. "As best as he can tell. I mean, we were at the Waldorf-Astoria. It's not like some vagrant attacked her or dragged her off. That place has security like Fort Knox, and anyone not decked to the nines would be considered suspicious. Although…" McCarthy frowned. "Dean said she went to the restrooms away from the gala because she didn't want to run into anyone who'd recognize her. So she wandered pretty far away from the party."

David narrowed his eyes. "Why?"

"Oh." McCarthy sighed. "Damn it. I am not in peak performance tonight." She tucked a strand of smooth blonde hair behind her ear. "Cat was upset. Dean said the two of you had split, but she wanted to reconcile. She was crying when she was with Dean and that's why she wanted to go somewhere away from the gala to repair her makeup."

Dean felt sick. He set aside his scotch. "She did break up with me, and I let her because I was just so stunned and… stupid. I've been trying to reach her all week. When she called tonight, I just…" He shook his head, feeling emotion well inside him. "I thought everything was going to be okay with us. And then—" David could still hear her scream echo in his head. "If anything happens to her, I—" He reached for his glass and downed the scotch. "Damn it."

McCarthy rested a hand on his arm. "She loves you, too."

He nodded. "That's the first thing she said. It just popped out of her mouth." David could barely breathe now. "Goddamn it. We have to find her." He set down the glass and prowled Cat's apartment. Were there clues here that might lead them to her?

He started sifting through papers on her desk, then magazines in the rack next to her chair. The shrill ring of the phone made him draw up short. McCarthy snatched up the receiver on the coffee table.

"Yes?" She paused a moment, nodded her head. "Okay. See you then."

David knew from her tone that it wasn't Cat. Or her captor.

"Dean's on his way over. He wants to go through Cat's stuff." She eyed

David as he held magazines in his hands. "Great minds think alike." She gnawed her lower lip a moment, then said, "I want to help, but I don't know what to look for."

"Neither do I. I'm just hoping something will jump out at me."

"Okay. I can go for that. I'll start in the kitchen."

David moved onto Cat's bedroom. When he entered the room, he couldn't help but smile. It was exactly how he'd imagined it would be. A big, four-poster bed with a thick, plush purple velvet comforter over crisp white sheets. A large antique armoire in rich cherry wood stood in the corner. Her vanity table and bench matched in era and wood. Two comfortable-looking chairs were situated in front of a bay window. They were covered with clothing, which made David laugh, despite the rock that sat in his gut.

He could picture Cat standing in front of the full-length mirror next to her dresser, holding up outfit after outfit, trying to find the right clothes to fit her mood *du jour.*

Just thinking about how versatile she was, along with her free-spirited, passionate nature, made him ache for her.

David had never felt so utterly consumed by love. He could kick himself in the ass for not admitting it sooner, for not acknowledging his feelings and telling Cat, when he'd had the chance, that he loved her.

Damn it. David suddenly realized that if anything happened to her, it would be the most profound loss of his life. And he would never forgive himself for not being with her at the gala when he'd had the chance to be.

He should have never let her step off his boat. He should have done everything in his power to keep her there until they'd both admitted their feelings, and their fears, and agreed to work through them.

Why the hell couldn't he have seen that back then?

As he carefully sifted through her clothes, looking for lord only knew what, he heard the front door open and then slam shut. David left Cat's room and encountered Dean in the hallway.

"David Essex," he said as he thrust his hand out.

"Dean Hewitt." They shook hands. Dean said, "You look like hell."

David nodded.

"You look like a man in love."

Again, David nodded.

Dean's jaw tightened for just a moment before he said, "We'll find her."

Following the brother-meets-sister's-lover exchange, they stepped up the search of Cat's apartment. David was in the laundry room when he heard Dean yell from the foyer, "You know who this Carl Henry guy is?"

David joined Dean, who was going through Cat's mail on the hallway table. He handed a letter to David. After reading it, he shook his head. "She never mentioned him." David considered the hard look on Dean's face and asked, "You don't think he has something to do with her disappearance, do you?"

Dean opened two other letters, scanned them, then handed them over to David. His gut took a dive south. "Oh, shit. This guy says he'll blame Cat if his wife dies."

Keys in hand, Dean was already heading to the front door, one of the envelopes tucked in the inside pocket of his tuxedo. "It's the best lead we have. You coming?"

"Hell, yes."

"I'll stay in case she calls," McCarthy said, having joined the men.

David followed Cat's brother out the door and climbed into his car. He should feel relieved that they had a lead; instead, dread consumed him.

Chapter 20

Cat had no idea how long she'd been held captive. It hadn't been easy using the restroom with her wrists bound together—wearing an evening gown, no less—but she'd managed. Lydia Henry had yet to open her eyes and Carl sat diligently by her side. Cat wondered how much sleep he'd had in the past few months.

Sitting on the sofa, she tried to think of a way out of her predicament. Reasoning with Carl hadn't worked. Offering to help Lydia hadn't worked. He insisted if anyone found out he'd kidnapped her, the police would haul him away and no one would care for Lydia.

So… what? He was planning on holding her hostage indefinitely?

The thought sent a chill up Cat's spine. She didn't think Carl would abuse or harm her. She wasn't afraid of that. What she was afraid of was being holed up in this tiny studio apartment until Lydia passed away.

She wondered if anyone was looking for her, wondered how the hell they'd find her.

David forced himself to let Dean take the lead when they pulled up in front of the building Carl Henry lived in. As much as he wanted to take the steps two at a time up to the third floor and kick in the door to apartment 310, he knew he had to keep his cool. There was no telling how Henry would react if Cat was inside, held hostage.

The thought made David ball his hands into tight fists as they bypassed the "out of order" elevator and ascended the narrow stairwell with concrete steps and a hand railing that the paint had all but fallen off of.

"She'd better be here," David said around clenched teeth. "And she'd better be okay."

Dean glanced at him over his shoulder. "There's no telling what we're going to find." His expression was grim, his jaw set in a hard line.

David knew he wasn't the only one desperate to find Cat, desperate to ensure her safety. Of course, her brother was just as concerned about her well-being.

David felt compelled to say, "I fucked up when I let her cut me loose. But if there's one thing I've learned from that experience, it's that I love your sister. And I would do anything to protect her. I *will* do anything to protect her."

Dean looked away. They reached the landing on the third floor and he stopped, turning his attention back to David. "You can't blame yourself for this. You didn't know about the letters or about Carl Henry. And you know what? Even if you did, you might not have been able to protect Cat from him."

Dean scratched his jaw. He looked grief-stricken and ill-at-ease, but determined. David guessed he looked the same way. Dean continued, "There's no telling how people will respond in dire situations. When Cass was being stalked last year, I tried to prepare myself for any conceivable scenario. But unless I kept her handcuffed to me, there was no way to protect her 24/7."

David groaned. "Cat would never let me keep her under lock and key. Nor would I want to. Her free-spirit is one of the things I love about her. But, damn it, if I had been with her tonight—"

"Look," Dean said in a sharp tone. "Blaming yourself isn't going to help Cat." In an unexpected move, Dean reached out to him, clasping David's shoulder with a large hand. "We'll find her. Just promise me that when we do, you'll tell her what you just told me."

David nodded. He'd just received "big brother approval" and that meant something. Speaking around the lump that had suddenly swelled in his throat, he said, "I'll tell her every day for the rest of our lives that I love her."

A look of satisfaction and approval crossed Dean's face before his expression turned grim again. "I have no idea if we're going to find Cat alive. You need to prepare yourself for the worst."

David gave a slight shake of his head, let out a low sigh. "Goddamn it."

Chapter 21

Dean gave two swift raps of his knuckles on the apartment door and then called out, "Open the door, Henry."

David forced himself to unclench his fists and his jaw. He tamped down the raging anger that had suddenly built inside him at the thought that the man on the other side of the door might be holding Cat hostage. That he might have harmed her.

"Last warning," Dean shouted.

Something deep within David slipped. His control, his sensibility, his patience, his civility… All gone. His shoulder slammed against the door, connecting with the hard wood. The door and the doorjamb creaked loudly. The brass plate that held the deadbolt in place pulled away from the wood as David hit the door one more time with his shoulder, the screws beginning to work out of their holes. He'd caused enough damage so that one swift kick had the door flying open, squeaking on its hinges.

Dean let out a short laugh. "That takes away all lingering doubt. You really are in love."

David merely grunted. He stepped into the apartment and drew up short, his eyes instantly landing on the curled up, motionless ball on the sofa.

Cat!

The commotion had brought a small, wide-eyed man rushing toward the door, but David ignored him. Cat didn't stir. The ruckus David had created by kicking in the door hadn't disturbed her in the least.

Was she unconscious?

Dead?

His heart constricted.

Behind him, Dean reacted quickly by grabbing Henry by the arm and pushing him face-first against the wall, his arm pinned at the small of his back. The man let out a sharp squeal, then began to plead so incoherently, David couldn't make out his words. Still, Cat didn't stir.

David crossed the room and sank to his knees before her. She was dressed in a formal red, strapless gown. Her hair spilled over her shoulders and down her back as unruly strands escaped their clips. David gently pushed a thick mass of chestnut hair off her face and whispered, “Sweetheart? Cat?”

She let out a soft moan. Her eyes fluttered open and she stared at him, groggy-eyed, a questioning look reflected in the whiskey-colored pools.

Then suddenly, she smiled. A soft, sweet smile that touched her eyes. “You found me.”

David’s heart jumped into his throat. He could barely breathe. “Yeah,” he managed to whisper.

Cat sat up. Her wrists were bound together, but other than that, she looked unharmed. She licked her lips and cleared her throat. “I need some water.”

David stood and crossed to the kitchen, passing Dean and the whimpering, sobbing Carl Henry along the way. They exchanged looks. Dean looked confused and David could understand why. Carl Henry looked like a man who wouldn’t squash a spider or swat a fly. Why the hell had he kidnapped Cat?

David got his answer when he returned to Cat with the water. He held the glass for her and she took slow sips. In between, she explained about Lydia Henry. When her voice was less raspy, David set aside the water and unbound her wrists.

He rubbed them for her as she stared at him, wide-eyed and smiling. “You came all the way from San Francisco to make sure I was okay?”

“I’d come all the way from the ends of the earth to make sure you’re okay.”

Tears filled her eyes and slid down her cheeks. “I’m sorry if I scared you.”

“Don’t apologize.” He cupped her face in his hands, stared deep into her eyes. “It’s not your fault. I should have been with you—”

“That *is* my fault.” Her hands covered his. “I wanted everything to be perfect between us. I wanted everything neat and tidy, and that’s unrealistic. Life isn’t neat and tidy. Look at the Henrys. Jesus. Talk about people with problems. Ours don’t even compare.”

More tears streamed down her cheeks, seeping beneath his hands, wetting his skin. David’s own eyes grew misty. “Cat, I love you. We were meant to be together. Tell me you want us to be together.”

Her head bobbed up and down. “I do.” She choked back a sob. “With all my heart.”

David pulled her into his arms and held her tight.

Chapter 22

"This is *way* too much!"

Cat laughed as she eyed the ten-carat diamond resting atop a gorgeous platinum Tiffany setting. David had slipped the ring on her finger while she'd slept.

She'd awakened to the rich aroma of coffee and one of his fabulous breakfasts. Rolling onto her side, the enormous rock on her finger had caught the glittery rays of sun that filtered through the opened patio doors. The prism of color caught her eye and Cat stared, in awe, at the gorgeous engagement ring.

Holding her hand up in the air as she lay on her back in the rumpled sheets, she continued to admire the diamond as David entered the bedroom with a tray of food.

Following her rescue, David had whisked Cat off to Paris. She had chosen not to press charges against Carl Henry. He had enough to worry about, and besides, she felt his pain. Dr. Kevin Conner returned from a prolonged trip to Asia, which Cat had not known about. He agreed to treat Lydia Henry. The fees associated with her care and her pacemaker were covered by an anonymous benefactor.

Cat smiled. Providing care for Lydia had been David's idea. She had asked him to let her contribute monetarily as well, but David had selflessly offered to pay for the best care possible.

His generosity, and his forgiving nature, made her love him all the more.

"So, what are you hungry for?" he asked as he lifted the lid off a plate of apple-filled crepes. "Look good? Because I also made stuffed French toast with raspberry sauce and strawberry blintzes."

Cat's stomach growled. She giggled. "Even my stomach loves you."

David's gaze softened. He set aside the lid and crawled onto the bed with her. She wrapped her arms around his neck as he settled between her legs. He dropped kisses on her throat, her jaw, her cheek. Then he drew her into one of his long, sexy kisses.

When he finally pulled away, she whispered, "I'm hungry for you."

David groaned. "I'm all yours."

Cat wrapped her legs around his waist. "Make love to me."

"Every chance I get." He kissed her again, then asked, "Will you be my wife?"

Cat could think of nothing better. "*Oui, monsieur.*"

About the Author:

Award-winning author Calista Fox divides her time between the beautiful desert of Arizona and the gorgeous bay of San Diego. Her ultimate goal is to become a citizen of the world, living and writing for months at a time in exciting locales like Paris, the English countryside and Japan. She is the author of erotic romance novellas and short stories as well as romantic suspense and paranormal novels. Calista also writes erotic romances as Ava McKnight.

Visit the author at www.calistafox.com *or email her at* calista@calistafox.com.

Birthday Wish

by Elisa Adams

To My Reader:

Have you ever had something you've always wanted to do, but have never had the courage to follow through with it? Anna has wanted Dean for a long time, but she's never told him. When he asks her what she wants for her birthday—and tells her she can have anything—she knows it's not an opportunity she can pass up. Birthday Wish is about what happens when one woman has the courage to go after her fantasies.

Chapter 1

"If you could have anything for your birthday, Anna, what would it be?"

Anna Kelly's gaze snapped to Dean, her hazel eyes sparkling with curiosity in the pale moonlight. The beginnings of a smile etched her full lips. "Anything?"

"Absolutely anything." Dean Harrison raised his eyebrows in silent challenge. "No boundaries. What would it be? A quiet night alone, away from this party you don't want?"

He'd take her away from the chaos. All she had to do was ask.

"How do you know I don't want the party?" She tucked a strand of glossy brown hair behind her ear. He followed the movement with his gaze, absorbed by the innate grace in her small hands. Hands he'd love to feel on *him*. Everywhere. He swallowed hard.

A chorus of laughter drew his attention to the French doors behind them. Light filtered through the sheer drapes, casting squares of bright yellow on the balcony floor. Inside the house, forms in silhouette moved and danced, mingling with each other as muted strains of jazz music floated out through the closed doors.

"Because if you wanted to celebrate your birthday, you'd be inside dancing and laughing with everyone else rather than standing out here in this heat with me."

He brushed the back of his hand across his forehead. It came away coated with sweat. Another relentless summer night in New England. Hot and humid, air so thick it made something as simple as breathing seem like a chore.

He should have turned down Molly's invitation to her sister's birthday party. But he hadn't, for one reason. She was standing right next to him.

"Okay, so maybe I'm not in a party mood right now." Her husky laugh sent a rush of warmth through him. "It's just an excuse for Molly to set me up with one of her single male friends. I don't know when she's going to learn that I'm not interested."

"Ah, the blind date in front of a group." He understood her need to hide out all too well. Since his divorce, he'd had more than a few well-meaning friends try to set him up. He grimaced.

"That's what it amounts to." She laughed, shook her head. Her dark, glossy curls fanned out across the back of her dress. "I'm not interested in a relationship right now, but even if I was, it would be with someone I picked out rather than a person someone else thinks would be *perfect* for me."

"I see your point." He grinned. "And I understand completely, but that still doesn't answer my original question."

She rolled her eyes, let out a dramatic sigh. "I'm still thinking."

She leaned forward, propping her elbows on the wooden railing, and dropped her gaze to the yard below. Dean took full advantage, letting his gaze sweep the length of her petite figure, her soft curves encased in some sort of light colored, flowing fabric that ended at mid-thigh. Her lips… he had plenty of fantasies stored up involving those full, incredible lips. Six months' worth.

Dean blew out a breath. The thoughts made his body ache, made his mind threaten to shut down. Made him think about how easy it would be to push her skirt up, move her panties out of the way, and slide inside her hot pussy.

Fuck. He ran a hand through his hair, desperate to get control of his libido before he scared her away.

"A new car?" he prodded. "A bigger house? A better job? Come on. If you had no limits, what would you choose?"

A night of amazing sex with a man who would worship your body the way it deserves to be worshipped?

A soft peal of laughter escaped her. She kept her gaze trained on a spot somewhere below them, but he didn't have to see her face to imagine the blush creeping up her cheeks.

"Anything at all? That seems like kind of a personal question." She glanced at him, her brow furrowed. She tugged her lower lip between her teeth, an unconscious gesture that told him she was deep in thought. The gesture carried back to when they'd been kids and it had taken a monumental effort to get more than three words at a time out of her.

"Depends on how you look at it." He winked. "You scared to tell me your biggest fantasy?"

At just the mention of the word, his already semi-hard cock stirred to full attention. Anna and fantasy together–a dangerous combination that made his mouth run dry and his heart thump against his ribcage. He closed his eyes and drew a deep breath, inhaling the soft, feminine scent of Anna mingled with Molly's rose gardens. His balls grew heavy, an ache spreading out through his limbs. He shook his head, trying to shake off his burgeoning arousal.

It was all her fault, really. He'd escaped the party because he hadn't been able to take another second looking at her in her sexy dress. And then she'd followed him outside.

"Dean?"

His eyes snapped open. "Yeah?"

"What are you doing?"

"What do you mean?"

She sighed. "This question. Where did it come from?"

"Just making conversation. When you stepped out onto the balcony all alone, you looked like you needed someone to talk to." Though the thoughts running through his mind weren't nearly so innocent.

"Conversation, huh?" A spark of amusement lit her eyes. "For a second there I thought you were flirting with me."

His breath caught in his lungs. Was he being that obvious? He searched her face for some hint of anger or irritation, but found none. Her gaze had softened, that lower lip pulled between her teeth again.

He narrowed his eyes, put his hands against the rail and leaned forward. "Would it bother you if I was?"

"No. I really don't think it would."

"Good, because I have to admit I'm enjoying this."

"Me, too. More than I should be, I think." She glanced over her shoulder. "It's a lot better than being inside."

"There's air conditioning in there."

"Yeah, but…" Her voice trailed off, her gaze lighting on his before dipping away.

"But what?"

"I've never really minded the heat." She turned around, her back against the rail and her hands resting on either side. "I know exactly what I'd want for my birthday if I could have anything in the world."

"What's that?"

"A weekend with you."

He let go of the railing, his hands clenching into fists. The blood roared so loud in his ears it drowned out all other noises around them. A weekend with him. That was almost, *almost*, his biggest fantasy. His gaze snapped to hers, looking for some sign that she was joking with him. He found none. "Really?"

She blinked, twice, her lips parted. "I can't believe I just said that."

"Do you want to take it back?" *Please, please don't want to take it back.*

"I, uh…"

"Cause if you mean it, I think something could be arranged."

She pushed away from the rail and walked to the darkened corner next to the door. She faced the wall, her shoulders rising and falling. Soon her laughter reached him across the balcony.

"Anna? Are you okay?"

"I'm just waiting to wake up from this twisted dream. Because if I really just said that to you, then I might as well jump off the balcony right now."

He walked over to where she stood and put his hands on her shoulders, turning her around to face him. "What's wrong with what you said? I asked, and you gave me an honest answer. It was honest, right?"

She started to look down, but he cupped her chin in his palm. She blinked up at him, her eyes half closed and her lips parted. The pink tip of her tongue darted out to wet that full lower lip.

The urge to kiss her almost overwhelmed his common sense. "Anna?"

"Yes, it was honest. Okay? Are you happy now? Go ahead and shoot me down. Tell me you're not attracted to me at all. Tell me what an idiot I am for even thinking you might be interested based on the first real conversation we've had since we were kids."

Her speech stunned him for a brief second. Her words held a healthy dose of insecurity, but they also held something else. Challenge. She was daring him to deny his attraction.

He stopped fighting the urge that had plagued him since seeing her walk outside fifteen minutes earlier. He leaned down and brushed a kiss across her lips. The light contact sent a jolt through his body. "I'm interested." More than interested. His body had tensed to the point of snapping.

"You are?"

He nodded.

"Are you sure? This isn't just some pity thing, is it?"

A rough laugh rumbled up from his chest. "No. *Hell* no. Pity isn't even involved. Ever since you walked into my office six months ago, I haven't been able to stop thinking about you."

He'd been in the middle of a messy divorce at the time, but he was a free man now and she'd just made him an offer he wouldn't be able to refuse. He'd always been fascinated with her quiet introspection, and with those eyes that seemed to take everything in, not missing a single detail.

She reached up, her fingers tracing the line of his jaw. He shuddered. "What are you doing?"

"Something I've wanted to do for a long time."

Her fingertips brushed his chin before moving across his lips. His groin tightened. He grabbed her wrist to still her movements.

"Now probably isn't the best time to be doing that." He cast a glance at the balcony doors.

"They're busy having fun in there. I think we're safe." She smiled, stood on tiptoes and pressed her lips to his.

The sensual touch of her mouth against his sent electricity sizzling along his nerves. Heat built from where they were joined, spiraling out to his limbs, to damned near every part of his body. She parted her lips and he dipped his tongue inside the warmth of her mouth.

He reveled in the taste of her, hot and sweet and exactly like he'd expected. A groan built up in his chest. He held her face in his palms and tilted her head to deepen the kiss. Her hands came up to his wrists, her fingers circling them, holding him close rather than pushing him away. He'd known it would be like this with her. Scorching, explosive. *Perfect.*

With a final, soft brush of his lips against hers, he broke the kiss and stepped back.

Her fingers flew to her lips, a slow smile curling the corners of her mouth. "Wow."

He slumped against the wall, shoved his hands into his pockets and clenched them into fists. The only way he could make sure he didn't grab her and pull her back into his arms. "You free this weekend?"

She nodded.

"Good. Don't make any plans. I'll be in touch." He pressed a small open-mouthed kiss to her lips before walking to the balcony doors and slipping back into the party.

Chapter 2

Anna's hands shook with nervous excitement as she stuffed her swimsuit into her duffel bag per Dean's instructions. She'd come home from work that afternoon to find that a note, written on his real estate company letterhead, had been slipped under her front door.

Tonight. Six thirty. I'll pick you up. Pack light. Don't forget a swimsuit.

A giggle bubbled up from her chest. Had she really propositioned him? It seemed that she had. The courage had been easy to come by with him standing there flirting, his heated gaze caressing every inch of her body when he thought she hadn't noticed. Of course, the glass of champagne she'd downed before stepping outside had probably helped her courage a little, too.

The giggle turned into a full-fledged laugh. All her adult life he'd fueled her hottest fantasies, but until three nights ago, he'd never shown any sign that he was interested. She hadn't been brave enough to voice what she wanted until he looked at her like he wanted to eat her alive.

She picked up a couple of thongs and bras from the pile she'd made on her yellow comforter and dropped them into the bag. A delighted shiver raced down her spine. It had been far too long since she'd had any sort of adventure in her love life. In the past couple of years, it had become the same old thing. Only the men changed.

Dean would be the one to fix all that. The one to break her streak of boring, ho-hum encounters. He made her want to be bad. To do things she'd never before been willing to try. Like proposition a man for a weekend of down and dirty, hot and sweaty sex.

Her pussy fluttered, her hands clenching into fists. Her face flamed. She'd been wound tight for three days, and finding the note had only made matters worse.

A quick glance at her watch told her she still had fifteen minutes to go. She'd be lucky if she lasted ten without imploding. She shoved the rest of her things into the bag, pulled the zipper closed, and flopped down on the mattress. Maybe she should have brought him home the night of her party. He'd obviously been willing. If she had taken him home then, she wouldn't be teetering on the edge of insanity right now.

She also wouldn't be preparing for what promised to be the most exciting weekend of her life.

She picked up the phone and dialed her sister's number. Molly answered on the second ring.

"I wanted to let you know I'm going away for the weekend," she told Molly. "Just so you don't worry. I'll have my cell with me so I can check messages, but I'm turning it off."

"Where are you going?"

"Away. I can't be disturbed. It's business." *Business* that had been getting her hot and bothered for years. Business she needed to take care of at the earliest possible convenience.

She bit back a smile.

Molly let out an indelicate little snort. "Since when do you take business trips?"

"Since now." She stood up and walked toward the mirror hanging above her oak dresser, combing her fingers through her curls. She studied her reflection and shook her head. She looked exactly like she felt—flushed, wanton, and ready to jump Dean's bones as soon as he walked into her house. "It's a weekend class I have to take. I'll be back Sunday night."

She dabbed on a coat of clear, shiny lip gloss and spritzed her neck and wrists with a summertime body splash she'd picked up yesterday afternoon. The scent of coconut and lime filled the air. She fastened a slim gold watch on her wrist, the only jewelry she'd need for the sensual weekend.

Molly laughed. "Yeah, right. Like I'm really going to buy that you're taking a business trip. What's his name?"

"Whose name?"

"Don't play dumb with me, Anna. I know you better than anyone. Who is this man you're running away with for the weekend?"

"You don't know him."

"Don't be so sure about that." Molly clucked her tongue. A dramatic paused stretched between them. "It's Dean, isn't it?"

"How did you know?"

"*Please*. I saw the two of you making out on the balcony the other night. Add that to your sudden secrecy… it doesn't take a genius to figure it out."

The blood rushed from Anna's head, her reflection blinking back at her. "You saw?"

"Well, yeah. You weren't exactly private about it, and I know how you feel about him, so it just makes sense. He's sexy. I don't blame you for indulging a little."

"Um… thanks?" Unable to look at her pathetic, embarrassed reflection any longer, she turned and stomped back to the bed to resume her packing.

"Where is he taking you?" Molly plowed ahead in typical working-mother-of-three take-no-crap fashion. "A romantic weekend in the country? A trip to some high-priced New York City hotel?"

"Gag. You know I'm not into all that romance stuff. We've been over that a hundred times before." She put her makeup bag into a large side pocket of the duffel, along with a zip-top plastic bag filled with shampoo, conditioner, and lotion. "Besides, this isn't about love. It's just… you know. A way to let off some steam."

"Sounds like fun. Just be careful, okay?"

"Of course, I will." She opened the top drawer of her white bedside table and pulled out a box of condoms. Family pack. She smiled. Yes, it would be a very good weekend indeed.

"Anna?"

"Hmm?" The box went into the other side pocket, along with the jar of chocolate body paint she'd gotten for her birthday—a joke gift from her cousin Alice.

A gift that would soon be put to good use.

"I'm glad you two are finally getting together. You make a cute couple."

Anna rolled her eyes. "Just because you have a storybook marriage doesn't mean that's what everyone else is looking for. I'm not ready to settle down. I just want a weekend away from the world before I have to settle back into the routine of work and real life again."

She'd just finished pulling the zipper on the pocket closed when the doorbell rang. "Molly, gotta go. I'll call you when I get back."

She disconnected the call. She glanced at the clock on the bedside table. Less than ten minutes had passed. She swallowed hard, took a deep breath and walked down the narrow hallway of her little cottage to the front door.

After she flipped the locks and turned the knob, the aging door creaked open on protesting hinges. Dean stood on her front porch, more casual than she'd seen since they were teenagers. Faded jeans hugged his taut thighs, a black v-neck t-shirt stretched tight across the expanse of his chest. A pair of dark brown hiking boots finished off the ensemble. Sexy in its simplicity. Her stomach quivered at the sight of him.

Gone was the sensible businessman, the owner of a successful real estate firm who ran his office with an iron fist. Gone was the silent, serious man she'd known since childhood. Now he was just Dean, the man she would be spending her entire weekend with.

A split-second of doubt flashed through her mind. Was she making a huge mistake? Though their mothers had been best friends since before Anna and Dean had been born, she really didn't know him all that well. She'd always been shy and he'd always been too solemn for his own good. Though that solemnity was the first thing that had attracted her to him. The quiet, stoic attitude had been a draw for her right from the start. His complexities intrigued her, made her want to get to know him better, but at the same time, he'd never given her a hint that he wanted the same thing.

Until the other night.

"Hi." One side of his mouth quirked in a sexy half-smile that heated her blood and pooled moisture between her legs. "Wow. You look amazing. I think I like this dress even better than the one you had on the last time I saw you."

She beamed, glad she'd decided to wear her favorite dress—a powder blue sleeveless number—rather than the shorts and t-shirt she'd originally planned. Seeing his gaze heat and a flush creep into his cheeks made it all worth it. "Thanks. You look pretty great yourself."

"In this?" His hand swept up and down in front of his body.

"Yeah. It's good to see you as something other than a stuffed shirt."

"You really thought of me that way?" He laughed. Stroked a finger down her cheek, leaving a row of gooseflesh in its wake. "I guess I'll have to use this weekend to correct that opinion. You ready?"

"Just about. Let me just grab my bag and put on my shoes. Why don't you come in for a second? I'll be right back."

"No problem."

She rushed into the bedroom, got down on her hands and knees and sifted through the closet until she found the shoes that would be a perfect compliment to her dress. She sat on the edge of the bed and laced the beige sandals around her ankles. The heels would put her a few inches above her barefoot height of five-foot-two. She might not have been born tall, but she could fake it with the best of them.

When she came back into the living room, Dean stood by the media cabinet tucked into the far corner, perusing her collection of DVDs. He glanced over his shoulder and smiled. "You like movies, huh?"

"Um, yeah. I guess I'm kind of an addict." She ran her hand down her arm, glanced down at the ground. "I'm all set. Should we go?"

"Sure." A soft laugh escaped him. He took her bag from her hand and started toward the front door. "I like what you've done with the place. It suits you."

A corner of her mouth lifted in a smile. After years of scrimping and saving, six months ago she'd finally managed to collect enough money to put a down payment on a house. Dean had shown her the four-room cottage in a busy but quaint downtown neighborhood, and she'd fallen in love with it. Since moving in, she'd added her own touches here and there, but the hundred-year-old dwelling had so many charming characteristics of its own she hadn't needed to change much.

"Thanks." She followed after him, grabbing her purse and keys on the way.

She locked the door behind them, glanced at the street and let out a soft breath. Parked in back of her trusty little ten-year-old silver sedan was a flashy red two-seater sports car. It looked brand new. "Is that yours?"

He nodded. "Just picked it up last week."

"Very nice. Did you trade in your SUV?"

"No. I'll need something to drive in the winter. This thing won't handle well in the snow." He put his hand on the small of her back and nudged her forward. "Let's get going before it gets too late."

He opened the door for her, and closed it once she was seated inside the car. The gray butter-soft leather enveloped her and she sank in, eyes closed and a smile on her face. She inhaled the unmistakable scent of new car, mingled with the equally unmistakable scent of the owner. Fresh, clean, masculine and spicy. Perfect.

Oh, God. If he had a long car ride planned to get to their destination, she'd never make it. Her eyelids snapped open.

He slid behind the wheel and turned the key in the ignition. The engine started with a rumbling purr. "You sure you want to go through with this?"

She touched her hand to his thigh, gave the hard muscle there a squeeze. "I was just going to ask you the same thing."

His leg jumped under her touch. "Good." When he spoke, his voice had taken on a gravelly tone. "I'm glad we're still on the same page."

He pulled the car away from the curb and headed out of town.

"Where are we going?"

"It's a surprise." He glanced at her and smiled. "It's not far. About an hour's drive north. I need you to do something for me before we get there, though."

"Sure. What's that?" Visions of maps or printed online directions danced through her head.

"Take off your panties."

Her mouth went dry, all the moisture flooding to other parts of her body. "Excuse me?" Her voice came out as no more than a whisper.

"Your panties. Take them off."

A tremor ran through her pussy at his blatant command. "What if I'm not wearing any?"

A soft groan rumbled from his lips. His gulp reached her across the small space inside the car. "Are you?"

"Maybe."

"Don't tease me, Anna. You might not be happy with the results."

"Okay, I'm wearing them." She licked her lips, willing to bet a month's salary that she'd be *very* happy with the results. "But just for future reference, I only wear thongs."

His palm smacked down on the steering wheel.

A short laugh bubbled up in her throat. She lifted her hips and slid her panties down her legs, her fingers trembling so hard it made the movements awkward. "Okay, they're off."

"Good. Put them in the glove compartment."

Her breath caught, all the blood rushing from her head to points further south. What had happened to the quiet Dean who barely said a word to her? He wasn't what she'd expected after a decade of lurid fantasies.

He was so much more.

With trembling hands, she opened the glove compartment, put the panties inside, and closed it with a click.

"Okay. Done."

His hand came down on her knee and gave her a light squeeze. "I need to know something before this goes any further."

A thousand possibilities flew through her mind, not all of them good. "What's that?" She held her breath waiting for his answer.

"Do you trust me?"

"Sure."

"I'm serious. If you don't trust me, this weekend is going to be a waste. I've known you since we were kids. You know me well enough to trust that I won't do anything to hurt you, right?"

"Of course."

"Good. That's just what I needed to know." He squeezed her thigh again, a little harder this time. "Spread your legs for me, Anna."

She squirmed in the soft leather seat, hesitating only a second before she did as told, parting her legs as much as she was able in the small space.

Dean pulled up the flowing hem of her dress, exposing her bare cleft to his gaze. The cool air from the air conditioning vent feathered over her pussy, sifting through the soft curls. A wave of heat pulsed through her clit and she moaned.

"Beautiful," he told her, his tone almost reverent. "This is going to be an incredible weekend. I can promise you that."

"I don't doubt it for a second." She leaned her head back against the seat, her pussy already throbbing and he had yet to touch her. Her breathing had grown ragged, her breasts rising with each sharp intake of air. The movements rubbed the rough lace of her bra against her peaked nipples, sending little jolts of pleasure-pain through the ultra sensitive buds.

He braked at a stop sign and glanced over at her, a crooked smile on his face. "How are you holding up?"

"That depends. Are you trying to kill me with arousal? If so, it's working like a charm."

A laugh escaped his lips. "Killing you is definitely not what I had planned."

His gaze dropped to her exposed pussy and his laugher died. "Put the seat back a little. There's a button on the side."

She found the button and depressed it. A low mechanical whir sounded as the seat lowered, exposing her more fully to his gaze.

"Oh, God." He spoke the words in hushed tones. "That's a beautiful sight."

He turned back to the road and pulled away from the stop sign.

He slid his fingers down the inside of her thigh until they brushed her labia. She shivered. He parted her folds and stroked his finger across her clit.

She arched into his touch, every stroke of his fingers sending sparks against her skin. Her head thrashed from side to side, her hips bucking against the relentless stroke of his fingers on the tight bundle of nerves. Her inner muscles quivered, her breathing an unsteady rasp.

A car approached, driving in the other direction on the quiet stretch of roadway, and she tried to school her expression.

"Don't. Let go. You'll never see any of them again."

Her body coiled like a spring, she gripped the door handle and thrust her hips against his hand. He stroked along the length of her slit, dipping his fingers into the moisture that flooded her pussy. When his fingers came back to her clit, she bit her lip and came with a low moan.

She squeezed her eyes shut as the spasms rocked through her body. Pleasure raced along her bloodstream, bringing every nerve to life. Stars danced on the backs of her eyelids, her mouth gaping, pants of breath escaping her lips. Still he continued to stroke her until he'd wrung every last shudder out of her sated body.

"You okay?" he asked, his tone husky with his own arousal.

Her eyelids drifted open and she glanced at him. Her lips rose in a small smile. "I think so. Give me another minute to be sure."

He brought his fingers to his lips and sucked them into his mouth. "You taste incredible. I can't wait to bury my mouth in your pussy."

She whimpered. Another tremor fluttered through her inner muscles. She'd be more than happy to let him. If she didn't die before they reached their destination.

Chapter 3

Dean let them inside the cabin and set their bags down on the pine floor next to the front door. He smiled, though he was so hard that walking from the car to the front door had been a challenge. His whole body screamed for release, his cock rigid against his zipper. Anna had to notice the bulge in his pants. There was no way she could miss it.

His fingers found the switch on the wall and flipped it up, bathing the living area of the cabin in soft light. His good friend Steve's weekend get-away hadn't changed a bit since the last time Dean had visited. The décor was plain, comfortable, with navy blue curtains and a dark red plaid couch and chairs. The cabin was small, but Steve hadn't bought it for the size. The three-room building sat on a large wooded lakefront lot with its own private beach. It was peaceful, and far enough away from civilization that Anna would feel safe letting go of all her inhibitions and be able to enjoy the weekend she'd requested.

He set the central air conditioner at sixty-eight to rid the air of the stale warmth. He glanced at Anna, standing in the middle of the living room, looking around. When she caught him staring, she smiled. Her gaze dropped to his obvious erection and the smile heated.

"Very impressive. And the house is nice, too."

He swallowed hard. "Thanks. The fact that I'm this hard is your fault, you know."

"How is it my fault? You're the one who ordered me out of my panties five minutes into the car ride."

"Guilty as charged." And he'd do it again if given the chance. Watching her come apart like that had to be one of the most arousing things he'd ever seen. He groaned.

She laughed softly and continued. "You're also the one who couldn't keep his hands to himself. I don't think I've ever been so turned on in my life as I was in that car."

That made two of them.

Oh, Jesus. There was no way he'd make it another five minutes if she kept talking to him like that. He fisted his hands and looked away, busying himself with turning on the few table lamps in the room. When he finished the task, he turned on the TV.

"Have a seat. I'll make us some dinner."

"Dinner?" The curiosity in her voice brought a smile to his face.

"Yeah, you know, the meal eaten before lunch and bedtime?" Bedtime being the operative word there. She'd offered him a weekend to live out his fantasies, and he intended to do just that. But first, a little conversation was in order. To heighten the anticipation for both of them, yes, but also to let him get to know her better outside of the context of being longtime family friends. His fascination with her had only grown since the encounter in the car. She'd opened her body so completely to him. Would she open her mind to him as well?

He had to find out. Had to connect with her on a level that went beyond the physical. He left her sitting on the couch and walked into the kitchen. Sex with Anna would be amazing, but getting to know what made her tick first would make the weekend positively mind-blowing.

Mindless sex held no appeal to him. Never had, never would. The physical act was only part of great sex. Most of the sensations started in the mind. If he learned about her, he could understand what made her tick and turn her on like no one had before. The car ride had been a start. He didn't intend to stop until he'd stripped her free of her reserve. Only then would she get what she was truly looking for out of their weekend.

He went to the fridge and began pulling out the makings of a simple dinner. Pizza dough, fresh vegetables, cheese and seasonings. Something light. Something that wouldn't require much work since his brain had shut down the second he'd touched her soaked pussy.

He slammed his fists onto the countertop. Getting through this meal might kill him. But he wouldn't act like a wild animal. Not yet. Not until he'd shown her at least a sliver of the civilized man she no doubt expected him to be.

Soft footsteps sounded behind him. *Damn.* Didn't she realize how close to the edge he was? If she'd thought his demands in the car had been rough, she had no idea what sort of pleasure he had in store for her.

"Do you need any help, Dean?"

He took a deep, calming breath to steady his frayed nerves. He'd promised her this weekend. He could hold it together long enough to make sure he didn't scare her away. "Sure, you want to chop vegetables?"

"Okay." She walked over to the counter and he handed her a knife and a small white cutting board.

He stole glances at her as he smoothed out pizza crust and brushed it with olive oil and garlic. While she worked chopping peppers, mushrooms, and onions, her lips drew into a flat line of concentration and a furrow creased her brow. His lips itched to kiss the crease away. He chopped fresh basil and oregano and put that on top of the crust, still determined to ignore the more basic urges plaguing him with Anna so close.

Fighting the urges got easier as he watched her and the familiar fascination took root. The grace of her movements, the focus etched on her face awed him. She was beautiful—but it wasn't just physical beauty. It was something he couldn't explain. Didn't want to explain. But whatever it was, it captured his attention and refused to let go.

She piled the chopped vegetables into a bowl and passed it over to him. "I have to say I'm impressed. I didn't realize you could cook."

He winked at her. "It's one of my dirty little secrets."

"Are there more?"

"Quite a few. I promise to let you in on a couple of others before the weekend's over."

He layered the veggies on the pizza, and then topped it with provolone and parmesan cheese. He slid the tray into the oven and set the timer.

Dean turned to face her, determined to ignore the heat in her eyes for a little longer. Anna would expect him to be a gentleman. A gentleman didn't jump on a woman the first chance he got. He fed her first. Romanced her. Gave her a little chance to acclimate herself to the situation before he made his move.

If he didn't look at her, he just might make it through the meal.

A half hour later they sat at the table, finishing up their dinner. Anna popped her last bite of pizza into her mouth and smiled. "That was really good."

Dean returned the smile with an easy one of his own. Thanks to the meal and the casual conversation, his erection had lessened to a much more manageable state. At least now he wasn't worried about losing the button on his jeans. "I'm glad you liked it."

"Where did you learn how to cook like that?"

He took a gulp of water and set the glass down on the table with a thump. "I got sick of eating out all the time, so I decided to take a few classes."

She watched him for a few seconds, her gaze curious. Her tongue darted out to wet her lips.

He braced himself for the questions sure to come next. Very personal questions that would put an instant damper on the sensual tone of the weekend. But she didn't ask. She just shrugged.

"Well, the lessons must have taken."

"What made you decide to go into nursing?"

She squirmed in her seat, a sharp reminder that she had no panties on. Under that dress, her lower half was naked and hot and ready for him to thrust inside. His cock pulsed back to life at the thought.

An answering lust lit her eyes. He leaned forward and took her hand, kissing each knuckle in turn. Even her skin tasted sweet.

She let out a shuddering sigh, her eyelids drooping. His gut tightened. The only things separating them were his jeans and boxers.

He could have them off in five seconds flat. "Anna?"

She blinked up at him with glazed-over eyes. "Huh?"

"Nursing. Why did you decide to go into the healthcare field?" He placed an open-mouth kiss in the center of her palm.

"I..." She whimpered, rocked forward slightly in her chair. "I wanted to be able to help people."

She was helping him right now. Right over the edge of reason.

He released her hand and stood, starting to clear the plates off the table.

Anna stopped him with a hand on his shoulder. "You did most of the cooking. I'll do the dishes."

"They can wait."

"No, it's fine. I don't mind." Her hips swayed enticingly beneath the flowing, thin fabric of her skirt. His balls hung heavy between his legs, his dick hard to the point of pain. Waiting wasn't going to be an option much longer. Who could think about dishes at a time like this?

He walked over to her, settling his hands against her hips.

She jumped. "You're lucky I didn't drop one of these plates. You'd have to pay for it."

"Nah. A buddy of mine owns the place. He'd understand the fact that I couldn't keep my hands off you for another second." He leaned in and pressed a kiss to the tender spot where her neck met her shoulder.

She shivered. "Um. That feels good."

To his dismay, though, she continued to wash the plates and flatware and set them in the drainer next to the sink.

He splayed his hands across her stomach, his fingers trailing down until his fingertips rested just above her pussy.

She let out a quiet puff of air, grabbed a dish towel, and started drying the dishes.

He slid his hands higher, cupping the firm mounds of her breasts. They filled his hands and more, spilling over. He'd love to strip her out of her dress, push her breasts together, and slide his cock in between them. Later, he just might. He gave the mounds a firm squeeze.

Her nipples beaded, pressing against the center of his palms. He licked his lips. What he wouldn't give for a taste of her…

He nipped at her skin, her neck, with light touches of his teeth. She let out a soft moan. "If you keep touching me like that, I really might drop a dish. There are things I'd rather spend the evening doing than picking glass up off the floor."

He chuckled, though the sound came out strained. Lust had twisted his gut into knots and every nerve had snapped to readiness. "Okay. I'll back off. For now. But you have two minutes and then all bets are off."

She glanced at him over her shoulder, a sly smile on her face. "A little bit impatient?"

"Hell, yes. You've had me hard as a rock for three days."

"Then why don't we do something about it?"

She was tempting him, teasing him, trying to control the situation. His mind fought to take back that control while his body wanted to allow her freedom to do whatever she wanted. Damn, he loved a confident woman. If all went as planned, they were in for one hell of a wild weekend.

"In a little while." He opened a bottle of wine and poured two glasses. "It's cooler tonight than it has been in days. I'm going to sit outside and enjoy the break in the humidity. Care to join me?"

"Sounds great." She took a glass from his hand and followed him out to the deck and into the bright light from the early evening sun. "I have an idea for dessert, if you're interested."

"What's that?"

"You'll see. Trust me, Dean, you'll love it."

Why did he feel like his power over the situation had just slipped from his fingers?

Ever since the night of her birthday party, he'd been in a frazzled state of semi-arousal, his baser instincts threatening to shut down his mind and take over his actions. Everything Anna said, everything she did, pushed him closer and closer to the edge.

"Okay. I'm game." *I think.*

She laughed. "Good. I'll be right back."

She ducked back inside and a minute later returned carrying a small white paper bag.

He gulped. "What's in there?"

"Just something I thought would be fun."

"A game?"

"Sure. Works for me."

He rubbed a hand down his face. What did she have planned? He'd gone into their arrangement assuming he'd be the one to surprise her, to show her what her sex life had been missing. That was why she'd asked him for the weekend, wasn't it? To experiment with sex in a safe environment with someone she trusted?

Maybe he'd gotten her reasoning wrong. He hadn't counted on shy, quiet Anna Kelly to have a surprise or two of her own.

She settled onto a chair and took a sip of her wine. "Nervous, Dean?"

"No." Nervous wasn't the right way to describe his emotional state. Aroused beyond belief would have been a more apt description. He flopped down into the chair across from her, drained his wine in a few gulps and set the glass down on the deck.

She set her own glass down after only a few sips and turned to him with a sexy, confident smile. "Wanna play?"

Did she even need to ask? "Sure. What do you have in mind?"

"I think it's time for dessert." She lifted the bag and pulled out a small jar. A black label with gold lettering caught his attention. Chocolate body paint.

A shudder ran down the length of his spine and he bit back a groan. So much for shy and quiet. The woman was a veritable sex kitten. The contrast stoked the fire burning inside him. "Where did you get that?"

"Actually, it was sort of a joke gift I got for my birthday, but I thought we could put it to good use."

He reached for the jar, but she pulled it away. "Uh-uh. You had your turn in the car. It's my turn to play now."

Oh, shit. He gulped, his lungs so tight he could barely draw in a full breath. It wouldn't take much more than a strong wind to make him come.

"Maybe we should save this for later. At the rate I'm going, I won't last much past a few seconds."

She lifted one shoulder in a casual shrug that belied the lust in her hazel eyes. "Thirty-two isn't ancient by any stretch of the imagination. I'm sure you could get it up again with the right… coaxing. And Dean, I know how to coax."

He muttered a curse, grabbed the seat of the chair with both hands to keep from grabbing her, unzipping his pants, and ramming into her pussy. The temptation was almost too strong to fight.

He squeezed his eyes shut. *One… two… three… four…*

"Take off your shirt, Dean."

Five… six… seven…

"Dean?" Her voice was a warm, silken caress over his sensitized skin.

"I did as you asked in the car. It's your turn now."

He opened his eyes on a sigh. "If you intend to tease me mercilessly with that stuff, let me warn you now that I may not be able to control myself later."

"Oh, I'm counting on that." She unscrewed the jar with a pop and set it down on the wicker end table. The rich scent of chocolate filled the air between them. "And before you even suggest it, I have to tell you I'm not looking for a gentleman this weekend. I've had gentlemen. They bore me. This weekend I want something more."

That did it. He stood, hauled her out of her chair, and crushed her against him.

One of his hands threaded through her hair. The other went to the small of her back, pulling her tight against him. Her belly cradled his cock, her nipples stabbing against his chest.

He thrust his tongue into her mouth in a claiming, possessing kiss. Her tongue met his thrust for thrust, her fingers wrapping around the back of his neck. Her other hand pulled the hem of his shirt from his waistband. Her fingers worked their way up his chest, pushing the shirt along as they went.

Her nails raked his abdomen and he thought he'd come out of his skin. He broke the kiss, panting, and let her go.

He couldn't take this. Not another second. Lust curled around his brain, shutting down most thought processes not involving Anna and her sexy little body. "You're playing with fire, Anna."

Her smile was nothing short of wicked. "That's what I'm counting on."

Chapter 4

Anna hid her giddy smile as the heat flashed across Dean's expression. He stood in front of her, shoulders hunched, breath wheezing in and out of his lungs. His lips were parted, his cheeks flushed a pale red, and his hands were clenching and unclenching.

The kiss had been scorching. So much stronger than their first kiss on Molly's balcony, and her body craved more of what he had to offer. But first, she wanted to play.

Her gaze flickered to the body paint before returning to his. "What's the matter, Dean? Afraid to show me your body?"

He gave a quick, hard shake of his head, stripped off his shirt and tossed it to the ground.

Her pussy muscles quivered. Lord, she'd reduced him to a silent, animal-like state that made her nipples bead even harder against the satin cups of her bra. "Good. Now the pants."

His chest heaved with his deep indrawn breath. His Adam's apple bobbed as he swallowed. With slow deliberation, his gaze never leaving hers, he kicked off the loosely-tied hiking boots and brought his hand to the waistband of his jeans.

She dropped her gaze to watch him work the button free and draw the zipper down, exposing the length of his hard cock encased in tight black cotton. Her heart skittered, a curl of lust forming low in her belly. Without thinking, she licked her lips.

Dean muttered a curse, drawing her attention back to his eyes. His gaze was hard and scorching, holding more than a hint of warning. She let out a breathless little laugh, ran a hand through her hair. It was going to take every ounce of willpower she had to keep ordering him around instead of begging him to forget dessert and just take her.

She whimpered. The thought of making Dean dessert would keep her in control for a bit longer. "Keep going."

He pushed his pants down, letting them drop to the deck. His socks followed, and then his thumbs hooked in the waistband of his boxer briefs. He pulled them down slowly and kicked them off. The briefs landed somewhere on the deck, but she couldn't be sure where. She heard the swish of fabric as they fell, but she was too busy looking at what he'd just uncovered to pay much attention to anything else.

His cock bobbed in front of him, long and thick, a drop of fluid leaking from the tip. Without giving it a thought, she caught the drop with her finger and brought it to her lips.

His ragged groan made a rush of moisture drench her pussy. She licked her lips and smiled up at him. "You taste good."

"Is this payback for the car ride?" he asked, his tone harsh with his arousal.

She shivered. That voice did it for her every time. Smooth and rich as honey, yet rough as gravel at the same time. The sound of his voice hit her right where it counted and threatened to bring her to her knees. A tremor ran through her inner muscles. "No. It was just too much of a temptation to pass up."

He reached out for her, but she shook her head.

"Keep your hands to yourself. It's my turn now." She cupped his balls in one hand, used the other to stroke his cock from root to tip. Once. Before she dropped her hands. "Very nice. Is this for me?"

"You know damned well it is. Are you going to tease me all night?"

He had to be the most beautiful man she'd ever seen. Not feminine in any way, but the symbol of all-male perfection. From his hard pecs to his six-pack abs, the man had the body of a gym god. And those arms… she was a sucker for muscular arms. She swallowed hard to clear the dryness in her mouth. "You know, I just might."

He muttered an indecent string of curses that had her smiling. She had no intention of teasing him all night. Twenty minutes, max. But Anna doubted even she would last that long. She'd wanted him for too many years to keep either of them waiting any more time than necessary. Her pussy ached to be filled. Her clit begged for attention from those warm, strong fingers.

Soon. She'd have him inside her soon. They both knew that and she wouldn't deny it was the whole reason behind the weekend trip. For now, she just wanted to have a little fun.

"Go lie down over there." She gestured to a chaise lounge across the deck.

"Are you fucking kidding me?" He took a step toward her, then another, stopping only when she lifted her hand in the air in front of her.

"Do you remember what you asked me about trust in the car?"

He nodded.

"It works both ways. You have to trust me. Put yourself in my hands."

She laid her palm on his chest, right over his heart. "I promise you, this will be good."

With a heavy sigh, he stalked over to the chaise and lay down on the taupe cushion. His cock stood at proud attention, his stomach rising and falling with every ruthless breath. His gaze locked with hers and she couldn't break the hot spell as she leaned down to grab the jar of body paint and made her way over to the chaise.

Anna knelt down next to him and dipped her fingers into the jar. She coated them with the rich dark chocolate paint and brought her fingers to his skin, painting a swirling pattern on his washboard stomach, just a few inches above the root of his cock. He grabbed fistfuls of the soft mesh cushion beneath him, his eyelids slamming shut.

She dipped her fingers back into the jar. This time, she painted his sculpted pecs. She ended with a swirl over each nipple. She'd enjoy licking the chocolate from his skin in a few moments.

She dipped her fingers in the paint again. This time, her focus was on the part of his body she most wanted to taste. His big, thick cock. She swirled her fingers up the length in a spiral pattern before coating the head in the sweet syrup.

Little groans escaped from his lips. His hips thrust against her fingers. She glanced back up at his face to find his eyes open, his expression darker and more aroused than she'd seen it yet. Anna sucked in a breath. Instinct warned her to move away, but she smiled instead.

She rocked back on her heels to admire her masterpiece. Swirls, dips, and circles of chocolate covered him from his chest all the way down to his cock. "You know, Dean, I have to say you look good enough to eat."

He drew a shuddering breath, more fluid leaking from the tip of his erection. "I thought you were going to let me plan this whole weekend."

"I don't remember agreeing to that." She laughed, though she knew her moments of control were numbered. "Now I think I'll have dessert."

She leaned in and licked his skin above his flat nipple. He tasted of hot fudge ice cream topping mixed with the hot, potent flavor of the man himself. She licked the circles from his pecs, trailed her tongue lower, slowly making her way to his nipples, gathering every drop of chocolate as she went.

Her tongue grazed the ridges of his firm stomach, tracing the lines and dips of his defined abs, moving lower and lower until she reached his cock. His hand came down on her head, tangling in the long strands of her hair.

"Don't even think about it," he warned. "I won't last."

"That won't be a problem." She rose to give her better access, darted her tongue out and licked the head of his cock.

His hand tightened in her hair, a rough groan spilling from his lips. His hips bucked toward her, the muscles of his thighs taut beneath the tanned skin.

Anna smiled. She'd always wondered what Dean would look like when he lost that legendary control. Now she knew. A heady sense of power filled her. She'd been the one to turn him into a primal, basic animal. A flood of her juices coated her pussy, her inner muscles quivering. Dean under her command—that had to be one of her biggest fantasies.

She licked the length of his cock, swirling her tongue to collect as much of the body paint as she could. His musky taste was stronger here, so much more enticing. Her tongue traveled from root to tip again, over and over, each lick pushing her mounting arousal closer to the breaking point.

Anna started to dip her hand between her legs, intent on alleviating some of the pressure, but she stopped herself. This was for him. She could find her release later. She had no doubts that he was already working on some sort of payback.

His fingers squeezed her scalp. "You've got about five seconds before I can't hold back. You sure you don't want to stop this now?"

"Positive." She parted her lips and took him inside her mouth.

A harsh curse flew from Dean's lips, his hips arching to meet her every time she brought her mouth down over him. She stroked up and down his length, swirling her tongue over the head on each upstroke. She cupped his balls in her hand, testing their weight against her palm. Heavy and full.

She circled the base of his cock with her thumb and forefinger, tightening her grip until he moaned. With short strokes of her fingers, she matched the rhythm of her mouth. He came with a long, ruthless groan, hot jets of his semen spurting into her mouth. She lapped and swallowed, cradling the hot length of him until he'd started to soften. Then she released him and rocked back on her heels, her pussy aching to be filled, her face hot and her head spinning.

Dean's intense gaze rested on hers, his chest heaving with each breath he took. "Wow."

Anna gave him a self-satisfied grin. "You liked that?"

"Liked it?" A rough bark of laughter escaped him lips. "Loved it is more like it. That was incredible. I thought you were going to kill me." He sat and pushed out of the chaise, grabbing her hand and pulling her to her feet. "Now it's my turn to play. Lose the dress and the bra."

Her heart skittered to a stop before resuming its beat, pounding against her ribcage. "What about my shoes?"

He glanced down at the strappy high-heeled sandals and licked his lips. "Those stay on."

Chapter 5

Anna's blood pounded in her eardrums. She reached back and pulled down the zipper of the dress, pushed the straps off her shoulders. The material slid to the deck boards at her feet. She started to undo the front clasp of her bra, but Dean pulled her hands away.

"I want to do this."

He pulled the clasp open and peeled the lace cups away from the mounds of flesh they covered. Her breasts sprang free, her nipples peaked and begging for his touch.

"Beautiful," he murmured, his tone reverent. He cupped them in his palms, drawing them together. He pressed a soft, open-mouthed kiss to each nipple before releasing her breasts and pulling her bra down her arms. It joined her dress on the deck floor.

He reached down and grabbed the jar of chocolate paint.

Her whole body shook with nervous excitement. She glanced up at the sky. Exposing herself to him so fully in such bright light had her wanting to cover her body. She wrapped her arms over her breasts.

"No, don't." He tugged at her arms until she dropped them away. "You have no idea how beautiful you are. How sexy. I want to see every inch of you."

His heated gaze traveled up and down her body, raising goose bumps on her skin. Dean dipped a finger into the body paint and brought it to her chest, swirling the thick chocolate sauce over her nipple. The other nipple received the same treatment.

Her legs wobbled. "Dean, I don't know how much longer I can stand."

He gave her a sexy half-smile. "I'll catch you if you fall."

He coated his finger in more paint and brought it to her stomach, drawing patterns with the chocolate. His touch grazed first one hipbone and then the other, stopping to collect more paint before he brought his fingertips to her mound.

"Spread your legs apart a little." He punctuated the command with soft touches against her thighs.

She shifted her feet and moved her legs apart, her knees threatening to give out and her pussy throbbing. She was soaked. There was no way he could miss it.

He leaned in and pressed his mouth against her, sliding his tongue along her slit.

"You taste incredible. You're so wet for me."

She whimpered. She'd had sex—good sex, great sex even, but she'd never had sex like this. With Dean it involved the mind as much as the body, and she was loving every second.

He stroked his fingers along the folds of her slit, painting her most private places with the edible paint. She shivered, her breath catching in her lungs. She'd never been so aroused, didn't know if she could make it another second without him inside her. "Dean, please."

"Patience, Anna. I want to admire my masterpiece first." He set the jar down and stood back, appreciating her with his arms crossed over his chest and a thoughtful expression on his face. She glanced down to see his cock rising again from its bed of crisp, dark hairs, and she smiled. *That* was what she wanted.

Inside her.

All night long.

"Take a look at yourself," Dean told her, his gaze encouraging. "Do you know how beautiful you are to me?"

She looked down at her body. He'd painted a large flower on her midsection, its petals reaching up to her breasts and across each hipbone. The stem trailed down the center of her abdomen, disappearing between her thighs.

Her gaze flew to his. He smiled and shrugged. "It suits you."

He leaned in and licked the chocolate from one breast, sucking her nipple into the warm cavern of his mouth. He rolled the nipple gently between his teeth. Panting breaths escaped her lips at the hot, wet sensation.

He moved to the other breast, his tongue collecting the chocolate along the way. This time, he nipped the soft skin on the underside of her breast. He sucked the chocolate-coated nipple between his lips and laved it clean. She brought her hands to his head, gripping him, wanting to hold him in place and pull him away at the same time. It was too much pleasure for her to take without some sort of release.

His tongue traced the petals of the flower, licking the chocolate away from her skin. Dean's tongue dipped into her navel to swipe at the center of the flower, traveled out to her hips to clean the petals there. Then he moved to the stem, his tongue and lips getting closer and closer to her mound.

Every muscle in her body tensed. Whimpering breaths built in her chest before breaking free from her lips. Her pussy fluttered in anticipation. And then he was there, his tongue working along her slit, delving into her pussy, stroking along her clit in a pace so fast it made her head spin. He was relentless, driving her closer and closer to the brink of orgasm until she toppled, her hands gripping his hair hard as the spasms rocketed through her body. Her vision grayed, her inner muscles contracting, little explosions shooting from her clit up to her core, then out to her limbs.

Just when she didn't think her body could take anymore, Dean stood in front of her, pulling her into his arms. His erection pressed against her belly, sending another tremor through her sated body.

He kissed her forehead. "Remind me to let you take care of dessert all the time."

She laughed. "That was pretty amazing."

He cupped her chin in his palm and drew her gaze up to his. "Are you okay?"

"I'm fine. A little wobbly, but fine."

"Good. Let's clean the leftover chocolate off. I can't wait too much longer to get inside you."

Another tremor raced through her body and she moaned. "I don't know if I can take any more right now."

His fingers reached between her legs, the tips grazing her clit in light circles. Moisture seeped from her pussy and a curl of arousal built in her belly. She dug her fingers into his shoulders.

He laughed, the sound rough and grating. "I think you can."

Dean took her hand and led her into the house, making a quick stop near the door to get their bags before heading into the bedroom. He dropped the bags on the bed.

"Why don't you take a shower first?"

A wicked idea hit her. Her lips curled in a smile and she ran her finger down the center of his chest. "Maybe we should shower together instead."

His gaze heated, his throat working as he swallowed hard. "Sounds like a plan to me."

A few minutes later they stood in the bathtub under the hot shower spray. Steam floated all around them, along with the scent of the chocolate that washed from their bodies.

Anna grabbed a washcloth and poured blue shower gel onto it, bringing it to Dean's chest. Her hand worked in small, slow circles. She was intent on arousing him as much as cleaning up the mess they'd made. She grazed his nipples with the cloth, stroked the leftover chocolate from his stomach, then reached between their bodies to wrap the soft cloth around his cock.

He groaned. "I'm clean enough. You, however, need a little attention."

He smiled and took the cloth from her hand, adding more shower gel before he began to wash the stickiness off her body. He made quick work of what was left of the flower—until he reached the juncture of her thighs.

His hand dipped and stroked, his fingers pressing against her clit. Soon she was clinging to him, rocking against him. She was close to coming again—*too* close. She let out a ragged moan. "Dean, please. I can't take much more of this torture."

He laughed, shook his head. Water droplets sprayed out into the steamy air around him.

"Hold on for a second, okay?" he said just before he ducked out of the shower. When he stepped back into the curtained enclosure, a condom covered his cock. He beckoned her with one finger. "Come closer."

She walked over to him and he pulled her close, crushing her slick body against his. His lips brushed her hair, her cheek, her lips in brief caresses before he turned her around and moved her hair off her shoulders. He kissed her neck. Along the line of her shoulder. One of his hands rested on her hip, the other between her shoulder blades.

"Bend forward."

She did as told, leaning over until her hands rested on the shelves on either side of the tub, her ass raised in the air. Steam and water brushed her pussy, sending a shiver through her body.

"Can you hold this position?" he asked, his voice husky with lust and urgency.

"I think so." Though her legs had already started to protest.

"Good."

That was all the warning she had before his cock prodded the entrance to her pussy, plunging inside.

She pushed back against him, meeting his thrusts until he'd seated himself fully inside. He pulled back, igniting fire inside her inner muscles, before he thrust in again. His strokes were hard, unmeasured, his balls slapping her clit with every thrust.

"You feel just like I thought you would," he said in a grating whisper. "So. Incredible."

He reached a hand between her legs, his fingertips circling over her clit. That was all it took for her orgasm to flood her body, pulling her along on a tide of sensation that threatened to drown her. Her elbows and knees buckled and she would have fallen had he not been holding her up. Her whimpers were uncontrollable, her breathing, too. It was so much. *Too much.*

She'd never survive the weekend at this rate.

She sensed his release seconds before it happened. Felt it in the tightening of his hands on her hips, in the short hard thrusts of his cock inside her body. She pushed back against him, encouraging him, welcoming him deep inside. For endless minutes time seemed frozen. Then he pulled her up and dragged her into his arms.

She slumped against him, every muscle in her body quivering. She needed to lie down and sleep. Needed hours of regeneration in his arms.

Anna bit back a smile. Tomorrow would be his day to live out his fantasies. She couldn't wait to find out what he had planned.

Chapter 6

"It's so beautiful here," Anna said, and Dean watched her gaze sweep around the backyard and to the lake beyond. "Your friend is lucky to have a place like this."

"Yeah, it's pretty great."

Trees lined the private yard, the grass a thick carpet of plush green. A few hundred feet from the house the grass met sand, and the sandy shore gave way to the rippling water of the lake. A tranquil, serene setting. Perfect for relaxing, sitting back, and taking a break from life.

Perfect, also, for finally taking the woman he'd been dreaming of for six months.

A soft breeze rustled the leaves on the tree branches. The wind feathered through Anna's shiny curls, sifting the them around her face and neck. Did she ever *not* look sexy?

Anna glanced up and gave him a soft smile. Something clenched in the region of his heart. It had been a day, not even a full twenty-four hours and already he knew he was in trouble. She was beautiful. Incredible. And his… for the weekend.

He wanted longer. Friday to Sunday wasn't nearly enough.

Her smile dipped into a frown. "You okay?"

"Yeah. I'm fine."

"You look… deep in thought."

He slumped down in the chair and clasped his arms over his bare stomach. "I guess I am. I was thinking about how incredible last night was. I want a repeat."

Her eyes glazed over and she licked her lips. "Me, too."

"Soon." As appealing as the thought of getting her out of her clothes was, sex wasn't the only thing on his mind. He'd suggested they move out onto the deck after lunch under the guise of wanting to enjoy the warm, dry summer afternoon before the predicted humidity hit again early the next week.

Beneath the simple excuse had been a deeper reason. He wanted to be with her, sit next to her and hold her hand, inhale her scent for a little while and just enjoy being with her.

What would she think if she knew? She wouldn't be happy. She'd made it clear to him that she wasn't looking for anything permanent. She wanted sex. With him. And he was all too happy to oblige.

For now, it would have to do, but he could also use the wickedness of the weekend to show her there could be so much more between them. He'd established trust. This afternoon, he intended to take that trust one step further.

"You brought your swimsuit, right?" He took her hand and brought it to his lips, his fingers brushing across her knuckles.

She shivered, glanced toward the lake. "Uh-huh. Are we going swimming?"

"Later. There's something I want to do first."

Her gaze drifted to his. Excitement flashed in the hazel depths of her eyes. "And what would that be? Wanna use up the rest of the body paint?"

His breath stuck in his throat. He coughed to clear the lump away. The woman was insatiable, and damned if he didn't want her all over again. His cock stirred to life, a rush of electricity racing through his bloodstream. "Not this time. I have something better in mind. Come over here and straddle my lap."

With a curious glance, she did as he asked. She put one leg on either side of his, her hands on his shoulders, and leaned down to brush her lips over his.

Her fingers tightened against his shirt, her tongue playing at the seam of his lips until he parted them and let her into his mouth.

The taste of her washed over his tongue, warm and sweet and mingled with the mint tea she'd had at lunch. He brought his hands to her ass and pulled her down on top of him. Still, it didn't bring her close enough. He ached to bury his cock inside her again. One time hadn't been nearly enough.

Her breasts bumped against his chest, her tongue stroking the insides of his lips, his cheeks. He splayed a hand across her back, loving the feel of her skin under his palm. He'd waited months to feel this way with her.

Anna broke the kiss, licked her lower lip and smiled down at him. "What do you have planned?"

"It's a surprise, like you surprised me last night." He pushed aside the strap of her tank top and kissed his way down to her breast. She hadn't put on a bra, and heat tumbled through him at the sight of her bared nipple. He blew a stream of hot air across it and the pink flesh beaded. Beautiful. He leaned down to place a kiss right on that spot.

Anna whimpered. He smiled against her skin. He loved how responsive she was to him, loved how sensitive her breasts were to his hands and his lips. She didn't try to hide her responses. She reveled in them instead—and so did he.

He pushed the other strap off her shoulder and pulled the fabric down. The neckline of the top pushed her breasts together and up like an offering too tempting to refuse. He cupped the firm mounds in his palms and brought his mouth down to them again, laving the nipples with the tip of his tongue until she was squirming in his lap.

Her movements drove her hot pussy against his cock and made his gut tighten. He lifted his mouth from her skin. "Why don't we move this inside?"

She nodded, a corner of her lip tipped up in a hesitant but sexy smile.

He helped her off his lap and led her into the bedroom.

After he closed the door, he turned to face her. She hadn't adjusted the straps of her tank top, leaving her breasts exposed. The cool air from the central AC had beaded her nipples even more, turning them into hard little pink points he wanted to wrap his lips around. His mouth watered. "You trust me, right?"

Anxiety flashed in her gaze, her shoulders shaking as she drew in a breath. "Sure. We went through this in the car on the way up here."

"I just need to make sure you haven't changed your mind." Because for what he had planned next, he would need all her trust. Every bit of it, and then some.

"Yes, Dean. I trust you." The determination was back in her gaze, along with a healthy dose of curiosity. "What do you have planned?"

"You'll see."

He stepped over to his bag and pulled out a white handkerchief and two silk ties, both with dark red patterns. This scenario had been one of the first things to come to mind when Anna had proposed their weekend, and he'd made sure to come prepared. The deep red tones would look magnificent against her tanned skin and dark hair. *She* would look magnificent on her knees in front of him.

His body tensed, already expecting her to shoot down the idea of putting herself so completely in his hands. But she had to know that he only wanted to make her happy. Anna's happiness was all he'd ever wanted.

He turned back to her, lifting the items in front of him. "This is something I've been thinking about for the past three days. Are you game?"

The rejection he expected never came. She studied him, her gaze moving between his and the ties in his hands, her teeth worrying her lower lip.

"Anna?"

"You want to tie me up?" Excitement tinged her voice, sparkled in her eyes. A flush crept up her breasts, staining her chest and neck.

Every muscle in his body was leaden. “Yeah.”

“Okay.”

The breath left his lungs in a whoosh. “Good. Get undressed.”

Her gaze locked with his, she stripped out of her clothing and piled it on the floor. She drew in a shaky breath, gave a nervous smile and glanced away.

He’d never get enough of looking at her body. She was incredible. Sexy and sweet. His for the weekend. Maybe more, if he played his cards right.

“Do you want me to lie down on the bed?” she asked.

“No. I want you right where you are.”

He walked behind her and pulled her hands to the small of her back, using one tie to secure her wrists in place there. She let out a soft sigh that hardened his cock against the front of his jeans.

“Tell me now if you want me to stop.”

“Don’t stop. I’m fine.” Her voice shook with desire, her shoulders trembling. “More than fine. I’m curious.”

“Good. Then for the rest of the afternoon, you’re going to listen to what I say. Every word. Is that clear?”

“Yes.”

“Good.” He stepped around her, cupped her chin in his palm, and brought his lips down on hers in a quick, hard kiss. He rolled the handkerchief into a long strip and secured it over her eyes.

“When you can’t see, all your other senses come alive.” He brushed a kiss over her earlobe. “You’ll feel every sensation so much stronger. I can make you feel so much.”

“Dean?” Anxiety. Maybe a little fear. But stronger than everything else, lust.

“Have you ever been tied up before, Anna?”

“No.” She licked her lips. “Have you ever… have you tied anyone up before?”

He pressed a quick open-mouthed kiss to her throat. “Yeah.”

She shuddered. “Oh.”

He held back a burst of laughter. “You don’t sound happy about that.”

“It’s just that I… I don’t even know how to explain this. Playing around is one thing, but if you’re serious about this…”

“It isn’t a lifestyle for me, if that’s what has you worried. I just like to play.” He stroked a finger across one of her nipples. “I’ll be gentle, I promise. You trust me. Don’t forget that.”

“I do trust you. But…” She sighed. “What are you going to do with that other tie?”

“I’m glad you asked.” She might fight him on this, but he wanted to give her an experience she'd never forget. He walked around to her back and lifted the second tie over her head, bringing it to her lips. "Open your mouth."

After a surprisingly short hesitation, she did as he'd ordered. He slipped the tie between her parted lips and secured it at the back of her head. "This is just a reminder that you aren't going to say a word unless I ask you to speak. Nod if you understand."

She nodded.

"I want to bring you more pleasure than you've ever imagined. Allowing me total control over the experience, putting all your trust in me, will enable me to do just that."

He moved to face her again, ignoring his aching cock as he looked her over. "I wish you could see how sexy you look right now. I've never seen a sight so beautiful. Your nipples are hard, ready for my mouth. Your skin is such a becoming pink. I can't wait to get my mouth on your pussy."

She whimpered.

"If you get uncomfortable at all and want me to stop, I want you to say your name."

She gave a short, vigorous nod of her head.

He smiled. Good girl. She wanted this as much as he did. He just hoped he didn't let her down. "Say it."

"Anna."

A little muffled, but still understandable. He'd needed to pick something she could say even around the tie. "Good. Use it if you need it. At any time. Understood?"

She nodded again.

"Excellent." He couldn't hide his smile, and there was no reason to even bother. No longer comfortable in his constricting jeans, he unzipped them and stripped them off.

Her wants and desires were a perfect match for his. Smart, quiet Anna wasn't nearly as shy in the bedroom as she was everywhere else. Exactly the type of woman he'd been searching for. He had been so right to accept her invitation this weekend. It might well turn out to be the most amazing time of his life.

Dean brought his lips down to Anna's shoulder and trailed a path of soft, hot kisses along her skin. She shuddered. Never in her life had she thought that something so extreme would turn her on this much. She'd been curious, but had never found the right man to experiment with. Dean had experience… a thought that shocked her and thrilled her at the same time.

He wouldn't hurt her.

He cupped her breasts, rolling her nipples between his thumbs and forefingers. A light pinch, the barest hint of pain, and a jolt of pleasure. She cried out, her pussy muscles clenching at the sensual touch.

"Silent, Anna. No sounds."

Oh, God. He was going to kill her. Her pussy was slick with her moisture, her clit throbbing between her legs. Without her sight, without the use of her hands she felt helpless, floating on a sea of emotion and sensation with Dean at the helm, taking care of her ultimate pleasure. She arched her back, needing more of his touch.

He dropped his hands away.

She bit down on the tie to keep from whimpering again. She couldn't see him, but she felt the heat of his body, heard his movements as he walked up next to her. He pushed her hair off her shoulder and leaned in, his lips closing over the tender skin where her neck and shoulder met.

And then he bit her.

A cry escaped her lips this time. She couldn't help it. The slight sting of his teeth sent a jolt from that spot right down to her clit. Her knees buckled from the pleasure.

"Shh." He pressed a finger to her parted lips.

She nodded, though staying quiet wasn't easy with the way he touched her. Not just his hands, but his gaze. She *felt* it on her skin like a heated caress. Heard his deep, ragged breaths and knew he was just as turned on as she.

"I want you on the bed now, Anna." With his hands on her shoulders he walked her to the bed and helped her down on her stomach on the mattress.

The position left her more helpless than before, her arms secured against her back and her cheek pressing against the firm mattress. He moved her legs apart, ran a finger down the length of her slit.

"So wet already. I have a feeling you're enjoying this."

What was your first clue? She bit back the retort and the accompanying laugh, knowing it would only get her scolded again. He wanted her quiet, and even if it killed her, she'd do it. If she did as he asked, he'd promised to make it worth her while.

The flick of his finger across her clit had her bucking against the mattress. She was too raw, too sensitized, and the feel of his hand on her sensitive flesh bordered on pain. She didn't think she'd be able to take much more of his sensual torture.

And then his palm came down on her ass with a gentle smack.

She couldn't help the noises now, a half-whimper, half-cry bursting from her throat. *Holy—*

No one had done that to her before. Ever. Part of her warned that she shouldn't enjoy such actions, but a bigger part of her wanted to beg for him to do it again. She wriggled her rear in the air.

He laughed softly, his palm coming down on her again. She moaned. The pleasure she derived from the action overrode the slight sting. A gush of moisture flooded her pussy, a low throb starting from there and working its way to her clit. He'd been right when he said sensations would be magnified. If he touched her again, she might come out of her skin.

"How are you holding up?" His voice was a low whisper, his fingers sliding into the slickness of her channel. Two, three—she couldn't tell. But she felt *full*. "Anna?"

She nodded, unable to form words past the guttural groans rumbling up from her chest. He twisted and turned those fingers inside her, his thumb pressing down hard on her clit. Her back arched. Her pulse pounded in her ears. She became a ball of sensation, unable to do anything but feel. Every inch of her skin hummed with tension, the stroke of his fingers inside her was a touch she felt everywhere.

All it took was one brush of his thumb nail over her clit and she came with a scream.

For a few harrowing seconds everything around her stopped. Her body bucked against the mattress, bucked against Dean's touch. Her inner muscles clenched and unclenched around his fingers, trying to draw him in deeper. Little pinpoints of light exploded behind her eyelids, the blood rushing so loud behind her eardrums it drowned out the world.

With his free hand, he caressed the length of her back, stroking and kneading softly. When her shuddering became small tremors, he withdrew his hands and moved away from the bed.

The sound of plastic ripping filled the silence and soon he was over her, between her thighs, working the head of his cock into her pussy.

When she'd asked him for this weekend, she hadn't expected this. She'd known him for most of her life. Their mothers had been best friends since grade school. But most of the time, she'd avoided him. It was either avoid him or risk mooning over him like some adolescent schoolgirl.

He was just so… potent. Virile. Sexy and powerful. Something indefinable about him turned her brain to mush and dampened her panties whenever he got within ten feet of her. Ignoring him had been easier—until he'd started flirting with her on her birthday. With that simple act, he'd changed the rules. Rules that had been set by him, many years ago, with his aloof and serious nature.

His body half-reclined over hers, her hands stuck in between them as he thrust inside her. When he came, he leaned down and pressed his teeth into her shoulder. Pain wasn't his intention. Even in her hazed, sated state, she recognized it for what it was. A mark of possession. Primitive and basic, it made her body tremble. It was in that moment that the first inkling of trouble raised a red flag in her mind.

She'd just wanted sex with him, but it seemed like she was going to get so much more, whether she chose to accept it or not.

Chapter 7

Anna walked down to the lake, her towel slung over her shoulder. The slow descent of the sun bathed the horizon in a wash of pinks and oranges. A cool breeze sifted through the tree branches. Her flip-flops slapped against her feet as she moved through the lush grass. A delicious ache thrummed through her body—satiation rather than lust. In just twenty-four hours, Dean had worn her out.

He'd also taken her to new heights, shown her pleasure she'd never before imagined. Going back to her real life, the humdrum sex that hadn't excited her before now, held no appeal at all. She'd never find a man who turned her on like Dean did. It wasn't just the sexual acts that had been intense. It was the chemistry between the two of them that had made it all so incredible.

She'd made a mistake in coming here with him. Before, he'd been nothing more than a fantasy in her mind. Now she'd never be able to walk away without it ripping her heart out.

After dinner, she'd fallen asleep on the couch and had woken up to a note asking her to put on her swimsuit and meet him outside. In desperate need of a break from the new reality of their situation, she'd happily complied.

When she approached the lake, Dean swam toward her and stood up in the waist-deep water. He ran a hand through his hair and slicked the wet strands back against his scalp. Tiny water droplets glistened on his chest and arms. She shivered, and though she wasn't sure she could take any more pleasure right now, her nipples beaded and a little gush of moisture trickled from her pussy. He had a body that would fuel her fantasies for a long time to come.

He smiled and waved. "I was wondering if you'd decided to ignore the note."

She laughed. "No, I just woke up. *Someone* has really worn me out. I guess I needed the sleep."

"Sorry."

"Don't be." She kicked off her flip-flops and dropped her towel onto the sandy beach.

"You coming in?"

"Yeah." She dipped a toe into the water and instantly recoiled. A chill raced up her leg. "Or maybe not. It isn't as warm as I thought it would be."

"Wimp." Dean chuckled, shook his head. "We had a lot of rain this spring and it's still early in the season. Once we get into July, the weather will warm the water. It's not bad now, though, once you get used to it."

"Yeah, right." But she took his quip as a challenge and stepped into the water, ignoring the shivering in her limbs and the numbness that stole over her legs. She wrapped her arms around herself. "You know, I'm really not noticing much difference."

"You didn't give it enough time yet." Dean smiled a devilish smile. Then he raised his hands in the water and splashed her.

Sprays of frigid water bathed her face and shoulders, trailing down the front of her swimsuit. She narrowed her eyes and bit back a laugh. "That was cruel."

One big shoulder lifted in a shrug. "Nah. I'm just trying to help you get used to the water, that's all."

"You think you're funny, huh?" She launched herself at him, wrapped her arms around his neck and knocked him into the water.

His arms came around her waist and he took her down with him.

The cold water hit her face, freezing the breath in her lungs for a moment. They both came up sputtering, and then soon the sputtering had turned to laughter.

Dean leaned in and kissed her hard on the lips, his lips cold and wet. His tongue slid into her mouth, brushing against hers before he pulled away, a smile in his eyes.

"I wasn't really going for funny. I was going more for something along the lines of cute."

"You think that was cute?" It *was* cute, in a way she'd never expected. It heartened her to see him having fun. Even as children, when their mothers had gotten together, he'd spent most of the time hiding away in his bedroom. Smiles didn't come easily to him—at least she hadn't thought they did. But she'd seen him smile more this weekend than she had in all the years she'd known. It only added to his appeal.

He was more than just a sexy guy with a killer body now. He'd become a real person to her. Someone she might even consider a friend.

The thought doused her mood more effectively than the chill of the water. She was in deep trouble. She'd asked for this little weekend get-together as a birthday present to herself, to assuage the need that in recent months had threatened to burn out of control, but the pull between them was starting to turn into so much more. To her dismay, warm feelings had started to develop, and not in the annoying-big-brother way she'd felt about him as a child, or the avoid-him-at-all-costs way she'd started to feel as an adult. This was different.

Now she'd started to think about him as a person. A person with hopes and dreams, feelings and emotions. A dangerous way to think. Because the man she'd once thought equally sexy and aloof was nothing like she'd imagined. He was sweet, kind, caring, and he put her needs and emotions first. Every single time.

That just couldn't be good.

He arched his brows. "What are you thinking about?"

"This weekend isn't what I expected."

He stepped back and crossed his arms over his chest, a wary grin on his face. "You thought it would be a weekend of nonstop sex and nothing else. No fun that didn't involve a bedroom, no conversation. An extended one-night stand."

"Yeah, I guess I did."

His grin widened, a sensual heat building in his eyes. "I guess I should have warned you sooner. I don't do that sort of thing. I'm not built that way."

A tremor ran down her spine, both anxiety and hope. She quashed the hope, reminding herself that she didn't want attachments. It seemed she'd been doing a lot of reminding over the past day or so. "Dean…"

"Don't worry. I'll give you the weekend we agreed to. But I just wanted you to know where I stand."

He turned and dove under the water, leaving her mind in more turmoil than it had been before his confession. Her head ached from thinking too hard, her heart ached from denying the emotions inside her.

What was she supposed to do? No solutions came to her, no matter how long she thought about it. She wasn't ready for more than the weekend, but at the same time she wanted to wrap her arms around Dean and never let him go.

She reached down and gathered cold lake water in her cupped palms, brought it up and splashed it on her face. Anna shivered. She'd moved back home six months ago, after the abrupt end to a long-term relationship that had been rocky right from the start. She and Jeremy had weathered through four years, three of those years living together, but they had never really been able to stop the arguments, stop the hurting and the fighting.

And then there had been the other women. His side affairs had been what had finally pushed her into letting go of the sinking ship and moving on with her life. She'd be damned if she was going to move right into the arms of another man. She wasn't ready to commit again. Wouldn't be for a long time. Enjoying single life was at the top of her list. With just his presence, Dean threatened to break apart the new life she'd started to build. She needed to push him away, but at the same time she craved to let him in.

Though her heart denied it, it was a good thing they were leaving tomorrow.

When Dean swam back to her, he stood and pulled her into his arms for another kiss. "What's on your mind, besides how I don't meet your expectations?"

"Don't be hurt, please. I—"

He cut her words off with a hard, wet kiss. "We aren't going to talk about it anymore. I know how you feel, and you know how I feel. Let's just leave it at that before we get into an argument and ruin the rest of the weekend, okay?"

She nodded.

"Good. How was your nap? You still look tired."

"I guess I still have some sleep I need to catch up on." And a great deal of emotional turmoil to ignore.

"Yeah, me, too." He laughed, though it sounded strained. "What do you say we take it easy tonight, watch a movie and relax on the couch? Steve has a DVD collection almost as big as yours. I'm sure we can find something interesting to watch."

He might as well have just said "cuddle". Did she really want to cuddle with him? The surprising answer was that she did. "Sounds like a plan to me."

Dean sat on the couch, Anna in his arms, the action flick she'd picked out flashing across the screen in a vivid sequence of movement and colors. He leaned in and kissed the top of her head, then immediately regretted the action. They'd already moved into territory too intimate to be comfortable, at least as far as emotions went. By cuddling on the couch with her, he was only adding to the problem.

But he couldn't help it. For as long as he could remember, he'd had a strange need to hold her, to keep her safe. Now he felt that need intensify to something he wasn't sure he could manage. A lifetime of protective feelings mixed with six months of physical longing brought out a side of him he rarely showed anyone. She made him want things he'd never wanted before.

Most of all, he wanted more time with her, and it had nothing to do with sex. He chuckled, remembering the way her body fit him so perfectly. Okay, not *only* to do with sex.

Anna glanced up at him, her eyelids half closed. "What's so funny?"

"Just that I never imaged we'd be here like this. I always thought you hated me, until your birthday."

She laughed. "And I thought you looked down on me."

"Why would I do that?"

"Because I don't make money like you do. I work in a nursing home. I love it, but I'm never going to get rich from it."

He brushed a lock of hair off her forehead. She looked so sweet and innocent. She might not be innocent, or particularly sweet, in the bedroom, but in many other areas she was. Somehow her heart had remained untouched by the ravages of the world. It was pure, innocent, and good. His own heart clenched. He'd give anything to be able to take her out on a real date, show her what they could be together if she just gave it a chance… but she wouldn't. She'd made it clear from the beginning that she only wanted a weekend of sex. If he wanted to see her once the weekend was over, it would take some convincing.

He blinked. He *did* want to see her again. And he *would* convince her. It would be difficult, but not impossible.

Courtship. He had a romantic streak buried deep. He rarely showed it, but with Anna, she deserved everything he had. Every part of him. It would take time, but he was a patient man.

And he had all the time in the world.

"Personally, I think what you do for a living is amazing. Not many people have such a caring nature that they can do that sort of work."

She smirked. "Yeah, right."

"Seriously. I admire you. Why do you find that so hard to believe?"

"Oh, I don't know. Maybe because you have a huge house, a killer wardrobe, and two very expensive cars?"

If he didn't do something, this conversation would deteriorate quickly into something neither of them wanted. He took her hand and brushed a kiss across her knuckles. "We've always been close, our mothers are like sisters. How much money you make is not going to lower my opinion of you. Believe me, Anna. I'm not that shallow."

The last sentence came out with more exasperation than he intended. He closed his eyes and pinched the bridge of his nose.

"I'm sorry. I didn't mean to upset you." Her fingers brushed his cheek. "I seem to be doing a lot of that today."

"It's fine." He opened his eyes and looked down at her, trying to hide the tenderness in his expression and hoping she saw it at the same time. "My ex-wife was always worried about status. She came from old family money, and it bothered her that I didn't make as much as her father did. I would never put you through that."

"Is that what caused your divorce?"

He sighed. He never talked about what had happened between him and Kathy after only a year and a half of marriage. Everyone around him knew not to ask. He didn't love her anymore, didn't want back the fractured relationship he was better off without, but the entire experience had left him bitter. He'd gone into it expecting so much, and had left with nothing.

"Yes, the money was an issue for her, among other things. She didn't want children. I did. That was a big cause of tension between us."

"You want children?" The surprise in her voice was enough to make him chuckle, despite his suddenly somber mood.

"Yeah, I'd love to have a couple of kids someday. It's the reason I bought the big house. It came on the market at a great price, and I couldn't pass it up. At the time I'd thought…" He hesitated. "She and I just weren't compatible. We rushed into marriage to fix a relationship that was already in trouble. Instead of getting married, we should have just split up."

She looked at him a long time before a slow, wary smile spread over her face. She didn't say a word, and he decided it was time to change the subject, and to give *her* a chance in the hot seat where she'd just grilled him to a crisp in a single question. "What about you? How come you're not married?"

She made a face. "Not even close to ready. I still have a few more years before my biological clock starts complaining."

He laughed, though it speared a pang of hurt through his chest. He'd finally found a woman he could see spending forever with, only to have her ready to run away.

Chapter 8

"Well, this is it." Anna shoved her swimsuit and the rest of her clothes into her bag. She did a brief walkthrough of the cabin, looking for anything she might have forgotten.

Sunday evening had come and it was time to go home. After cuddling and talking under the guise of watching a movie, they'd spent a good deal of Sunday in bed, catching up on sleep. Then in the afternoon, they'd swum in the lake again, laughing and joking like teenagers.

Now they'd packed to leave and he'd barely touched her all day. Anna was beginning to worry. Had he shut her out of his life early? Was it because he wanted more than she was ready to give?

She brought her bag out into the kitchen where Dean stood leaning against the counter, looking out the back window at the glassy surface of the water.

"Hey."

He turned around and faced her, his lips unsmiling and his jaw set. "Hi."

Her breath caught in her throat. She wasn't ready for the weekend to end, and it appeared neither was he.

She sighed, running a hand through her hair. There was nothing she could do about his feelings. She would have to be the one to make sure they stuck to the original agreement.

He pushed away from the counter and walked over to her, his finger tracing the line of her jaw. "I guess it's time to leave."

"I guess so." Though it pained her to even think about it. This place, an ordinary single bedroom cabin in the middle of nowhere, had become magical. It was in this place that she had realized how easily she could fall in love with Dean, if she let herself.

Which she would not, under any circumstances, allow herself to do.

A tense silence stretched between them, one that wasn't broken until they'd been on the road for half an hour.

Dean finally spoke, his tone hopeful. "Can I call you sometime?"

She almost laughed. It seemed like the wrong thing to say at a time like this. They were poised to walk out of each other's lives, and now he was asking if he could call her? It couldn't happen. He'd just gone through a divorce, and she'd just walked away from a relationship that had been longer than his marriage. They both needed time. Jumping into anything more than a fling wasn't the smart thing to do.

"The deal was for one weekend." Though every fiber of her being ached for more.

"I was hoping you'd be willing to explore other possibilities."

"I don't think that's such a good idea."

"Why not?"

He braked for a stop sign. She glanced around at the thick groups of trees lining the road. Quiet and perfect.

She let out a watery sigh, her gaze trained outside the window so he wouldn't see how he affected her. "I told you, I'm really not ready to settle down. I just got out of a bad relationship and I don't want to rush right into something else."

His hand slammed down on the steering wheel. When he spoke, irritation laced his tone. "I'm not asking for forever. I'm just asking for a date, and we can see what happens from there."

"Dean."

"Okay. Okay. Fine. I fucking give up. Happy now?"

The pain in his voice damn near broke her heart. It wasn't possible that she'd come to care about him so much in such a short amount of time. It *wasn't* possible, but somehow it had happened and it was going to take everything she had to ignore what she felt.

For the remainder of the drive back home, neither of them spoke a word.

When they got to her house, Dean didn't even get out of the car. He turned to her, a sensual, yet cool, smile on his face. He touched his finger to her jaw, brushed the back of his hand across her breasts. He licked his lips. "Thanks for the awesome weekend. It was a blast."

The fact that he could shut off his emotions with such speed only strengthened her resolve to walk away without a backward glance. She murmured her own thanks, grabbed her bag and got out of the car. She'd hurt him. He didn't have to say it for her to know it was true, but if he could ignore it, so could she. She couldn't get away from him fast enough.

She walked up the path to her little cottage and opened the door. When she turned around, it surprised her to see Dean just pulling away from the curb. Always a gentleman, even when she'd cut him down and rejected him in such a ruthless, harsh way.

Would it really have been so bad to accept a date with the guy? He was everything she'd ever looked for in a man.

And that was part of the problem.

He was too perfect. There had to be some defect she'd been blinded to by the weekend of debauchery. All men had their faults, and Dean with his quiet nature probably hid some deep, dark secrets.

But she couldn't think of a single thing she'd noticed over the years, not even when she wracked her brain. He was what he made himself out to be. Open and honest, fair. Tender when he wanted to be, tough when the situation called for it.

And a master in bed.

She'd miss that the most.

She wandered around her house, acclimating herself to being alone again. In just a few days, he'd torn her world apart. The burning drive to be alone, to enjoy the single life, had faded to almost nothing.

It would be nice to share her life with someone. Maybe having a man around again would stave off the boredom that had slowly been gnawing away at her insides for the past six months.

Or maybe she should just get a dog.

Dogs were easy. Unconditional love. No guilt trips into attachments she wasn't sure she wanted. No emotional baggage, no staying up all night worrying if they'd gone out to find someone else.

No deep emotional connection, but she could live without that. She'd done it before—in the last year or so of her relationship with Jeremy.

If it meant saving her heart from another fracture, she'd do it again.

Chapter 9

Dean walked out of the florist shop with a swing in his step. It had been a week since his fling with Anna. He'd given her that time to cool off, to come to realize that they really would be good together.

He smiled. Now her break was over.

He would approach winning her over as he approached everything in his life—with carefully planned precision. During the past week, he'd mapped out his strategy. Gifts like the bouquet of wildflowers he'd just ordered to have delivered to her at work. Phone calls. Visits. Whatever it took. He wanted her in his life, as more than someone he'd known forever but really didn't know at all.

Now that he'd learned more about her, one thing had become clear. She was perfect for him. Vivacious and fun and she'd breathed new life into him when he'd felt he was aging too fast at thirty-two.

He wanted her back in his arms. Wanted her in his bed, all night long.

His cock tightened at the thought. Damn, he really wanted her in his bed. Needed her there. On her back on his mattress, under him while he rocked inside her. They'd fulfilled their fantasies with each other. Now he had to prove to her that the reality of them together could be better than any fantasy she'd ever imagined.

He slid behind the wheel of his car and pulled away from the curb. He'd made the first move. The only thing left to do was to sit back and see if Anna would make the second.

Anna slid her timecard through the slot on the machine. It gave two short beeps, letting her know the action had been recorded. She stuffed the timecard into the pocket of her scrubs, wrapped her stethoscope over the back of her neck, and pushed open the side door of the building. Time to go home. She sighed. *For another night alone.*

She hadn't heard from Dean in a week. Either she'd hurt him more than she'd realized, or he'd decided she just wasn't worth the trouble. Either way, the thought of not seeing him again made her heart feel like it would burst.

"Anna, hold on a second."

She turned to see Nancy, the shift manager, rushing toward her. "Did I forget to finish my documentation?"

Nancy stopped in front of Anna, her short, round body shaking with both exertion and laughter. "No. Someone just delivered a huge bouquet of flowers for you. They're sitting on the counter at the nurses' station."

Hope flashed in Anna's chest. "Really?"

Nancy nodded. "I didn't want you to leave without them."

Anna followed Nancy to the nurses' station. The sight that greeted her there nearly took her breath away.

He'd remembered.

For her sixteenth birthday, her boyfriend at the time had sent her a dozen red roses when football practice had kept him from the party her parents had thrown for her. She'd been glum, and Dean had asked her what was wrong. She'd told him she preferred bright, mismatched flowers to the standard dozen red any day.

And that was what he'd picked out for her. The bouquet was huge, a rainbow of gorgeous colors and scents. It brought tears to her eyes that he'd remembered after all this time.

She took the card off the card holder, tore open the envelope, and read.

You had your fantasy, and now I want my turn. Call me.

He'd added his home, work, and cell phone numbers to the bottom of the card. She hiccupped.

"That's an incredible gesture."

Anna turned to Nancy, tears welling in her eyes. "Yeah, it is. But I can't accept these. It wouldn't be right, since I told him I don't want to see him again."

Nancy raised one blonde eyebrow. "You don't look like you don't want to see him again."

"It would be a bad idea."

"Why is that?"

For too many reasons to explain. "Because I might fall in love with him."

"And what's wrong with that?"

"So many things. First, I'm not ready for a relationship. I'm not easy to deal with. I always screw things up. And second, he's a friend, and that's all."

"That's such a lie. I haven't even met the guy and I know that." Nancy laughed. "What does he look like?"

"Tall, broad shoulders, sexy as all hell." *He's perfect. Absolutely, utterly perfect. In every way.*

"Then what are you waiting for? Put yourself out of your misery. Go home and call the guy."

For once, she couldn't agree more.

He hadn't expected her to call so soon.

Dean sat up straight in his chair, braced himself against the hope swelling inside him. She might be calling to tell him to leave her alone, that the flowers had gone unappreciated.

Her next words negated that possibility. "I can't believe you remembered."

"Believe it or not, I do have a pretty strong romantic streak."

Anna laughed in that husky voice of hers. "Maybe some of yours could rub off on me. I don't think I have a romantic bone in my body."

He let out a breath. There was a lot about herself that Anna could still learn. A lot he could teach her.

And Dean thought there was a lot about himself that she could teach him.

"Did you like the flowers?"

"You knew I would. They're the most beautiful things I've ever seen. They must have cost you a fortune."

"Have dinner with me," he blurted, unable to hold back another second. The urge to see her again had grown to something overwhelming in the past week.

She hesitated so long he was afraid she'd deny his request, but then she let out a soft little sigh. "When you said you wanted your turn for a fantasy, what did you mean?"

His fantasy, his *biggest* fantasy, involved something that would scare her. Commitment. Courtship and love and trust, and eventually a ring on her finger. It would take time, but he was a patient man. They had all the time in the world. "Have dinner with me and you'll find out."

"How can I say no to that kind of an offer? Okay. I'll have dinner with you."

He resisted the urge to jump up and punch his fist into the air. "Excellent. Are you free tonight?"

"It just so happens that I am."

Epilogue

"OhmyGod," Anna breathed, a wave of pleasure rolling over her body.

"You like that?" Dean ran his hand down the center of her back, making her arch like a cat. He thrust into her again, this time the angle of her hips making his cock stroke along her G-spot.

She only managed a low moan in reply.

He chuckled. "I thought you would."

His hand wrapped in her hair and he held her in place while he thrust in and out of her waiting body, each stroke making little jolts of electricity race through her core. She was close. So damned close and he still held her back.

"This kind of torture has to be illegal," she ground out, pushing her hips back against him.

"You love it and you know it." He gave her ass a little smack.

She laughed. She did love it. Loved *him*. It had only taken her a few weeks to realize it, though she'd waited quite a bit longer to voice her feelings. "Dean, please. I need more than this. *Now*."

"Anything for you." He reached between her legs and found her clit, stroking over the sensitive nub with the pad of his finger.

The touch spiraled up through her core, sending her into a slow, shimmering orgasm that had her bucking against him. Her elbows gave out and her forearms hit the mattress under her. In the past few months, the sex, as well as the emotional bond, had only gotten better. He knew exactly what she wanted, and exactly how long to hold back before giving it to her.

How had she lived this long without him? Even after only a few months, she couldn't recall a time in her life when she didn't need him. He'd become everything to her in such a short time.

She wouldn't have it any other way.

Sometime later, when they were both sated and worn out, Dean curled her into his arms on the soft mattress. His mattress. His bed. Where she seemed to be spending more and more time lately. Earlier in the evening, he'd asked her to move in with him.

Though she hadn't told him yet, she'd decided she would.

"I love you, Anna," he said, his voice clogged with emotion.

She snuggled deeper into his embrace, loving the warmth of his strong body wrapped around hers. "I love you, too." She stroked her hand down his arm. "You still have yet to tell me what your fantasy is. Remember? The one you wouldn't tell me over dinner on our first real date."

He pressed a kiss to the top of her head. "This is it, baby. This, right here, is the best fantasy in the world."

About the Author:

Born in Gloucester, Massachusetts, Elisa Adams has lived most of her life on the East Coast. Formerly a nursing assistant and phlebotomist, writing has been a longtime hobby. Now a full time writer, she lives on the New Hampshire border with her three children. Visit Elisa's website at www.elisaadams.com.

Feel the wild adventure, fierce passion and the power of love in every ***Secrets*** Collection story. Red Sage Publishing's romance authors create richly crafted, sexy, sensual, novella-length stories. Each one is just the right length for reading after a long and hectic day.

Each volume in the ***Secrets*** Collection has four diverse, ultra-sexy, romantic novellas brimming with adventure, passion and love. More adventurous tales for the adventurous reader. The ***Secrets*** Collection are a glorious mix of romance genre; numerous historical settings, contemporary, paranormal, science fiction and suspense. We are always looking for new adventures.

Reader response to the ***Secrets*** volumes has been great! Here's just a small sample:

> *"I loved the variety of settings. Four completely wonderful time periods, give you four completely wonderful reads."*
>
> *"Each story was a page-turning tale I hated to put down."*
>
> *"I love* ***Secrets****! When is the next volume coming out? This one was Hot! Loved the heroes!"*

Secrets have won raves and awards. We could go on, but why don't you find out for yourself—order your set of ***Secrets*** today! See the back for details.

Secrets, Volume 1

Listen to what reviewers say:

"These stories take you beyond romance into the realm of erotica. I found ***Secrets*** absolutely delicious."

—Virginia Henley,
New York Times Best Selling Author

"***Secrets*** is a collection of novellas for the daring, adventurous woman who's not afraid to give her fantasies free reign."

—Kathe Robin, *Romantic Times* Magazine

"...In fact, the men featured in all the stories are terrific, they all want to please and pleasure their women. If you like erotic romance you will love ***Secrets***."

—*Romantic Readers* Review

In ***Secrets, Volume 1*** you'll find:

A Lady's Quest by Bonnie Hamre

Widowed Lady Antonia Blair-Sutworth searches for a lover to save her from the handsome Duke of Sutherland. The "auditions" may be shocking but utterly tantalizing.

The Spinner's Dream by Alice Gaines

A seductive fantasy that leaves every woman wishing for her own private love slave, desperate and running for his life.

The Proposal by Ivy Landon

This tale is a walk on the wild side of love. *The Proposal* will taunt you, tease you, and shock you. A contemporary erotica for the adventurous woman.

The Gift by Jeanie LeGendre

Immerse yourself in this historic tale of exotic seduction, bondage and a concubine's surrender to the Sultan's desire. Can Alessandra live the life and give the gift the Sultan demands of her?

Secrets, Volume 2

Listen to what reviewers say:

"***Secrets*** offers four novellas of sensual delight; each beautifully written with intense feeling and dedication to character development. For those seeking stories with heightened intimacy, look no further."

—Kathee Card, *Romancing the Web*

"Such a welcome diversity in styles and genres. Rich characterization in sensual tales. An exciting read that's sure to titillate the senses."

—Cheryl Ann Porter

"***Secrets 2*** left me breathless. Sensual satisfaction guaranteed… times four!"

—Virginia Henley, *New York Times* Best Selling Author

In ***Secrets, Volume 2*** you'll find:

Surrogate Lover by Doreen DeSalvo

Adrian Ross is a surrogate sex therapist who has all the answers and control. He thought he'd seen and done it all, but he'd never met Sarah.

Snowbound by Bonnie Hamre

A delicious, sensuous regency tale. The marriage-shy Earl of Howden is teased and tortured by his own desires and finds there is a woman who can equal his overpowering sensuality.

Roarke's Prisoner by Angela Knight

Elise, a starship captain, remembers the eager animal submission she'd known before at her captor's hands and refuses to become his toy again. However, she has no idea of the delights he's planned for her this time.

Savage Garden by Susan Paul

Raine's been captured by a mysterious and dangerous revolutionary leader in Mexico. At first her only concern is survival, but she quickly finds lush erotic nights in her captor's arms.

Winner of the Fallot Literary Award for Fiction!

Secrets, Volume 3

Listen to what reviewers say:

"***Secrets, Volume 3***, leaves the reader breathless. A delicious confection of sensuous treats awaits the reader on each turn of the page!"

—Kathee Card, *Romancing the Web*

"From the FBI to Police Detective to Vampires to a Medieval Warlord home from the Crusade—***Secrets 3*** is simply the best!"

—Susan Paul, award winning author

"An unabashed celebration of sex. Highly arousing! Highly recommended!"

—Virginia Henley, *New York Times* Best Selling Author

In ***Secrets, Volume 3*** you'll find:

The Spy Who Loved Me by Jeanie Cesarini

Undercover FBI agent Paige Ellison's sexual appetites rise to new levels when she works with leading man Christopher Sharp, the cunning agent who uses all his training to capture her body and heart.

The Barbarian by Ann Jacobs

Lady Brianna vows not to surrender to the barbaric Giles, Earl of Harrow. He must use sexual arts learned in the infidels' harem to conquer his bride. A word of caution—this is not for the faint of heart.

Blood and Kisses by Angela Knight

A vampire assassin is after Beryl St. Cloud. Her only hope lies with Decker, another vampire and ex-mercenary. Broke, she offers herself as payment for his services. Will his seductive powers take her very soul?

Love Undercover by B.J. McCall

Amanda Forbes is the bait in a strip joint sting operation. While she performs, fellow detective "Cowboy" Cooper gets to watch. Though he excites her, she must fight the temptation to surrender to the passion.

Winner of the 1997 Under the Covers Readers Favorite Award

Secrets, Volume 4

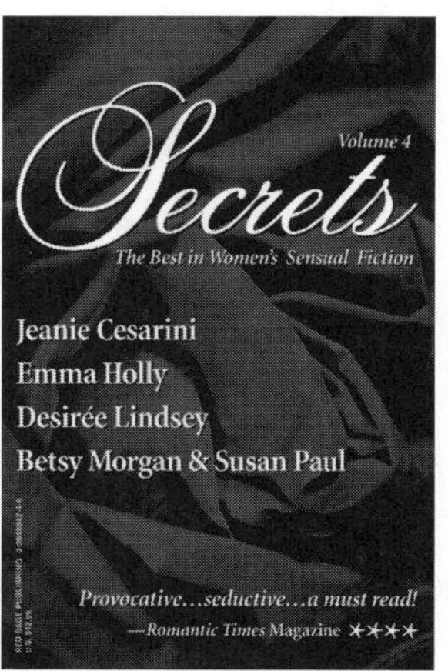

Listen to what reviewers say:

"Provocative... seductive... a must read!"

—*Romantic Times* Magazine

"These are the kind of stories that romance readers that 'want a little more' have been looking for all their lives...."

—*Affaire de Coeur* Magazine

"***Secrets, Volume 4***, has something to satisfy every erotic fantasy... simply sexational!"

—Virginia Henley, *New York Times* Best Selling Author

In ***Secrets, Volume 4*** you'll find:

An Act of Love by Jeanie Cesarini

Shelby Moran's past left her terrified of sex. International film star Jason Gage must gently coach the young starlet in the ways of love. He wants more than an act—he wants Shelby to feel true passion in his arms.

Enslaved by Desirée Lindsey

Lord Nicholas Summer's air of danger, dark passions, and irresistible charm have brought Lady Crystal's long-hidden desires to the surface. Will he be able to give her the one thing she desires before it's too late?

The Bodyguard by Betsy Morgan and Susan Paul

Kaki York is a bodyguard, but watching the wild, erotic romps of her client's sexual conquests on the security cameras is getting to her—and her partner, the ruggedly handsome James Kulick. Can she resist his insistent desire to have her?

The Love Slave by Emma Holly

A woman's ultimate fantasy. For one year, Princess Lily will be attended to by three delicious men of her choice. While she delights in playing with the first two, it's the reluctant Grae, with his powerful chest, black eyes and hair, that stirs her desires.

Secrets, Volume 5

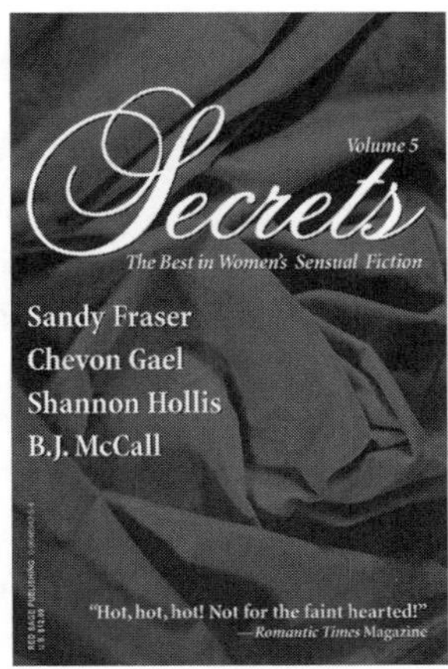

Listen to what reviewers say:

"Hot, hot, hot! Not for the faint-hearted!"

—*Romantic Times* Magazine

"As you make your way through the stories, you will find yourself becoming hotter and hotter. ***Secrets*** just keeps getting better and better."

—*Affaire de Coeur* Magazine

"***Secrets 5*** is a collage of luscious sensuality. Any woman who reads ***Secrets*** is in for an awakening!"

—Virginia Henley, *New York Times* Best Selling Author

In ***Secrets, Volume 5*** you'll find:

Beneath Two Moons by Sandy Fraser

Ready for a very wild romp? Step into the future and find Conor, rough and masculine like frontiermen of old, on the prowl for a new conquest. In his sights, Dr. Eva Kelsey. She got away once before, but this time Conor makes sure she begs for more.

Insatiable by Chevon Gael

Marcus Remington photographs beautiful models for a living, but it's Ashlyn Fraser, a young corporate exec having some glamour shots done, who has stolen his heart. It's up to Marcus to help her discover her inner sexual self.

Strictly Business by Shannon Hollis

Elizabeth Forrester knows it's tough enough for a woman to make it to the top in the corporate world. Garrett Hill, the most beautiful man in Silicon Valley, has to come along to stir up her wildest fantasies. Dare she give in to both their desires?

Alias Smith and Jones by B.J. McCall

Meredith Collins finds herself stranded overnight at the airport. A handsome stranger by the name of Smith offers her sanctuary for the evening and she finds those mesmerizing, green-flecked eyes hard to resist. Are they to be just two ships passing in the night?

Secrets, Volume 6

Listen to what reviewers say:

"Red Sage was the first and remains the leader of Women's Erotic Romance Fiction Collections!"

—*Romantic Times* Magazine

"***Secrets**, **Volume 6***, is the best of ***Secrets*** yet. …four of the most erotic stories in one volume than this reader has yet to see anywhere else. …These stories are full of erotica at its best and you'll definitely want to keep it handy for lots of re-reading!"

—*Affaire de Coeur* Magazine

"***Secrets 6*** satisfies every female fantasy: the Bodyguard, the Tutor, the Werewolf, and the Vampire. I give it Six Stars!"

—Virginia Henley, *New York Times* Best Selling Author

In ***Secrets, Volume 6*** you'll find:

Flint's Fuse by Sandy Fraser

Dana Madison's father has her "kidnapped" for her own safety. Flint, the tall, dark and dangerous mercenary, is hired for the job. But just which one is the prisoner—Dana will try *anything* to get away.

Love's Prisoner by MaryJanice Davidson

Trapped in an elevator, Jeannie Lawrence experienced unwilling rapture at Michael Windham's hands. She never expected the devilishly handsome man to show back up in her life—or turn out to be a werewolf!

The Education of Miss Felicity Wells by Alice Gaines

Felicity Wells wants to be sure she'll satisfy her soon-to-be husband but she needs a teacher. Dr. Marcus Slade, an experienced lover, agrees to take her on as a student, but can he stop short of taking her completely?

A Candidate for the Kiss by Angela Knight

Working on a story, reporter Dana Ivory stumbles onto a more amazing one—a sexy, secret agent who happens to be a vampire. She wants her story but Gabriel Archer wants more from her than just sex and blood.

Secrets, Volume 7

Listen to what reviewers say:

"Get out your asbestos gloves — ***Secrets Volume 7*** is... extremely hot, true erotic romance... passionate and titillating. There's nothing quite like baring your secrets!"

—*Romantic Times* Magazine

"...sensual, sexy, steamy fun. A perfect read!"

—Virginia Henley,
New York Times Best Selling Author

"Intensely provocative and disarmingly romantic, ***Secrets, Volume 7***, is a romance reader's paradise that will take you beyond your wildest dreams!"

—Ballston Book House Review

In ***Secrets, Volume 7*** you'll find:

Amelia's Innocence by Julia Welles

Amelia didn't know her father bet her in a card game with Captain Quentin Hawke, so honor demands a compromise—three days of erotic foreplay, leaving her virginity and future intact.

The Woman of His Dreams by Jade Lawless

From the day artist Gray Avonaco moves in next door, Joanna Morgan is plagued by provocative dreams. But what she believes is unrequited lust, Gray sees as another chance to be with the woman he loves. He must persuade her that even death can't stop true love.

Surrender by Kathryn Anne Dubois

Free-spirited Lady Johanna wants no part of the binding strictures society imposes with her marriage to the powerful Duke. She doesn't know the dark Duke wants sensual adventure, and sexual satisfaction.

Kissing the Hunter by Angela Knight

Navy Seal Logan McLean hunts the vampires who murdered his wife. Virginia Hart is a sexy vampire searching for her lost soul-mate only to find him in a man determined to kill her. She must convince him all vampires aren't created equally.

Winner of the Venus Book Club Best Book of the Year

Secrets, Volume 8

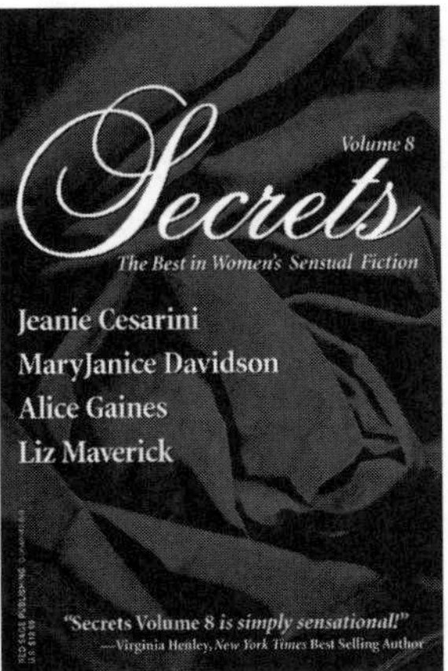

Listen to what reviewers say:

"***Secrets**, **Volume 8**,* is an amazing compilation of sexy stories covering a wide range of subjects, all designed to titillate the senses. …you'll find something for everybody in this latest version of ***Secrets***."

—*Affaire de Coeur* Magazine

"***Secrets Volume 8***, is simply sensational!"

—Virginia Henley, *New York Times* Best Selling Author

"These delectable stories will have you turning the pages long into the night. Passionate, provocative and perfect for setting the mood…."

—*Escape to Romance* Reviews

In ***Secrets, Volume 8*** you'll find:

Taming Kate by Jeanie Cesarini

Kathryn Roman inherits a legal brothel. Little does this city girl know the town of Love, Nevada wants her to be their new madam so they've charged Trey Holliday, one very dominant cowboy, with taming her.

Jared's Wolf by MaryJanice Davidson

Jared Rocke will do anything to avenge his sister's death, but ends up attracted to Moira Wolfbauer, the she-wolf sworn to protect her pack. Joining forces to stop a killer, they learn love defies all boundaries.

My Champion, My Lover by Alice Gaines

Celeste Broder is a woman committed for having a sexy appetite. Mayor Robert Albright may be her champion—if she can convince him her freedom will mean a chance to indulge their appetites together.

Kiss or Kill by Liz Maverick

In this post-apocalyptic world, Camille Kazinsky's military career rides on her ability to make a choice—whether the robo called Meat should live or die. Meat's future depends on proving he's human enough to live, man enough… to makes her feel like a woman.

Winner of the Venus Book Club Best Book of the Year

Secrets, Volume 9

Listen to what reviewers say:

"Everyone should expect only the most erotic stories in a ***Secrets*** book. …if you like your stories full of hot sexual scenes, then this is for you!"

—Donna Doyle Romance Reviews

"***SECRETS 9***… is sinfully delicious, highly arousing, and hotter than hot as the pages practically burn up as you turn them."

—Suzanne Coleburn, Reader To Reader Reviews/Belles & Beaux of Romance

"Treat yourself to well-written fiction that's hot, hotter, and hottest!"

—Virginia Henley, *New York Times* Best Selling Author

In ***Secrets, Volume 9*** you'll find:

Wild For You by Kathryn Anne Dubois

When college intern, Georgie, gets captured by a Congo wildman, she discovers this specimen of male virility has never seen a woman. The research possibilities are endless!

Wanted by Kimberly Dean

FBI Special Agent Jeff Reno wants Danielle Carver. There's her body, brains—and that charge of treason on her head. Dani goes on the run, but the sexy Fed is hot on her trail.

Secluded by Lisa Marie Rice

Nicholas Lee's wealth and power came with a price—his enemies will kill anyone he loves. When Isabelle steals his heart, Nicholas secludes her in his palace for a lifetime of desire in only a few days.

Flights of Fantasy by Bonnie Hamre

Chloe taught others to see the realities of life but she's never shared the intimate world of her sensual yearnings. Given the chance, will she be woman enough to fulfill her most secret erotic fantasy?

Secrets, Volume 10

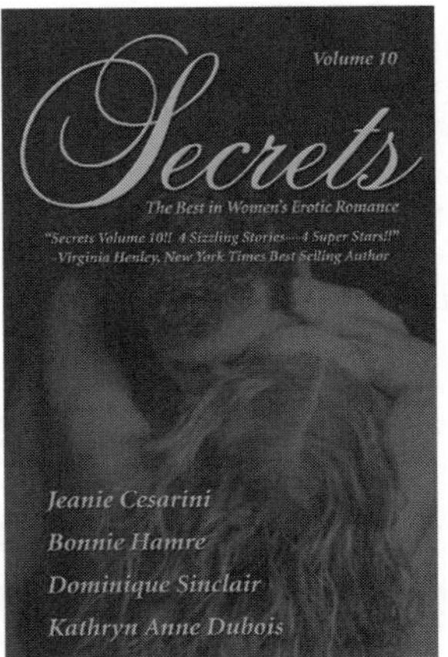

Listen to what reviewers say:

"***Secrets Volume 10***, an erotic dance through medieval castles, sultan's palaces, the English countryside and expensive hotel suites, explodes with passion-filled pages."

—*Romantic Times BOOKclub*

"Having read the previous nine volumes, this one fulfills the expectations of what is expected in a ***Secrets*** book: romance and eroticism at its best!!"

—*Fallen Angel Reviews*

"All are hot steamy romances so if you enjoy erotica romance, you are sure to enjoy ***Secrets, Volume 10***. All this reviewer can say is WOW!!"

—*The Best Reviews*

In *Secrets, Volume 10* you'll find:

Private Eyes by Dominique Sinclair

When a mystery man captivates P.I. Nicolla Black during a stakeout, she discovers her no-seduction rule bending under the pressure of long denied passion. She agrees to the seduction, but he demands her total surrender.

The Ruination of Lady Jane by Bonnie Hamre

To avoid her upcoming marriage, Lady Jane Ponsonby-Maitland flees into the arms of Havyn Attercliffe. She begs him to ruin her rather than turn her over to her odious fiancé.

Code Name: Kiss by Jeanie Cesarini

Agent Lily Justiss is on a mission to defend her country against terrorists that requires giving up her virginity as a sex slave. As her master takes her body, desire for her commanding officer Seth Blackthorn fuels her mind.

The Sacrifice by Kathryn Anne Dubois

Lady Anastasia Bedovier is days from taking her vows as a Nun. Before she denies her sensuality forever, she wants to experience pleasure. Count Maxwell is the perfect man to initiate her into erotic delight.

Secrets, Volume 11

Listen to what reviewers say:

"***Secrets Volume 11*** delivers once again with storylines that include erotic masquerades, ancient curses, modern-day betrayal and a prince charming looking for a kiss." **4 Stars**

—*Romantic Times BOOKclub*

"Indulge yourself with this erotic treat and join the thousands of readers who just can't get enough. Be forewarned that ***Secrets 11*** will whet your appetite for more, but will offer you the ultimate in pleasurable erotic literature."

—*Ballston Book House Review*

"***Secrets 11*** quite honestly is my favorite anthology from Red Sage so far."

—*The Best Reviews*

In ***Secrets, Volume 11*** you'll find:

Masquerade by Jennifer Probst

Hailey Ashton is determined to free herself from her sexual restrictions. Four nights of erotic pleasures without revealing her identity. A chance to explore her secret desires without the fear of unmasking.

Ancient Pleasures by Jess Michaels

Isabella Winslow is obsessed with finding out what caused her late husband's death, but trapped in an Egyptian concubine's tomb with a sexy American raider, succumbing to the mummy's sensual curse takes over.

Manhunt by Kimberly Dean

Framed for murder, Michael Tucker takes Taryn Swanson hostage—the one woman who can clear him. Despite the evidence against him, the attraction between them is strong. Tucker resorts to unconventional, yet effective methods of persuasion to change the sexy ADA's mind.

Wake Me by Angela Knight

Chloe Hart received a sexy painting of a sleeping knight. Radolf of Varik has been trapped for centuries in the painting since, cursed by a witch. His only hope is to visit the dreams of women and make one of them fall in love with him so she can free him with a kiss.

Secrets, Volume 12

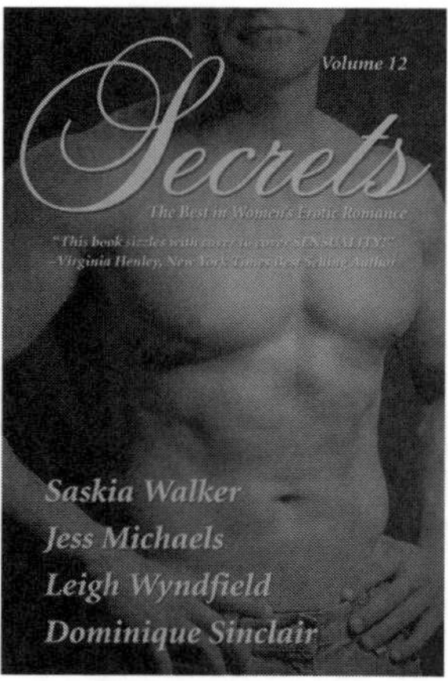

Listen to what reviewers say:

"***Secrets Volume 12***, turns on the heat with a seductive encounter inside a bookstore, a temple of naughty and sensual delight, a galactic inferno that thaws ice, and a lightening storm that lights up the English shoreline. Tales of looking for love in all the right places with a heat rating out the charts." **4½ Stars**

—*Romantic Times BOOKclub*

"I really liked these stories. You want great escapism? Read ***Secrets, Volume 12***."

—*Romance Reviews*

In ***Secrets, Volume 12*** you'll find:

Good Girl Gone Bad by Dominique Sinclair

Reagan's dreams are finally within reach. Setting out to do research for an article, nothing could have prepared her for Luke, or his offer to teach her everything she needs to know about sex. Licentious pleasures, forbidden desires… inspiring the best writing she's ever done.

Aphrodite's Passion by Jess Michaels

When Selena flees Victorian London before her evil stepchildren can institutionalize her for hysteria, Gavin is asked to bring her back home. But when he finds her living on the island of Cyprus, his need to have her begins to block out every other impulse.

White Heat by Leigh Wyndfield

Raine is hiding in an icehouse in the middle of nowhere from one of the scariest men in the universes. Walker escaped from a burning prison. Imagine their surprise when they find out they have the same man to blame for their miseries. Passion, revenge and love are in their future.

Summer Lightning by Saskia Walker

Sculptress Sally is enjoying an idyllic getaway on a secluded cove when she spots a gorgeous man walking naked on the beach. When Julian finds an attractive woman shacked up in his cove, he has to check her out. But what will he do when he finds she's secretly been using him as a model?

Secrets, Volume 13

Listen to what reviewers say:

"In ***Secrets Volume 13***, the temperature gets turned up a few notches with a mistaken personal ad, shape-shifters destined to love, a hot Regency lord and his lady, as well as a bodyguard protecting his woman. Emotions and flames blaze high in Red Sage's latest foray into the sensual and delightful art of love." **4½ Stars**

—*Romantic Times BOOKclub*

"The sex is still so hot the pages nearly ignite! Read ***Secrets, Volume 13***!"

—*Romance Reviews*

In ***Secrets, Volume 13*** you'll find:

Out of Control by Rachelle Chase

Astrid's world revolves around her business and she's hoping to pick up wealthy Erik Santos as a client. Only he's hoping to pick up something entirely different. Will she give in to the seductive pull of his proposition?

Hawkmoor by Amber Green

Shape-shifters answer to Darien as he acts in the name of the long-missing Lady Hawkmoor, their hereditary ruler. When she unexpectedly surfaces, Darien must deal with a scrappy individual whose wary eyes hold the other half of his soul, but who has the power to destroy his world.

Lessons in Pleasure by Charlotte Featherstone

A wicked bargain has Lily vowing never to yield to the demands of the rake she once loved and lost. Unfortunately, Damian, the Earl of St. Croix, or Saint as he is infamously known, will not take 'no' for an answer.

In the Heat of the Night by Calista Fox

Haunted by a century-old curse, Molina fears she won't live to see her thirtieth birthday. Nick, her former bodyguard, is hired back into service to protect her from the fatal accidents that plague her family. But *In the Heat of the Night*, will his passion and love for her be enough to convince Molina they have a future together?

Secrets, Volume 14

Listen to what reviewers say:

"***Secrets Volume 14*** will excite readers with its diverse selection of delectable sexy tales ranging from a fourteenth century love story to a sci-fi rebel who falls for a irresistible research scientist to a trio of determined vampires who battle for the same woman to a virgin sacrifice who falls in love with a beast. A cornucopia of pure delight!" **4½ Stars**

—*Romantic Times BOOKclub*

"This book contains four erotic tales sure to keep readers up long into the night."

—*Romance Junkies*

In ***Secrets, Volume 14*** you'll find:

Soul Kisses by Angela Knight

Beth's been kidnapped by Joaquin Ramirez, a sadistic vampire. Handsome vampire cousins, Morgan and Garret Axton, come to her rescue. Can she find happiness with two vampires?

Temptation in Time by Alexa Aames

Ariana escaped the Middle Ages after stealing a kiss of magic from sexy sorcerer, Marcus de Grey. When he brings her back, they begin a battle of wills and a sexual odyssey that could spell disaster for them both.

Ailis and the Beast by Jennifer Barlowe

When Ailis agreed to be her village's sacrifice to the mysterious Beast she was prepared to sacrifice her virtue, and possibly her life. But some things aren't what they seem. Ailis and the Beast are about to discover the greatest sacrifice may be the human heart.

Night Heat by Leigh Wynfield

When Rip Bowhite leads a revolt on the prison planet, he ends up struggling to survive against monsters that rule the night. Jemma, the prison's Healer, won't allow herself to be distracted by the instant attraction she feels for Rip. As the stakes are raised and death draws near, love seems doomed in the heat of the night.

Secrets, Volume 15

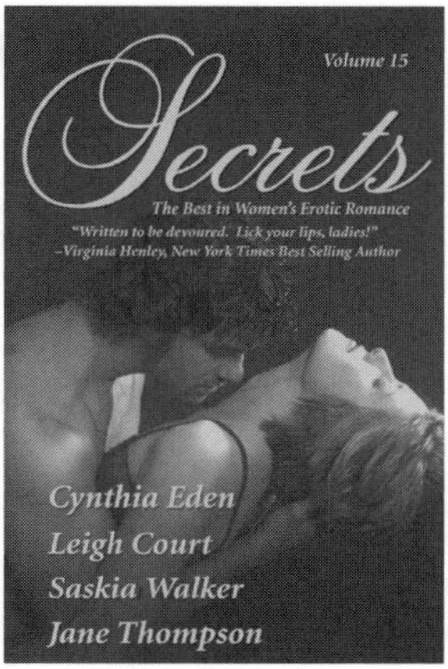

Listen to what reviewers say:

"***Secrets Volume 15*** blends humor, tension and steamy romance in its newest collection that sizzles with passion between unlikely pairs—a male chauvinist columnist and a librarian turned erotica author; a handsome werewolf and his resisting mate; an unfulfilled woman and a sexy police officer and a Victorian wife who learns discipline can be fun. Readers will revel in this delicious assortment of thrilling tales." **4 Stars**

—Romantic Times BOOKclub

"This book contains four tales by some of today's hottest authors that will tease your senses and intrigue your mind."

—Romance Junkies

In ***Secrets, Volume 15*** you'll find:

Simon Says by Jane Thompson

Simon Campbell is a newspaper columnist who panders to male fantasies. Georgina Kennedy is a respectable librarian. On the surface, these two have nothing in common... but don't judge a book by its cover.

Bite of the Wolf by Cynthia Eden

Gareth Morlet, alpha werewolf, has finally found his mate. All he has to do is convince Trinity to join with him, to give in to the pleasure of a werewolf's mating, and then she will be his... forever.

Falling for Trouble by Saskia Walker

With 48 hours to clear her brother's name, Sonia Harmond finds help from irresistible bad boy, Oliver Eaglestone. When the erotic tension between them hits fever pitch, securing evidence to thwart an international arms dealer isn't the only danger they face.

The Disciplinarian by Leigh Court

Headstrong Clarissa Babcock is sent to the shadowy legend known as The Disciplinarian for instruction in proper wifely obedience. Jared Ashworth uses the tools of seduction to show her how to control a demanding husband, but her beauty, spirit, and uninhibited passion make Jared hunger to keep her—and their darkly erotic nights—all for himself!

Secrets, Volume 16

Listen to what reviewers say:

"Blackmail, games of chance, nude beaches and masquerades pave a path to heart-tugging emotions and fiery love scenes in Red Sage's latest collection." **4.5 Stars**

—*Romantic Times BOOKclub*

"Red Sage Publishing has brought to the readers an erotic profusion of highly skilled storytellers in their Secrets Vol. 16. … This is the best Secrets novel to date and this reviewer's favorite."

—*LoveRomances.com*

In ***Secrets, Volume 16*** you'll find:

Never Enough by Cynthia Eden

For the last three weeks, Abby McGill has been playing with fire. Bad-boy Jake has taught her the true meaning of desire, but she knows she has to end her relationship with him. But Jake isn't about to let the woman he wants walk away from him.

Bunko by Sheri Gilmoore

Tu Tran is forced to decide between Jack, a man, who promises to share every aspect of his life with her, or Dev, the man, who hides behind a mask and only offers night after night of erotic sex. Will she take the gamble of the dice and choose the man, who can see behind her own mask and expose her true desires?

Hide and Seek by Chevon Gael

Kyle DeLaurier ditches his trophy-fiance in favor of a tropical paradise full of tall, tanned, topless females. Private eye, Darcy McLeod, is on the trail of this runaway groom. Together they sizzle while playing Hide and Seek with their true identities.

Seduction of the Muse by Charlotte Featherstone

He's the Dark Lord, the mysterious author who pens the erotic tales of an innocent woman's seduction. She is his muse, the woman he watches from the dark shadows, the woman whose dreams he invades at night.

Secrets, Volume 17

Listen to what reviewers say:

"Readers who have clamored for more ***Secrets*** will love the mix of alpha and beta males as well as kick-butt heroines who always get their men."
4 Stars

—*Romantic Times BOOKclub*

"Stories so sizzling hot, they will burn your fingers as you turn the pages. Enjoy!"

—Virginia Henley, *New York Times* Best Selling Author

"Red Sage is bringing us another thrilling anthology of passion and desire that will keep you up long into the night."

—*Romance Junkies*

In ***Secrets, Volume 17*** you'll find:

Rock Hard Candy by Kathy Kaye

Jessica Hennessy, the great, great granddaughter of a Voodoo priestess, decides she's waited long enough for the man of her dreams. A dose of her ancestor's aphrodisiac slipped into the gooey center of her homemade bon bons ought to do the trick.

Fatal Error by Kathleen Scott

Jesse Storm must make amends to humanity by destroying the computer program he helped design that has taken the government hostage. But he must also protect the woman he's loved in secret for nearly a decade.

Birthday by Ellie Marvel

Jasmine Templeton decides she's been celibate long enough. Will a wild night at a hot new club with her two best friends ease the ache inside her or just make it worse? Well, considering one of those best friends is Charlie and she's been having strange notions about their relationship of late… It's definitely a birthday neither she nor Charlie will ever forget.

Intimate Rendezvous by Calista Fox

A thief causes trouble at Cassandra Kensington's nightclub, Rendezvous, and sexy P.I. Dean Hewitt arrives on the scene to help. One look at the siren who owns the club has his blood boiling, despite the fact that his keen instincts have him questioning the legitimacy of her business.

Secrets, Volume 18

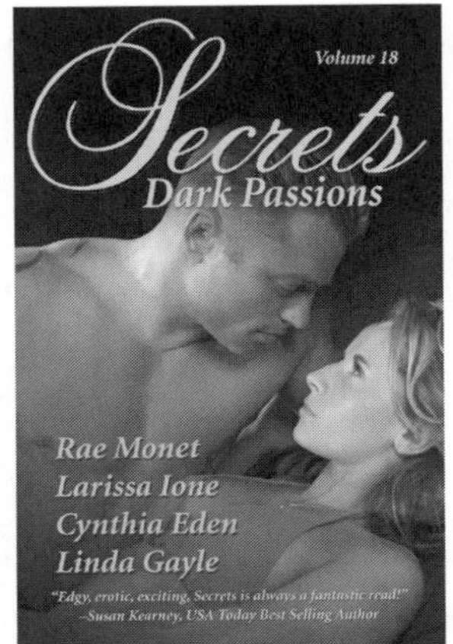

Listen to what reviewers say:

"Fantastic love scenes make this a book to be enjoyed more than once." **4.5 Stars**

—*Romantic Times BOOKclub*

"***Secrets Volume 18*** continues [its] tradition of high quality sensual stories that both excite the senses while stimulating the mind."

—CK^{2}S Kwips and Kritiques

"Edgy, erotic, exciting, ***Secrets*** is always a fantastic read!"

—Susan Kearney, *USA Today* Best Selling Author

In ***Secrets, Volume 18*** you'll find:

Lone Wolf Three by Rae Monet

Planetary politics and squabbling over wolf occupied territory drain former rebel leader Taban Zias. But his anger quickly turns to desire when he meets, Lakota Blackson. Focused, calm and honorable, the female Wolf Warrior is Taban's perfect mate—now if he can just convince her.

Flesh to Fantasy by Larissa Ione

Kelsa Bradshaw is an intense loner whose job keeps her happily immersed in a fanciful world of virtual reality. Trent Jordan is a laid-back paramedic who experiences the harsh realities of life up close and personal. But when their worlds collide in an erotic eruption can Trent convince Kelsa to turn the fantasy into something real?

Heart Full of Stars by Linda Gayle

Singer Fanta Rae finds herself stranded on a lonely Mars outpost with the first human male she's seen in years. Ex-Marine Alex Decker lost his family and guilt drove him into isolation, but when alien assassins come to enslave Fanta, she and Decker come together to fight for their lives.

The Wolf's Mate by Cynthia Eden

When Michael Morlet finds Katherine "Kat" Hardy fighting for her life in a dark alley, he instantly recognizes her as the mate he's been seeking all of his life, but someone's trying to kill her. With danger stalking them at every turn, will Kat trust him enough to become The Wolf's Mate?

Secrets, Volume 19
Released July 2007

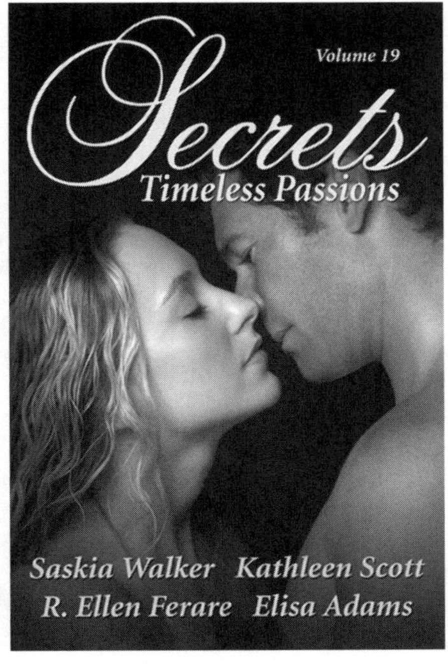

Affliction
by Elisa Adams

Holly Aronson finally believes she's safe and whole in the orbit of sweet Andrew. But when Andrew's life long friend, Shane, arrives, events begin to spiral out of control again. Worse, she's inexplicably drawn to Shane. As she runs for her life, which one will protect her? And whom does she truly love?

Falling Stars
by Kathleen Scott

Daria is both a Primon fighter pilot and a Primon princess. As a deadly new enemy faces appears, she must choose between her duty to the fleet and the desperate need to forge an alliance through her marriage to the enemy's General Raven.

Toy in the Attic
by R. Ellen Ferare

When Gabrielle checks into the top floor of an old hotel, she discovers a life-sized statue of a nude man. Her unexpected roommate reveals himself to be a talented lover caught by a witch's curse. Can she help him break free of the spell that holds him, without losing her heart along the way?

What You Wish For
by Saskia Walker

Lucy Chambers is renovating her newly purchased historic house. As her dreams about a stranger become more intense, she wishes he were with her now. Two hundred years in the past, the man wishes for companionship and suddenly they find themselves together—in his time.

Secrets, Volume 20
Released July 2007

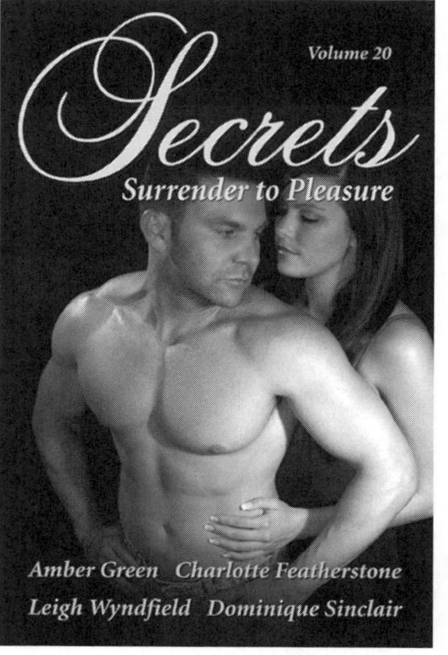

The Subject
by Amber Green

One week Tyler is a hot game designer, signing the deal of her life. The next, she's on the run for her life. Who can she trust? Certainly not sexy, mysterious Esau, who keeps showing up after the hoo-hah hits the fan!

Surrender
by Dominique Sinclair

Agent Madeline Carter is in too deep. She's slipped into Sebastian Maiocco's life to investigate his Sicilian mafia family. He unearths desires Madeline's unable to deny, conflicting the duty that honors her. Madeline must surrender to Sebastian or risk being exposed, leaving her target for a ruthless clan.

Stasis
by Leigh Wyndfield

Morgann Right has a problem. Her Commanding Officer has been drugged with Stasis, turning him into a living, breathing statue she's forced to take care of for ten long days. As her hands tend to him, she suddenly sees her CO in a totally different light. She wants him and, while she can tell he wants her, touching him intimately might come back to haunt them both.

A Woman's Pleasure
by Charlotte Featherstone

Widowed Isabella, Lady Langdon is tired of denying her needs and desires. Yearning to discover all the pleasures denied her in her marriage, she finds herself falling hard for the magnetic charms of the mysterious and exotic Julian Gresham—a man skilled in pleasures of the flesh. A man eight years her junior. A man more than eager to show her *A Woman's Pleasure.*